THE MOON TEAR

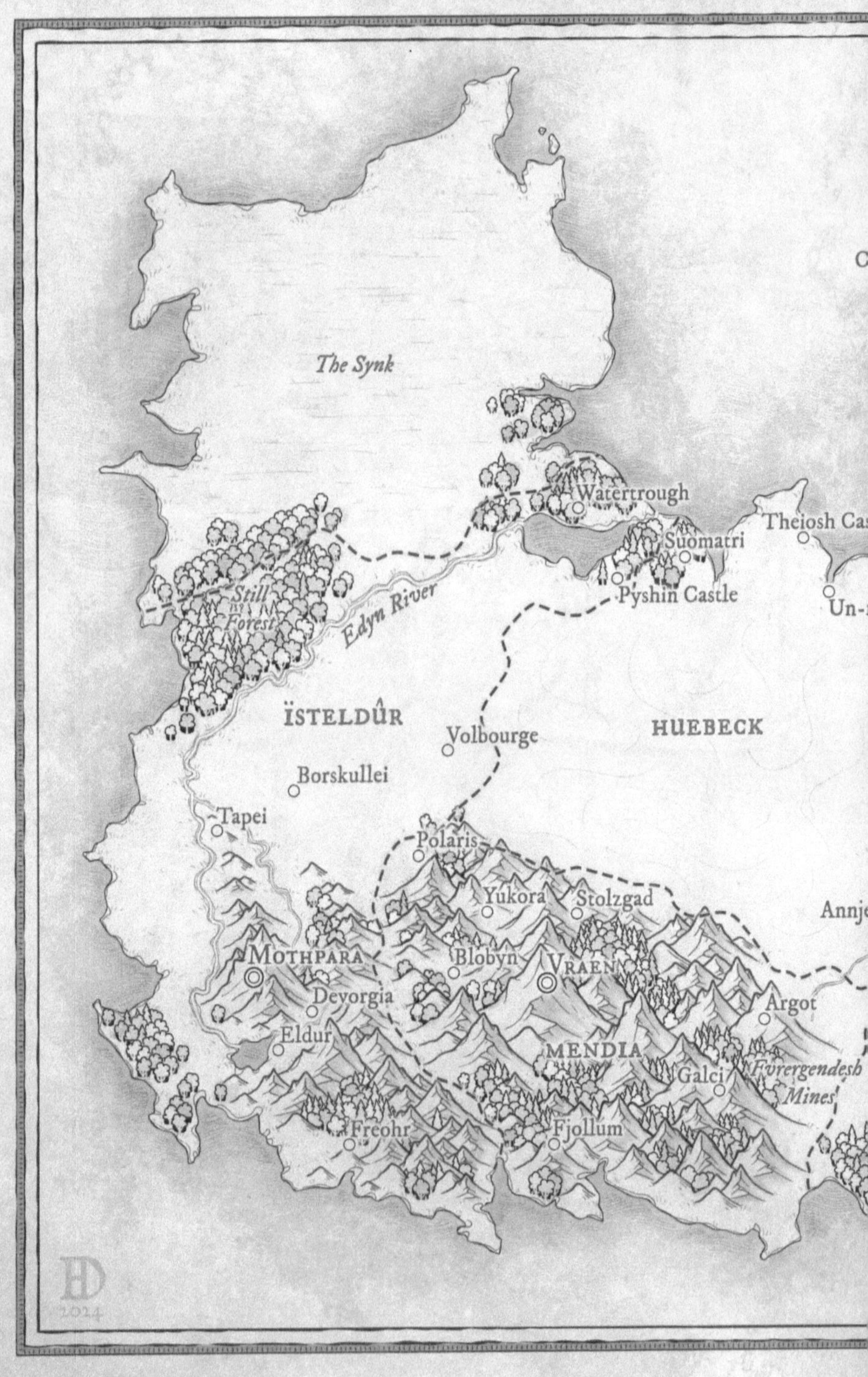

The Synk
Watertrough
Theiosh Cas
Suomatri
Pyshin Castle
Un-
Still Forest
Edyn River
ÏSTELDÛR
HUEBECK
Volbourge
Borskullei
Tapei
Polaris
Yukora
Stolzgad
Annje
Mothpara
Blobyn
VRAEN
Devorgia
Argot
Eldur
MENDIA
Fvrergendesh Mines
Galci
Freohr
Fjollum
C
HD
2024

THE REALM OF
ALAGANA

Keeyto
Tiur
Llyria
PUANOULACUE
Othios
Cilliet Delois
Soruna
LESAH
sh
Mi-svetlo
Amber Castle
Aldeyn
AIDEIL
Ûnsigra
Siochanta
Ismay
Galeisia
MAINWOOD
Ryn Village
Weibow
ver
ANIÖM
Auran River
Meyarei
Alagour
ODELLE
Slétum
Datia
Grosgir
Theony
River
Ethryn
Foxwood
Letteran
Hägenveihr Forest
THREINSFOLD
Jothya
Riggole
FARINDOR
Seclaine

THE MOON TEAR

ALAGANA TRILOGY

M.E. ROYCE

To facing what fears us most head on—this is for us.

Gifts of Alagana

Gifts are the specific combination of magikal energies
that exists within certain members of the elvish race,
channeled through Gemstone conduits
Granted by the Realm's deities.

Scariyai

Elemental Gifts manifesting through energies that occur
in nature fall into the categories of water, fire, earth, and air
in any of their derivatives.

Scarox

A skill and mind Gift focused on enhancing an elf's agility
and strength while providing the channeler with immediate
intuition of an opponent's thoughts. They are the soldiers and
commanders.

Beiythron

A skill and mind Gift that pushes the boundaries of
knowledge and science. These are the engineers and
creators and architects.

Contents

Prologue

Cara squinted through the gale, cursing the day she accepted her Gift of magik. For all the good her golden healing magik was worth, nothing stopped her body shaking from the deep chill. Her ears—pale, pointed, red-tipped—poked out from auburn hair frosted with rime. She rubbed her thumb and forefinger together absently to encourage a sliver of feeling.

Air whipped around the summit of the mountain and Cara's feet skidded across the slick, spiraling path. She climbed while flanked by two Silver Elvish guards from the castle nestled into the base of the bare mountain. A Silver man and woman shuffled a few paces ahead, heads bowed against the gale.

If Cara dared look down the unforgiving cliff to her left, she could just see the lush green valley below between breaks in the unrelenting storm.

At the base of the mountain, carved stone outlined the fortress of Ûnsigra where the rock had been manipulated by elvish scariyai Gifted with mineral magik. The castle housed one of the greatest scholarly institutions in the realm and offered its services to human and elf both. Those willing to learn were granted sanctuary. It was for the potential knowledge within those stone walls that Cara bothered volunteering for this trek up the mountain. That is, if she survived this perilous hike.

She squinted at the two guards clad in smooth iron. Through the flurry of snow, she made out gold leaves inlaid into their metal shoulder plates. Steel glinted at their hips and elegant wood bows were strung across their backs, hewn from the Greywood forests in the south. Their backs were straight with the tell-tale pride of the eastern Silver Elves, their noses always tilted up in the presence of Amber Elves like Cara.

Beneath the guards' forged metal was fabric, tightly sewn to defend against the cold. Two braids circled their heads in the style traditionally worn by Northern Aideillians.

Cara wrapped her thick cloak tighter. Neatly cut wraps and tinctures in small glass vials pressed into her ribs, threatening to throw her off balance. Every muscle ached. She found herself repeating an old Farindor nursery rhyme to pass the time of a forest that walked and a queen who commanded it. She would give anything for the softness of the forest floor. Anything to be rid of the precarious mountain trail and blustering winds. The additional weight from all the options she wouldn't use only made her body scream more. The head scholar of Ûnsigra had insisted that her pockets be filled with the best the academy had to offer. *Just in case,* he had said, nose up and beady eyes staring down at her through narrow spectacles. His reasoning was that a healer needed all instruments available to her. She should not rely on the Gift of magik alone, channeled as it was through a little gemstone.

A tiny pop sounded under Cara's armpit as a flute of nectar cracked from the force of her shivering. *These vials will be the first to go,* Cara thought, tucking in her chin, and pressing on. Ûnsigra medicine—all Aideillian medicine, for that matter—fetched a handsome amount of gold rykes at market, more that she could expect to see in a year's wages.

The delicate figure dropped back to Cara's side. Madame Kyenz-eihra, the woman Cara was hired to aid, rested a hand on her swollen belly and shuddered. The elvish woman was in her late thirties, an age considered early adulthood for the Silver Elves. If all went smoothly, Madame Kyenz-eihra would look the exact same in eighty years, maybe longer since she was Gifted. But now, her lips trembled from the climb and her breathing came in long stressed pauses. Her husband slowed his pace until he was able to wrap an arm around her back to keep her from slipping down the mountain.

Though Cara couldn't alleviate her own discomfort, she linked her arm through Madame Kyenz-eihra's. As a healer, she felt the woman's pain as her own, despite the many layers of hides and furs between them. A prick of warmth at Cara's sternum was followed by a golden light that passed from Cara's arm to the other woman.

"Madame Kyenz-eihra," Cara said encouragingly. "Vialett, you can make it. Just a little further."

The Silver guards, having trudged on ahead, paused to look back. Cara waved them on through the snow. "We're coming."

The Ûnsigra guard had offered a feeble escort to protect the pregnant Silver Elf and her husband as they scaled the cliffs of Keystones, the name of the ghastly mountain. Recent riots in outlying castles along the Auran River had consumed the fort's resources, before even accounting for the ongoing thirty year war waging between Aideil and its western enemy.

A particularly vicious wall of snow and wind slammed into the band of elves. Cara shifted Vialett closer to the cliff wall and away from the deadly drop. In doing so, Cara felt a string unravel around her waist and winced as a bound parcel of dried herbs slid away, vanishing before she could untangle her arms and grasp it. Both women had prayed that the storm would ease up prior to the climb, but the four-hundred-year-old blizzard hadn't answered their pleas.

Some Aideillian law decreed that in order for a first-born child of elvish nobility to be declared legitimate, the mother was to bathe in the faërfalls at the top of the mountain, the pools tucked away, deep within the rock, accessible only from a single tunnel that opened at the pinnacle of Keystones. The faërfalls would offer a glimpse into the bloodline's future. An assurance to the High Council that there would be Gifted children, or reason to convict. A successful journey wiped past transgressions clean and would situate the Kyenz family back into high society after the scandal of their union.

If Aideil didn't have such a stringent class system that restricted love, Cara would never have had to put on more clothing than a merchant peddler had in the back of their wagon at a winter market. But tradition was tradition and the long-lived elves were not about to change their ways now. As it was, Cara found herself counting the rykes each step forward made her and her twin sister.

The path ahead widened, the slope tapering off to near flat.

Stepping onto the plateau, the snow froze, each flake floating suspended in the air. The blizzard raged a few paces behind them, but on that stretch of ice-coated stone was an eerie cloud. Even Cara's breath hung in a suspended frozen sphere in front of her nose.

If the maps were accurate, they'd find a cave nestled in a nook a few lengths ahead. From what Cara could see, there was only a dark silhouette of sheetrock that promised ancient magiks and prophecies.

Cara glanced at the woman at her side and suppressed a shudder of emptiness as her body regenerated the healing magik she had used to soothe Madame Kyenz-eihra. Vialett didn't look particularly fond of the weather either, her face mirroring Cara's own thoughts.

Vialett's mouth moved, and Cara nearly missed her murmured words. "No matter what the waters reveal, Sky give me strength to raise this child in love, without the prejudice that will be forced upon them. Give me the strength to shape them with integrity and grow them into a being worthy of serving the Old Throne."

The words were tinged with sorrow. It was a prayer to the High Elvish gods of old, reminiscent of a time long past, when magik flowed into all living beings and a High Elf sat on the Old Throne of Alagana.

The distance to the mouth of the cave shortened. Cara bit her tongue to keep from whispering the words in Ancient Elvish that Vialett would have to say to request entrance. The woman knew her duty. Cara need not pester her, and risk angering the Guardian. If the Guardian be willing, Cara and Madame Kyenz-eihra would enter the mountain alone. There was some magik woven into the stone that only female elves could enter without physical Trials. Men endured all manner of tests until they were broken. *Thank the Old King I wasn't born a man*, Cara thought with a shiver.

A cold grey slab of stone angled into a pitch-black crevice. The entrance to the cave of Keystones tunneled into darkness so solid that it gave Cara vertigo. A mottled wolfhound sat on a slight ripple at the base of the entrance. The Guardian of Keystones. The sketches the scholars had shown her when she volunteered did not do justice to the sheer size of the beast. Its paws were rough and splintered from centuries of patrolling the mountain. Patches of fur had been seared off with fire that burned to the bone. Decades of souls darkened its eyes and a long tail of thick black fur wrapped across its feet. On its haunches, the wolfhound towered four heads above the two Ûnsigra guards who both dropped to a knee and bowed their heads.

Cara shrank back, releasing Vialett's arm. The hound's inky eyes had the same color as the ocean floor. Within the course of a slow blink, the wolfhound saw into her. The creature was magik itself. Every fiber of its being was woven from the magik that built the realms. And it devoured her thoughts. It inhaled her darkest secrets and fears. How she was too young to be accompanying a Lord of Aideil and his wife on a journey that could bless them as surely as it could condemn them. Cara's twin sister's face flashed before her, laughing, then crumbled to ashes. Then it was over. No physical pain. The wolfhound retreated from her mind and its attention shifted elsewhere.

She felt a brief squeeze on her arm where Vialett comforted her. The two women shared every uncertainty of what lay ahead, and approached the Guardian of Keystones.

Vialett dipped into a low bow, her knee brushing the snow. A snowflake melted on the blue gem of her earring with the faintest pulse of magik. Cara shifted her gaze away from the conduit of a Gifted water lily. The Silver Elvish woman took care to look directly into the Guardian's eyes, likely experiencing a similar analysis of her past. Cara flinched down into a similar bow a moment later.

"Guardian, anointed by trial and set to protect the faërfalls of the Sky," Vialett began. "I, Vialett Kyenz-eihra, ask pardon for the blessing of Sight upon my child and bloodline to be."

A deep rumbling echoed off the planes of stone as the wolfhound replied. "And this is all you ask?"

"Yes." Her voice did not waiver, a feat that Cara would not be confident of in herself. *Another reason to return to Hågenveihr Forest,* Cara thought to herself.

The wolfhound shifted its weight forward. Dense muscle clenched as it rose onto all fours. The Guardian lowered its head level with Vialett's. The woman met its gaze, her breath fogging in front of her.

Cara felt the shift then, from a Trial to an aura of peace. The scarred eyes of the Guardian did not threaten them, as they did not threaten it. The wolfhound opened its jaws. Long pearl-while canines curled down inches from Vialett's forehead. There was a shuffling of footsteps behind them as Lord Kyenz started forward, stopped by the two Ûnsigra guards.

A delicate paw rested on Vialett's shoulder. Cara's body was frozen to the spot, but she gathered a kernel of healing magik into her chest. Just in case.

The tips of the wolfhound's canines brushed against Vialett's wild hair. Its warm breath melted the ice that had built up around the crown of her head.

"To you, my little water sprite, you may enter." The wolfhound's voice was of nature and of the wind, soft and deep. The voice of ancient magik. The tiny sapphire that pierced Vialett's right ear glowed in response. Cara felt her own amber gemstone warm as well.

Both women released a long breath and stood as the Guardian stepped to the side, the cave open.

Looking back, Cara glimpsed the three male elves shifting snow-drifts to form a shelter. The Guardian of Keystones circled the mouth of the cave, resting, finally, as motionless as the mountain around it.

The Silver Elf and Amber healer left the white light of the mountain, engulfed in an atmosphere of oppressive darkness. Light by torch was futile due to the strong draft that spiraled around them at regular intervals. The two relied on touch to guide them along ice-coated walls.

Their journey twisted and dipped, carrying them deep into the mountain. Soon Cara became truly lost. The walls gradually lost their icy coating. The stone tunnel dried, smooth rock emanating warmth. A pale blue-green light radiated where their hands touched, casting shadows that danced on the walls around them. The passageway narrowed drastically. Their thick cloaks were left abandoned in the dim light.

The heavy silence made Cara twitchy and restless. She preferred the constant buzz of life as it existed in the forest. Insects and rustling and the scraping of tree branches. This silence seeped into her mind. "What do you imagine is at the end of this tunnel?" she finally asked. "What will it look like? I could never get a definitive answer."

Vialett took a moment to think. "I suppose..." Her words drifted off as the path took a sharp left turn. Ahead, the tunnel emanated its own light, clear and crystal.

Beyond was a vast cavern. The ceiling glittered with the reflections of luminescent water ripples and stones. Stalactites reached down toward undisturbed water that flickered with greens, blues, and purples. Silky ribbons of water fanned out from minuscule holes up above and tumbled over rocks at the far end of the cave. Whenever a tendril of water landed on a rock, a soft burst of light emitted from that spot. The falls were divided into one main pool and then a multitude of separated pools of various depths.

It was like nothing Cara had ever dreamed of. She felt her magik sing and soar through the currents of energy that flowed through the space. Each pool flickered a different color. A single vial of this water would prove invaluable, leading her kingdom into a new era of medicine and magikal studies . This had to be one of the only places left that maintained its magik over the centuries, when every other aspect of life dulled and magik faded.

Vialett unwound her forest green wrap. She handed the fabric to Cara and stood before the pools with not but a breast bind and loosely fitted cream under layer.

She made her way into the waters. The rocks ignited into color under her feet, a speckle of light dancing across the stone. When she was waist deep, Vialett dipped her head beneath the surface. The pool spiraled with pearly coils of magik and encased her body.

Cara's eyes were transfixed. Threads of magik and swirls of color reflected in her eyes. She fingered a leftover glass vial she hadn't surrendered in the tunnel with her thick fur coat. It was the greatest honor in Aideil for a healer to be accepted for the Keystone Journey, and a rite of passage for the famed Farindor healers. She was the youngest healer to have been selected and Cara vowed to take in every detail to share with her twin.

After a smooth dip into the water, Cara tucked the filled flute of water in her belt. With so much raw energy around her, Cara pinched a strand of magik from a drop from a stalactite. She expanded her range of power and linked to the Silver Elf. Her amber ring glowed in response. To monitor what Vialett saw and when Cara needed to pull her from the waters, she needed to keep a constant stream of linking magik flowing. Once they left the mountain, Cara would never speak of what she witnessed through the eyes of the pregnant elf, as was the agreement.

Cara counted the minutes as they passed, only wanting to dip into her bond with the water lily and encroach on the privacy of the vision if utterly necessary. Some elves ventured too deep into the waters and were lost to the mountain.

She rubbed the cloth of her tunic between her fingers. Time was up. Vialett didn't come out of the pools of her own accord. Bubbles surfaced, disrupting the pool's glassy surface.

Cara abandoned her clothing at the lip of the pool and dove down. She wrapped her arms around Vialett and kicked up. Later, she would wonder how deep these pools went for Vialett to have been so far down.

She snapped her fingers once they were at the edge of the water, simultaneously laying down the shivering elf. A spark of daisy yellow magik ignited. Cara's palms heated, and she blew on the spark until her hands glowed with a vibrant golden light.

The healer placed her hands on Madame Kyenz-eihra's stomach and circled across her torso in runic patterns. Her blood raced from fear, a knot curling in her stomach. A kernel of doubt seeded—was the rune correct?

Cara allowed for the panic to take hold and she poured more of herself into the magik. More power flowed through her hands than she had ever accessed, almost as if the waters themselves were amplifying her Gift.

She swallowed and dragged a finger up from the diaphragm to Vialett's chin. The familiar aching chill of expending her stored magik spread up her shoulder, leaving gooseflesh in its wake.

Vialett's eyes flew open with a ragged breath. Alive, Cara released her own breath. She felt Madame Kyenz-eihra's skin warm and cheeks flush. The elf leveled a steely gaze on the healer and Cara saw crackling strength in the woman's eyes. The water lily shoved the vision down the bond and burned it into Cara's mind.

"She must never come to use magik, or she will destroy us all."

Part One

Remnants of Old Magik

Chapter One

Spring bloomed in the elvish capital of Aideil in all manner of glory. White and light pink flowers nestled in dense beds of moss while warm light streaked through the thick canopy above. Vines raced up the trunks of trees that towered up and out hundreds of feet into the air, the branches fading away into the clouds.

Eyolin waved away a cascade of pollen falling from the archway above her and swerved to avoid a wooden wagon teetering precariously on the road that spanned the width and length of the tree branch. Normally, the limbs of the city were wide enough to carry two to three wagons comfortably, but that morning every avenue and bridge was packed with merchants hoping to establish themselves among the deep pockets of the elvish aristocracy. For today was a day of celebration. Or it was for the rest of the city's residents.

Tiny birds dipped and fluttered overhead, dropping tiny trinkets for children to grab madly at. Eyolin's hand plucked one from the air and examined the little soldier with his fist raised victoriously. She tipped it into the cupped hands of a young child with slenderly pointed ears and silver hair.

Cheers and raised voices yipped and hollered from each of the five levels of the city, from the gates on the ground, to the fifth tier bridges that were nestled near the crown of the trees.

Two more birds carrying beiythron-made children toys rustled a wall of flowering ivy. Eyolin shook her head in a muffled sneeze, her light brown curls poking out of their loose braid. She would rejoice the day when the bark of the city wasn't coated in a film of glittering allergies. There was a time when Eyolin and her sister would have dragged their mother out into the market on the first day after the new moon of springtime. It appeared slowly as a figure moving toward her through fog might. Her raven-haired sister in a cream-colored fitted blouse fastened down with handmade armor and an old, beat-up cloak. A bag of spare change for the postman and a red strand of licorice. That was before—all before.

A dull throb pounded the back of Eyolin's eyelids, and the mist cleared. She thought of her family distantly, as though those memories were a dream, and she routinely woke up to cruel reality. She had a loving home once, a mother and a sister and a father. But one day they were all gone.

A posse of young Academy students barreled past her, ducking beneath the wagons in a coordinated slide. The boy at the back, an elf no more than twelve, poked a slim blade into the canvas cover of the merchant's wagon, retrieving a fat plum, before disappearing into the throng. Eyolin smirked to herself; she would have done something similar.

Bracing a hand on the wagon to prevent her feet from slipping over the edge of the branch, she maneuvered against the flow of stalled traffic.

Officers in spotless armor blocked any progression further up into the city's tiers, demanding papers and declarations of wares.

Eyolin pulled her hand out of her pocket and bit into a plum with a smile.

A shop window flew open in front of Eyolin as she turned a corner, the wooden shutter missing her head by a hair. If not for the natural swiftness of a Silver Elf, she would be nursing a nasty bump.

She straightened and glared at the shopkeeper. Any ill-mannered retort dissolved on the tip of her tongue as she met the gaze of an old man with wrinkled, human skin, showing his years plainly in the crow's feet that peeked out of the corners of his eyes.

"Careful, little one. Almost got you before the big parade." He spoke in a rasp and blinked a handful of times to clear his milky eyes.

Eyolin glanced inside the shop and her stomach flipped. Rows of letter boxes lined walls of honey-colored wood. She cursed herself softly for allowing her feet to carry her to the spot of her latest day-dream. Twelve years she had avoided the postman's shop, the very smell of damp paper a bitter reminder of a life lost.

She fiddled with the two bronze rykes in her pocket. It was enough, she knew, to cover a search of archived letters. Or enough to send a bird out to locate a sister who did not want to be found.

Her eyes snagged on the scars in the wood that stuck out like blood on blanched wool. Nausea swelled and this time the memory could not be pushed down.

Two scariyai worked on the exterior of the post shop, their vibrant cloaks glinting with silk patterns unique to the magik-wielders they adorned. Each of their hands glowed a dim, luminescent green as they wove a protec-tive nature spell to keep the trees that supported the city alive and healthy.

The larger of the two scariyai released a breath and stood, brushing off the bark from his knees. He turned his head and beamed down at seven-year-old Eyolin, her head still a bit too big on her small body.

"Mageiyro, Mageiyro!" Eyolin squealed, hopping and grinning.

"How is my little warrior today?" Mageiyro asked. He held her out at arm's length in a good-humored assessment and nodded. Eyolin pulled her fists into her sides and stood tall.

"Ah, yes. Magnificent form. Crotha," he conceded. Eyolin released her fists having been given the formal command to relax and bounced back and forth in pride. "You should be very proud of your little sister, Arden. She has the makings of a fine soldier," he added with a wink. "Though your progress at the Academy is not to be overlooked. Your aptitude for knives and cryptology is most impressive."

The figure of Eyolin's older sister Arden came into view. She had their father's long, angular face with almond eyes and a lean, stringy figure. Even at her young age, Arden scowled with years of accumulated distaste.

Eyes narrow, she responded, "Very fine, Scariyai Mageiyro. Though Academy discipline is sorely lacking. Nothing gets done."

The scariyai regarded them both before speaking. "Things were different when magik was stronger in the world. Elves had their Gifts as an outlet, with a purpose. Now Gifts are mere trifles, if that, and used for the petty vices of war, a disgrace. An elf's blood needs drive, to create."

"Enough blood has been spent." Arden had Eyolin by the arm and was directing her into the shop away from the knowing gaze of the magik-wielder.

"Indeed."

Eyolin blinked her eyes to clear the past from the present, finding herself to have slid down the outside of the post shop with her knees tucked to her chest. These images were too clear, too lifelike to be a dream, weren't they? But they existed only in her mind. A result of too many years spent on her own.

The whinnying of a pony brought Eyolin's attention back to the tree-road. A dark-skinned Amber Elf wrestled the steed forward, the animal unused to the web of bridges and branches. Their saddle was piled high with tent fabric and woven baskets of the grassland kingdom of Aniöm. Farther down the road, a tanned Gold Elf from the seas of Velesah strode with an entourage of lesser magikal servants with skin the color of the plum Eyolin had stolen. A syket, if Eyolin remembered correctly, though she had never seen one in person. She couldn't get a good look at them, for large sacks weighed down on their backs.

She lost sight of the sykets as a barefooted couple spun into the avenue, breathless and disheveled. A sickly sweetness wafted off them. Eyolin recognized it as dwarvish spirits. The couple's joy carried them through the crowds toward the heart of the market where the parade was set to end in a giant celebration.

Trumpets blared twelve times and Eyolin bolted, arms pumping with a sudden burst of adrenaline. The events following the fanfare were bound to bring patrons, and she would be thrown out of her slimy bar of employment in an instant if she didn't show up on time.

Glancing up through the tiers she realized there was no way she would make it to the middle tier before the soldiers got there.

Without another thought, Eyolin dove into a narrow cranny between a spiraling staircase and a low hanging bridge linking two tiers of the city. She squeezed through, shuffling sideways as she went.

The bark was rough against her scratchy clothes, the knees already thinning to the point of needing a patch.

Her hand reached up instinctively, finding a notch in the wood where she could start the climb. If only her mother could see her now, she thought bitterly. Her little girl scrambling up the side of a tree of Mainwood like an animal. There was a law somewhere about climbing unregulated parts of the city, but frankly, she'd never been caught and therefore, the rule didn't apply.

Eyolin rested a third of the way to the middle tier, her grip on the wood unwavering. Every avenue, branch, and bridge were packed shoulder-to-shoulder with the citizens of Mainwood. Soldiers in glistening armor led groomed horses through the throngs, their grins wide and helmets off. Perhaps a dozen scariyai walked in their patterned robes, having little use for the metal of the scarox and foot soldiers. Not when their elemental Gifts could shield them much more efficiently. Eyolin glimpsed a scattering of scarox with what looked like an entire armory strapped to their backs.

Ever so slowly, the militia spiraled up the tiers. Those they passed dipped their heads with tears of gratitude on their cheeks. Children searched the ranks of soldiers from the shoulders of their mothers, scanning for a familiar face. Eyolin tore her eyes away, her arms shaking from holding her body flush against the tree and climbed the last lengths to the middle tier.

Eyolin dipped her head behind the counter of the pub, only half a horn late, and twisted a platter of sparkling elvish wines and olives onto her shoulder. A basket of crisps sat half-eaten at her back as she moved toward the packed tables of customers taking a break from the hypnotic symphonies of celebrations out in the main square.

She passed a table of Aideillian officers lounging along the far wall. Their attire, clean but worn and scratchy, singled them out as members of an outlying township or castle rather than the elaborate elite who lived and trained in the capital. Mainwood was the heart of the kingdom. Without it, there would be no governance. No order.

A pile of roughly polished helmets toppled over, the sound making her flinch. She needed focus. Eyolin drowned out the buzz of business, listening instead to the exchange of words at each table. She was behind on paying the owner of the bar her due in exchange for his silence and discretion. He'd caught her stealing from him. When she'd begged her tears dry he'd offered her a chance. Just one. She'd been living that chance for years, despite how taxing it was on the meager earnings she made.

She did quick arithmetic. One more moon and she would have enough to purchase a decayed plot that sat on the lowest elvish tier of the city. It had once been a family home until the magik that sustained the branch died. It was possibly the only place in that tree-city where magik had no foothold. And that was precisely where she wanted to live.

She'd prepared lies about a tragic journey from the war-ridden grasslands and her aspirations in the welcoming branches of Mainwood. A new name. A new identity. Every detail was prepared for the moment her chest of rykes was full. No more seedy half-elvish men whose jowls were larger than even the laziest of hounds. One more grand lie.

Two slender Silver men slid past Eyolin and out into the thoroughfare of afternoon revelry, their torsos tapered and clothed in spider silk, the overlapping panels fluttering in the gentle breeze. Nobility,

Eyolin noted from the star insignia that adorned the cuffs of their sleeves. The lineage of an elf was strength, for with it one could claim the power of the stars—of the gods and High Elves of old. Of magik.

Eyolin stopped finally at a table of three men with their boots propped on the flat space between them. Their helmets lay discarded by their chairs, along with their weapons. Half-elves, Eyolin deduced with a sniff. And of the kind a woman wouldn't want to run into at night. There was a stark divide between the elves of the higher branches and those who lived below. Most would say it was due to the concentration of magik that prolonged the lives of the three elvish races. Others said that humans were only ever meant to be ruled, hence the lack of magik they attracted.

A human woman employed by the barman straddled the soldier on the left. She wore a dress that consisted of two panels of black fabric, connected by a strip of cloth bound around the waist. The woman ground against the officer and tossed her hair from side to side. The officer heeded her little notice, being rather engaged in the smooth conversation in the Aideillian dialect with his companions.

"They're waiting for us to turn our backs on them, Huebeck and Ïsteldûr," said the one in the middle, looking particularly bug-like with his pointed ears sticking out from his head, his face consumed by wide eyes.

Eyolin's ears perked up and she schooled her features. Odd that they would mention the kingdom of Ïsteldûr, whose ruler had started the forty-year War of Uhura only to vanish and surrender the fortnight prior, leaving Aideil and her allies victorious. Eyolin had to admit that there was something off about it all but couldn't bring herself to care.

"You don't think the peace will last?" the third soldier mumbled, almost as if to himself.

"You didn't see Annjeih Castle, but I was there," the middle bug replied, hungrily. "They were winning. You must've not heard the commanders talking about deserting, running somewhere—I don't know, into the mountains."

"The Mendian Mountains? But those have been cursed ever since the dwarves disappeared," the right soldier said through a mouthful of olives.

"Why not go to Huebeck? Surely a bunch of fine Silver Elvish deserters would be welcomed into the underground sand cities. Everyone there is a mercenary or a murderer."

The soldier on the left spoke up at last, his fingers circling the woman's lower back as she ground harder—closer to a dog on a tree, Eyolin noted absently. "If they survived the labyrinth of tunnels filled with unimaginable beasts, the warlords of the desert would mount their heads on spikes for their sand-caea to feast on."

"Not to mention," the bug chattered eagerly, "Huebeck and Ïsteldûr have always stood on the same side of conflict. Magnogogue would doubtlessly go to the High Lord of Huebeck for aid. Wouldn't want to get caught there as an Aideillian."

"Magnogogue has been receiving aid from other sources of late," the soldier with the woman said. "Other realms whisper in his ear, pulling his soul from the land of the living."

Eyolin dropped off the sparkling wines and dipped away from the table, filing away the snippets of information to be traded later. An empty vial slipped beneath her belt, the clear powder it once contained now dissolved in the three flutes of wine already near empty in the hands of the soldiers.

"You truly are my best investment," the owner said with a clap on Eyolin's shoulder as she returned to the bar to refill her tray. She fought back the urge to cringe away from the film of slime on his meaty palms. "I don't care what you do or how you do it, as long as you keep our patrons paying."

Eyolin turned away from his wink with a pinched smile and slipped away before he remembered her dues. He believed she spiked drinks to keep people addicted and buying. The untraceable and illegal powder simply muted an elf's ability to keep their mouth shut. Words bought power. When one was incapable of keeping secrets, what was said could be converted into gold rykes. Eyolin only drugged elvish men who couldn't keep their hands to themselves, those who treated the staff with self-righteous biases. She excelled at identifying the good ones from the rotten. And if she got it wrong and they grew a spine the next day, it was a bar in the largest city of Aideil. Getting drugged was bound to happen.

She twisted through the crowded space toward a table near the entrance. The elves there wore sleek dress robes in black, beige, and dark green, their silken hair brushing past their shoulders. Young fourth or fifth tier aristocrats, Eyolin figured. Ages anywhere under two hundred from how smooth their skin was. They observed other tables and the crowds beyond the open widows with haughty prejudice, leering down straight noses.

"Anyone up for a trip to the ground?" The elf in black asked.

"On market day?" the beige-robed elf replied. "And risk a slapped wrist for tormenting the humans? Say when, brother."

Sensing his intention to stand, Eyolin stepped down on the corner of beige cloth pooled on the floor. She kept her weight on the ball of her foot as she bent the tray toward the table.

The elf stood as she anticipated, pitching backward as he stumbled on the caught robe. Eyolin fumbled the tray, feigning clumsiness, the short glasses of amber liquid clattering across the table. Hands moving swiftly, she righted each of the three glasses before they could spill all over the robes that cost the equivalent of her entire savings.

A long string of flavorful expletives tore out of the elf's pretty little mouth and Eyolin hurried to put on a frightened face.

The beige-robed elf's face reddened with fury, his eyes falling on the bowed barmaid.

It was the man in dark green that met Eyolin's gaze from where she stood bowed over the table. Her heart leapt to her throat; the fear no longer wholly fake. He was the same perfectly molded Silver aristocrat that she encountered daily, every surface decadent and flawless. Black hair and crystal blue eyes almost white. But there was a hungry glint that bore into her, raking across every decision she ever made and acting as executioner. He knew—something. Anything, if it damned her. Her most guarded secret felt projected on her outstretched hands.

When the beige-robed elf gripped her by the back to the neck, her breath hitched. Still, the white eyes of the seated man bore into her. She was lost in them. They betrayed an endless sort of wisdom, one that Eyolin could never comprehend.

Eyolin felt the grip on her neck tighten and her back straightened involuntarily. The corner of the beige robe was still lodged underneath her muddy shoes. The elf was yelling at her, yet she didn't hear one word. She was lost deep within the gaze of the severe blue-white eyed man.

A rush of fear as chilling as a frosty wind raised the hair on her arms. The ice settled on her skin as sure as snow and prickled painfully. Something wrong oozed from the elf who held her captive with his penetrating look.

It was an inner voice almost lost to her that confirmed what perturbed her so.

Magik.

She flicked her eyes around his collar and hands. No gemstone was immediately visible, though the marking of a Gifted elf could be beneath his green robe.

Eyolin had enough sense to jerk away from the fuming elf holding her by the neck, flicking her arm back to dislodge the man. She swiped the tray from the table and batted the shoulder of the standing elf. She disappeared into the crowd before any of them could pursue.

She meandered back to her table of drugged soldiers an hour or so later, their laughter heightened as they swapped war stories.

There was not only one but three human women swaying in front of the soldiers. A growing stack of bronze rykes piled on the corner closest to the scantily clad women.

"What do you think of the news of the border cities?" It was the bug-eyed elf who spoke, always the inquisitive one. "You think it's Ïsteldûr?"

The man on the right eyed the women with his bottom lip between his teeth. Eyolin watched his hands slide up and down his thighs with barely contained restraint. This wasn't the proper venue for what he wanted to do.

"Raids and kidnappings isn't a tactic the great necromancer is likely to sully himself with. He's more of a..." the elvish man tore his eyes away from the three human whores in front of him, noticing Eyolin tiptoeing up to the table. His eyes narrowed, void of the prior haze of bliss.

"More of a what, sir?" Eyolin chirped before her mind could catch up to her mouth. She hastily cleared away the empty wine glasses, replacing them with full ones. She turned to leave when his voice stopped her again.

"Magnogogue," he replied, his eyes shadowed. "High Throne of Ïsteldûr, the last true Gifted fire scariyai. Some might even call him the Heir of Matthieus, of the Old Throne." He paused, letting the words sink in as if Eyolin should have any idea what he was talking about. A bunch of High Elvish religious hokum and old news.

"Oh, he's the necromancer," Eyolin guessed, her tone a tad condescending. "We still won. He's gone, crawled back into whatever hole in a volcano he came from."

Once again, Eyolin winced internally. Her mouth ran off on her. This man was too far involved with this line of inquiry for her to pull back now.

"One of many, girl," the man growled. "The border between the realms is slipping. For centuries now, as magik grows weaker, things drip into our realm from the others. With Gifts fading, where else does power turn to? Dealing with the hell realm comes at a cost. But where will we be when those that dip into dark necromantic arts learn to not only create tears in the realms but also control what comes out?"

Eyolin felt the eyes of the white-eyed aristocrat boring into her skull. Magik may fade, but it will always exist. The five realms were created from magik. From magik life comes, without it nothing remains. It was the first thing they taught her during her two short years at the Academy. The reason anyone exists at all. And the reason so many do not. Magik.

The soldier flicked a ryke from the top of the stack meant for the whores. Eyolin snatched it from the air, not daring to take her eyes off him.

"To cease your questions," he spat. A gold ryke balanced in between his knuckles. Eyolin eyed the metal coin hungrily but backed away with a slight bow. He pressed the ryke into the thin strip of cloth at the nearest whore's waist. "We're leaving. The girl here will clean up."

His two companions sputtered into their nearly full glasses of sparkling elvish wine. The man on the right whispered into his whore's ear, her face blushing. She maneuvered around the crowded table to the wall, her arms straining under the weight of the soldiers' helmets and belts.

Eyolin melted into the crowd once more, losing sight of the trio tipping back wine like water.

Chapter Two

The tub of dirty water in the backroom was near to overflowing when Eyolin shouldered through the curtain. Eyolin unloaded the glasses into it, her mind spinning with how easy it would be to snap a man's neck. That gold ryke should have been hers for the cost of six flutes of elvish wine. Instead, she was given a mere bronze, hardly a third of what she was owed. Granted three of the drinks were drugged, but that should have opened their pockets more.

Eyolin's hand clenched and a glass shattered. She swore under her breath and quickly picked out the shards and wrapped up her bleeding fingers in a towel. From her position in the bar, she eavesdropped on Aideillian ministers after meetings, researched events happening across Alagana when she could, and ran her mouth at inopportune moments. Regardless, the stories of others turned into profit for her, especially now that she had a contact on the ground.

At the rear of the backroom was a tapestry of a dirt sprite, its spindly arms hugging a root for a pillow as it slept. Eyolin regarded the tapestry while massaging her cut hand, then reached to pull it aside.

It wasn't solid wood that lay behind it, but rather a nondescript door. A small indent sat where the sprite's hands were. Eyolin hooked her hand into it and the door popped toward her.

She felt a familiar buzzing as she stepped through the wards surrounding the herbalist's shop. Two deep breaths steadied her heartbeat, the sting of magik always bringing up unwelcome memories and headaches.

The owner wouldn't notice her absence. He never did with his only care for the extra coin she supplied him with. Had he been attentive, Eyolin might never have discovered the doorway tucked behind the tapestry.

Eyolin tiptoed up the curving staircase on the far edge of the shop, taking care to not disturb her master as she weighed out a flammable fungus behind the counter.

Bulbous jars hung in rows from untrimmed branches, each of them labeled with careful script. Tiny lamps nailed to the walls provided a warm flicker of fire across the space.

Ducking into the upstairs room, Eyolin stripped off the patched and damp apron, wiping from her waist to her toes with a spare towel to rid herself of the stink of the bar. Feeling satisfied she no longer stuck to the floor, Eyolin donned her prized leather armor. It had taken four months of earnings to buy. The pieces came from the old armory within the Fvrergendesh Mines for seventy silver rykes—a fortune for an unnamed elf in Mainwood. It's what set her back from purchasing a plot of land for her home. But the weight of the leather on her shoulders was as close to a hug from a mother as she would ever have. Even better was the benefit of people not ogling her when she wore it or purposefully trying to run her off a branch with a cart.

Her armor gave her a sense of authority when she had none. The herbalist didn't mind her wearing it. In fact, the old woman quite encouraged it. The cut was an outdated Farindor style, ensuring that she wasn't mistaken for an Aideillian solider. Aideil's southern neighbor was starkly different from them. Farindor's monarchy was ruled by Queen Daetheiri and her court, with all positions of power filled by elvish women. The woodland kingdom was guarded by a female militia that rarely ventured into the rest of the realm.

Here in Aideil, isolation and brutality was what the militia praised. As such, it was predominately filled with men who could better survive the harsh conditions. Those elves Gifted with magik were collected as children to be trained. There was no choice whether to return one's Gift to the realm on one's twentieth birthday. Such stringency made the Court of Farindor seem almost utopic.

As with every thought of magik, Eyolin's head had developed a severe pounding. The bitter scent of tea eventually pulled her back to the small room she'd lived in for the past few years.

The front door of the shop opened with a delicate bell. From the outside, the entrance appeared as an unmarred expanse of tree trunk thanks to a glimmer made by one of the herbalist's many illegal connections.

Eyolin appeared at the top of the stairs to catch a glimpse of the newcomer. The woman made subtle gestures and murmured softly to the cross-looking herbalist. The name of a rare herb drifted up—esthyri. Eyolin's master stood from her scales and shook her head in disagreement.

The customer turned in exasperation. The hood of her cloak fell from her head revealing ginger hair pulled into a loose braid. Her eyes flitted up to Eyolin and froze. The woman pursed her lips and brought the hood of her cloak up once more.

It wasn't anything out of the ordinary. Most of the clientele of the herbal shop wished to keep themselves anonymous.

Now that Eyolin was farther down the steps, she managed to catch the line of conversation.

"They're dying, what do you mean you can't sell it to me?"

Eyolin's master sighed, massaging the bridge of her nose. "Esthyri is strictly regulated. If I lower the price for you, I'll be unable to pay my source and this entire establishment will lose its reputation. This is the last of the herb for the remainder of the season."

"I need that esthyri," the woman said through gritted teeth.

"You don't need anything," the herbalist said. Eyolin could nearly feel her master rolling her eyes. "I've the right to refuse insufficient payment. This isn't a charity."

Although there was a glimmer on the front of the shop, there wasn't anything to dampen sound. The thought of a wandering drunk following a woman's voice to the hidden door behind the tapestry moved Eyolin the rest of the way down the stairs.

Eyolin reached into her pocket. The stem of a capper mushroom was wrapped tightly in a strip of fabric next to the empty vial of powder. Alone, the stem was extremely valuable. Eyolin had been meaning to sell it to the merchants at today's celebration. She was always allowed to collect extra on her foraging excursions as long as she met the requirements set by her master.

She reassessed the mushroom stem. It would be a fair trade for the amount of esthyri the woman needed. With a decisive nod, Eyolin slipped the parcel onto the counter in front of the healer.

"I found it in the mountains near Kletahr Valley," Eyolin explained, her master picking open the fabric gingerly. "It's worth the esthyri you need, and enough for us to pay for another partial shipment of the herb to restock."

"I suppose this was to be bartered elsewhere," the herbalist inquired. Eyolin kept her eyes down. The herbalist released a sigh and turned to the customer. "Very well. This will do. I'll wrap your things up."

The deal done, Eyolin noticed the steaming cup of tea on the counter. She glanced up at her master and the old woman nodded her chin at the tea with raised eyebrows.

Rolling her eyes, Eyolin snatched it up and took a sip. The nagging headache dissipated in moments; the bitter herbal tea saturated with thick honey.

She went to return it to the counter when her eyes met the narrowed glare of the herbalist. Eyolin pleaded with her eyes, but found no mercy in her master's stern face. Eyolin opened her mouth to protest, the cup of tea dangling above the counter.

"Does it help?"

Eyolin scowled. "Yes," she grunted.

"Then drink it."

Eyolin slurped pointedly and clunked the cup down. The herbalist looked Eyolin up and down, noting the armor and old dented sword at her hip.

"Be back for our evening tea, child. We have a few matters to discuss."

The afternoon air flushed the haze of the herbal shop out of Eyolin's sinuses, the door closing behind her and vanishing from sight. The middle tier of the city and its main square lay before her.

Wide, waxy leaves dripped water all the way to the ground. Thick branches twisted and curved outward. The bark disappeared into a blur of green vines and lichen speckled with budding flowers.

The shops and pubs around the main square of the middle tier were small and packed close together. Store-fronts with open windows and doors oozed conflicting smells, with the sounds of revelry soaring above all else. The upper two tiers were far more spread out with sprawling residences, the Academy, and Great Hall. Street vendors had their tents pitched in any available nook.

A flash of light reflecting off the hilt of a broadsword caught her eye as an Aideillian general shoved angrily out of a tent on the far side of the square. Eyolin's eyes went wide, and she faded into a shadow, her eyes glued to the one person not enjoying the celebrations.

As if sensing her attention, he angled his shoulders her way, eyes narrow, scanning the crowds. The air around him rippled, obscuring his features in a mirage. Eyolin squinted to get a better look and black eyes peered back. She watched his nostrils flare before green spread from his belt, the magik blinding. Once the light faded, the general stood taller; his shoulders rolled back and persona genial.

It was a trick of the light. Perhaps a scariyai glimmer meant to mask undesirable traits such as a nasty scar. And yet...

Eyolin started off in the other direction, but only made it a few paces until her gut pulled her in the other way. Her curiosity would one day be her doom.

She reached a hand out to pull aside the black tent flap the general had exited. The entrance was black velvet stitched with red and gold patterns. A heady incense sparkled in the air as she stepped inside.

An old woman in purples and reds was on Eyolin immediately, ushering her to a cushion in the center of the foyer.

"Oh," Eyolin sputtered. "Really, I'm not here for your services."

"Nonsense," the woman said with a wave. "Everyone who visits is drawn by the prospect of speaking with lost loved ones."

A vein popped in Eyolin's neck from how violently she recoiled. A seer—a witch who communed with the souls trapped in Midriel. The corruption of magik stank the air as much as the smoke.

Eyolin's flicked her gaze around the space, breathing shallowly through her nose to minimize the fogginess in the incense. It was a standard seer's traveling tent with minimal adornments and flowing panels of velvet dividing the room into sections.

From the way the seer fiddled with her bone bracelet, she *knew*. It was impossible, but this old woman knew the tragedies that followed in Eyolin's wake. She could see it plainly in the old woman's crinkled smile and milky eyes.

"For two silver rykes," the seer crooned, "you can talk to the man who waits for you beyond the veil of our realm."

Eyolin curled a lip. "What use have I for the dead?" *Or magik,* her mind added.

Eyolin made to stand but was stopped by the seer's old knobby fingers balling in Eyolin's sleeve. Something in the seer's demeanor drew Eyolin back into the cushion. What use had a general with a woman who communed with the hell realm?

"The dead may already be with you." The seer pulled Eyolin back to seated, her eyes vacant. "Even when the body decays, the soul lives on."

"What about that scariyai?" Eyolin pushed. "The man who came before me? He just left. What did he want?"

"Once a king walked among us. A god among sheep. Then, he split his power. Too weak."

The woman was speaking in riddles. Still, Eyolin lingered, an explanation nudging at the back of her mind.

"Now he hunts from below, in a skin not his own."

A chain rattled in the far corner of the tent, breaking the trance that held the seer to Eyolin's sleeve. Through the haze and darkness, Eyolin glimpsed slender blue legs and bare feet.

The velvet panels shifted.

"What is this?" Eyolin demanded.

A young girl drew her knees up to her chest. The chains rattled where they were clasped around her ankles. Yellow eyes blinked out at her, wide and frightened. Two soft feline ears flicked back defensively. Panic swelled in Eyolin's chest as the conversation from the bar she was on her way to transcribe and sell to the spinner merged with the truth before her.

Slavers. Raids. The kidnappings. They had reached the capital. They were in the main square under everyone's noses. And there was at least one officer who did nothing.

The seer jerked Eyolin's wrist, commanding attention. When Eyolin managed to tear her eyes off the quivering blue-skinned girl, black veins inked the seer's neck and cheeks, bleeding into haunting eyes.

"It's time for you to leave, Silver girl," the seer hissed.

There was nothing Eyolin could do. The seer may very well shred into her with whatever unnatural magik she pulled from the hell realm of Midriel.

Eyolin, lost for words, backpedaled out of the seer's tent.

Immediately, the swirling world of cheers and trumpets crashed into her.

A peddler with an assortment of candies and dried fruits yelled, "Branch Market! Get your Branch Market candies here! Celebrate the victory over the west with the finest of goods!"

Eyolin committed the shape of the girl to memory, adding it to the list of intel she would sell to the dwarvish spinner. She never asked what he did with her words, but if the stories were true—and more often than not they were—the captive would be free within a fortnight.

Surveying the crowds, Eyolin spotted an open path leading towards the spiral staircase to the ground. She cut through the throng, passing shops carved from unique knots in the wood and repeating the conversation from the bar until it was imprinted perfectly in her mind.

Eyolin treaded lightly on the sloping length of Weinthr Tree. She detoured down a set of floating stairs to the right of the main tree to avoid a congested segment of the elvish market. This particular path brought her past one of the old hiding spots she shared with her sister, Arden, who used to tuck letters and treats into the notch in the wood. Visiting the secret hole was a small reminder of her past that Eyolin could never seem to shake. She brushed her fingertips against the dotted wood that curled around a small opening. Eyolin removed a neatly folded parcel of blank parchment and a stick of hard charcoal. In the back of the hole lay a tattered square of cloth with seemingly random holes and notches in it. Arden's favorite cypher for sending messages to Eyolin while they were students in the Academy. A rag to most. A world of secrets for the two of them to share.

Pain blossomed behind Eyolin's eyes as memories pounded through her efforts to suppress them.

"House Kyenz, please," said Eyolin, speaking to the old postman over the counter. Her sister, Arden, stood at her shoulder, snatching up the bundle of envelopes in the postman's hand before Eyolin could peek at the senders.

Letters fluttered to the floor, save for one dusty piece of parchment which Arden clung to so violently her fingers crinkled the edges. Moments later, Arden's chest was rising rapidly from the words she read. Her eyes flicked to her little sister who regarded her quietly while nibbling a strand of licorice.

"Don't follow me, Eyolin. This is only for big kids."

Eyolin puffed out her chest, "I am big. I'm Year Two."

Arden knelt, forcing a serious face. "Yes, and I have a very important mission for you..." A handful of bronze rykes jingled in Arden's palm, outstretched for Eyolin to grab. "Get us tickets for the theater. There's a show in an hour. I'll meet you there."

Eyolin knew she should have done what Arden asked. Knew that she should have just gone to get tickets and forgotten about the letter, but she was seven years old and incredibly curious. She had watched Arden disappear around the side of a tree from her spot in the postman's shop, and it had unnerved her.

So, she followed.

There Arden was, walking toward a cluster of soldiers making their way up a set of stairs to the Great Hall, their armor glistening. The now balled-up letter was held tight in her fist.

A woman approached from behind wearing some straight, deep green dress. Ancient grey hair was braided down her back. From where she stood, Eyolin saw skin stretched thin over bone where the woman reached out to grab Arden's shoulder. A black design stood out on the wrist. Something serpentine.

Two more figures appeared at the old crone's sides, both human and about as old as Arden. The two girls wore clashing apparel. Where one wore a pale orange ball gown that young socialites wore in human cities, the other wore a fitted black, stretchy leather jumpsuit with thick-soled boots.

The ancient elvish woman spoke demandingly at Arden, her words draining the blood from Arden's face. From where Eyolin stood, telltale signs of panic pinched her sister's lips.

Perhaps she should have heeded Arden's advice and stayed away, but Eyolin's feet tiptoed closer all the same.

"Perhaps you lie, little elf," the woman cooed. "The Sisters will have her collected one way or another, this is simply us asking reasonably."

"Eyolin is not for sale."

"She will be when all the realms know what she is, and no amount of running will keep her from the claws of the highest bidder. But with me—with us she will be safe."

Her family's greatest secret, which they'd tried so hard to hide, had been their undoing. It was Eyolin's fault that the Sisters came for Arden. Her fault again for not speaking up when she had the chance. There was no one left for her to call family, just an emptiness in her soul and a determination to rebuild what she lost.

The memory blurred, twisting with whispers and accusations. Pain and fear as biting as a snake lashed at her from her subconscious. Arden's words the day she ran away from home and the soft lullaby of their mother broken intermittently by sobs. Screams and the cracking of wood flooded her mind.

"You can't rely on magik, Eyolin. It is forbidden to do so."

"That! Can't you even control that?"

"How special you are to be Gifted."

There was a line from a text Eyolin had once stolen from her father's collection of books that read: "To bind one's magik to a gemstone was to cultivate the magik before the energy is returned to the earth." It was in times such as now when she clung to those words.

She was so close. So close to that threshold—the only way she could atone for what happened to her family. In just under a year, whatever lay twisted inside her would be released back to the land in the cycle of life.

Eyolin's magik had not manifested itself in any way for twelve years. Be it a miracle or dutiful dedication to suppress it, she was one turn of the world away from being free.

Chapter Three

It took minutes for Eyolin to complete the transcription. At the bottom edge of the page was a loose sketch of the girl with blue skin and the chains that marred her too-thin ankles. As with all great puzzles, the location of the seer's tent was left for the spinner to decode in hashed lines and swirls around the parchment's border.

Once done, she returned the rest of the bundle and charcoal, concealing Arden's rag cypher.

Eyolin set off from her hidden spot and descended the remaining tiers of the city until her feet hit the ground of the human districts. She wove through the narrow streets of old, stone houses, pushing away the unwelcome memories from earlier. It was pressing late-afternoon and by this time the ground of Mainwood was near dark.

Dirty tents were propped up on rotting posts and wedged into stinking alleyways. The familiar breeze was thick with oil and horse manure brushed off the branches of the higher levels.

Eyolin perused various human vendors, absently pulling strands of hair over her pointed ears. It was easy to disappear in Mainwood, but on the ground to be an elf was to be a target. She had no intention of joining the ranks of the abducted.

The humans that resided in the city were private in their affairs until something elvish affected them. Eyolin noted their avoidance of eye contact, their minimal dialogue amongst themselves, and bent backs from attempting to keep the streets clean without the aid of magik.

She ducked around the side of a tent, scooting around a handful of empty sickbeds. A human with sagging, veined skin stood from his spot behind a chest of medical supplies, the brief alarm at her appearance melting into a smile.

"Any help today?" Eyolin inquired with a nod to the half-empty jars in an open chest.

"Not today, lass. Check back tomorrow. Tonight's celebrations will surely bring some business."

Eyolin folded a few rags absently while she nodded. "I'll be by in the morning then."

"Good girl," he replied. He was half-turned away when something lit up his eyes. "Say, you found any fresh tools in the upper tiers? Mine seem to have rusted overnight."

"Elven-forged metal still gets tarnished you know."

He seemed to deflate at that and Eyolin backtracked.

"I'll take a look in the morning, see if anyone has a fair deal."

"One of the good ones you are, and you still won't tell me your name."

That was the way it worked between the elves and humans in Aideil. Eyolin had been running errands for the kind human doctor who had once patched her up after a beating by a group of elvish boys, but they never exchanged names lest he get exiled for association with a Silver Elf.

They fought the same wars and lived in the same kingdom, but the humans long ago demonized the elves and the elves rose to the occasion. For all the glittery wealth in the elvish tiers of Mainwood there were multitudes of unspoken cruelties and hatred between the two races. The humans never stood a chance.

Thinking of this, Eyolin spoke up. "Elves and humans aren't so different you know."

The doctor grunted. "Tell that to the pointy bastards using us as cannon fodder in every petty disagreement. I've buried more of ours than there are elves to begin with."

"At least the War of Uhura has come to a close," Eyolin offered.

"I'm sure you folk will figure out something else to squander our lives over." He dismissed her with a wave, taking particular interest in a crease on a sheet. Eyolin took the cue and dipped into a slight bow on her way out.

With her first stop out of the way, Eyolin stepped onto the main avenue of the human district. A fat swine squealed at her ankles, and she stepped sideways into a puddle of liquid she didn't care to identify. The squat stone buildings on the main avenue were well kept, though moss and grass occasionally peeked through the cracks. A constant gloom only broken by torches and lamp-posts made everything seem laced with secrets.

Secrets were what she planned on dealing in. Straight on and two lefts would take her to a little dwarvish friend who ate gossip like a dragon with treasure. He could spin a song out of any half-truth and enchant crowds to dance until all their secrets came spilling from their lips. A true dwarvish spinner, rare even before the dwarves of

Mendia disappeared. Dwarves weren't Gifted with elemental magiks like the elves, but rather a magik of other means.

A warm wind lifted her long sleeves from her shoulders and the shadows danced across the mud. Eyolin listened to the growing music and clinks of coin on wood, smiling from the familiarity. The ground was as much her home as the second floor of the herbal shop.

She turned onto the market avenue tucked away behind the human's Hall of Policies. Vendors weighed coins and passed off their goods. A food tent down the way creaked and leaned from the number of men packed inside.

Above curved the main staircase that led up through the heart of Mainwood. Eyolin paused and watched elves move up and down like ants. Perspective warped the higher up she looked, vertigo flipping her stomach. The nearest curve of stairs looked as fresh as the day they were carved, having been preserved by nature scariyai and the Master of Aideil throughout the centuries.

The rest of the Greywood forest stretched into the distance, the ancient trees housing the vast expanse of the capital. The parchment tucked into her tunic grew heavy. Those soldiers in the pub said the land was withering away. If magik was the lifeline of Alagana, where would they all be when it vanished for good? Would the branches crumble to dust? Would the air turn toxic?

With a shrug, Eyolin shoved through the dense crowds.

The spinner had his crowd transfixed when she arrived. Children spilled out into the street their cheeks rosy and eyes glued to the dwarf with a harp on his knee.

His eyes were wide and animated as he plucked a chord. His spectacles glinted red in the firelight that spilled from the hearth. The spinner lifted his eyes to meet Eyolin's.

Words washed over Eyolin and the world around her fell away into the song of the spinner.

Suddenly, she was surrounded by a different room, from a different time. Her childhood bed soft as down. Morning light glinted through the trees. Within a breath, the spinner's magik ensnared her inside a memory of song and legends. His words were her mother's.

"I haven't been the mother I should have been." The tone made Eyolin's lip tremble. "There are so many things I was supposed to teach you."

"Can you tell me a story, then?" Eyolin asked. It was the only thing she could think of to say. "A story I should know."

Her mother took a long pause, eyes catching the sun rays peeking through the leaves. "There is one, actually, a tale that every magikal creature knows in their own way. It's about how even the worst acts have the power to shape a bright future."

Eyolin propped herself up on her elbows. "What is it?"

"To some they call it the Betrayal. But my people always referred to it as the Beginning, when our history was written. The great king of old, King Jenthius, ruled time and space from a palace in the Sky realm. He was the first High Elf in our world and ruled during an age when time itself did not tick.

"There were eight children born of the king, but only two belonged to the king and queen—Matthieus and Alaina, who despised one another most ardently. The other six had different mothers and were not in line to inherit the throne. They were Taurien, Sameun, Stoikgard, Elliena, Agualen, and Lila.

"During a fight between Matthieus and Alaina, Lila—a babe at the time—was killed. Rumor suggests that it was Matthieus' doing. Lila's mother, a sun sprite, pleaded for retribution. To honor his youngest child, King Jenthius created the Middle realm to be her burial grounds. The ashes were blessed to grow into a great tree. The magik of this new realm preserved the spirit of Lila who would one day serve the kingdom of Aideil.

"Lila's mother was pleased but would only be content if King Jenthius named Alaina his heir, changing the line of succession from the eldest, Matthieus, whose hands were stained red with the blood of Lila.

"To be High King was to have the power of all magik, to be used and shaped at will. Matthieus had all but claimed that power for his own. To shift that energy to Alaina was no easy feat.

"In a show of good faith, King Jenthius agreed, but only if Alaina had the spine to claim the throne. The result was something called a Choosing, where both candidates would present themselves before the Sky realm. The King's magik would then Choose whoever the rightful heir was. Alaina had the support of many, but she was notoriously submissive.

"Matthieus' jealousy and clever tongue drove him to reach out to his half siblings, urging them to draw upon their own talents and abilities to distract the King's magik during the Choosing. Some say he planned to murder Alaina. But the Choosing never happened.

"The other children of King Jenthius leapt at the opportunity to seize power for themselves. They saw an opportunity to establish themselves as gods in the realm of Alagana and all those who inhabited it. It would have taken them centuries to implement their schemes, for time still did not tick as it does now. However it happened, Alagana became dependent on the magik of the High Elves—a land where the children of King Jenthius were seen as gods.

The dwarvish spinner paused, his audience enraptured. An older boy closer to the front flipped a copper ryke into the pot at the dwarf's feet to continue the story. When he spoke next it was both Eyolin's mother speaking, as it was the spinner.

"Matthieus hated the joy of his half siblings as they spread their blood into the mortal Gold, Silver and Amber Elves, granting the lower races of elves access to the longevity of life and lesser magiks. He wanted to force the hand of his father, bend the will of the Council. The throne was meant to be his.

"One night, he slew every guard in the palace. If King Jenthius refused to initiate the Choosing, Matthieus would eliminate the only other option and ensure no other would follow. Matthieus crept into the royal chambers, driving a dagger through his mother's heart, carving it out and sticking it to the headboard.

"He made his way to Alaina's rooms, drawing a blade glistening with poison. She wasn't there. Alaina had gone to the throne room where King Jenthius and the Council had gathered and told him of the murder. All the magik within him couldn't save his queen when he heard what his child had done. King Jenthius collapsed at her bedside and unleashed the full breadth of his Gift. His grief tore through him, whipping his magik into a vortex that threatened to consume all that lived. Two new realms split off from the others—one from the Sky and one from Alagana—both imitations of hell: grief and loss, thus completing the five realms under the control of the High Elves.

"Jenthius saw his magik as the cause of his family's slaughter and betrayal and sought to expel all magik from the elven race..."

A collective gasp rippled through the crowd and Eyolin blinked away the visage of her mother seated on her bed. Everyone was looking at her standing along the far wall.

She'd been speaking in sync with the spinner, knowing this tale by heart.

The spinner blinked slowly at her. Eyolin swallowed and pinched her mouth shut, nodding that she would stay quiet. Satisfied, the dwarf struck a series of strings that recaptured the attention of all who listened.

"But magik has a mind of its own. It felt the blood ties to King Jenthius' children and crept into the skins of the six Betrayers—the title for the children of King Jenthius who knew of Matthieus' plan but did nothing. Feeling his power split, King Jenthius severed the ties before each of his children gained their full share of the High King's magik. Instead, the elements and skills were divided between those six children so that no being could ever hold the power of the King again. Magik follows bloodlines, and since it comes from the Sky realm and the High Elves, only elves are Gifted with innate magik beyond that of lesser magiks.

"The Betrayers were expelled from the Sky realm. The magik they now possessed drew them to various regions of Alagana—the lands that they had desired to rule over. With the waning magik he had left, King Jenthius shaped the seven kingdoms of Alagana, isolating his children from one another so that they could never again rise as one and further protecting Alaina with a gift of Prophecy.

"As there were six Betrayers, six elemental forms of magik were shared: water, fire, earth, air, mind and skill. Whatever remained, died with the king, whose spirit was too depleted to go on."

Silence lingered in the space where the story had been spun, weaving into the minds of the children who listened.

Satisfied that the performance was at an end, the children filed out, flicking rykes into the spinner's direction, until Eyolin was left alone with the dwarf.

He shrugged on a patterned quilt and squatted over the scattered coins with a wave over his shoulder to Eyolin.

"Remind me to have you lead a tale one of these days," he said. "You certainly bring me enough as is."

Eyolin folded her legs into a seated position at his side.

"I do not think these children wish to hear about abductions and shackles," Eyolin replied.

The spinner hummed. "It is precisely these words of warning that keep us from wandering too far from the road."

Eyolin unfolded the parchment and sighed. "Then let us hope your magik leads another to safety."

The dwarf paused, looking sideways at Eyolin. He carefully plucked the page from her fingers and scanned what Eyolin had transcribed. The corner of his lip quirked. He tapped a nail on the drawing as he asked, "You know this creature?"

"Someone taken without their consent."

The spinner pushed to standing and shuffled over to a stack of books tucked in the corner.

"Where one goes, so do they all follow." He glanced up at Eyolin's confused face and gestured grandly. "Their skin is not always their own, blue at birth, then otherwise unknown." He flipped through a tome, closed it, then moved on to another.

Realizing Eyolin still sat near the hearth, the spinner said, "Thank you, my little Silver. I will see what I can do." He glanced at the pot of earnings from the performance. "Take a handful, but don't be greedy."

Outside, the afternoon had stretched late into the evening. Market Avenue swelled with families clutching large slabs of roasted meat and the sloshing of mead filled the air.

The spinner had been generous with his payment, if not a little distracted. Still, Eyolin felt pleased with her day's work. She wove back the way she'd come, taking a side road to avoid the heaviest of the congestion. If she could skirt up the main staircase, she would make it to the herbalist's scheduled teatime.

Navigating around a cluster of wagons, the air around her cooled preternaturally. She could have stepped into a meat cellar from the fog that puffed in front of her, a stark contrast to the sticky warmth of the main avenue. The hairs on her arms stood on end. Her breath drew in shakily. She had felt something similar once. But just as she pushed to identify the memory, she felt emptiness. Like the memory was hidden behind a waterfall.

She angled her eyes to the sides, finding nothing out of the ordinary. There were closed tents to her right. A merchant with his head wrapped in purple silk and gold teardrops jangled a puppet with ruby eyes in front of a giggling child.

A group of young men stumbled by laughing, oblivious to the change in temperature.

The sensation intensified until Eyolin thought her skin might frost. Her feet were frozen and heavy. She took a step, slow and unsteady. Every instinct screamed to run, but to run would create panic. And there was no use alerting the crowds of a threat and causing the little child begging her mother to purchase the puppet to get trampled.

Eyolin moved to resume her walk through the human district when a bony hand wrapped around her wrist, yanking her sideways through a slit in a closed storage tent.

Her hip throbbed where she landed, the dirt hard and her old sword digging into her side. The pocket with the rykes split, the coins scattering around her.

The tent flap swooshed twice allowing Eyolin to quickly take stock of her surroundings. The inside of this tent was musty and void of boxes or merchandise—no thickly embroidered rugs or plush cushions for patrons to rest on.

A thick, black fog billowed up from the dirt too dense and pillar-like to be coincidental. *No*, Eyolin thought. *No, this isn't real.* It was a test of her resolve to bury her magik, this hallucination threatening to rip open old wounds and flood her with memories. It had happened before; on the morning she lost her mother. A black fog.

The entrance flap settled, leaving Eyolin prone in total darkness. She needed to get up. Get up and out onto the main thoroughfare before the magik hidden somewhere in her rotting body surged to the surface. She had to get back to the herbalist. Their evening tea would wipe away the fear that paralyzed her.

Yet her body refused to move.

She felt the air heave a breath the way a storm swirls around in circles. The sword at her waist jerked, ripped from its sheath by a hand Eyolin could neither see nor feel. An invisible hand closed around her throat cutting off any chance at a scream.

The chilling grip tightened the more Eyolin thrashed and kicked and scratched, scrambling to breathe. It was so dark, her vision blurred, and it made no difference. Unconsciousness tipped closer.

No, she thought with a clarity that startled her. *I survive.* It will take much more for this realm to be rid of me.

Stand.

The voice could have been her own, but it sounded too deeply within her bones to have been spoken aloud, in too deep a tenor, commanding a primal instinct to obey. Her weight shifted in response, hesitant and wobbly against the pressure at her throat.

Telekinesis, the voice spoke a second time, firmly masculine. With feet planted, Eyolin pushed off the ground, rolling her shoulders and closing her eyes to match the darkness that suffocated her. The muscles in her neck tensed to adapt to the loss of oxygen, a slight defense against her attacker.

Somewhere, from deep within Eyolin's core, the same masculine tone rumbled with rage. She did not hear it so much as feel the reverberations chattering her ribs. The telekinetic hand released her throat and retreated. The lesser magik had broken.

Eyolin swallowed down stuffy air, her eyes flying open. Her knees buckled involuntarily. She crumpled atop her unsheathed sword, the metal cool and familiar with its dents and dullness. Her fingers wrapped around the hilt, shaky but strong.

Dark flame blossomed in a sphere in the corner of the tent. Black flickers of light smoked with a power not meant for this realm. Where there was darkness, cold black fire swirled through fog as solid as stone.

Shadows writhed, a figure forming from fog, stepping through space. It cupped the dark flame greedily. There was no face or body, but a cloak of night and arms that shifted in the gloom.

Eyes that were not there focused on Eyolin's body curled on all fours.

Eyolin tensed, shifting back on instinct as the fire expanded and launched at her face. The dirt where she had knelt darkened into ash. Where the darkness spread, so did the pit.

A second sphere of dark flame, twice the size as the first, ignited to Eyolin's dismay. Eyolin felt the old steel in her hand and knew that one touch of that dark flame and her blade would crumble to ash.

The figure made of shadows hissed in a series of clicks and guttural scraping sounds. Eyolin couldn't help but note the similarity to an insect.

A grey lightning bolt zoomed through the tent from the outside. The popping in her ears signaled the presence of an exceedingly powerful scariyai.

The grey light collided with the dark fire. The two elements writhed and flicked at one another. To Eyolin, the competing energies resembled cats brawling. She choked down the laugh in her throat at the image.

The lightning expanded until the flame was contained in the center. With a final circle, the bolt emitted a powerful blast of light.

Darkness settled alongside silence.

Eyolin stumbled backwards. The fabric of the tent rippled at her back, bolted down and thick. She angled the tip of her blade into the canvas.

A figure burst through the tent's entrance at the same moment Eyolin pushed her sword through the back. The flash of light from the torches outside illuminated a creature cloaked in darkness. Lunging at her.

Grey light flowed off the figure so brilliantly that the creature recoiled back into shapeless black fog.

Eyolin pushed her sword down, the tent tearing. She was almost free to slip away and vanish. But her hands paused, the edge of the blade angled flat for the final slice. She was intrinsically drawn to the figure illuminated by sparkling power, curious to who they were, why they were in the human district, and facing off against a creature without a solid form.

The figure, a man from the broadness in his shoulders, drew a semi-translucent blade that emanated its own light. He cracked his neck with a jerk to the side and deflected an onslaught of dark flames spewing from three directions. The hand not clutching the hilt of the short sword splayed open. Little stars of magik twinkled at his fingertips and the shadows retreated.

Power radiated from him as intoxicating as any drug she could have slipped into sparkling wine. It contrasted the daunting evil that boiled in cloaked darkness. The man's power was crisp and direct, alluding to a song of magik and light that she had long ago given up hope for. She was enchanted.

An unholy snarl tore her attention back to the primal mass of dark matter. The creature took on a larger form, this time with legs far more solid than wisps of shadows. It slithered from side to side, assessing the man.

The shadow screeched and lunged, engulfing the man in fog. Stars of magik twinkled and sparked, grey ribbons of power coiling around the fog like reins.

The metal in her hand tingled in response, shooting through her fingertips and onto the blade of her sword. In a burst of light, Eyolin's sword ignited with crackling lightning. She flinched back, trying to shake the sword from her grip, but her hand held tight. The glowing weapon felt like a natural extension of her arm. Twelve years without magik melted away and her blood sang with savage delight. One year left to dance with magik, to arm herself with that seductive blanket of power before she reached twenty.

The voice deep in her chest chuckled. This was what it wanted.

Whatever hellish creature had attacked her now stood over her rescuer. The man had been knocked on his back in the skirmish. A torch of black fire extended from the creature's hand, catching on the canvas of the tent. The man's blade, no longer aglow, lay knocked to the side just out of reach from the man's outstretched hand. Bright sparks pulsed from his chest, absorbed by the growing mass of fog. Eyolin knew what it was without a question. The man's life force.

He moaned while his foot twitched, hand inching toward a dagger tucked into a fold of leather. It wasn't defeat that pursed his lips, but ecstasy. He did not sense the nearness of death that each pulse of light brought him closer to.

Eyolin, emboldened by the electricity that sizzled on her sword, lunged.

The shadow burst into a burning red vortex around her blade, crumbling like parchment to a flame. Swiftly, it disintegrated, the suffocating pressure dissipating.

Once Eyolin was sure that the fog would not return, she turned her attention to the still figure that lay in the entrance of what was left of the tent. He looked young with his eyes closed. In his current state of unconsciousness, his features were soft with no creases or worry on his forehead, his jawline sharp and skin smooth of stubble.

A spasm shuddered through his body and his eyelids twitched causing a narrow blade to fall from its hiding spot along his ribcage.

The sword dropped from her own grip, the electricity vanishing as soon as her touch lifted. Magik prickled at the back of her neck as she knelt next to him. Without thinking, she hovered a hand above his chest. Dark energy leapt up to meet it. Her body pulled back, but her hand stayed rooted to the space above his solar plexus. The energy wrapped itself up to her shoulders like a vine. It burned with blistering heat. Smoke hissed near her shoulder.

Eyolin closed her eyes, wishing for the pain to simply go away. As if listening, the snaking energy faded.

Opening one eye, Eyolin saw that the dark matter had vanished, but she gave a squeak, nonetheless.

The man's eyes were open.

Eyolin recoiled only for him to catch her wrist. He was clad in black leather armor, light, Eyolin noted, but strong. Pliable enough to accommodate movement, but not too soft as to allow a knife. The belt as his waist wove through black pants. A curved dagger was looped through one of the sheaths.

His broad shoulders shrugged in discomfort, and he released his grip on her wrist. The absence of his touch left a poignant tingling. The magik pushing against her skin urged her to touch him again.

It was then Eyolin realized that most of the tent had burned away, exposing them both to the throng of people packed onto market avenue.

Not a single head turned their way. It was as if they didn't exist at all. That nothing out of the ordinary had transpired.

The prickling in Eyolin's hands intensified and spread. She stretched out an arm. A web of shattered glass splintered upwards in the shape of a bubble covering the tent area.

"Mirroring spell." Eyolin swore it was the voice in her head giving her useless pointers, but then it spoke again, very much so in front of her. "Sort of like seeing into the minds of those passing by and altering their impressions to the mundane, concealing whatever is inside. Tricky right?"

Eyolin gaped as the man propped himself up on his elbows, a slight wince flickering across his face.

"Was that you?" Eyolin demanded.

"Sure, I'll take credit." He winked. Eyolin's lip twitched in agitation, and she had the thought to call lightning to her knuckles and smash his pretty face in. His face softened. "Thank you."

He vanished. Like the popping of a bubble. Just gone.

Eyolin reached over where his body had been and waved her arms out wide.

"Elf's gone mad isn't it," a gruff voice mumbled. Eyolin snapped her head up. An old human man in a dusty navy suit coat spat on her face in passing, being sure to kick a bit of dirt into her hair to match. No more mirroring spell, she deduced. Just a grimy elvish girl on her hands and knees fisting at the air looking mad.

"I do look ridiculous," Eyolin muttered.

She stood, wiping the spit off on her sleeve. She snatched up her sword and the slim dagger, tucking both into her belt and dusting off the dirt from her knees. Her mind reeled as she replayed the events from the tent. The black shadow monster, its insect clicking and black fire. Equally as disturbing was her unlikely savior evaporating the moment the mirror spell broke.

Eyolin shuffled in the general direction of the spiraling staircase, but her mind was leagues away.

Chapter Four

Distracted by the realization that she'd forgotten the coins littered on the ground, Eyolin ran into an enormous officer on rounds. She reeled back, noting the stature of the half-giant. Her head hovered slivers away from the large assortment of knives hanging on his belt like a butcher.

"Sorry, sir, I'm—" Eyolin blustered. "Sorry."

The officer's hand clamped down hard on Eyolin's forearm. His fingers could snap her in two. Eyolin glanced up at the half-giant's face then lost the nerve, focusing intently on her dirty clothing.

She risked a glance up, putting as much innocent fear into her face as possible. He wore a traditional Aideillian uniform of brown-on-brown wraps and leathers. He had a square face covered with a rust-colored cropped beard. His mouth was pulled into a permanent scowl between burn scars and sunspots.

His frown deepened. "You're cold as ice."

"I've been working in the shade," Eyolin replied, the lie falling off her tongue.

"Like you've been in a meat locker for a week." His tone was flat.

"It's chilly on the ground."

His grip didn't loosen. Rather, he pulled her toward him. "You're awfully young for an elf to be alone on the ground. *Speak your name.*"

Eyolin's mind bowed to the authority of the command. A piercing pain in her head confirmed that the half-giant was using Soft Tongue. She bit her cheek to hold back the words.

"I go by the name of Eyolin Kyenz-ustheira."

The officer's brows quirked. "Of the late Silver Kyenz line? How fascinating. *Tell me more.*"

This was why she hated magik. It forced obedience and punished those who stood in opposition. No matter how hard she willed her body to resist, it would bend for a talent as meager as commanding a few words.

"I cannot lie to you, can I?"

"Unfortunately for you," the officer replied, "the Kyenz line doesn't exist anymore. There are no survivors."

"You're familiar with the family?" Eyolin chirped. Her palms slickened with sweat.

He frowned. "I recall the incident report when the Kyenz's *eihra* and girls were declared dead. Such a tragedy."

Now Eyolin's heart was in her throat. She was going to vomit all over this officer's polished boots. She had never heard the words out loud. And to group her father into the deceased was to confirm what she assumed for years. Everyone in her bloodline was dead.

"The Lord Kyenz and his wife, both trained scariyai," the officer said to himself. "And two unGifted daughters, erased from the records."

"As it is," Eyolin started. "There must be more than one family who share the same last name."

"You're evasive and adept at skirting my questions." He spoke bluntly and without sympathy, though why she was expecting some level of kindness from an officer in the Aideillian army she couldn't say.

"Would you prefer I tell you I was dragged into an empty tent by a shadow that hurled fire at my face while turning the dirt to ash?"

"Yes."

Eyolin stumbled over what to say next. The half-giant bristled, but the hostility wasn't directed at her. He seemed intent on the space behind her, like he was glaring her attacker into existence by sheer will. His grip on her arm lessened.

"Do you often frost over?"

Eyolin gave a little yelp noticing how her skin had paled to light blue. The officer tipped her face up with a finger under her chin.

"I'm really quite well." Though the wobble in her voice betrayed her.

"Age?"

"Twent—nineteen." Every word was a blunder. The weight of Soft Tongue coerced her into revealing truths, and the truth was precisely what she could not afford to speak aloud.

"On the threshold," he mused. "Gifted?"

Eyolin's mouth opened to reply honestly, acknowledging that resisting his questions was futile, but the rumbling voice that guided her earlier returned sternly.

No, it commanded.

Just like that, the Soft Tongue lifted.

"I am not," Eyolin said, plastering on a smile.

"Then what could possibly have frightened you about speaking to me?"

"There was a creature, back in the tent where I was attacked."

Eyolin had no reason to believe this officer hostile. Perhaps she could convince him to escort her to the stairs and lose him in the branches.

"*Did it ever leave you?*" Again, the Soft Tongue drifted over her mind and did not affect her.

"I'm not possessed if that's what you mean."

"You don't need to be possessed for a dark creature to be with you."

Eyolin's mind flickered to the voice swirling within her. Was it dark energy? Or magik itself clawing to be freed?

"How did you escape?"

Eyolin weighed her words. She had the power to answer freely, and she suspected the officer was wholly unaware of the change.

"I cut a hole in the tent," she started. "At first I was knocked to the ground, but I found this dagger next to me and threw it." Eyolin drew the slim dagger she retrieved from the man and offered it to the officer. "Whatever attacked me burst into flames at the touch."

The officer glanced at the blade and hissed through his teeth. Eyolin realized too late that whoever she stole that blade from may not be friendly to the kingdom.

"Then a Grey cannot be far."

"A Grey?" Eyolin repeated.

The commander angled the blade, its tip to the pad of his finger. Even in the gloom of the night—heady and black on the ground aside from the periodic spheres of torchlight—the blade sparkled with its own luminescence. Slightly opaque and gleaming. A weapon of magik.

"An order that wields magik of a different realm. Mixed-bloods who are responsible for tearing kingdoms apart for sport."

Eyolin could have rolled her eyes if the officer's face hadn't looked so serious. She sighed.

"Do they realize there are other colors to choose from? Why Grey?"

The officer chuckled darkly. "Light and dark, black and white. Both are bound into the Grey." He tucked the blade into a fold in his belt. "In a different age, they could manipulate the folds of space in between color and light. Now they just meddle for money."

"So they dropped a dagger. Doesn't sound that dangerous." Eyolin didn't mention how the man had lost a kernel of his life to the creature. How dark energy had crawled up her arm when she got too close. She knew that an inquiry was imminent for claiming the name of Kyenz where everything she said would damn her. She would have to lie her way out of it, or own up to the truth. Both had little room for error.

"I have witnessed the carnage that follows in their wake. It is enough to make a grown man wretch. They kill without feeling. Without thought." The officer pulled Eyolin into the torchlight. "The Binding that holds their magik together lets darkness fester until it wraps around their spine and snaps it in half."

He held her head still, gripping her at the jaw.

"So what did a Grey want with you?"

Eyolin shrugged, casting off an air of indifference.

"We didn't exchange words," she offered after a pause. "Again, I found the dagger, not the man."

"And when did you realize that a frae can only be killed by a fatal hit using magikal means?" The officer jerked her head to either side, checking her ears for a gemstone. His glance flicked down to confirm she wasn't wearing a necklace or other obvious stone. "As you say you are without Gift, you have no magik."

The realization sunk her stomach. "So the frae can't be dead."

The officer's face blanched at the same time as a scream sounded from a nearby building.

"A frae and a Grey have breached the borders of the city," the officer commented gravely.

One scream multiplied into a chorus of terror.

"To hell with it." The officer gripped Eyolin by the shoulders and shook her a little. "When I say run, you run, and do exactly as I say. Get to the Great Hall, take the tunnel entrance on Theorist that will take you up the center of the tree and away from the haze. Frae are most powerful after sunset and we are nearing the twilight hour."

"I have a safe place to stay," Eyolin started, thinking of the herbalist's wards.

"*You will go,*" the officer commanded with such force that Soft Tongue settled on her mind, persuading her that it was in her best interest to flee to the Great Hall. Nowhere else. Taking the exact route he told her. Whatever voice was aiding her was silent.

"Are you going to escort me?" The question was more fearful than a retort. Eyolin squinted into the darkness of the street. The blackness billowed and moved, swelling.

The screams registered at a pitch just beyond the nearest building. Eyolin's eyes fixated on the corner of the avenue and the cracked window above a dull painted sign.

"One last thing," the officer said, ignoring her and drawing two blades. "Don't think of a soul, or there will be none left in this city by morning."

Eyolin realized with a rush of dismay that there were no security details reporting to the cries, save for this one burly half-giant. The human division comprised a large portion of the Aideillian army and controlled all ground patrol within city limits. Not one was in sight. Shouldn't there be some alarm for threats?

Dust floated through the air with all the time in the world. The wind held its breath. Movement slowed to a halt until only the echo of a scream hung overhead.

The temperature dropped to well below freezing, turning Eyolin's nose pink and her breath cloudy.

A wall of black haze shot from the hard packed dirt. The cloud thickened, covering the sky and ground until the flickering torch-lights were blotted from view and Eyolin couldn't see her own boots. Vertigo upended her sense of direction.

Red dotted eyes blinked at her from the murk. With each blink a new memory surfaced, flipping through the pages of Eyolin's childhood. Her mother. Her sister. An old man scooping her off the floor as she sobbed. Her father. Darkness. Pain. Blood-red pain. Muffled words sounded in her head, though no matter how hard she strained, she could not discern the phrases.

The officer's voice called to her from behind. "Go! Kyenz-ushteira, now, *go!*"

Eyolin launched herself forward. Her arms went first, scooping and clawing at the swirling black fog. It smelled of death. Of the rotten corpses of slaughtered animals piled in the woods where a predator stashed its kills. The scent latched onto her skin until she felt marked as already dead.

A screech echoed around her. She swam harder. The fog stung her eyes. She took a quick right turn and skidded sideways, trusting the years of navigating the ground of Mainwood. A tree root caught her ankle and she sprawled out on to the ground. Her sword came loose and clattered into the black fog.

Eyolin lunged after it, but the fog had faces. Each distorted in and out of focus without any distinguishing features. They whispered in a melancholy harmony of death and despair, of prisoners trapped in a ring of fire. Moans and wails. Sobs and fear. A feminine voice sang words of a different realm that left traces of frost on Eyolin's cheek. She sounded lonely; a mother trapped in a guilt-ridden hell. The faces bobbed up and down around Eyolin's body. A nightmare haunting from another life. A few gripped at her as they drifted past, hands dissolving where they would have touched her.

She scraped her hands along the ground. It was wet. Slick. The black haze stuck to her palms as Eyolin looked at her hands. Blood. Her mind reeled. The memory of her mother's death flashed in and out in detail. The bones. The light.

"*Eihra...*" Eyolin whimpered, calling out for her mother involuntarily.

The black fog froze and all the changing faces converged into one. The gentle face of her mother emerged from the stillness, the same as the last time Eyolin saw her with frazzled hair and a purple nightgown.

"Eyolin," cooed the voice, a perfect mimic to her mother's. "Come, Eyolin. I've missed you."

Her face was exactly as Eyolin remembered down to the soft smile that relaxed her eyelids.

Eyolin's instinct to flee dissipated. It was her, years after death. Alive. Eyolin could reach out and touch her. A calmness settled on Eyolin's shoulders, one that she hadn't felt in years. Safe, she told herself, her own mind clouded. She was safe here.

"Nothing can harm you now, dearest." Her mother held out her arms, the skin smooth and flawless. "Eyolin, come to me."

Eyolin fell to her knees, reaching toward the visage of a life lost. She clasped her fingers around her mother's delicate hand. It felt thinner than it should. Her mother's eyes flickered black long enough for Eyolin to clear her mind of the frae's bewitchment.

She jerked her hand back, only for the frae to clamp down on her wrist, nails digging into Eyolin's flesh. The face of her mother curled into a snarl.

"I told you to come, child."

The voice dropped any pretense of love, ticking into an ear curling snarl. Eyolin scratched at the hand holding her down, her feet scrambling to find traction. The creature's hold on her mother's image was slipping. The skin snagged and twitched, and the solid eyes of her mother blinked black. Taloned feet clung to the haze like a raven on a branch.

She couldn't get away.

The frae's telekinetic magik wiped a tear from her cheek.

"You think you're innocent. That you can stop the deaths of those who love you. But you were always meant to destroy."

New sets of red eyes winked from the fog.

"Is this her?" they whispered.

"Her blood is fresh as the air in this realm."

Eyolin's chest ached from the pounding of her heart. Though the frae held her to the spot, it was not alone in the mist. There were more things out there.

The frae did not like that at all.

"She's been claimed," the frae clacked, the mouth of Eyolin's mother peeling away from bone. Its black eyes flicked through the mist and Eyolin felt ribbons of magik snaking through the haze. The red eyes shut, only to reopen in front of Eyolin's nose.

Voices resonated around her. "We have defied far greater bargains than a simple blood debt."

Eyolin screamed at whatever gods once existed to, just this once, save her, though she knew she did not deserve it.

The voices fell silent and Eyolin glimpsed a figure, lean in stature, and cloaked in night, fade in and out of the fog. She briefly thought of the Grey from the tent and waited for a flash of his blade to cut through the darkness, or a tide of sparkling magik to wash away the walls of black around her. Neither occurred.

This figure shifted from solid to mist much as the frae had done in the tent, sending a shiver of fear that there was a second monster stalking her. If this was her god, he was no High Elf of the Sky.

One by one, the red eyes vanished.

Only the frae remained.

Its eyes were glazed from extending its magik out and for a moment it looked sad, or wistful, every gruesome part of it. Eyolin opened her mouth then, to say something, or thank it for not killing her, she didn't know.

"Master doesn't know," it spoke, sputtering into a jagged cough with each breath. "He's after her too."

Eyolin quivered on the ground, her body still and fatigued, any words escaping her breath. *He.* An ominous and unnamed *He.* A master and a debt and a monster.

The frae opened its mouth wide and inhaled. Eyolin's life energy pooled in a dense wad in her throat. She envisioned it absorbing her energy and flying away, leaving her body cold in the dirt.

Its hand flew to its ribcage and Eyolin's vision cleared. A wide blade pierced the frae's chest from the back. The hand that gripped Eyolin's fell away as a rotten clump with rags of skin dangling off the bone.

Black eyes shuttered and the creature collapsed. The half-giant twisted his sword and yanked it from the corpse of the frae. The metal dripped with black blood. Eyolin gagged from the smell. Where the blood touched, steel crumbled away. He took his second blade and drove it into the frae's skull where it stayed.

"I thought you said mortal means can't kill a frae," Eyolin said her vision tilting.

The officer grimaced. "This isn't a mortal blade."

He took a fist of the frae's stringy hair and picked it up, the short blade sticking out of its forehead. Eyolin stared into a face with a skeletal hole for a nose and empty crevasses for eyes. Flesh dangled off the bone in shreds. The bone that shone was decayed. Eyolin tried to find fear or anger to channel at the monster, but she couldn't stop seeing the sadness in its eyes moments before its death.

"Did it say what it wanted with you?"

Eyolin stayed silent, lost in the empty gaze of the frae.

"The frae don't target at random, there isn't enough free thought in them. It was being controlled by someone. Did it mention who?"

Every fiber in her being told her to run, that though the frae dangled lifeless before her, the red blinking eyes would find her if she didn't move. She didn't trust that this officer would keep her safe or that the frae was truly dead. And, for some reason, she wouldn't mind if the frae lived. She had believed the frae as it spoke with her mother's face that it wouldn't harm her. It wasn't rational, but she trusted that as long as it had held her, whatever else lurked in the fog couldn't touch her. The frae's crushing telekinetic strength would have eased once she lost consciousness. Whoever had sent it wanted her alive. Which meant that someone knew who she was. They could know her father, how to find her sister—a family she'd lost. Just as the seer said. There was a man trying to reach her from Midriel. The face of her mother flashed before her and she knew that she owed it to the memory of her mother to track down whoever was after her.

The half-giant was waiting for her reply. Eyolin winced and looked down. A gash ran down her forearm, dripping blood onto scuffed knees. She needed somewhere to recover and think things through, and she couldn't burden the herbalist now. Not with an officer too invested in her well-being. She needed somewhere safe to hide, somewhere right in the open.

"I'm no one," Eyolin said. "There isn't anything good to gain from me."

"Even no one is always someone."

"You said Professor Einsfar would find me a room until it's safe?"

"That will be up for discussion if you are deemed to be not a threat."

"I'm not..." Eyolin started, but her vision went black, and she crumpled to the ground.

Chapter Five

Eyolin woke to a deep throbbing in her head. She groaned and reached a hand up. A sharp pain shot through her arm. The gash from the day before was wrapped in cloth and lathered in salves that cleared her sinuses.

She massaged her neck. In doing so she noticed colossal wooden arches that met at a point high above her head. The wood glowed with vitality, but Eyolin felt sick. She shouldn't be there. What was she thinking allowing herself to get caught by an officer and dragged into the one place where secrets were extracted by scariyai without mercy?

The rising panic ebbed the longer she let her eyes wander. She'd never been in the Great Hall of Mainwood. The sunlight filtering through stained glass windows fell in dappled rays, putting her above the third tier of the city where the leaves didn't blot out the sky. Narrow beds stretched to either side of her in two neat rows.

Eyolin waited for the burning sensation of a scariyai digging through her memories as they were rumored to do to prisoners, but felt only her headache. Her wrists were free of chains—a small relief. Though when she didn't show up at the bar, the owner would surely follow through with his threat of alerting the authorities of her transgressions, elaborating where necessary. An inquiry would expose the herbalist, Eyolin's comings and goings with the spinner, her associations with the human doctor on the ground. It would be an unraveling of secrets and a life she had been so close to leaving.

One thing scared her above all others. She had given that officer her name—her true name, before the Soft Tongue had broken. Those damning words alone opened up old wounds with worse consequences.

Symbols and murals were carved into deep red wood. Eyolin fixated on the typography hidden in the symbols rather than dwell on her present situation. Her mind clicked into gear and the symbols arranged themselves into words and pictures in Ancient Elvish. They were the most exquisite pieces of art she had seen in years, so lifelike that they appeared to move.

There was a young woman that stood beneath a tree. It was in full bloom with a carved door at its base. The next panel illustrated the great tree burning. Flames ate away at the thick branches. The expanse of its limbs crumbled away into the smooth wood. Petals fell in puffs of ash and the young woman's face twisted with savage satisfaction.

The third panel had the young woman in the center of a wave, controlling it to extinguish the fire. The tree was left scarred. Dark streaks were etched into the tree's trunk and marred the door. The woman turned away with a look of malice.

In the final panel, the wave swallowed her whole. Only the tree remained.

Eyolin squirmed and searched for an explanation in the symbols. The story wasn't anything she had heard or seen before, and she strongly disliked not comprehending what looked to be a monumental historical moment. There was text she decoded at the end of the illustrations: *The fall of Lara: the fourth Sarom.*

Lara... Eyolin didn't recognize the name from any books or tales.

"Look who's finally awake. I would have never heard the end of it if you died on my watch from a scratch."

Eyolin jumped and the cot creaked. A boy stood next to her in white smocks. His black hair was buzzed to stubble, and his dark brown eyes twinkled with amusement.

"I'm Dale."

"Hi," Eyolin said, her voice wary.

"I'm not a nurse," he said hastily, waving his hands. "Just the kitchen runner, so don't bother asking what happened." He pretended to hold a note pad and pencil. "Need anything?"

He spoke fast, which didn't help her headache a bit. Her mouth was tacky, and she found herself wishing for the herbalist's disgusting tea—the herbalist who no doubt would be worrying for her, but could not go looking.

"How'd you end up working here?" she said finally. Eyolin gestured at the glass of water that lay just out of reach. Dale nearly threw it at her.

"You mean because I'm a human?"

Eyolin didn't respond. She hadn't immediately noticed his rounded ears, her mind still catching up to her situation. His tone dropped the hospitable front from the moment before.

"Look, we all slave around for the Silver Elves. May as well get paid for it. Free food and shelter. All we lowly humans need. Is that what you want to hear? What do you want, your highness?"

Eyolin's mouth pinched into a scowl, and she cozied into the cot with the glass of water. She was too achy to be pleasant.

"Go hungry then. I'll take whatever you don't eat."

Her stomach made a loud gurgle and Dale snorted.

"Bread," she said quietly. "Would be nice, thanks."

Dale spun around and vanished through a servant gate without further comment.

Discomfort settled in as she waited. She was exposed in every way. Her armor, cheap as it was, had been stripped away, along with her dented sword. Everything itched and all she wanted was to wake up anywhere else, preferably before the frae and the magik and the haunting feeling that she was being observed caught up to her.

Sitting up to better look around, Eyolin spotted an older elvish man standing by two great oak doors with his hands clasped across his round belly. Wrinkles disappeared into a long, white beard. His fitted armor gleamed where the sunlight glinted off his middle. A deep purple cape fell over his shoulder, clasped at his throat. Full formal regalia in an infirmary suggested that his status in the Great Hall was that of a general. Or higher. Eyolin recalled the general and the seer, but no amount of squinting could confirm that this was that man or not. He didn't have black eyes, that much was certain, but neither did the general after that flash of green magik.

Glancing at his sword seeded enough doubt that Eyolin abandoned the comparison. An ornamental blade—not a broadsword—was looped through his belt and topped with a diamond-shaped blue topaz. Expensive, but not the weapon of the general she'd spotted. Eyolin narrowed her gaze on a small satchel looped next to the sword. The air around it buzzed and blurred.

His attention fell on Eyolin's cot.

Within a blink, he had crossed the space to stand at the foot of the bed.

"*Galilee kahnai*, Eyolin. So good that you've woken. You gave Traik quite a fright."

Eyolin offered him a weak smile. Already she was identified and at a severe disadvantage in the Great Hall. She didn't know the faces of dignitaries and higher-ups, or who to avoid and who to shield herself from. This man assumed correctly that she understood the Old Language of the elves, meaning he knew of her father's love for literature and language, or made a lucky guess. Though, here under the same roof as the best of the kingdom, luck likely had little to do with it.

"*Sahbiet ney out shou*," Eyolin opted to say, her words filled with honor and grace, everything a Silver Elf should be. "*Dallahnyai et cout tohw.*" She threw in a quick bob of her head in the motion of a bow. Her mind worked up a lie, some explanation as to how she disappeared all those years ago, where she has been, keeping any mention of the herbalist far from her mind.

"*Sahclute ah chlœ. Gheflan la shaflow et far.*" It took Eyolin a moment to translate, catching something about loving, sounds, and the old tongue. She'd never cared for linguistics as her sister and father had. She needed only the local dialect. Any instruction from her father and two years in the Academy were lost to her.

"*Isthrashiriaie*," Eyolin said, her tongue struggling to shape the word.

"Remarkable," the old man commented with a warm smile. "But your father wouldn't have left you without all the tools to succeed with us, would he?"

"You..." Eyolin swallowed. "Knew him?"

"One of our best, Lord Kyenz was." His eyes shone with emotion. "His was the voice of reason on the High Council. Ah, to see his words at work."

Eyolin did not trust her voice, so she remained quiet. It seemed plausible that Arden had been rushing to the Great Hall that fateful day to see someone of importance—someone like this man. He may yet be an ally.

"Do you remember him, Eyolin?"

Yes, she thought. Every detail of his face, the strength of his jawline and the depth of his laughs.

"Not really. It was all so long ago." Her voice didn't waver.

"Of course, you were not expecting to be found," he said as a fact. "So why stay in Aideil? What kept you tucked right under our noses?"

Eyolin paused. She thought she knew the answer, but not what it was this man wanted her to say. She held the power to shape her own story and mold it to one that suited her. But it would have to be woven with the truth.

"When a branch fell and destroyed my home, it took my mother with it. Father was away fighting for Aideil during the War of Uhura. I never heard from him. Stopped looking. I didn't have anywhere to go."

"Why not come to one of us here in the Great Hall, or run away somewhere new?"

Eyolin picked over the words on her tongue until they felt right.

"This city, the trees, are the only place I've ever known. The leaves are the same that caught the water my mother gathered after the rain, making the drops dance, and I feel that it is my responsibility to stay, to make sure that her memory is honored rather than forgotten."

"You aren't waiting for anyone?" His look was expectant. Eyolin knew the answer he wanted to hear—a confirmation of Arden's death. Eyolin could not give him that. It was too final. Arden was still alive. It was a certainty Eyolin clung to.

"There is no one left for me to wait for."

"You're right I suppose. Lord Kyenz did not return to us."

It was now that the tears threatened to spill. Deep down she had known, but to hear the confirmation that her father was well and truly gone was a grief so profound that she briefly had to tuck her knees into her chest and press her fingers to her temples until her emotions were suppressed.

When she recovered, the old man was studying a column of script on the nearest wall.

"He never mentioned your aptitude for magik," he said as dully as stating the weather.

"I have no Gift."

"I beg to differ," he said with a raised eyebrow. "The air around you is a radiant aura of untapped potential. I had my doubts when Traik brought you in, but seeing you here... It is magnificent."

Eyolin glanced at her arms. They were as ordinary as always, the bandages scratchy, her skin speckled with a few sunspots. No shimmering magik, despite the awe in the old man's eyes.

"Traik?" she inquired, hoping to draw the conversation away from herself. "Was he the officer who killed the frae?"

"The very same. Commander Traik's write-up was quite interesting to say the least."

"And what was in that report?"

"He claims to have identified the frae's master, and it puts all of us in harm's way." He paused, looking Eyolin up and down before continuing. "The frae was sent by Magnogogue. Long has the king of Ïsteldûr sought a way to free fire from its cage. Whatever magik lies in your blood might be the key to unlocking his god from Midriel. And that is simply something that cannot come to pass."

It made sense, adding a layer of clarity to one of the forces from the fog. The illusive *He* the frae mentioned and the figure walking through the black fog. Eyolin had called for a god to save her. Perhaps a demon rose to the occasion instead. The fire god imprisoned for eternity.

"And he wants me?" Possibilities fractured in Eyolin's mind, each one more monstrous than the next. It couldn't be true. She had been careful to conceal her power, even more so to ensure that when the time came, she had every lie in order to start a new life. Every action was well thought out, calculated, and carefully executed. For a god and a king to have her in their sights brought more dread than any cell could inspire.

"He must have some way to sense your power where I cannot." The man cocked his head at her. "Do you know your Gift, child?"

Eyolin didn't even know this old man's name. The longer she stared, the more familiar he became the same way characters in a painting do when you stare at them long enough. There was a curl to the ends of his silver hair that a memory pressed at, but she couldn't place him. His posture seemed to be at war with itself; proud and strong one moment, hunched and furious the next. His age did not match the power he exuded. His eyes both fearsome and genteel. Something didn't add up, though she couldn't say what.

"Are you Professor Einsfar? The one I was told to find?"

The side of his mouth quirked and his beard twitched. "Do I look like the librarian?"

Eyolin swallowed hard. He moved with a fluidity that contrasted the bulk of his middle, his neck swiveling almost serpent-like as he squared his shoulders.

"My name is Master Tequerra Arendt, Master Scariyai of Aideil. One of three left in Alagana who remember what it felt like for magik to flow as freely as a river in spring. Unfortunately for us, my rival has a nasty habit of lighting my earthen magik on fire and has recently revealed that he can get past my wards."

"You've fought him?" Eyolin perked up. "Magnogogue?"

His nod confirmed it. Master Arendt had fought a necromantic Master of Fire and lived. He knew how to survive and lead a kingdom to war. From the glint in his eyes, Eyolin could almost see the full breadth of his Gift, a magik as old as the land, a Master. Uneasy respect settled in the pit of her stomach. She could no longer hide from the High Council, on which Tequerra sat as its head, but if she endeared herself to him, through whatever means necessary, he would prove to be a formidable ally, especially in the face of Ïsteldûr's monsters hunting her down.

There will always be monsters. It is when they show their face in the light, we realize that we knew them all along. It was the voice of Master Arendt, speaking directly into her mind in response to her thoughts. The telepathic magik was a scorching fire in her head.

"Get out of my head."

Block me out yourself. Others will not be as gentle as I am. It is how the frae saw your fears and manipulated you into seeing your mother.

Eyolin's grip tightened on the edge of the cot, her knuckles white as the touch of magik burned her from the inside.

Still, Tequerra did not cease.

What are you so afraid of losing? His voice was a drum, echoing through her eardrums. *You have a Gift, and I am giving you the opportunity to claim it.*

"I. Don't. Want it," Eyolin ground out.

I'm afraid you don't have a choice. Magnogogue is coming to collect you. I intend to make sure that never happens.

"There is always a choice," Eyolin replied, steadying her voice to prepare for what she was to say. There was no room to waver. No time to second guess the damning words. "I claim the name of Kyenz, and with it, immunity from the transgressions of my past that led to this point. If you are so adamant that I cultivate whatever magik lies within me, then I want you to personally oversee my training so that when Ïsteldûr attacks, I can murder the man who killed my father."

"A murderous politician in our midst," Master Arendt said fondly. "I dare say you will fit in wonderfully among our ranks."

"And what of her transgressions she so vaguely referred to, General?" Commander Traik stepped around the side of her cot, his arms crossed and face rosy. "Kyenz or not, she's a gutter rat. I looked into her dealings in Mainwood."

"And?" Tequerra inquired, not at all concerned, his hands rubbing together at his belly.

"She doesn't exist," Traik said with a glare. "No employment, no housing, no record of her at all."

"Well, if she's a spy, all the better to keep her close." A rush of relief flooded Eyolin at Master Arendt's defense. Something about her fascinated him. She intended to find out why. Maybe she was a spy.

Metal clinked in Traik's palms. Handcuffs. "Are chains not more appropriate for our lying patient?" The commander took a step closer. "How many years have you defied Council law?"

Eyolin stuck her chin out. Weakness now was not an option. "For me to defy a law and be held accountable for it, shouldn't I first be made aware of it? I am a gutter rat after all, and last time I checked, rats are unintelligent creatures."

"Sir, I am of the belief she has associations with the Grey who have historically been known as sympathetic to Ïsteldûr. Topped with countless other allegations I intend to bring to light—"

"May I stop you there, Commander?" Tequerra hooked his thumbs in his belt. Traik's mouth snapped shut, though his jaw worked in circles. "She is not Lara. That girl did not take well to being shackled, and we lost her. I vowed to not make the same mistake a second time, not when we are nearing the third cycle without magikal regeneration. Alagana will not last another cycle if Eyolin is thrown beneath the Great Hall in a cell with no doors."

"What do I have to do with that?" Eyolin's mind reeled. "I don't even have a gemstone."

"You will." Master Arendt turned from her, beckoning a fuming Traik to follow. "And I accept your terms. I will train you."

She had the word of a Master, in a kingdom where promises and bargains were not easily broken. She would learn to wield magik.

Chapter Six

"Wait," Eyolin called out before she could bite her tongue.

Master Tequerra Arendt paused with his back to Eyolin and nodded Commander Traik on. He waited until the thick doors of the infirmary shut completely, then turned with an unearthly smoothness. He approached slowly, as one might a frightened doe in the forest.

"I know you," she said. "From before, but the memory isn't clear."

His face did not reveal a thing when he replied, "I am the Master of Aideil, a common face even to those on ground."

Eyolin didn't want to push the master's goodwill, but she was so close. She remembered rainwater pelting those same ancient features, straightening his beard. The harder she pushed, the foggier the image became. She was about to give it all up when an energy surged in her chest, burning her insides as it went. She saw it all—the man in the rain, the master, holding her tight to his chest as she screamed and kicked. Low words spoken in a language not heard in the realm in centuries. The thick cloak he draped over her as she nestled in a small crevice of a tree. A biscuit and leather pouch of coins left in the pocket of a delirious seven-year-old child. It was undeniably the same man, but he gave no inkling of recognition, so Eyolin let the thought go, pondering over the clarity of a memory she had no recollection of until that moment.

"Forgive me," she said eventually. "That must be it."

"Is there something on your mind you would like to share, Eyolin?"

"Who is Lara? The one you said you lost?" Eyolin couldn't deny she was curious. First, the engravings of the tree and the girl on the ceiling of the infirmary, then her name again when Traik had wanted to snap metal around her wrists.

"You mean the Fourth Sarom," Master Arendt said gravely. "Did you ever hear the story of the Betrayers? How the five realms came to be?"

Eyolin shrugged, the spinner's performance vivid. "The story, sure, but I don't practice the religion."

"The High Elves never deserved such a devoted practice for the harm they created." He took a moment to regard Eyolin. "Every three hundred and fifty years or so, a being of immense magikal capabilities emerges in order for the five realms to remain and for life to exist in equilibrium due to the upset the High Elves caused during the Betrayal. Lara was the fourth Sarom. I believe we have found the fifth."

He spoke of legends and myths as if they were tangible historical facts, of prophecies spun by bards and dwarvish spinners about reincarnation and magik. The Sarom were sung as mystical anomalies, as escaped souls, and omens of war. The Sarom were supposed to hold Fate in their palms, to mold it as they deemed fit. Certainly not the start of a happy ending, but it explained why the western kingdom was adamant on collecting her.

Eyolin would know if Fate favored her, and she knew that from her past that Fate mocked her and was not her ally.

She was at a loss for words. The title of 'Sarom' stuck to her teeth like licorice.

"Alas," Tequerra started. "We will know for certain a day after tomorrow when you are tested for magik, as you should have been years ago. During the interim, you will remain here in the infirmary under the watchful care of our nurses and staff. If all goes well, you will be set up in a more suitable living situation within the week."

No further explanation was given. Master Arendt spun on his heel and strode through the doors of the infirmary with long strides. The moment the doors shut in his wake, a sharp pop cracked in Eyolin's ear, a veil of magik lifting. Master Tequerra Arendt had not wanted anyone to overhear them.

"The Sarom, huh?"

Dale ducked out from behind a curtain with a plate balanced on his fingertips. Eyolin's blood pressure spiked uncomfortably, eyes flicking to the empty beds around her. The servant merely shrugged.

"Look, I was trapped inside the silence bubble from the get-go. It kept both sound and objects from passing. I tried—nearly lost a finger."

Eyolin was at a loss for words, her fear mounting that this human was about to shout for a supervisor, spreading word of her newfound predicament.

"We all have secrets. Now you get to trust me with one of yours. Keeps life interesting." Dale deposited the plate of scones and juice onto her small bedside table, then slipped through a hidden doorway in the wall.

The smell of the pastries was tantalizing and Eyolin swiped at them greedily. She only looked up when a young nurse tiptoed over, dressed in a blue-grey dress with a crown of flowers adorning her head. The nurse's straight honey hair was braided down her back. An uncut golden gemstone sat on her pointer finger, the air around it shimmering—a Gifted healer, Eyolin deduced.

The nurse set a vial of amber liquid next to the now empty plate and lay a cool cloth on Eyolin's forehead, though she didn't have a fever.

"The tonic will put you to sleep."

Eyolin nodded her thanks but did not touch the vial.

A great commotion awoke her the following day. She blinked the sleep from her eyes and noted the lateness by the afternoon sun. Gifted healers scurried between beds, weaving like ants around bleeding shapes that groaned and twitched.

The infirmary was overcrowded with soldiers, their armor blackened from exposure to fire, some breastplates splintered in random patterns that still smoldered. Blood soured the air, but was cleared by wisps of daisy-yellow magik streaming from the hands of the healers.

Pushing herself to her feet, the world swayed, and she collapsed back to the cot. Her body felt sluggish in a way it never had been, every joint stiff and aching. A bowl of soup lay cold on the bedside table.

Eyolin, sensing that her body would crumple if she attempted to stand, caught the arm of one of the nurses.

"What happened? Where are these men coming from? Are we under attack?"

The nurse turned, her face agitated. "An outpost just south of Mi Svelto was assaulted in the night. The scariyai who survived the initial attack blinked back as many soldiers as they could."

"Has Ïsteldûr made a statement? Is this an act of war?" Gods, it had only been two days since the War of Uhura came to a joyous conclusion, Aideil victorious. Unless Ïsteldûr never intended to surrender.

"From what I've heard between their screaming, the attack was made by a breed we haven't seen in this realm or any other," the nurse said swiftly. "They had elvish bodies, but their skin was ash-grey with eyes as red as the blood they spilt. Wiped out an entire battalion in under an hour. There has been no correspondence with the west yet."

The nurse nodded at the untouched vial by the soup. "You'll want to sleep through the worst of it. They always get louder at night."

This time, Eyolin didn't hesitate to tip the glass to her lips, hungry to escape the gruesome sights around her. Darkness swirled into her head and she tumbled into a restless sleep full of nightmarish scenes and fire. A lullaby sung by her mother in the old language hummed in the background.

Tu di szaer sthi ya,

Pour di haeth.

Nei da wour,

Key sha ti bah.

Nei di wour,

Cuai sha ti vour.

Nei di thtae,

Se trop ti bah.

"Now rest your head,

Upon my chest.

For every morn you wake,

I'll be right at your side."

A figure cloaked in curling flames strode through her dreamscapes, watching the carnage of Mi Svetlo with a grim satisfaction—Death incarnate. He looked as if he'd been pulled from a famous painting and given horrible life. He was a being of legend: the god of fire and hell. Yet, within the dream, Eyolin did not fear him.

Other gods of lore leapt through smoke-filled skies. The three-eyed stallion of the plains kingdom galloped after a scorpion god of the desert, both tortured and injured in ways that gods should be above.

The smoke turned to trees, far more wild and fierce than the Greywood of Aideil. Eyolin drifted above them, focusing on her mother's lullaby.

Arms wrapped around her, holding her close. The night sky cleared of smoke, the stars twinkling so magnificently that the entire cosmos lit up in brilliant clusters. She was flying through them, the stars. All Eyolin had to do was dip her fingers into them and she could scoop up the stars like tiny pebbles in a stream.

A loud bang jolted Eyolin out of her sleep. She shot up, gasping, convinced in her grogginess that she would find the skeletal head of the desert god perched over her cot.

Nurses and staff backed away from her, eyes wary and fearful. Vibrant green tendrils of energy snaked from her fingertips, swirling around in a ring above her head. The tingling of magik itched under her skin. *Foreign,* Eyolin thought. It felt so wrong. Her magik had never surfaced so potently, or with such intention.

The wood of the Great Hall drained her magik until the green strands dissipated. Eyolin couldn't tear her eyes from her hands, stunned by the lingering nightmare and public display of power. She had held pain and loss close to her heart for years, but never had such shame crippled her. No real scariyai would lose control.

Determined to retreat from the lingering stares, Eyolin swung her legs off the cot and rested bare feet on the stone floor. Unlike the day before, her body felt light and energized.

A rustle to her right caught her attention and a small human girl no older than twelve placed a plate of cheese and berries onto the nightstand. Her other arm was full of a bundle of clothes that she deposited on Eyolin's pillow.

"Where's Dale?"

The girl's bottom lip wavered and Eyolin softened her voice.

"The servant who was here a few days ago. He was my kitchen runner, but I haven't seen him."

"I only just got here this morning," the girl whimpered. "All able-bodied human men were taken away during the night. Decree of the High Council."

Eyolin's chest ached and she regretted asking. A tiny alarm in her head reminded her that Dale knew what she was. She would need to locate him to ensure his silence.

A nurse arrived and shooed the little girl away briskly. "Master Arendt has been delayed. He will meet you in a few hours. You are recommended to stretch your legs in the meantime. I do ask that you not disturb or speak to anyone while you roam and be mindful of where your feet wander. As long as you remain a guest, the Great Hall will not harm you."

She had forgotten about the ominous test that Tequerra mentioned, and her mind ran wild with the possibilities as she picked at the dry cheese. In Aideil, Gifted elves visited the Grandmother Tree, and it varied between kingdoms which presiding magikal deity they pledged themselves to through a series of tests to receive their individual conduits for magik. Jewels marked the scariyai. Scarox received metal pendants. Grandmother Tree bestowed the gift of magik on them all, having deemed them worthy to house an elemental channel of energy. Black lava rocks and obsidian channeled fire. A topaz or azurite for those Gifted with water variations, or the water lilies like Eyolin's mother. A tiny token of a hammer would mark the beiythron. The individual would then wear that gem every moment of every day without fail. To remove it would unhinge the wielder's magik, threatening to splinter and cut off the Gift entirely. Without a gem, a Gifted elf couldn't control their magik and the land of Alagana would reabsorb the Gift. The worse the break, the more destruction would erupt. It was that gemstone through which magik could be harnessed and molded to the bearer's wishes.

The reason they tested elves so young—Gifts evolved as they got closer to twenty years old. The threshold when unbound magik returned to the earth was the most dangerous time to be tested, for the five realms would already have their claims to one's magik. Now that Eyolin thought about it, that must be why there was such interest in the magik of her ancestral High Elvish blood. She had turned nineteen just four days prior. This was the last year her magik would remain before Alagana took it back, and the process would not be painless.

The Grandmother Tree was rumored to be the essence of Lila, the youngest daughter of High King Jenthius. Her grave grew into the deity of Aideil, Eyolin's kingdom. The opening of the creaking infirmary doors lifted her attention from the spiraling terror at the prospect of facing a magikal deity.

The doors of the infirmary opened to the rest of the Great Hall. A line of high-class parchlim in deep blue suit coats whirled by in a tightly knit unit. Their gold buttons blinded Eyolin's adjusting eyes. She was especially dazzled by their spotless velvet cloaks with their circular pendants marking their social status.

Around the rest of the circular room beyond the infirmary were evenly spaced hallways that tunneled deeper into the Great Hall's various levels. The unit of parchlim zipped in and out of the many arched side doors. Again, the hive mentality was astonishing.

Scattered among the crowd were scariyai, sticking out with their vibrant colored robes of reds, purples, and greens. Each robe indicated the elemental Gift they manipulated. Visible gemstones sat affixed on rings, looped onto necklaces, though a few hid their marks out of shame or modesty.

The doors closed, snapping Eyolin out of the dazed revery. She tugged on scratchy linens with a light leather-bound tunic that mirrored other acolytes rushing about with books—likely where she would have ended up if her Gift wasn't not a curse and her mother was never murdered. Eyolin fixed the laces on the leather boots and slipped out of the infirmary into the heart of the kingdom.

She glanced at the acolytes in matching attire, searching for a hint of what specialty they studied. All of them were young men. It struck a nerve to see the only women in the Great Hall be servant children, not elves or dignitaries or correspondents, and certainly not acolytes strolling haughtily through the space like gods-forsaken peacocks. At least the scariyai were wizened enough with age to have mastered masks of indifference.

The main doors that led to the rest of the city were open, the warmth captivating Eyolin's attention. It was so much brighter at this upper tier of the city.

Moving closer to the entrance, Eyolin let the sunlight blanket her cheeks. She could have spent all day breathing in that crisp air had someone not run into her shoulder, knocking her off balance. Rather than acknowledge the slight, Eyolin righted herself and turned back to the rays, her ears tuning in to the conversation of a passing pair of elves.

"I told you, Princess Cortese," a man was saying, "there simply are not enough resources to be chasing after every creature who goes missing."

Eyolin kept her eyes closed, unwilling to move into the shade and out of range of the intriguing line of dialogue. She had a history trading secrets and stories. That habit wasn't about to fade overnight.

"They are not a *creature*, dear parchlim," replied a snipping voice. "They are kin. Gone missing in *your* city and thus *your* responsibility."

Interesting, Eyolin thought. The blue-skinned girl in chains came to mind. She'd given the spinner directions and a description but would that be enough?

The parchlim and princess paused—directly in front of Eyolin. Blocking the sun. She pasted on a face of indifference, keeping her eyes closed to allow herself some level of deniability.

"You are a guest in our halls, Princess. I suggest you start acting as one."

"My kin will be found, parchlim, with or without you. When she is, all of Velesah will know of your disagreeable nature. You will be barred from ever speaking in our courts or traveling through our waters."

Eyolin heard delicate feet stomping down the steps and into the city. It was then Eyolin opened her eyes and faded into the shadows.

There was a Velesian royal in the Great Hall. And they were inquiring about the kidnappings. Eyolin wracked her brain for what she knew about the sea kingdom and their ways, already missing what knowledge the herbalist would undoubtedly share over tea.

Tea. The thought jolted her back to the present. Eyolin never made it to tea.

She wondered how long it would take for her name to join the list of disappearances. She wondered if anyone would search for her at all.

Eyolin skirted the main foyer in short steps, ridden with nervous energy. Elvish soldiers stood stationed next to three of the eight archways. Their armor possessed a fierce elegance as if long feathers of metal flowed over their chests and backs, ending around their knees. Aideillian angels, with birdlike helmets that caged in their faces.

The domed ceiling curved high above her head where a gorgeous chandelier shone a warm light over the busy hall. Eyolin bumped her way through a thick group of parchlim jostling one another angrily in the midst of a heated discussion. A certain cluster of soldiers with their helmets tucked under their arms caught her attention and her fingers felt particularly sticky with the thought of studying one of the contraptions closer.

The closest elvish soldier with his helmet off looked shockingly ordinary, without an excess of muscle or a murderous gleam in his eye. His face was plain and skin a neutral sandy color. There was a cluster of scars along his exposed forearm that Eyolin contemplated sliding her hand under to nick the helmet.

His arm twitched ever so slightly and Eyolin suddenly lost her nerve. She swayed backward, one foot behind the other, looking to put distance between them. The sudden density of people had other plans.

There was no crack to slip through as she was pushed into the guarded hallway, away from the warm chandelier and drafty space of the hall.

It was dark for only a moment before torches of light purple and green flame flickered to life. Two robed scariyai slunk through the crowd, a faint coil of magik swirling at their feet an indication that they controlled the illumination. Eyolin half expected Master Arendt to be one of them due to the presence of earthen magik, but the green scariyai was far slimmer with black hair. For her to switch direction now would bring unwanted attention.

A door opened into an oval space where scariyai, parchlim and elvish soldiers filtered through in a sea of colors. Inside, four scariyai with gold circlets around their heads flicked through pages of thick books as they paced, each an elected representative of the kingdom's Gifted. Three parchlim sat at the head of the central table, their hands crossed in their laps, faces pale. Eyolin recognized those three as members of the High Council who spoke for the top three tiers of Mainwood. The lower two tiers, and the ground, were represented by an elected Silver commander who changed every ten years and never knew a thing about politics, choosing to use the platform to promote an agenda generally focused on terrorizing the humans. Eyolin's father had been different, though no less vicious on the human district. He increased the revenue of the elvish tiers three-fold, and opened lasting trade routes with Farindor—all during peace times. The moment the War of Uhura struck, Lord Kyenz was pulled to the front as a general, his title on the High Council falling to an unseasoned commander who left the lower tiers to manage themselves. It was how Eyolin had gone undetected as long as she had.

More familiar titles filled the room, distinguishable by their clothes and adornments. Eyolin felt a mounting a suspicion that she had wandered straight into a meeting of the High Council. The heads of Aideil's two Academies had seats at the table next to a selection of fully armed officers. Heads of Aideil's noble houses remained standing in draping clothes with long flowing sleeves, along with a suffocating number of soldiers.

The chair reserved for the Master scariyai sat notably empty and remained so as the doors leading back to the Great Hall closed.

Eyolin was stuck in a room with the most powerful men in the kingdom, and arguably the realm. The din of whispers and conversation fell to silence. She was a lamb trapped in a room with monstrous creatures.

The attack on Mi Svetlo was the center of the meeting as those with a seat at the table initiated the roundtable discussion on available courses of action.

"When we meet Magnogogue on the field, it won't be one army we face, but three," the parchlim at the head of the table said. He represented the top tier of Mainwood, the houses with the strongest

Gifts and bloodlines. "Where do you think the bodies of the lost have gone? Ïsteldûr has given themselves over to the darkest of magiks. Necromantic. A power that does not have a soul. If war knocked today, we would be outmatched."

Eyolin wished to be a mouse at that very moment. Metal armor and sweat-soaked leather pressed into every side. But everyone was enraptured by the High Council table. She opted for taking slow and shallow breaths.

"Their continued experiments are what is tearing our realms apart," a minister spoke, his age matching the yellowed pages of the books stacked in front of him. "Their practices do not have the spine to hold the realms together. Not only have the dead risen, but demons themselves. Livestock slaughtered. Our scariyai missing. The best of our legions. Not so much as a bone found."

Eyolin was going to be sick. It was the Gifted who were going missing. A targeted attack.

"Until we control the narrative, these disappearances must be kept quiet." It was the scariyai in the purple robe who spoke. "Dare I suggest we need a delicate touch?"

The second parchlim blanched. "Traik's report included that a Grey had breached the walls. Going to them now is feeding a double-edged sword our unguarded throats."

"Not them, they will be dealt with." Eyolin could just see the scariyai as he hovered in the space where the Master Scariyai should have been. "I meant the veins of magik that run beneath the forest here in Mainwood. Or have you forgotten about the power bestowed on this land by the gods?" He paused, hands on the back of the chair, making eye contact with each member of the High Council. "Magik is meant to be pure. The land is begging to be cleansed of the Dark magik seeping from the west. If we release a single artery of the realm's blood, there is every possibility that the cracks would heal and all those tainted by Darkness would no longer be able to exist on this plane."

The second Academy minister interrupted. "Forgive my bluntness, but there is no magik strong enough, nor Gift with the breadth to direct it should such a force exist. We need to match Ïsteldûr and turn to the other realms—might I recommend our closest neighbor, the Middle?"

The other officers seemed to agree from their nods. A general at the table raised a hand to command attention. "Aideil's patron deity has never intervened or meddled in our mortal wars and will not start for the sake of our lives."

"Other beings call the Middle home, not just the ashes of Lila, may she bless our Gifted for centuries to come." The scariyai wore a look of deep contempt. "Let the west call up from the hell realm. We shall match it by introducing the birds and predators of old. We just need enough power to create a fold. Our scariyai are trained to blink our armies leagues at a time. Imagine transferring that energy into a new device."

The dwarvish spinner would be absolutely giddy to be listening in on this High Council meeting. Eyolin imagined his spectacles falling off as he gasped in shock. Maybe his toe got burnt by an ember he didn't see. He'd hop around on one foot over to his chest that contained all his best stories. Then, Eyolin would be offered gold rykes. Then, Eyolin would be free.

The two ministers exchanged a glance and opened their books. "Need we remind you that though we elves can breathe and exist in the other realms, the creatures born of the other realms cannot survive in ours."

"Take the pluket," the other said, spreading his hands to project the image on the page above the heads of those seated. The air popped with the lesser magik and a black feathered bird with razor sharp teeth flapped its three-dimensional wings, the minister's handwritten notes pointing out various anatomical anomalies scrawled in the air alongside it. Eyolin couldn't read the script, but it was the size of a horse. "Residing in the Dead Forest of the Middle realm, the pluket's body metabolizes a very specific compound in order for its organs to function." Scholars to the core, Eyolin noted. They would take any excuse to lecture. She tuned out the voice until something interesting was said. She was starting to get fidgety. By the time her mind rejoined the discussion, the general was making gestures at an enchanted map that had risen from the smooth wood of the table.

Clouds drifted over the map where the mountains of Mendia sank into the wood. Waves foamed against the shores of Aniöm. The seas surrounding Puanolocue crashed and writhed against the archipelago. It was the ominous black stain that drew the eyes of everyone in the room.

"We centralize our scariyai around castle-cities," the general declared. "Galeisia and Soruna have the most valuable assets. Move our seasoned scarox there. They cannot touch us here in Mainwood, but any full-scale attack will be on where our resources lie. Amber Castle will host a training camp to assist both Soruna and Galeisia should anything happen." The parchlim were nodding along while the ministers took notes. "Battles are fought with magik first. Ïsteldûr is waiting for something. We must anticipate and prepare for every possibility. Our beiythron in the forges have a few innovations to incorporate into our ranks here in Aideil. While we draw fire from whatever we face on the border, we send a small guard up along the coast, taking care when passing Watertrough, and into the Synk to locate Golryk Castle."

Only one shook his head—a noble in all white, from the silver of his hair to the snowy jewel on his ring. "If we take the seat of the Old Throne first, Magnogogue will have full authority to bring down the wrath of his god. It is not unknown that Matthieus seeks Golryk for the power it would grant him. The King's Power to rule the five realms." He paused and Eyolin assessed the room. They were enraptured, albeit all a bit paler with nerves. The noble took a long breath, savoring the attention. "Assuming Magnogogue's connection with his fire element is intact, Golryk Castle would potentially create the rift needed to release Matthieus."

"The past fourteen-hundred years of degeneration," one of the ministers pointed out, "may very well have leeched the Old Throne of its magik. Two cycles have come and gone without the sacrifice. This is our last chance. Without magik to aid us, Ïsteldûr and their dark magik will have free rein to conquer the six kingdoms."

"Which is why we need our best to skirt up the coast and into the Synk."

Eyolin tunneled into a memory before a fire, the herbalist demonstrating the properties of plants when boiled. Each herb came from a different kingdom with varying potencies of magikal energies in the soil. Velesian wateroot turned muddy liquids pristine in an instant. Illusive mirage herbs from Huebeck secreted a purple-hued substance that cured skin diseases. The Synk, from Eyolin's knowledge, was a great expanse of land, void of magik. Barren and dead. *It wasn't always that way,* the herbalist had told her. Once, the Synk was a natural well of energy linking it to the Sky Realm where Alagana's royal family had built their palace. Plants only seen in the Sky flowered in the Synk and twisted into the clouds. The throne in Golryk Castle was said to have been built by weaving together the magiks of the seven children of King Jenthius following the Betrayal, drawing upon the abundance of energies in the land. That act, without the King's Gift to maintain the realm, drained the earth surrounding the throne until nothing could remain. But there was still a hope that one day, an elf would assume the Old Throne and unify the elvish armies of the seven kingdoms. A True Heir, a title reserved for the High Elf who claimed the throne. The High Elves were all gone now, the royal family reduced to fickle deities of magik, forever trapped into serving the mortal races of elves.

The third parchlim spoke out at last. "No one enters the Synk. Not even Magnogogue."

Two of the officers opened their mouths to respond when a guard of Amber Elves burst into the room. Eyolin was jostled to the side, and she made as little movement as possible while the bodies blocked her from sight.

The newcomers were spitting angrily in the dialect of Farindor, the kingdom bordering Aideil's south. She would have given anything to understand what the guard of elvish women garbed in gold and bronze were saying, their presence demanding respect from every man in the room.

Eyolin eyed the open door and, ever so slowly, slid her way to it, using the distraction to her advantage. Despite the urge to stay and hear the council out, she'd pushed her luck far enough.

Cold fingers wrapped around her arm and tugged her back the moment she got her foot out the door. The torso she was trapped against was hard despite being unarmored.

A low, growling voice brushed her earlobe. "Hello, little doe. Enjoying the show?"

Eyolin risked a glance behind her. The man was younger than those closer to the High Council table, his arms tanned and riddled with white scars where they showed above his rolled up sleeves.

The arguing elves from Farindor faded into the background as his grip tightened, fingernails digging into Eyolin's forearm. He angled her towards him, leaving little room for escape. She was trapped staring into cold, ice blue eyes rimmed with grey.

Eyolin's mouth opened and closed like a fish out of water. No one paid them any notice. The pain in her arm reached an unbearable threshold that threatened to squeeze a cry out of her, but to cry would draw the attention of every powerful person in Aideil.

"I could have any part of you removed for sneaking into this war room," the man purred into her ear. "Does that excite you?"

When Eyolin's lip shook from the effort not to cry, he grinned.

"Women always seem to get themselves into the most precarious situations," he sighed. "I think your tongue will go first, to prevent you from talking your way out of a good lashing." His eyes flashed, and his thin smile quirked a singular dimple in his right cheek. "The mutilated always scream so beautifully."

The soldier's gaze flicked to the table where a scariyai had a mud-colored tendril of magik pushing one of the Farindor elves toward the door—toward Eyolin. She needed to get out of there.

His attention on the Amber Elves provided just the opportunity for Eyolin to slip his loosened grip with a spin. Two steps to escape the war room. One step.

And she was crashing into a body entering through the crack in the closing door.

Eyolin stumbled, tripping over her feet.

A sharp tug in her gut pulled her upright, her weight dragging her back a step and into the war room. The sting of magik pricked her mind as Eyolin followed the sensation until the tension went taut. The body she'd ran into wore plain Aideillian armor at odds with the rich commanding officers and nobles in rich attire. But thanks to the commotion over the table with the Amber guard, no one noticed as he slipped through.

His body went rigid. His shoulders rose rapidly as he angled his chin back to look directly into Eyolin's eyes. Sandy-white tips peeked through partially dyed black hair. The hazel eyes were as bright and fierce as they were that night with the frae.

The Grey, Eyolin realized with a jolt.

The doors creaked shut, cutting Eyolin off from the war room.

Chapter Seven

The hallway was cold, empty, and devoid of the warm torchlight granted by the scariyai. Glancing between the darkness to her right and the light to her left, Eyolin started towards the main foyer where the infirmary entrance lay.

Her hand wouldn't stop shaking where the soldier had squeezed. The quiver spread into her shoulders remembering his threats. She couldn't trust him to forget her face, to not seek her out and exact whatever punishment he deemed worthy or report her to any one of the men in that room. She would be ruined before she had a chance to start. He was a young officer, no older than she was. He would have been a year or two above her in the Academy had she remained. If that was the sort of personality that succeeded in Aideil, Eyolin wasn't sure she would last very long at all.

The Grey she crashed into was another loose end. The swirling in her gut intensified, the allure of his presence nagging her. His posture acknowledged that he felt the string of energy pull at the same time. It was undoubtedly the man who saved her from the frae. Which meant that an assassin was in the High Council meeting.

Eyolin eyed the closed doors, assuming any attempt at reentry futile. She needed something to occupy her hands with and suddenly, the thought of waiting patiently on an exposed cot in a public infirmary didn't seem all that appealing.

Talk of the Old Throne and tactical movements of war had shaken her significantly. They had just concluded the War of Uhura. Their resources and armies were already depleted. They were tired. If what Tequerra had said was true, and Magnogogue intended to collect her, what sort of Gift was the Sarom supposed to possess? How was she supposed to make a difference when the forces at play were death and magik? She'd had her fair share of both and wouldn't be used as a weapon in Aideil's war.

She skirted around the circular room of the Great Hall, admiring the tiny balls of magik that lit each hanging orb.

An adjacent hallway, lit with regular flame torches, had expertly crafted paintings and murals stretching around a curving corner. Having apprenticed briefly with an artist named Rova Bayhallow, Eyolin took interest and turned in. She was thirteen all over again, the proud Rova taking her off the streets in exchange for assistance around her studio. During those months, Eyolin witnessed the creation of masterpieces. The one in front of her now was one of those frames.

When the memory surfaced with a splintering pain at her temples, Eyolin did not fight it.

Rova's nephew, Fox, was in town on a visit, his parents having moved to Datia for his schooling. He and Eyolin had gotten along for the first two nights, sharing the attic of Rova's studio, but on the third evening, Fox took the role of tormentor. While Eyolin cleaned the studio for Rova, Fox tipped over ink wells and swapped paint tubes with oil. The tipping point for Rova was discovering that her cherished paintbrushes were replaced by enchanted ones that did precisely what the artist wished not to do.

Always an expert liar, Fox pinned each transgression on Eyolin's shoulders. She was expendable and took each strike of Rova's wooden staff without so much as a tear.

"Tree trash of an elf," Rova spit at Eyolin's back. "For my generosity and kindness, you play tricks. You deserve the mud you crawled from."

Fox and his two friends had chased her through the winding tree roads to the ground where Eyolin had hidden among a pile of fresh linens in the tent of the human physician.

She hadn't thought about the Bayhallows in years. Even now, admiring the artwork of her brief master was muted by a lifetime of believing that everything her hands touched died. The strong characters depicted on a battlefield would never be her. Perhaps her deal with Tequerra would change her Fate. To rise from her place in the mud would be worthy of its own painting.

The memory didn't release her. The jeers and hatred. The pounding of feet as Fox and his friends pursued her. Eyolin pinched the bridge of her nose, the pain associated with her vivid memories piercing. Despite the agony, she hesitated on a detail. Something in the face of Fox's friend struck her as horribly familiar.

There he stood, a head taller than Fox, with pale skin and a weasel-long face. His hair was more unkempt, but the eyes threw Eyolin from the memory with their icy imprint.

The soldier in the war room, with his soft, deadly words...they had met. He was Fox's friend.

Even from around the bend, Eyolin felt the wood shake from the force of the High Council doors being thrown open. It didn't take long for severe-faced parchlim, ministers, soldiers and scariyai to fill the Great Hall.

Eyolin looked for the Grey assassin, or an indication that a kill had been made, but no sandy-haired figure with stolen armor passed.

A hand slammed down on her mouth, muffling her scream. Her assailant's arm curled around her torso lifting her up.

"Stay quiet, little doe," Fox's friend murmured in her ear.

His breath was sour as he carried her away from the lit canvases and main hall. Eyolin caught sight of the infirmary doors, the safety too far away to be a comfort.

Around the corner, he spun Eyolin around, pressing her back into the cold wall.

"You stuck around," he said, face bent down over her. "Is your face naturally so plain, or is it a stylistic choice?"

Eyolin met him with a defiant exhale. He realized his hand was still clamped over her mouth and made a show of moving it, pressing her tight to the wall. "Already mute? You know, I haven't heard a single word leave your lips since I caught you spying on the High Council."

A knife flipped into his hand. The metal tip dragged up Eyolin's thigh. *No, no, no,* Eyolin repeated in her mind, wishing for anything or anyone to come around the corner and stop whatever torture this soldier deemed appropriate.

"Exciting, isn't it?" The knife reached Eyolin's armpit. "To be completely and utterly under another's control."

Footsteps echoed off the inside of the tree. Eyolin dared to hope.

"Evening, Maximus."

Hope fell to the wind as the Grey assassin strode into Eyolin's periphery. Out of all the people she wanted to see, he was the last on her list. And he was smiling.

"Enjoying your playtime?"

"Back away, soldier," Maximus snarled without a glance. "This one's misbehaving, and I intend to teach it a lesson as I would a disobedient bitch."

The Grey met her gaze. There was the same nauseating tug in her gut.

Maximus curled the edge of the knife around the soft part of her throat, enjoying the goosebumps that jumped in its wake.

A dark spark twinkled at the Grey's fingertips. He could leave her at any time, and Eyolin prayed that he wouldn't.

"Is she?"

Maximus pinned Eyolin by crushing her windpipe in his hand with the knife flat on her skin. Neither man moved. They hardly breathed. Veined bulged in Maximus' forehead. The Grey's eyes didn't drop from Eyolin's for a moment. There was a smugness to his mouth that flipped her stomach.

Finally, the Grey took a step back.

The string in her stomach jerked tight and the Grey blinked from existence.

Maximus' mouth pinched in a malicious smile that fell when the Grey assassin materialized between him and Eyolin. A white, luminescent blade glinted in the darkness.

The Grey's back was flush against Eyolin's stomach, and she couldn't help her hitched inhale of breath. The magik flowed from him in waves, pulsing between them in a dizzying array of lightless force. He was, in every way, the personification of night, and of death. The Grey were fighters bred in blood. Eyolin realized that his help may not be her salvation at all but rather the very thing that tore her life apart.

The Grey's head turned to the side, his profile full of sharp angles and shadows. His nostrils flared and he flicked his eyes to meet Eyolin's.

Maximus stumbled back a step. His grip on his knife never wavered and a second, longer blade dropped from his sleeve.

"You're messing with my meal," Maximus snarled.

"Good for you, objectifying the female sex," the Grey assassin commented, his blade pointed lazily at Maximus. "What a winning sentiment with the ladies, though if you'll pardon my advice—I don't think this one likes you very much."

The hallway remained empty. Noise from the Great Hall sounded far away and underwater. Far away. Removed. Sluggish. How long would it take for anyone to notice she was missing? A couple hours, perhaps. She could make a dash to the infirmary—but that would trap her in a room, albeit a large one with plenty of witnesses. She was fairly confident she could outrun Maximus. The Grey, on the other hand, had staggering magikal abilities that she personally was not interested in testing.

A vein twitched in Maximus' neck, and he was moving. Toward the Grey and Eyolin.

Enough with 'the Grey this,' 'the Grey that,' a low male voice spoke into Eyolin's mind. *It's Kipp.*

"*Kaerisetay uncah,*" the same voice murmured aloud. Kipp spoke so quietly that a whisper would have been too loud a characterization.

Maximus' head jerked to the side, his muscles relaxing. His smile dropped, dimple filling in, leaving him with a vacant, if not slightly bewildered, look on his face. His two blades clattered to the floor. Kipp's fingers twitched at his side. In response, Maximus flinched and scooped up the weapons, tucking them into their sheaths. A single dribble of blood trailed to the tip of his hand.

He turned and walked away without a second glance.

Eyolin stared at the back of Kipp's head, feeling the predatory stillness in the Grey's shoulders. He hadn't moved. Only uttered two words that were not elvish, or dwarvish, or any dialect known to the realm. The otherworldly phrase danced off the air around them like sprites. His whispered incantation had turned a threat into a puppet.

Kipp removed himself from Eyolin's immediate person, his white blade blinking into the folds of space that he manipulated with whatever unnatural magik his kind possessed.

"He will have no recollection of this encounter. Your face has been wiped from his mind with a block directing him to prick his thigh with a knife if he sees you again. Should last a few months at least." Kipp winked and blinked out in the same manner as before. The shadows shuddered in his wake.

Chapter Eight

Kipp released the breath he was holding. The surge of energy he felt from her left his head spinning. The enchantment on the officer had escaped his lips before he had had a chance to think things through. He laughed to himself; he's going to have a limp for ages before he finally figures it out. Scarox never saw him coming.

Her mind was so fragile and haunted. He hadn't even been able to properly introduce himself before whispering his damning enchantment. He regretted only not taking more time for that.

It wasn't often that he dipped into the Twilight while in Alagana. Twilight's physical existence was as powerful as its magikal one, and the Grey's magik could manipulate the space separating the realms.

His detour during the assignment was sure to be noticed by the Regent when he arrived for his report. The girl's unbounded energy had frozen his Passing from Alagana to the Twilight realm, the force of her fear dragging him through the shadows.

Officially, he needed to provide strategic intel on Aideil's troop movement with the newest developments pushing the eastern and western kingdoms to a bloody meeting. He had sworn the Binding vows which guaranteed he kept to the exact terms of the assignment. A convenient catch-all for the Grey. He had a knack for pushing the boundaries of the Binding magik, but he could not break it completely. Only the Regent had that power. And Kipp was his Second.

The meeting in the war room confirmed that Magnogogue and his court were behind the frae attack in Mainwood, but why that frae wanted a taste of that girl was a mystery. The creature had slipped from the Twilight into Alagana and Kipp wanted to know how many others went with it. The client would be pleased to have the frae back home where it belonged anyhow, but the troop movements to Aniöm would be a problem. Alagana was not ready for war. Not quite yet. But it would be once Kipp set each piece in motion.

Kipp materialized from the Passing in a crouched stance. He picked at the pollen on his shoulders and stood. With a roll of his neck, his armor rippled into black leather and grey fabric. He shook his head, running his fingers through his hair.

Two steel-grey towers rose to either side. The diamond platform he Passed onto was made from the same ore as his luminescent blades.

Kipp tucked a white crystal disk into the folds of his leather tunic. The flickering blue light faded when his fingers left it inside the pocket. The portal's crystal was grown from within the Twilight's tower, and was the only sure way to and from the realm to Alagana.

The land ahead was flat and cast in a muted grey, everything a different shade of dusk. The Twilight realm remained a sheet of ash at all times of day and the drab color felt of home. The sun indicated high noon.

Two shadowed creatures stood guard at the base of the towers. Their cloaks were made of dark shrouds that fizzled into the air and breathed of their own accord. The two frae nodded to Kipp who walked past with hardly any acknowledgment.

Beyond the gates, the only semi-habitable city in the Twilight realm peeled into view. The silver Pipassê rose on the horizon. The design of the stronghold was blocky with slits of windows adorning the exterior walls to allow archers a protected shot at the wraiths and creatures who occasionally snuck through the inner-city wards. Squat two-story buildings webbed out from the Pipassê. Shingles slid off roofs at varying intervals.

Kipp drifted his hand along his empty belt. A seraph blade and daggers built themselves from the surrounding air and space. Each clinked against his thighs. The tiny bat demons huddled in his path scattered in a flurry of hisses.

The streets were quiet save for a black-beaked creature with spindly legs who flipped human hands through the leaves of a book. Its black feathered wings twitched in wariness when it noticed the Grey.

A white-eyed witch turned her head from the bloody bones littering her porch and curled her lip back from decayed teeth.

Kipp prowled through the street and the creatures of the Twilight realm recoiled from his presence. *Power*, Kipp thought. All the power in the five realms doesn't beat the fear in the eyes of demons when they behold their executioner.

Heavy footsteps clomped around the corner. Kipp narrowed his eyes at the seifyr. Four thin horns curled on top of its hairless head. Red beady eyes blinked above pointy, ebony teeth. Its hardened breasts connected to a flat abdominal as the seifyr bowed. Kipp nodded to it. He recognized the beast by where one of its arms ended in a ragged stump. *A disobedient pet*, Kipp mused. Seems to have learned its manners.

The Pipassë loomed overhead, a flat sheet of rock with swirling fog at the top. Kipp fingered the hand portal in his pocket. The girl unnerved him. Her proximity fueled his magik and made him want to level that cursed tree city where it stood. He had given her his name. She'd seen him in that room. She was a liability. But that rush felt good. Sparks twinkled off his fingernails, an afterglow of the power from having her breath on his neck back in Alagana.

Kipp passed through the titanium doors like they were liquid. The foyer beyond was empty. A stone staircase led to the upper floors of the Pipassë.

"Show off," muttered a voice to Kipp's right.

"Shut it, Jet," Kipp said in a bored tone without turning his head. He moved towards the stairs. A hand gripped his forearm and twisted him off course. Kipp looked at the figure dressed in the same grey and black tunic and black leather pants. Eyes of coal set in a dark complexion stared back.

"What do you want, Jet?"

Jet looked Kipp straight in the eye. His gaze was wary.

Kipp's brows came together as a headache splintered through his mind. He gripped his head, fingers digging into his temples. The girl. Laughing on the edge of a cliff. A tree in the center of a glen. And power. Swirling. Pulsing. Kipp pushed the vision further. A moon. Red. And darkness. So much darkness. Something slick rubbed on his palms. He looked down to see what it was. Nothing.

He stood in the Pipassë. He was in the Twilight realm. The fog of the vision faded. Jet shook his shoulders.

"Kipp! Kipp, come on buddy, snap out of it."

Kipp shrugged off Jet's hands. He was on his knees.

"You saw something." Not a question.

"I didn't."

"Fine, if you want to play difficult." Jet's eyes surveyed the foyer. His typical quiet personality was far too tense for things to be alright.

"What?"

"You know what the Regent told me?" The Regent: Jet's least favorite person and the man responsible for Jet being stuck as a scout rather than moving him up into the ranks of the targisha.

"Do spit it out. I'm utterly enthralled."

Jet cleared his throat and cracked his neck. "That you're on your last assignment."

That made Kipp pause. He was the Regent's Second, in line to inherit the Grey and all the power that went along with it. To be sent on a last assignment was taking away everything Kipp had worked towards. Killed for. Already a bitterness was carving a hole in his chest. He was undoubtedly the strongest member of the Grey so this had to be political.

"Any reason for this unwelcome development?"

Jet wrung his hands. "Something about the frae you tracked into Mainwood... there was another one, or you didn't actually kill it."

"You think I didn't properly kill a Twilight mutt?" Kipp's voice was lined with silver fury.

"Well, it went back to Alagana either way. Whether it's learned to cross realms is now a serious issue. With witchcraft and necromancy pushing towards destroying the barriers—"

Kipp cut his friend off. "Necromancy has never been strong enough to be a serious threat."

"Maybe it is," Jet insisted. "The Regent certainly thinks so and plans on using you as a test. To see if your magik is unstable, or if the Dark practices are tearing these realms to shreds."

"Never felt better, Jet," Kipp said with a grin that did not match the sinking feeling in his gut.

Jet leveled a stare on him. There never was any getting around Jet's perception. That's what made him so damn good in the field. Give him another fifty years and he would have the makings of an excellent Second. Maybe even Regent.

"You had a vision slip." Jet wasn't wrong. "That hasn't happened since..." Jet trailed off.

Kipp's body relaxed. The Regent didn't know about how his name had slipped out of his mind the same way the witching curse had. And within the same breath. He had room to negotiate. The Regent didn't know about her either, he took it. Her magik. Untapped. No, Jet was referring to an old screw-up of his that he could never shake.

"I haven't touched the book since I retrieved it from Ûnsigra. My magik is stable."

Jet tugged at a loose thread near his hips. "What did you see?"

"It was just a bout of nausea from the Passing. I've had four in the past week with no time in between to recharge." Skipping between realms was similar to getting dropped into the center of a hurricane. His stomach was more than a little queasy.

"And you say you're fine?"

"When have I not been?"

Jet studied him in a way that made Kipp want to itch his neck.

"He knows," Jet said at last. "Whatever you're failing to mention right now. The Regent knows."

Kipp tunneled through every detail of the last few assignments for potential outs. There was always a loophole Kipp could exploit in saving his hide. The Regency was going to be his after all. Damn the 'last assignment' bullshit. He'd amassed more than enough power and respect to be the proper choice. The only choice.

"Kipp," Jet said, his face downcast in disappointment.

Kipp stood and brushed his knees. Of all the assassins, Jet was the only one who Kipp trusted. Right now, he would give him something—a secret truth. Not the *whole* truth, but enough for Jet to know that Kipp cared.

"It was darkness," Kipp conceded. "The vision slip. The same one I've seen for months. War is already in Alagana, and we have failed to prepare." He left out the face he now knew, the one who belonged to a pretty little elf hiding in the east. How she was at the center of it all.

Kipp rubbed his hands down his chest and settled them on the armrests of the chair. A man in a loose grey tunic tied at the waist by a leather strap stood on the other side of the table. A scapular draped over the man's shoulders. A cowl covered his white spiked hair.

"My, my Kipp, you have been busy," the man spoke through gritted teeth.

"Regent," Kipp said and inclined his head to the leader of the Twilight and the Grey, the man who controlled their magik-bound assignments and presided over the fear-enforced peace the Grey maintained with the creatures that called the Twilight realm home.

The Regent curled his upper lip in assessment of his Second before speaking. "How fare the kingdoms?"

"Bristling to slit one another's necks as always. There is movement toward the Old Throne of Alagana if Aideil can unify its forces. Farindor won't be a threat to either side. There is too much dissension among their ranks. Queen Daetheiri loves her woods too much to risk their burning. Aideil won't bother with an alliance anyways. They already strong arm Aniöm to their will. No word from Velesah or Mendia."

Kipp handed over sketches of commanders' faces who he deemed would be of importance in the ensuing war, notably that shark Commander Maximus. Among the sketches were notes on any physical weaknesses and which amongst them would be the best string to pluck if they wished to unravel their ranks and create discord.

"And the girl?"

Kipp's eyes narrowed. His mind worked to spin this away from that powerful little elvish girl. Unfortunately, the Regent was having none of it. As always.

"There was a girl in that war room, wasn't there? The hounds smelled her on you when you entered the realm."

"That was a girl?" Kipp toyed with amusement. She passed as masculine well enough; she might have been mistaken for a young soldier. He would have to see to it that the wraithounds be reminded of his rank before they sold him out again.

"What do we know of her?"

Kipp opted to surrender some ground. If the Regent was curious about her, that meant he already knew something. And therefore, Kipp wanted to know what he knew. "Clumsy, bumps into people, quiet type."

"The client wants her placed. A woman hasn't been seen wandering the Great Hall in the garb of an acolyte in decades."

Kipp stifled an urge to flinch back. "Placed?" Someone else knew how much power thrummed through that girl's blood and was willing to make deals with the Twilight devils to get it. Or, like Kipp, they could be chasing a hunch. Gifted elvish women in Aideil were somewhat of an enigma. They were either classified as harmless, or they were ushered away quietly. To where, he hadn't the faintest idea, and hadn't devoted any thought to the matter until now.

"It seems that your elvish girl has piqued their interest after the hounds brought word."

"From her scent?" Kipp smirked. Someone who knew how she smelled. An intimate perhaps.

"Precisely from her scent."

"What do I need to do?"

"She is your new target." The Regent's tone was clipped and Kipp knew to read the signs that pointed to a very difficult decision. "You are the best of us, I will not deny that. I have expressed that you are to be my successor, and I am hesitant to break that pact. However, we have a client who we cannot turn away. They have insisted that you are the only option—not to kill her. Not quite yet. Though it is imperative that you be the one to kill her when the time comes." The Regent tucked Kipp's field notes into a file on his desk. "The brief awaits you in the barracks. The objective is straightforward. Keep her alive until the Moon of Sanguis in a year's time. The rest will become clear in the brief." The Regent flicked a hand, dismissing him.

Kipp didn't budge. "Is this my last?"

The Regent's face ticked, but did not reveal a distinguishable emotion. No, he was too smart for that. They were an organization of killers and butchers. "You're out of line, Aisolon."

"This girl," Kipp snarled. "Is she my last assignment?"

"Kipp..." For the Regent to answer was to admit that whoever held the strings, whoever had bought Kipp to monitor the girl, controlled the Grey. They were supposed to be neutral, ambiguous, separated from Alagana's constant squabbling.

"As your Second, I demand you answer me." Kipp opened the lid of power that swirled just out of reach. Kipp had never dared threaten the Regent. The act alone was grounds to strip him of rank, but he didn't care. The injustice of it was laughable. A sleight of hand by a family he had grown proud of—a family of the worst Alagana had to offer. The Regent's face felt the hurt reflected in himself. He knew what this meant to Kipp and did it anyways. It is what the leader of the Grey should do, what Kipp would have to do once he claimed his place in a year. The Regent saw this—felt this in the crackling strength that swirled in Kipp's hazel eyes.

"For what's coming, Alagana needs your magik. Aisolon, you pulled more Grey magik than ever was recorded during the Binding since the establishment of the Grey a millennia ago. It will take every last drop of it to do what is necessary in the coming months. You were the only option."

"Why tell them my magik is breaking?" He saw it in the way the Regent's eyes flickered to the mirror at his side. He was afraid of Kipp's influence over the others and had every right to be. Kipp was within his power to walk out right then and take the Regency for his own. It would take minutes.

"That wasn't a lie," the Regent replied. "Power like yours is not meant to be contained within a single being. Perhaps once, in an older age, your magik would be one of many. A great display of grandeur. But those times are gone. Alagana, in all her beauty, is dying, and magik can no longer be relied upon to save her."

"Then this is my last." Kipp felt it as a certainty. He expected rage, not the crack in his soul that swirled with the image of the elvish girl surrounded by a sea of blood.

"Take care in the coming months, my friend. The Moon of Sanguis has only been seen five times since the creation of this world. It is a day when Fate holds no power, and every world bleeds the color of hell. "

The Moon of Sanguis. Kipp's mind reeled. Images from the pages of a book flickered through his mind. All those years ago. A necromantic celestial ritual, trapped in a celestial event that occurred every three hundred and fifty years, give or take a few. The original curse that finally tore the royal family of High Elves to shreds. Calculations flew through his mind until he was certain. The girl was the key.

"*Hershkata*, Kipp Aisolon. I'll see you on the other side."

Chapter Nine

Eyolin elbowed her way through the Great Hall's massive main chamber, her mind reeling. Maximus hadn't come looking for her, the enchantment the Grey—Kipp—had placed on his mind seemed to do the trick. Twice. He had saved her twice, and yet she felt more threatened now than when she had been alone in that tent facing the frae.

She tucked a strand of hair behind her ear. The end of her braid was unraveling. Eyolin tugged at it as she spun towards the infirmary doors at last.

Master Arendt stood leaning against the outside of the high doors flanked by Traik. Eyolin stepped behind two parchlim before either of them saw her. Slowing her steps, her eyes settled on the half-giant. The air rippled to his left. Eyolin watched the shape of a body flicker into view. Long legs with pointed toes floated a hair off the ground. *A glimmer*, Eyolin thought. A type of illusory magik that manipulated the light to the welders bidding. Some stronger illusionary Gifts could shift appearances or disappear all together.

Eyolin caught flickering glimpses through the haze of the glimmer, a side effect of her own haywire magik. Her every nerve felt rubbed raw and electrified, seared from the inside out the longer she focused on seeing through the glimmer. Her Gift had been amplified somehow, even if just by the mere proximity to so much magikal energy. Now she was seeing distortions wherever magik existed. She was in the center of the city's power and thus felt the disorienting headache pound at the base of her skull.

She blinked away the rush that rose into her throat.

Whatever drifted at the shoulder of the half-giant looked like nothing more than a shadow on the wall. But it moved with such intention that it couldn't be a trick of the light.

Two feline ears flicked atop the shadow's head, a slim tail flicking out one moment and gone the next.

It stalked Traik's person like a predator. A predator Master Arendt paid no attention to. The green panels of the master's tunic cast his face in a sickly pallor. Tequerra's fingernails curled ever so unnaturally each time he passed a small satchel between his hands. He was distracted. Distant. Lost in his mind.

Traik angled his shoulders to face the wall for a moment, caging in the glimmer. Eyolin saw his jaw move and shoulders rise. The commander was speaking to it. He turned back to Tequerra with a frown and the shadow disappeared.

Tequerra's head snapped up. Eyolin's mouth opened for an audible gasp. A green vein forked up his neck and into his brow. He took a long breath and the darkness receded.

This magik is going to my head, Eyolin told herself. She looked closer at the master and every muscle was relaxed and poised. His hands were clasped at his belly. Nothing amiss.

"Commander Traik," Eyolin said as she finished her slow approach. "What are the qualifications to become a soldier of rank, say, a commander such as yourself?"

Traik grunted and crossed his tree-trunk arms. To Eyolin's surprise, Tequerra answered.

"The talented rise." Master Arendt pushed off the wall to close the distance between them. "Our leadership candidates go through rigorous training, both mental and physical."

"And how long does that typically take?" Eyolin asked. She spoke from fear that Maximus would come for her, but she masked her worry well.

Tequerra's eyes were amused. "Are you interested in taking up a mantle?"

"Curious," Eyolin said. "Everyone that I see is so young. Even the officers."

"The cost of war," Traik growled. "They're all green now."

"You can look into it when we return." Master Arendt ushered Eyolin out of the stream of bodies.

"Return?"

He smiled. "From the Middle."

Words failed her. *A different realm.* The Middle held more than just monsters, but ancient histories and horrors. The Grandmother Tree, once High Elvish royalty as King Jenthius' youngest child, now the Gifting deity of Aideil.

Her Gift. Everything would be lain bare—her years of hiding stripped by energy that was neither good nor evil. Eyolin's mind reeled with the suddenness of the trip. She should study. Learn about the trials and know what to expect.

Eyolin had been so caught up processing her run-in with Maximus and the Grey that she'd nearly forgotten the topic of the High Council meeting. Had the master and Traik been filled in on the developments? She should come clean before she lost control of the narrative, yet she found herself holding her tongue.

The minister's projection flashed in her mind, the birdlike pluket already stalking toward her. That was one creature of the Middle realm. She hoped that she wouldn't encounter anything worse. She hadn't left the forests surrounding the city. Suddenly she was about to jump realms with a Master of Magik. She could already see the story of her life weaving together at every new development.

She was in utterly over her head.

"Is there no time to prepare? I—"

"Children journey to the Middle when they are half your age," Tequerra interrupted. "There isn't a moment to lose."

He sounded almost giddy.

"You'll hardly know you left," the master said. He extended his right arm for her. Traik squared his shoulders with a pointed look that made Eyolin pause. She should mention the glimmered creature she'd seen Traik speak with. She eyed the knives at his belt and opted to remain quiet.

The moment Eyolin touched the master's arm, she was sent tumbling into a dizzying sensation. Her feet left the ground, and it felt as if a large hand squeezed her lungs. When she feared her vision would go black, she felt solid land beneath her.

Eyolin squinted to adjust to the bright glare of the sun. Her first blinking left her lightheaded and nauseous with a heavy sense of vertigo.

Around her, everything was muted in sepia tones. The grass of the circular glen was long and unkempt. The trees towered high, different from the ones in Mainwood. Harsher. More pointed. All cast in a deep shade of silt, like she was trudging along the bottom of a murky lake. Thick golden-brown foliage obstructed what lay deeper in the forest.

This was the Middle. Not the colorful realm of Alagana, but the ancient realm that lay just above it. The Middle rested atop Alagana like a blanket.

She turned to survey her surroundings and realized that she was alone. Master Arendt and Traik were nowhere to be seen. A heavy thump fell to her side. She felt the wet breath and heat emanating off it before she dared to look. She was nose to muzzle with a massive erixsay.

The beast had a head the size of a small boulder. When it snarled, Eyolin saw fangs that resembled ivory tree limbs. Its tan fur was tattooed with jagged scars. The pelt rippled over the erixsay's six strong legs. Eyes that glinted red as the sun revealed the hunger that rumbled through the beast's snarl. A forked tail twitched impatiently, and droplets of saliva splattered when it snapped its jaws. The moist ground had large indents from where it had raked its claws.

Fear inked itself on her skin through her sweat. Eyolin swallowed down the panic that bubbled inside. Adrenaline pumped through her. *Weapon*, she thought. *I need a weapon.* Cover, run, scream. The various commands held her body firmly in place. She frantically tried to remember the few times Arden had taken her to the training arenas when she was seven. All useless stances and blocks meant for hand-to-hand combat with something that stood on two legs. This creature had six. She had managed to ignite her sword when she fought the frae. Summoning magik through desperation wasn't the most reliable strategy. This wasn't Alagana, either. Magik worked differently in each of the realms.

Her indecision froze her until the erixsay pounced. Eyolin rolled out of the way. The snapping jaws missed her shoulder, its tail swatting her square in the chest. The hot stink of the erixsay reeked of spoiled blood.

She scrambled up and bolted. She couldn't outrun the beast but could buy herself time to come up with a plan. Her feet pointed toward the edge of the glen. Cover. If she gained enough momentum, the erixsay might crash into a tree and be dazed for a heartbeat.

The damned master, Eyolin swore. This wasn't the Grandmother Tree. This glen in the Middle was an arena of death. The erixsay's swift footsteps didn't follow her. She risked a glance over a shoulder.

There was nothing there. The glen was empty. Eyolin slowed, her heart pounding in her ears. The edge of the forest was a few lengths away.

A ripple in the air caught her eye. Four erixsay prowled out of the ether. Each stalked forward slowly. Assessing their prey. A tug in her gut almost made her sick. Her head ached but the feeling grew. It spread through her body. A shock rippled through her hand, making Eyolin flinch. That hand curled around a solid mass. She glanced down, taking her eyes off the erixsay. A sword crafted of white lightning. It crackled as she raised it, light as air but solid and humming with magik.

The four erixsay blinked out. They materialized nearly on top of her. Eyolin brought the sword up. The blade lodged itself in the jaws of the lead beast. It snapped hard. The tip of the sword snapped beneath a fang. A thrum of lightning jolted into the mouth of the erixsay who produced a high-pitched yowl and fell to the ground stunned and whimpering.

The next beast lunged at her. Eyolin held out her hand. A wave of energy flowed to her palm. A beam of fire wrapped around her hand, an otherworldly strength holding her arm strong against the blunt force of the beast. It railed into the fiery palm head-on. And dissolved into a flurry of sparks.

The remaining two erixsay bounded over the electrocuted body of their packmate. Eyolin caught one by the muzzle, its surface slick, and used its momentum to throw it into the other erixsay. Her blood was boiling, the magik singeing every vein. Her mouth felt parched, moisture leeched from her body from the use of her Gift. Magik used without a gem had no conduit. No buffer that saved the mortal blood. At this rate, she wouldn't last long enough to make a run for the woods.

Eyolin backpedaled. The sepia tinted forest grew above her. More snarls reached her ears from its depths. The rest of the pack.

The three erixsay in the glen regained their footing. Six more stepped from the undergrowth. They didn't attack. Their forms flickered like the glimmer in the Great Hall. Eyolin's eyes narrowed and she shifted her movements toward the open center of the glen. She made it a few steps before more appeared. They emerged from a fold in the air, stepping forward like walking through a waterfall. Like the glen was masked with its own form of a glimmer.

Magik, from what she felt so far, was much more fluid in this realm. It was like working with clay, an artist wielding a brush before a palate of paint. The energy within her was tangible, if only she willed it into being—much different from the magik of Alagana that required formal study and training.

Eyolin summoned a streak of lightning and flung it into the empty center of the glen. Her ears rang. There was wetness dribbling down her neck. Blood soaked into the cloth at her collarbone. The air shuddered around the lightning as it sizzled forward.

It hit something solid. Something that wasn't visible.

Lightning exploded upward, tendrils branching out like a tree. Exactly like a tree. The magik coiled itself around a thick tree trunk and snaked skywards.

The glimmer peeled away.

The erixsay dissolved into dust.

The twisted, knotted tree had branches that extended over the glen and cast everything in shadow. Its trunk was thicker than the largest home in Mainwood and its foliage bloomed out in a wide array of flowers, each in a different shade of tan and brown. Near the base of the tree Eyolin saw a jagged black charred line, just like the tree etched into the ceiling of the infirmary.

The Grandmother Tree.

Eyolin dabbed at the blood in her ear. The energy used in fighting off the erixsay and stripping away the glimmer left hollowness in her bones. She took a step towards the tree and fell to her knees instead.

The tree emanated a light shimmer in the sunlight. One of the tree's roots rose from under the earth and arched, taking the shape of a doorway. The air became cleaner and sweeter. A breath of warm air soothed the ache Eyolin's magik had left.

"Don't worry, my child. I will not harm you."

Eyolin gasped as a female figure stepped from the wood of the trunk. Leaves floated down across her body, rippling into a sheer dress. Her eyes sent shivers through Eyolin. They were solid wood, unblinking, like two knots of tree bark.

"Come."

The tree woman motioned for Eyolin to follow her as she vanished through the archway in the base of the trunk. Eyolin approached. A staircase cascaded down in a spiral. Wariness held her on the first step, despite growing up in a city high up in the trees. She placed her foot on the wooden stairs slowly. Dots of magik flickered awake like tiny flames and illuminated her descent.

After what felt like an eternity, Eyolin emerged into a large circular chamber. In its center was a levitating, almond-shaped orb. A voice seeped out of the wood like sap.

"I've been expecting you for a long time, Eyolin. It pleases me that you found your way to me, after all that you have endured in your few years."

Eyolin spun around trying to find the source of the voice, but the honey-colored wood vibrated all around her. "Who are you?"

The tree chuckled kindly. "You know who I am. I am the keeper of the Middle, this forest, and the grandmother of Aideil's Gifted."

The weight of the realization hit her like a club. This tree was as much a deity as it was a grave.

"Lila," Eyolin breathed. "You're—alive." It was beyond anything Eyolin had expected. To stand before the visage of a High Elf was to drink in the presence of a god.

"In spirit only, to honor my father's descendants with the means to control their magik."

The orb in front of Eyolin cracked open, and a bright white light filled the room. Beams of energy radiated out and bounced along the wooden walls, illuminating the wood at every touch. The sepia tones of the Middle were stripped away and swirled with the rainbow. After a few moments, the light dimmed. A transparent woman shrouded in a shimmering white mist stepped forward. The strings of energy fanned out around her slender face. A silk veil covered her. The murdered daughter of King Jenthius, buried in the Middle, whose essence grew to be the Grandmother Tree as a gift to the land of Alagana.

"Why is it you only Gift those who are able to access the Middle? So few have the strength in their magik to blink, and natural portals have been wiped out."

"Always so inquisitive, Eyolin." The spirit of Lila looked down with a warm smile. "Aideil possesses many scariyai who have learned to blink and thus, Aideil sources its gems from me. Other kingdoms have their own means of obtaining gems for their Gifted."

"And the glimmer? The erixsay that nearly bit my head off?"

"The test. If you possessed no Gift, you would not have survived. Your companions were aware, but not concerned." The spirit pursed her lips in displeasure. "Unfortunate that you cut through the glimmer so quickly. It almost reached the fun bit."

"Fun?" Eyolin had to pinch her leg to keep from snarling.

Lila drifted through the chamber, her arms wrapped around her middle. Where she went, magik shimmered in bright rays. This deity was pure and light where Eyolin was pain and deceit. "Where the full force of the Sarom is provoked. It's quite marvelous. I've the privilege of seeing it once before."

This was wrong. It was all wrong. She didn't deserve to stand before a god and argue, but still her mouth ran. "I can hardly maintain a spark of magik without pain."

"I would assume that's the wormwood still lingering in your blood, numbing your Gift."

Eyolin's ears turned pink. Wormwood—the distinguishing ingredient in the herbalist's evening tea. She had thought it only for subduing her migraines.

"I can smell it." Lila waved a hand. "Nasty brew, dismissing the Gift like an unwanted child. If you are to wield the power of the Sarom, you must yield wholly to the magik within. The King's Gift chose you where it has not chosen others. Are you up to the task?"

"I—I think so." Even as she said it, she knew it was a lie. Lila likely sensed it too. There were parts of herself Eyolin could never revisit. Memories that were as blocked as her magik.

"The path of the Sarom is never one I delight meddling with," Lila continued. "Things that cannot be said will inevitably come to pass. You must trust that your magik cannot fail you. Only your body can fail."

But her magik *had* failed her. Over and over again in a past that haunted her. Her sister cursing her and abandoning them all. Her mother murdered. Eyolin felt the terror of that moment every time she closed her eyes. The scream, the blast of light, her mother's apron. The joy of her life ripped from her.

Eyolin had been helpless against the frae, only sparking a zap of lightning into her blade long enough to stab an already injured creature.

She was a runner. She always ran. Away from people, from connections and any who could care for her. Away from magik. She had stayed with the herbalist as long as she had because the nightmares had been stopped—by the tea, as she now knew.

Even now, in the glen, before a magikal deity, a god, she took a shortcut, running from the trial at the first opportunity. And she would have done it again.

A single tear rolled down Eyolin's cheek.

Lila's spirit drifted down, and her translucent hand brushed the tear away. Lila lifted the tear, and a beam of light flashed from the orb to hover in her palm. Light spun itself into the tear, flickers of the rainbow bouncing off it.

Lila cupped her hands around the tear. "Do you claim your Fate, Eyolin Kyenz-ushteira, daughter of Lord Kyenz and Lady Kyenz-eihra, and take this moontear as your gem?"

Eyolin was numb as she answered. "Yes."

"This gem is the embodiment of your Gift. It contains the essence of your magik and a tether between the mortality of your body and the magik of the Sky realm where magik began. With it, you may grow your power, hone it, and control the energies that flow through you. But, if the surface is cracked or overwhelmed with power, it will not only extinguish the magik within you, but also consume your soul. Part with it, and your Gift is surrendered back into the earth as if it never existed at all."

A flash of light appeared when Lila placed the tear above the orb. When the chamber dimmed, Lila was gone.

Hovering in the center of the circular room was a crystal-clear gem in the shape of a water drop, wrapped in a delicate silver coil. Eyolin gazed in awe as light reflected in the gem like a prism. A warm light emanated from the moontear's center.

She wiped a second tear off her cheek and straightened. She had survived the test. The daughter of King Jenthius had greeted her. King Jenthius. This was the Grandmother Tree of legend, and she had spoken to it. Lila didn't see Eyolin's Gift as a curse.

Accepting this gem forever tied her magik to her very essence, forfeiting any plan to release it back to the earth. She had even convinced the Master of Aideil to train her, though whether he honored her wish was another matter. It was everything her younger self could have dreamed of—a spot among the scariyai. And yet, it was her mother whom her mind drifted to. Her mother had given up everything for her, to hide her Gift from the world. She had honored that for years, hiding and suppressing herself until she fit within the mold her mother built for her.

But what if she could be more? What if she could relinquish the fear that haunted her every waking breath? Perhaps there was a purpose for all of her suffering. It would be an insult to the gods, even the ones she didn't worship, to turn from her Gift now that she'd received the blessing of Lila.

Warmth spread over her skin. Eyolin opened her eyes to find the room filled with light. She was glowing.

The cuts on her knees and arms, all injuries from the erixsay, stitched themselves together. Her head ceased its constant aching as a tendril of healing magik snaked to Eyolin's temples, circling her head in a halo.

At the center of the light was the moontear. It radiated health and blazing energy. The power of the Sarom, linked to a tiny opalescent gemstone. The power to... Eyolin did not finish the thought. She didn't know where she stood amidst the machinations of her world, how she fit in. For every memory she held close to her heart, there was no place where she felt truly herself, truly at ease with simply being. But maybe, just maybe, she could discover that now.

Chapter Ten

E yolin stepped from the arched entrance of Grandmother Tree what felt like an eternity later. The sepia toned sky was richer, with its browns darker than they had been when she arrived. A soft breeze rustled the canopy. She glanced around to ensure that there were no signs of the erixsay, a glimmer mirage from Lila or not.

Master Arendt and Traik stood on the far side of the glen and Eyolin could have sworn the tree at her back shuddered.

Traik inspected his various blades for sharpness while Tequerra paced incessantly. He crossed in front of Traik, and a wave of hostility rippled from his person. It was Eyolin's turn to flinch. She retreated a step back into the shade of Grandmother Tree almost wishing for the branches to wrap her in an embrace she might never leave. The bitter emotions from the other side of the glen left a nasty aftertaste and her mind filled with anger and hate and... darkness. Most unnerving was that the thoughts were not her own.

I have not seen such darkness since the Beginning. Lila's voice trembled on a delicate wind. *You may be more at risk than those that came before. Be careful, Eyolin.*

Eyolin's lip trembled as she met Traik's gaze. Magik as she knew it was without individual thought, but that tidal wave of hatred was filled with an ancient undertone of pain. All of it pooled around the master and Traik.

The half-giant narrowed his eyes, noticing the elvish girl quivering in the shadows of a magikal deity. Eyolin was certain that the darkness came from him. He'd spoken with a glimmered figure. He'd been lurking on the ground of the human district at the same time as the frae. And he wanted her in a cell.

Tequerra spun on his heels and stopped pacing in the middle of the path he had worn. There was no sun or moon drifting through the sky of the Middle so Eyolin couldn't discern how hong she had been inside Grandmother Tree.

Giddy excitement lit up Master Arendt's face as he waved to her with both arms. Traik sheathed the sword in his hands and pushed off a trunk that groaned under his weight.

Crickets screeched in her ears, amplified into a cacophony of torture. She took a step from the shade, tentatively, waiting for a monster to spring at her or an enemy to make themselves known. The wind boomed like a drum and the scrape of Traik's chainmail felt like claws digging into Eyolin's mind. Every hushed sound blared in her head. It hurt. It all hurt so much.

Nausea swelled in her throat, and it was all she could do to stay standing. She would not fall in front of the Master of Aideil.

Tequerra, whose earth magik made all the land sing to him, froze.

"Kneel," he ordered. She might have recoiled at the command had she not felt so dizzy. His words broke through the tsunami of exposed nerves. "Steady yourself. Your magik hasn't adjusted to the gem."

In answer, the moontear prickled against the skin of her palm. One look at the gemstone sent blood rushing to her ears.

She felt the wave of power before it surfaced—a calm ocean before a storm.

"Get back, I don't—" Eyolin gasped.

"She's going to pull a Lar—" Traik started. Master Arendt cut him off with a glare sharper than any knife.

Neither man retreated as power coursed from her core into the moontear, wave after wave, crashing and boiling and writhing. It was alive.

Eyolin wanted to scramble back and away but the grass gripped her shins where she fell to her knees. It was the overwhelming fear of a decade without magik that frightened her so. She was a fool for believing she could control it. A miserable, stupid fool for putting herself here. The moontear didn't want her, or her magik. The master was wrong—Lila was wrong. And for their misstep, she would reduce the grave of a High Elf to dust.

Green magik swirled from Tequerra's hands. His knee brushed the earth, and his hand was soft where it planted itself in the beige grass. Vines and grass and dirt piled into a wall that pulsed and groaned. Eyolin felt the veins of energy extending towards her.

Master Arendt's voice called to her mind, a soft pressure that met no resistance.

Let it out, Eyolin. Let your magik flow.

"Brace, Commander," he called from behind the wall.

Blood flowed from Eyolin's nose. With the use of her magik, destruction would follow. She choked back a sob. Nothing had changed. She hadn't changed, only gained a gemstone with an empty promise.

Eyolin waited for the explosion of light. For her Gift to level Grandmother Tree and everything in it. Nothing prepared her for the searing column of energy that met such resistance that she thought her body would split in two.

Then emptiness. A hole so deep she couldn't see the top.

The earthen wall shuddered and Tequerra's magik withdrew, the green whips snapping back into his hands.

"The wormwood," Traik grumbled. "It must be lingering."

"A few days, weeks. We will wait. There is still time."

Traik cocked an eyebrow at Master Arendt and approached Eyolin. Her eyes swept past the half-giant and once again, a dark aura of emotion swept over her, though, this time it felt subdued.

"What did you see?" Traik asked, his hand extended to her. "Did you speak to Lila?"

Eyolin didn't answer. He referred to the spirit not the deity. The master shifted uncomfortably and broke the silence.

"May the bards take note: did the tree answer?"

Eyolin had to guess that he meant the moontear. Her fingers were stiff as she peeled them open. The jewel was hardly the size of the pad of her thumb, with a smooth teardrop shape. Its interior pulsed and swirled with pearly shades. She was lost in the gemstone when Master Arendt murmured a prayer in a language she did not recognize.

"The moontear of the Sarom, the fifth of its kind."

She had expected something akin to relief. Instead, it was a morbid finality. Her plan to build a quiet home in an unimpressive notch in Mainwood was so very far away.

Four others had claimed the title of Sarom before her, four other elves surviving a trial from a deity to walk away with a moontear. She could almost see her own story carved into a pillar in the infirmary.

Master Arendt said she had days—to do what? Master a Gift she had been prepared to relinquish the moment she turned twenty? A magik that caused her nothing but pain?

Her sister's face huffed in the background of her mind.

"It isn't nothing!" Arden exclaimed.

Eyolin stood at Arden's back in the living room. The pungent scent of spices wafted from the bubbling kettle by the fire. Their mother, surrounded by a breath of air that smelled of cinnamon and honey, looked near to tears, her hair frizzy where it exploded around her delicate face.

"It will always be that way, Arden," their mother replied. "Gifted women have no place in Aideil."

"Every day that passes poses a greater risk of her being discovered," Arden screamed. "Of the High Council finding out about our deception, of you being convicted of treason, and of Eyolin being locked away to be tested like a beast."

Eyolin had heard this argument before. Soon, her sister would slam the door and that would be the end of it.

The scene swirled beneath the surface of the moontear. The gemstone searched for the source of her pain. Eyolin wished to tell the gem that it was no use. The memory it wanted was erased from her mind. Still, it searched.

Eyolin's mother stood at the window that overlooked the jagged Terrot Mountains. Eyolin sat perched on the edge of her bed, rubbing the sleep from her puffy eyes.

"There is a darkness in this land that will consume everything, destroy everything, and take everything you hold dear away from you." Her mother turned, the bags beneath her eyes heavy from a sleepless night. "But I know

you. I trust that you will never stop looking for the light. Know that it is out there, that all is not lost. And you will survive."

Eyolin's heart pounded and all she wanted to do was curl up and cry for the sister she had lost.

"Magik can be a fickle thing," her mother explained. "It can betray us, the Gifted, even if we have mastered every facet. To be Gifted, is to humbly give yourself to a force that can twist your intentions beyond recognition."

"Eihra, your gem..." Her mother's azurite earring had frosted over into a layer of ice. She winced in pain and warmed the stone between two fingers.

Her mother's face faded as the moontear scoured Eyolin's years on the streets, drifting from apprenticeship to thievery to foraging. It had been so long since she'd allowed magik to flourish in her veins. Now each memory was faded and fuzzy.

Her mother's healing water transferred to curing broths for any illness and her father's stormy winds that upturned freshly folded laundry when he sneezed.

The lullabies of forests and magiks and legends lost over steeped leaves and honey.

A yelp from Arden as a pot toppled over and their mother's soft rain that erased the burns.

There was beauty in magik once. A delicate artistry that Eyolin had forgotten. In its place terror and pain poisoned her mind.

Sensing the shift in tone, the moontear dug for the moment it all changed. For the day when the power within her swelled too great. A scene from the same day magik proved to be as much a curse as a gift. That death and destruction followed in her shadow. She could have sworn that a low chuckle resonated from the moontear. *No,* Eyolin thought decidedly, feeling the splitting migraine that came from thinking about that day. No, she would not give the gemstone in her palm the power in her veins. Not completely. She would train to be useful, but never again will her magik take a life.

She must have said the last part out loud for Tequerra replied, "We will do what we can."

Traik and Master Arendt stood over her, transfixed with the moontear.

"You are the hope we needed," he continued. "With luck on our side, you will never lay a foot on a battlefield."

Traik's lip twitched. Eyolin couldn't determine if the lapse in his steely glare was due to hate or something else, but she found herself distrusting the half-giant more with each passing moment.

"She has yet to prove she has bonded to the gem. If her Gift does not manifest, it will have been a waste of a Sarom."

Tequerra hoisted Eyolin to her feet, making a fuss over cleaning the drying blood from her chin and neck.

"Keep that safe," he said with a nod to the moontear. "The destruction of a gem, even if you aren't bonded, breaks all connection to magik. A piece of you would be gone. Only the darkest parts remain. And we need you at your best."

Eyolin had half an idea to flee into the woods of the Middle. Perhaps her skin would take on the same color as the realm. There would be no dancing the chords of war or magik. Still, she took Master Arendt's outstretched arm to carry her back to Alagana.

* * *

Kipp slipped silently into the barracks, the sky forever grey in the Twilight realm. The pale moon never rose or set, only rotated around the horizon. He shared a room with Jet with one window as the only source of natural light in the rectangular cell. Two narrow beds lay on opposite walls and greylight shone from two bulbous balls that hovered near the ceiling.

Stepping cautiously over one of Jet's skeleton dogs snoring in the doorway, Kipp strode to his mattress. A folder was tucked into the creases of his sheets. Kipp hissed under his breath. The Regent's seal was pressed in black wax—the seal that belonged to Kipp by right. Kipp hovered his hand over it, feeling the magik woven into the oils. If—when he broke it, the Binding magik would seal his fate to that of the contents inside. He couldn't very well kill the Regent with Binding magik attaching him to a job. He'd be shredded from the inside out.

"Is this your last?" Jet stood in the doorway with his arms crossed, nodding to the folder. "Should I plan on baking you a cake for tomorrow, or give you some restless lessers who don't need a head?"

Kipp's mouth tilted up in a smile. The skeleton dogs rustled, their legs kicking out in their sleep. Tiny stars twinkled around their bony paws. They were one of many species of lesser creatures. Most of the Twilight's inhabitants fell into this lesser category, being unappealing to the elves in Alagana.

Kipp's hands had ended so many of the Twilight's lessers, from frae to wraiths and from demons to seifyrs. He'd even killed skeleton dogs, though Jet preferred to take them off the streets and make them pets. Jet's own personal patrol.

"I'm sure Erik can rustle up some candles from a witch to make it a real celebration. He'd be one elbow deep in the witch and the other arm deep in the batter." Jet paused, scrunching his nose at the thought. "Better pass on the cake. I've lost the appetite for witch fingernails."

"I could do with some slaughter."

Jet sucked in through his teeth. "That good?"

"That bad."

"No specifics needed, but should I call Erik and Po? It can be his initiation. Take your mind off tomorrow." Jet referred to Po, some new rookie the Grey had scraped off the streets in Huebeck. Sticky fingers and low alcohol tolerance that caused his red hair to stick to his forehead.

Erik had been recruited in Jet's cohort fifty years ago, the magik of the Grey preserving their half-human bodies like that of a Gold Elf so that they appeared in their early twenties. Kipp remembered the moment a snarky boy with blood caked under his fingernails was thrown in front of Kipp for assessment. Erik had murdered his parents, putting him on the run at an early age. For all that nastiness, he was the best pastry chef the Twilight realm could have hoped for. Each Grey would have died without the purpose the Regent gave them.

Kipp had years on all of them. He'd first come to the Twilight realm by tumbling through the portal at the bottom of the Keystones faërfalls. The cave had been his sanctuary from the guards. The elves had hunted the child with human blood and a curious magik that should not have been possible. His natural aptitude for the Grey's magik had earned him favor with the Regent almost immediately. Starved for power and praise, Kipp pulled more magik from the realm than ever heard of. When Jet and Erik were dragged in by their necks, Kipp had personally trained them, seeing himself beneath the blood and dirt on their skin and souls.

Jet and Erik were two sides of the same coin. Where Jet poked and prodded and came up with ill-timed jokes, Erik brooded. But where one was, so was the other in the shadows. It had been some years before Kipp had cracked Erik's walls and caught him with a plate of hot cookies. They never let him forget it.

"Po asleep?" Kipp asked, stretching out on his mattress.

Jet's eyes twinkled. "Just shut his door."

"Then I say we pay him a visit." Kipp tucked a pillow over the folder full of that girl's details. He'd deal with that later. This may very well be his last time in the Twilight realm, his last time with the closest thing he had to family. "Grab Erik. Check the pantry and make sure he hasn't touched my dwarvish spirits, then bring him and the bottle."

"We really gonna kill him off so early?" Jet grinned.

The room's door created open. A deep voice growled out, "I don't remember you complaining when my ass was stuck in a trough of witches bones."

Erik leaned against the doorframe. Tall, dark olive skin and eyes that cut as deep as his seraph blade. He wore the same black and grey leathers and tunic as Kipp and Jet but stood just taller than both. His shoulders were broader and his face harder, sharper. Kipp's eyes flicked down to his sleeves, all covered with powdery white.

"Are you mixing the ashes of your father into your brownies now?"

"Unfortunately, they wouldn't be an adequate substitute to flour." His face didn't reveal a single emotion. He raised the hand that had hung behind his back. "I brought the spirits. Figured Kipp would appreciate the sendoff, last assignment and all."

Kipp swiped the bottle from Erik's dangling fingertips. There was maybe a fifth of the bottle left. "If you saved any for me, that is."

Erik rolled his eyes and pulled out a newly opened bottle of dwarvish spirits from a fold in his leathers. Jet and Kipp eyed it conspiringly. If the humans made ale for the masses, and the elves made wines that altered one's vision, then the dwarves made spirits that made realities anew.

It pained Kipp to keep this assignment from them. The Regent was challenging his right to taking control by throwing him on a useless hunt. Any one of the men in this room could keep a girl alive for a year. He should be preparing to undergo the trials of succession, not chasing tail.

Erik's eyes flashed. "I have something better for Po."

Kipp fell face first into his pillow and groaned. Jet, Erik, and Po were still out on the outer streets of the city wreaking havoc. After Po slammed the bottle of magically enhanced dwarvish spirits, Jet had the brilliant idea to go bloody up some Twilight creatures on their hit list, a running tab of anyone or anything who didn't treat the Grey assassins with the utmost respect.

He pushed himself up, leaving bloody handprints on the sheets. They'd be thrown out along with the rest of his things when he left in the morning. The Grey were not sentimental or permanent in their philosophy. With each assignment, all traces of membership were stripped from the barracks. They could die, and no one would receive notice or explanation.

Maybe he'd just kill her, Kipp thought. Keep a bottle of her blood, find a witch to tie her essence to it. That could make the sacrifice work. He didn't need to actually babysit her. Or tend to her well-being. The client expected him to kill her in the end, so why not shortcut it and be done? Kipp hadn't read the specifics. The wax seal lay intact, waiting for him to Bind himself to the mission. His head spun too much to read it now anyways.

Sudden pain ripped through Kipp's body. He doubled over and fell to his knees. The contents of his stomach heaved onto the floor. It felt like his insides were melting. The amount of power made him heave again. *Power, power, power,* were the only thoughts that he could form. The energy rushed into a tight coil in his gut, and he knew where it stemmed from. The girl. It was the same tug that manifested in her presence that tickled tantalizingly strong magik. Except now, she was nowhere nearby. She was in Alagana, a different realm. *What sort of magik can cross space like that,* Kipp wondered. His chest was boiling.

The magik of the Grey lapped at the energy that flowed into him from her. In his drunken state, he envisioned the transfer of power that would occur if he pinned her against a wall. Another round of retching tore at his insides and the image vanished. A target, he reminded himself. She's the piece that he needed to place to ensure that Jet, Erik, and Po would have a livelihood as a Grey under his command. The piece that needed to die. How could he feel her? If she had this effect of him the next time he stood flush against her, he couldn't be sure that his magik would be contained to his body. Oh, how grand an explosion the two of them would make.

The nausea and pain subsided. Kipp remained on his knees in the vomit. Jet would be returning soon. He wouldn't appreciate the mess. Kipp groaned and pushed himself up. He focused on the liquid at his feet. Grey sparks twinkled up his arms as his magik came to life. He incinerated what was left of the dwarvish spirits to dust. With another swoop of his hand, the dust vanished. No sign of the surge of power that the girl had somehow channeled into him or his body's negative reaction to it.

Kipp tugged off his tunic and tossed it into a corner. He made his way to the washrooms to prepare for the state between sleep and death where he would regain his full strength. It would take all his effort to watch the girl and keep a safe distance until the game began.

Chapter Eleven

"**A**re you ready to begin?" Tequerra asked?

He and Eyolin stood on the steps of the Great Hall in Mainwood the morning after Eyolin received the moontear from Grandmother Tree. She'd spent the entire evening failing to calm the panic that surged with each thought of training. There wasn't a room set up yet in the hall of the scariyai, and she was silently grateful for these last moments when she wasn't formally tied to Aideil. Everything would change once she was presented as a female scariyai training among men. That brought her to another level of anxiety. The men were selected and tested during early adolescence. Each would have at least a decade—if not centuries—more experience and knowledge than her. Where some may be grateful to learn from such expertise, the thought of those men only filled her with dread.

The night before, Eyolin had stared into her milky gem until her eyes filmed over with exhaustion. If she had connected with the moontear, she didn't feel it. Her magik had felt muted the moment she blinked back to Alagana. In the Middle, magik was raw and limitless. Alagana felt wrong. Stifled and dull.

"You'll be training with Karok to start," Master Arendt was explaining. He had been overly exuberant as he debriefed her on training schedules, hours of study, and pointed out the hallway to the library. She would be traveling to and from the training grounds at the base of the Terrot Mountains every dawn, returning in the afternoon for mealtime, followed by guided study as Karok saw fit. Or vice versa depending on the day's focus. Then repeat, and repeat, until Tequerra was satisfied with her progress.

"You have yet to connect fully with the moontear," Master Arendt continued. "As such, Karok will work internally on freeing your Shoutka—or spirit form. It is a powerful mind magik that is rare enough that Ïsteldûr will not be anticipating it. Or you. It will also assist in bonding with your gem."

"What about lesser magiks?" Eyolin inquired. "When do I learn to fuel light?"

Tequerra gave her a sideways glance. "We have fire sprites for that. Our scariyai ranks have been grossly depleted with the recent disappearances. As such, we need to bypass the standard learning model you would have undergone after the Academy. A Shoutka will be our secret weapon."

Eyolin thought she must have nodded. There weren't any Aideillian scariyai with a mind Gift, so she was filling in the gaps. It made enough sense.

"From this point onward," Master Arendt instructed, "you are not to speak of your Gift to anyone. If your moontear is seen, it is an opal specifying your specialty as a mind scariyai. Understood?"

Eyolin scoffed. She'd kept her Gift a secret for years. This lie was as easy as breathing.

Tequerra held out his arm to blink the two of them to the training grounds.

When her feet hit the ground, she dared to open her eyes. Every expectation was swept away along with her breath.

She had been placed in the center of a stunning garden-like forest where thick, green vines wrapped around an assortment of trees. They were different from the carved towering trees of Mainwood and had twisted branches and long waxy leaves. It was as if the creators of this place couldn't choose a specific climate or ecosystem, so they mixed them all.

In front of her a crystal-clear stream gurgled, weaving around the trunks. Above her, she glimpsed white-capped mountains and sheer rock cliffs. Scattered here and there were moss-covered boulders of multiple sizes. She watched as elves flung themselves through the air performing acrobatics while wielding swords and demonstrating katas for scariyai dressed in cream robes who sat cross-legged near-by.

In one corner, a familiar shape stumbled about with a bow staff that was noticeably heavier than they were capable of wielding. A slender elvish instructor yelled a series of demands, smacking down a wooden stick on the trainee's back with a sickening crack.

Straining her eyes, Eyolin identified Dale, the human servant from the infirmary. Beads of sweat shone on his brow, and Eyolin glimpsed bruises on every visible patch of skin.

Dale's instructor's voice carried as he remarked, "The only reason I bother with you, human, is because you keep showing up."

"Not my fault," Dale wheezed. "Blame the High Council and their new *integrated* military."

The instructor's face reddened, and he whipped the stick at Dale viciously. Dale sloppily blocked, moving at a glacial pace compared to the elf.

As she watched Dale's human blood drip into the grass, Eyolin found her feet leading her toward the sparring pair. Dale was so much shorter than all those around him. His speed and strength were reeds to a scythe compared to the elves, but this was a training ground where weakness was beaten from thought.

Tequerra paused, calling Eyolin back to the path. "He'll be fine, Eyolin. Gueah has produced the finest officers for our legions. We hope to include the humans, starting with that one there."

Gueah's barking orders and stalking gait looked familiar. It took Eyolin a moment to realize why.

"He walks like my father."

That made Master Arendt halt. He collected himself quickly. "I don't recall them being familiar."

"Did anyone here know him?" Eyolin said before she could catch herself. She didn't miss the tightening of Tequerra's shoulders at that.

"Every elf under your father's command was slaughtered. No, I don't believe anyone here will ever speak of the name Kyenz, and I advise you not bring him up again."

The two of them fell into an uneasy silence, the path winding ahead endlessly. As she did during her foraging trips for the herbalist, Eyolin let her mind wander—away from the impending dread of magik, and to the grounds around her. The birds called to one another, and animals made their way through the thick ferns and bushes. Flowers of every imaginable color and shape carpeted the ground and dotted the trees. Water lilies, like Eyolin's mother, tiptoed throughout the flowers. Their healing water magik flowed out of their hands in a mist and onto the petals and grasses. The forest beds breathed with renewed life in their wake. The water lilies were Gifted fairies and elves that had the power to make liquids with nourishing and healing properties. Their water was rumored to make dying plants spring back to life.

Three small foxes came yelping through the underbrush and zoomed into the shade of a tree root. Eyolin craned her neck in the direction the foxes had come from and noticed a dandelion-yellow mother liponark. The large dog-like creature padded around a tree. Eyolin gasped as it stood to its full height, towering twenty heads above the forest floor. The liponark tilted its head and let its ears flop over to one side as it listened, then turned to look into Eyolin's eyes. Eyolin held her breath, waiting for the beast to charge. It dipped its head in Eyolin's direction before disappearing around a group of boulders. Tiny yips followed close behind.

Young pups bounded at the mother liponark's heels. They pounced at mushrooms and barked with delight. Eyolin saw a powder blue pup stick its head up and take notice of Eyolin. It opened its mouth in a grin, its tongue flopping out. The blue pup barked at Eyolin fondly and raced to catch up to its mother and siblings.

Master Arendt wove through the foliage and trees silently, his footsteps barely grazing the ground. Eyolin reasoned it had something to do with his earthen magik but hearing her feet shuffle along alone was chilling.

Eyolin followed him around a sharp bend, mouth opening in awe. This place breathed magik and energy and life in a way that the

Middle hadn't. It was vibrant, colorful, and shimmering. While she believed that the magik in the blood of elves was dwindling with each generation, the grounds around her were a testament that there was at least a little life left in the realm. Passing a tropical tree, Eyolin watched tiny creatures with bat-like ears hook their claws on smooth bark horizontally.

A group of scariyai sparred across a stream in the distance. Each used breathtaking techniques that combined magik, swordplay and acrobatics into a graceful dance of death. Whirlwinds were countered with icicles. Defenders threw pulsating plasma spheres off course using blasts of power.

Three elves whirled atop boulders, two Gifted scariyai, the third a scarox Gifted in weaponry. Each were masters in their specialties, graceful and poised. Again, Eyolin saw the hopes and dreams of a younger version of herself reflected in the water. This is where she had always wanted to be accepted—by people who knew what she felt. These elves had claimed their power, growing into weapons and artists of their crafts.

Another look confirmed that all were men. Male elves, Silver and Amber. No women, no Gifted scariyai who had the same figure as she did.

The farther in they walked, the less sparring pairs they encountered. Master Arendt and Eyolin crossed over a crystal stream that bubbled through the greenery, smooth pebbles shimmering as the glaze of water rippled over them. The clear surface sang with energy. Her mother had been able to instill water with healing properties as a water lily. She pictured how a simple stew could be enchanted with the Gift of a water lily to take away a fever, or how a single drop could revive a wilted plant. It was a peaceful magik, inherently gentle and good. It didn't flare and cut like the moontear looped at Eyolin's neck. Responding to her wandering thoughts, a ribbon of water coiled out of the stream toward Eyolin's chest where the moontear pendant sat.

Before the water could make contact, Tequerra snapped a twig under his foot, the first sound he had made in what seemed like hours. He stood still, bent over as he eyed a small bush of tiny berries. He waved her over with a hand.

"Sharcloe," Eyolin commented, warranting a warm smile from the master.

"Very good," he said with approval. "It can either kill the being that ingests it or cure the worst of poisons." His mouth twisted into a conspirator's smile. "It depends on how long it's boiled and at what temperature. A fascinating little fruit, isn't it?"

The sharcloe on the bush were small and grey, growing in clusters of four or five. Master Arendt picked one and squeezed his thumb and forefinger together. The interior was bright red on the edge and a deep purple toward the center. He wiped off the pink juice and resumed his silent trek through the forest. Eyolin had half a mind to mention that those sharcloe were too ripe to be dangerous and would make a lovely jam but opted for something less antagonistic.

"Sir, where are we going? Am I not training with the others?" The other women, or... well anyone.

"You will be taking an unorthodox approach to magik given the urgency of the matter at hand and the fact that you have clearly no instruction in the arts. Karok learned morphling magik as an adult and can best guide you to accessing your spirit form—thus bonding with your moontear. It is best this way."

"Will Karok be overseeing the rest of my training?"

Tequerra huffed. "There is no telling your aptitude for magik, despite the raw talent. Once I am satisfied with your control over morphling magik, then we can discuss further."

"What about weapons?" Eyolin knew she sounded childish, that she should keep her mouth shut and respect the master who could have chosen to punish her for breaking countless laws. But she didn't know when she might have an opportunity to speak with him again and simply wanted to know. Master Arendt read as much in her face and conceded.

"Traik oversees combat in the city. I can arrange for him to add you to a rotation once your fitness improves."

Eyolin opened her mouth to thank him but stopped when a prick pierced the back of her arm. She lost sight of Tequerra moving around a fallen tree covered in moss and fungi, and her mind turned fuzzy. Her feet felt heavier, and her eyelids drooped. In two more blinks, everything tipped sideways. She was alone.

Her breaths shortened. Panic made her lip quiver. She stumbled a few more steps, unable to discern whether she traveled forward, sideways, or backward. A root seemed to spring up from the ground. Eyolin tripped and fell hard. Dazed and disoriented, the taste of blood flooded into her mouth.

Her mind wasn't working. It was a swirling and empty chasm that swallowed the daylight from the bright forest. Then the ground moved. No—it slithered. A serpent's head shimmered with smooth rusty brown and green scales, resembling the forest in which it lived. Bile rose in her throat that she gulped down.

The serpent's head lowered until breath warmed Eyolin's cheeks. Her body wouldn't move, wouldn't flee. She had lost feeling in her arms and the numbness was spreading. Eyolin let out a gasp and the serpent recoiled its head. Its jaws opened. Row upon row of dagger-like teeth retracted in and out as it inhaled her scent and hissed.

Balls of saliva splashed off Eyolin's tunic. The serpent's throat vibrated with a low hiss that grew to a piercing scream. Magik. Eyolin grasped at whatever power she possessed, pulling at strings through instinct alone. Fire, water, air, something, anything. And nothing. One by one, the tethers to magik were snipped. She whimpered.

She tried, and failed, to calm herself. The promise of magik was as far away as ever and a certainty settled on her bones as sure as anything she'd ever felt—she was about to die.

A slithering sensation wrapped around Eyolin's torso and tightened. She was being crushed and she couldn't even scream. Her arms and legs prickled with pain as her circulation was cut off.

There was no miraculous explosion or hidden power. The venom took that all away. Master Arendt was not coming back for a girl who couldn't survive the walk through the training grounds and a single snake.

Two more heads, only slightly smaller than the first, slithered into view. They snapped and nipped at each other viciously and tugged at the fleshy restraints that kept them from biting their own necks.

Eyolin scanned the surrounding area for a way out of the serpent's grasp. If magik wouldn't come to her aid, old fashioned escape tactics would have to do. Her lower body was wrapped by coils of scales. Any branch or weapon was too far out of reach. She had just enough mobility in her toes to shift her heels in the dirt and slip her hands along her body to relieve the numbness and give her ribcage room to breathe.

She searched for anything sharp, cursing herself for not thinking of bringing even a fork with her as a weapon. A few days in the infirmary getting pampered by nurses had made her go soft.

The three heads of the serpent still nipped at one another, distracted from their prey. They'd return to her soon—there! Her hand wrapped around an angular stone next to her feet. Her thumb brushed a sharp, splintered edge. That could work.

The venom was hard at work in her body, every moment dotting her vision with black. With a last push, Eyolin kneed upwards into the body of the serpent and sliced the stone through the scales. All three heads snapped to her. Their slitted eyes narrowed.

Their attention was short-lived.

A roar raised the hairs on Eyolin's neck. Her hands were slick with the serpent's blood, and she lost her grip on the stone. The sound came from behind her. She didn't get a glimpse at what creature made it but the three headed serpent frantically released her and sprang away into the shadows of the woods. Eyolin wasn't particularly keen on sticking around herself, given Tequerra had abandoned her and her trainer, Karok, hadn't made an appearance yet.

She blinked, her vision blurring as she rolled into the bushes for cover. Venom. Antidote. Get it out. She grasped at the rational part of mind that screamed about plants. How many times had the herbalist drilled her on medicinal plants and roots?

Blearily, Eyolin scanned her surroundings. Blue flowers grew on top of white mushrooms on a nearby stump. Eyolin could just brush the soft underbelly of the fungus. Its juices dribbled down her fingers. As slowly as she could without disturbing the uneasy quiet, she lathered the slime on the arm that had felt the first pinprick.

She could have made a mistake. Whatever venom this serpent possessed could easily have distorted her vision.

Her breaths were little more than gasps at this point, her mind a puddle of darkness, the hallucinations warping color and shape.

The last thought she had was of a god cloaked in fire reaching down to her.

Chapter Twelve

"What purpose did you have leaving her in the tyrono's lair like that? She could have been killed!" The voice, deep and masculine, came from somewhere above Eyolin.

Sharp laughter followed, not humorous but critical. It was Tequerra. "She needs to connect with her gem. We don't have time to coddle her."

"Your best idea was having her wrestle a snake?"

Eyolin wanted nothing more than to sink into the soft ground and be swallowed up by a sleep so sound she forgot who she was. Instead, she felt consciousness sink in and drag her to the surface where the energy in the air was far from pleasant.

"Initiate fear," Master Arendt was saying. "Force her into a situation where she had no choice but to use magik or die."

"I'm proud to announce, she both lived and did not use magik."

"She would've had you not intervened."

Who had intervened? There must have still been lingering effects of the bite because her mind immediately conjured the image of the blue flowered mushroom fighting the three-headed serpent.

"The venom was killing her faster than the tyrono was!"

"Her magik could have healed her."

"She doesn't know how!" The voice arguing with Master Arendt was yelling at this point. Eyolin could hear the master hiss with displeasure at the affront. An instructor was far below a master of magik in the eyes of society. Eyolin would feel bad if her instructor lost his head on her first day—if she ever managed to open her eyes.

Eyolin, still pinching her eyes shut, pushed herself to her knees, wincing at the scrapes that seemed etched into her bones. Master Arendt's tone reached a crescendo.

"Then teach her. She's awake, no thanks to that slime she smeared on the puncture wound." Eyolin could practically see the master bursting a vein from frustration.

"You aren't going to make me suck out the may wasp venom myself and be hospitalized for the day?"

"Tempting, but we need you to get to work immediately. Get her into spirit form."

There was no reply. Electricity sizzled through the air, sending a shiver down Eyolin's spine. She smelled the tinge of magik in the air like burnt hair.

A large, white hare materialized on top of the log Eyolin was still crouched beside. It cocked its head at her and soared over her head, landing about two lengths away, giving her a nice view of a fluffy bunny butt. It chattered and clacked its teeth and Master Arendt stomped through a bush a moment later. Its white hind leg stamped incessantly.

"Shut your furry—" Tequerra began and stopped as he beheld Eyolin scowling at him. "Eyolin."

"Any other shockingly close encounters with death I should be aware of for the rest of the week?" Eyolin asked with an innocent lilt.

The hare thumped its foot and sat on its hind legs with its arms crossed.

"Silence, Karok!" Master Arendt's face was beet red. Eyolin looked from the master to the bunny—her... trainer?

Tequerra snapped his fingers, and a vine flicked the hare's ears. The hare—Karok, Eyolin corrected in disbelief—actually curled its paws into fists, pretending to flex biceps and air box.

"Do change back to your natural state. The girl can't hear your thoughts telepathically." Tequerra turned his back to walk away. "Not until the girl connects to her gem." Referred to as the girl now, a downgrade from the illusion of being the Sarom. He was a far cry from the kind and understanding master scariyai that had met her in the infirmary with Traik. She had left anonymity for degradation. All for the promise of a bed and answers. Neither of which she'd received.

The hare hopped over the log as Tequerra vanished around the side of a tree. The air around it shimmered, and an electric wave rippled through the air. A tall, lean man with tanned skin and soft chocolate eyes scratched at the layer of stubble that covered his face. His face was scrunched as if he was always laughing. Long dark hair fell in chunks around his head with light patches that lit up his features. His jaw was chiseled, giving him a crude handsomeness—for a human.

Eyolin couldn't believe her eyes. But it was his ears that confirmed her suspicion. Her trainer was human. Master Arendt had failed to mention that before he decided to throw her to a tyrono snake and leave her for dead.

A human—it was more than she could comprehend. A human who could channel magik was unheard of. Witches were humans who performed spells, but their power was bound to words and items; they did not have magik flowing in their blood. Rather, magik hovered around witches. Elves were the only magikally Gifted race thanks to the blood of the High Elves.

From the look of Karok, he didn't seem particularly concerned with the technicalities of magikal study. So why would Tequerra pawn her off on him, and so far away from everyone else?

Karok leaned forward and smiled, flashing bright white teeth. His gaze was assessing and inquisitive.

"Hello, love," he said, pulling Eyolin to her feet. "Hope Gerome didn't put you off snakes for the rest of your life, they're really quite liberating to morph into."

Eyolin couldn't control the way her mouth dropped. "It—that thing had a name?"

"She is actually quite sweet. Once made a pass at me when I was perfecting my dashing tyrono physique. Never could get used to the multiple heads, left me seeing triple for days. The may wasp venom in your body sent her into a bit of a frenzy, I'm afraid. I'll check up on her later."

Words failed her. She hadn't expected to understand magik immediately, but here a human stood prattling on about slithering around with three heads. Luckily, Karok was an expert at talking to himself.

"I'm gonna gamble that we'll get you to sprout a tail by the end of the day. Sound like a plan? Good. Me too. Let's go." He plucked a fern from nearby and fanned himself, walking in the opposite direction that Master Arendt had gone. Eyolin scrambled to keep up, not wanting to risk Gerome returning.

"Where did Tequerra go?" Eyolin asked at last, breaking the silence as they traveled further into the forest.

"High Council meeting." Karok noticed her confused look. "He's one of the prominent members. Makes all the big calls. Gods, don't you know who runs Aideil?"

A Master of Magik who didn't attend the meeting Eyolin had stumbled into. Questions of where he'd been swirled. They had been discussing troop movements and the growing tensions with Ïsteldûr, with a leading member absent without explanation.

Karok picked up on the flash of hurt and slowed a bit. "Hey, sorry, that came out wrong. I shouldn't have assumed, you of pure elvish blood and all."

He made a path through the thick underbrush for Eyolin to go through. He itched his neck as she passed. He wasn't wrong though. She might be the only elf in Mainwood who wasn't at least passably educated and well read. She was a nameless gutter rat recently given a badge of power and she was so far out of her depth that she might as well walk around with a sign.

A few flat rocks lay in the center of the small glen. Karok went over to sit cross-legged on the largest one. He nodded toward the smaller slab across from him. Eyolin sat down stiffly.

"I'm not connected with my gem... I can't access my magik." It sounded as lame out loud as it had in her head.

"Does it look like I need a gem to be a morphling?" Eyolin shrugged and shook her head. "Master Arendt assigned you to me because I don't use a gem. I never took the trip to Grandmother Tree, Midriel knows I'm not elvish. Being Gifted is the easy route, especially if you start young. You missed the path for 'easy' a while ago. So, we do things my way."

A falcon flew down and perched on Karok's shoulder. It dipped its head and a sound rumbled in its chest. The morphling nodded and gave it a pet before it flapped off. Karok turned his attention back to Eyolin, "Little guy's reporting on the liponark pups."

Eyolin chewed her lip for a moment, glancing in the direction of the falcon.

He sighed. "Ask it."

"Pardon?"

"I'm human, love. Third great-uncle was elvish maybe, giving me just the kick of elvish blood to survive the attack that turned me into a morphling. Most changed morphlings can't control the change to the body or mind. In those cases, the monster wins and there is no path back to your natural form."

Morphlings and humans and great-uncles. Eyolin wasn't sure she was equipped with the empathy required of her, but she nodded her thanks at Karok's story.

"It was a pack of werekeys." Karok pulled the bottom of his shirt up just enough to show a mottling of scar tissue. "The alpha's bite turned me into one of them, or it would have killed me. Survive the bite and get a choice—albeit a shitty choice. I give into the alpha's bite and live as a senseless beast, or I fight it and curse myself to a life of constant fear that I will one day lose control and slaughter every living thing in my way."

It sounded so familiar, the same haunting power lurking just below the surface. Eyolin recognized the strategic choice in matching the two of them together, but where Karok masked his agony in sarcasm and banter, she was cloaked in a horror that made smiles not quite reach her eyes.

"How long ago did you become a...?"

"Morphling? Four years ago, give or take, in Aniöm where the packs still roam." He exhaled and clapped his hands. "So, here's to the outcasts of magik who no one else will deal with. Shall we begin?"

The lesson was meditative, gently prodding Eyolin's consciousness with the hope of finding triggers to her magik. So far, the obstacles were numerous, each blocking any connection to the energy of the realm.

Karok was pacing on top of a boulder throwing around ideas to break through.

"Master Arendt mentioned you don't have experience with lesser magiks like mind fields and telepathy. Given our literal mental block, why don't we do some internal digging?"

Eyolin would rather rub salt in her eyes.

"Sure, how would I do... that?"

Karok leveled her with a deadpan stare. "That sounded as enthusiastic as I hoped."

She didn't know what else to tell him. It wouldn't take long in her mind to realize that it was about as toxic an environment could be. There was so much pain and grief boiling inside, threatening to spill over in a long overdue eruption. But somehow, she knew that Karok understood. She would give it a chance, just to see if there was a god out there who didn't believe she was cursed to destroy all she touched.

"First, imagine that your mind is a bubble," he said. The image clearly formed in Eyolin's mind. "Pull it inward like inhaling a breath. Focus that breath intentionally. Feel the moments in time it brushes and follow the draw of magik. It could be a trickle of water, a mountain slope, a piece of thread. Each mind is structured differently. What do you see?"

Eyolin saw a narrow beam of light that pulsed slightly. Her mind was a dark crevasse except for this beam.

"Follow it. Follow it to the end."

She did. The moontear glowed bright as a star in the far recesses of her mind. Eyolin reached toward it.

"Let it in. Let it light up your mind."

Upon contact, Eyolin's dark mental field erupted as bright as the sun. But she didn't pull out. She felt its warmth. Its joy. The moontear mapped out her memories on twisted branches like those of Mainwood. Golden light rippled off her six-year-old self, sprinting down a tree road with Arden at her side, laughing. The memory morphed into her harvesting for the herbalist in the forests surrounding Mainwood. Karok's voice brought her hurling back to the present. She opened her eyes, and he was beaming.

"Morphling magik isn't just physical, it's mental as well, allowing you to see your own memories, to relive them. To morph into your past, so to speak, utilizing the lesser magiks."

He nodded to her chest and Eyolin blushed, looking down and covering up with an arm. Her moontear was as bright on the outside as it was within her mind.

"That wasn't too hard, now was it?" Karok said with a smirk.

They spent hours in Eyolin's mind, following thread after thread until she had mapped out every possible route to and from the moontear that rested in the center of her soul. Not once did Karok ridicule her or make her feel less than for falling short of an expectation. It was a small relief. A tiny miracle that gave her enough confidence to welcome in the threads of magik that sang for the moontear.

The sun had dipped below the mountains when Eyolin gave herself over to the moontear.

Eyolin was reveling in the lightness of her chest, in the simple act of allowing her gem to breathe in time with her breaths and pulse to her heartbeat. Meanwhile, Karok discussed the following day's agenda.

There was already a reading list full of anatomies Karok thought she might be interested in learning to morph into. Histories and migratory patterns, even a few drawing classes, all to ensure that she would be comfortable weaving the shape into her own skin when the time came. Unless she could read faster than a drunk finishes a pint of mead, she calculated that the lessons would take approximately a month, maybe two.

The thought left her oddly sick. Two months among Aideil's elite, playing at power when all she worried about was finding a way to reclaim the little chest of silver and bronze rykes that would buy her freedom, now tucked into her abandoned room in the herbalist's shop.

How long had she dreamed of being accepted as a scariyai? This was an impossibility. A fluke. She should have ran the moment she woke in the infirmary. Instead, she'd let her mouth run and make a deal with the Master of Magik.

She went quiet on the walk to the paddocks. There were no ways to reverse time, to avoid the frae and the Grey or Master Arendt. Her life was not quiet or simple as she wanted. It was full of the constant warmth of magik, as dangerous as it was, an ever present mountain with a chasm of magma. But she thought about how beautiful it was to map her own mind in all of its complexities. Magik was beautiful too, a realization that startled her almost as much as the crash sounding from the paddock.

"Aniöm rider's dragon," Karok explained. "They only listen to the elf they're bonded to. They can be a bit testy when locked up."

Eyolin walked through the open paddock doors, wrinkling her nose at the smell of horse manure—and whatever else was boarded there. A crimson liponark yawned in its corner atop a mound of freshly cut grass. Behind a gate a prickly looking caea stretched spindly wings. Its bronze bridle jingled with the movement.

Finally, they arrived at the long post of saddled horses they would ride back to the city on.

Karok stroked the neck of a chestnut mare reverently.

"She'll take you back to the city."

Eyolin's eyebrows lowered. "You're not coming?"

"I live out here." Karok shrugged. "I'm both human, and an abomination of a morphling. I don't leave the training grounds."

"That's horrible!" Eyolin exclaimed. "What about your family? Friends?"

Karok winced and his eyes darkened. She shouldn't have pried like that.

"Sorry, I'll—" Karok broke off and turned on his heels, vanishing without another word.

The chestnut mare snorted over Eyolin's shoulder.

"Midriel take me," Eyolin cursed. She pulled herself into the saddle with a worrying thought that Karok didn't have any family left. That would explain why he lived in the secluded training grounds over an hour from the city rather than within it. It was quiet out here. Peaceful.

She nudged the mare to the road with a final check that she had the list of reading material tucked in her pocket.

The ride to Mainwood made Eyolin realize how exhausted and starving she was. Alone with her thoughts, on a road through the Greywoods, sleep pulled at her eyelids.

She nodded awake when the mare jolted to a stop, her neck stretched over a post just within the city limits. Around her was an ever-growing stream of elvish soldiers returning from the training grounds. She was surprised to see so many humans among them, clearly part of the same inclusive initiative as Dale, though they fared just the same with bruises staining their body under their gear.

Her ears perked at the discussion of a mess hall—also to include some of the humans. There hadn't been any formal instruction on what she was to do with her time other than train and study, but she reasoned she had earned a meal with the rest of the men.

Eyolin fell into step with the crowd, all weaving through the human district in equally sweaty attire. She stifled multiple giggles as humans gawked at the procession of elves.

A little girl pointed out the humans among them before her mother ushered her inside and closed the door.

The mess hall in the human district must have been a new development considering how shocked every shop keeper and passerby looked.

Eyolin let herself get swept up in the flow of scariyai, scarox, and soldiers. She tried to relax her mind into the same blissful lull she had been in with Karok when they worked on lesser magiks and mind fields.

The attempt only made her more anxious. Reflecting reminded her she had no point of contact within the city who she could confidently be seen with. Legally that is. She had wrongfully assumed that the scariyai she studied under would be her guide. She hadn't the faintest idea where Tequerra's offices or chambers were to barrage him with every question that came to mind. Frankly, his recent displeasure would likely make her presence unwelcome. She vowed not to seek him out until she had amassed enough skill and power to make him truly proud. He wanted her Shoutka to be Aideil's personal weapon against Ïsteldûr. She hadn't the faintest idea what that entailed, but she would prove to him and everyone else that she belonged.

As if on cue, her eyes landed on Dale shuffling beside a bored-looking Gueah. The other elves gave Dale a generous bubble creating enough room for Eyolin to slip through.

Eyolin trailed him for a few paces before making the decision.

A quick tug to his tunic where his bow staff was slung. The wood knocked into her shoulder when Dale flinched. He mumbled an apology but otherwise didn't look up. Eyolin persisted.

Eventually, Dale picked up his head to reprimand whoever kept bothering him. Words died on his lips, his mouth falling open. Eyolin waggled her eyebrows at him and motioned for him to keep walking lest they bring attention to themselves.

Neither of them spoke until they arrived at the mess hall. Eyolin noticed with a small amount of pride that he looked a little less miserable.

The mess hall, however, was wretched enough that they both gagged. It had to have been hastily built, the tent thrown over poles stuffed into freshly dug holes. They were farther into the human districts than Eyolin had ventured before, having stuck to markets where she could trade and stay in the shadows. Here, torches and lanterns lit every crevice.

Eyolin paused at the entrance with Dale, Gueah excusing himself without a glance. Long wooden tables sagged under the weight of the human and elvish soldiers. There was a notable divide between the raised dais where the elves sat and the long tables in the mud. The smell made Eyolin fight to not cover her nose. Dale looked positively giddy.

A flickering orb floated past her head, the one delicate thing in sight in the mass of bodies.

"Land of your people, ears."

She glared at him out of the corner of her eye. Dale pinched his lips to gather to contain whatever laughter twinkled in his gaze. She opened her mouth with a retort but stopped herself when the sinking realization hit her. There were no women in sight. Surely there should have been at least one other—unless this was a mess hall not meant for female elves, which was a ridiculous thought. She was a part of the same army now.

Dale picked up on the hesitation, reading it as something it wasn't.

"You going up or staying down?"

Up on the dais, a servant with a muzzle-like mask over their mouth poured Gueah a glass of amber liquid. A lip curl of disgust was Gueah's only acknowledgement of the human help. Every part of the interaction threatened to steal the hunger from Eyolin's stomach.

How were they able to get away with such casual cruelties while parading humans like Dale around as symbols of change? More and more elves filled the raised dais, each picking silently at their food, avoiding looking down upon the human ranks and their chattering laughter.

Eyolin's gaze slid to the man next to Gueah. She nearly bolted.

It was Maximus, looking the same as the last time she saw him with his white shirt open one button too many.

Kipp promised that he wouldn't remember her, but that was trusting a killer in every sense of the word. However, Maximus didn't glance at her, so she didn't need to test the Grey's handiwork. Coming to a quick decision, Eyolin pulled Dale into the buffet line meant for the humans.

"That your ex?" Dale cocked a brow toward Maximus.

Eyolin's face crinkled in confusion. "Is that code for something?"

"Gods above and below, you do live under a rock."

"Technically, I live in a tree." It had been so long since she'd made a joke that she almost thought someone else had spoken.

"An ex. Like dating."

Eyolin shook her head with a shrug. Dale's eyes went round and Eyolin was ready to catch the plate he had in his hands.

"Like me and Freya are dating," he said like it explained everything. "It'll never happen, but if we broke up, then we'd be exes."

"I genuinely thought you meant the letter."

Dale slopped a scoop of mush onto his plate. "I shall take this moment to declare that you are now my pupil, to learn all there is to know about humans and the intricacies of dating. We can use my and Freya's relationship as the case study."

"And what, pray tell, will I be learning about such behaviors?"

Dale looked far too pleased with her questions. "First and foremost, Freya and I hang out and have sex."

Eyolin felt the blood in her cheeks like it was painted there.

"Please tell me you've had sex, or this is going to get weird very quickly."

Eyolin opted to redirect. "How old do you think I look?"

"With your kind, it's hard to tell." Dale gave Eyolin the once over. "Fifty?"

"I'm nineteen!" Eyolin quickly lowered her voice. "Fifty? In what world are you living in?"

"Damn, not gonna lie, I thought elves took longer to reach maturity, and from the looks of you..." Dale nodded at her chest. Eyolin resisted the urge to tip the contents of her plate onto his head.

The two of them reached the end of the line and navigated to an open space of bench at the far edge of the tent. Upon further inspection of her plate, Eyolin curled her lip in disgust. There wasn't a single identifiable food.

"Don't tell me you're a virgin who's never have meat before. I don't think our budding friendship can survive you being a celibate vegetarian." Dale held up a bird leg and dangled it in front of Eyolin's nose. She swatted it away.

Looking over her shoulder, she whispered, "I could never afford meat in the upper tiers, alright? I haven't had it in years and this mush looks disgusting."

Dale's smirk vanished. Both of their attention turned to the food in front of them and Eyolin couldn't resist the gnawing hunger in her stomach. Both plates were licked clean before they spoke again.

"Did you ever figure out that kata you were learning today?"

Dale eyed Eyolin warily. He had no idea she'd watched him get beaten to a pulp with a stick, but she pushed anyways.

"It was the Gi kata, first of thirteen if I recall correctly."

"Sure, I guess." Dale cringed, no doubt reflecting on the day. "Gueah wouldn't show me what it's supposed to look like."

"Mhm," Eyolin hummed. Raw memories of Arden directing her through the thirteen sequences of swordplay and weaponry flipped by. She braced for the splitting headache these sorts of images produced and almost flinched when nothing happened. Curious. "My sister taught me them a long time ago."

"She here training with you?" It was a simple question, a reasonable assumption. And one that blurred her vision with tears. Some small part of her had hoped that her sister had been waiting in the shadows like an avenging deity, prepared to step in and whisk her away the moment she revealed her magik to Master Arendt. A stupid dream. Arden had left her, abandoned for the rest of their lonely lives. Maybe one day when Eyolin fulfilled her agreement with Tequerra she'd see if Arden existed at all, or if she was only a memory.

A human servant, with the same sickening metal mask, placed a goblet next to her and poured amber liquid into it. Normally, Eyolin avoided alcohol, even the sour mead that humans chugged by the gallon. At that moment she drained it in one go.

Dale quirked a slightly worried smile and did the same, then waved to another servant for a refill.

They repeated this process for a second round, then a third.

Eyolin broke the cycle once the mead had numbed any thoughts of her past. "Hey, do you know where I'm supposed to sleep?"

Dale stared at her over his goblet.

"You didn't get a room? Aren't you Master Arendt's little protégé?"

"I—don't think I am anymore. Anyways do you see any other women here who I would be staying with?"

"Anti-women. Very elvish." Dale took a long drink. "Is there a magikal nursery for your virgin self to sleep in? With little toys and everything?"

"Ha, ha. I could try for an inn, but it's not like I'm getting paid for a single day of failure."

"Midriel burn us all, you aren't going to an inn. You'd be eaten alive."

"There's got to be somewhere they keep their new recruits."

"Where did you live before the infirmary?"

"I can't go back there." Eyolin didn't elaborate. That wound was too fresh, and frankly she was too frightened to show her face there. The herbalist surely believed Eyolin had abandoned her. She also didn't know if she was being trailed and wouldn't risk the exposure.

"Understood," he said.

Eyolin was eternally grateful that Dale didn't push. She didn't like the look that lit up his eyes though. It was as conspiratorial as it could get.

"You can't morph into a guy like one of those Gifted freaks, can you?"

The mead caught in Eyolin's throat and Dale let out a whoop.

"I knew I heard the old master correctly! What kind of magik you got?"

"I'll let you know when I have it figured out," Eyolin said.

"Any way for you to get into highly secured areas?"

Eyolin gave him a look. "I tell you I need a place to stay and the first thing you think of is snooping through confidential information?" She couldn't blame him. It was just the thing she would have done a few days prior had she been in this same situation. Eyolin imagined all the coin she could pocket off of a well-placed ear to a wall in the Great Hall. The dwarvish spinner would have a field day. She could still write a missive with the information gleaned from the war room, but if leaked, it would lead a trail to her doorstep. And she didn't even have a door.

Dale nodded towards Gueah. "We can start by getting dirt on him. Something juicy enough to get him put in a cell beneath the city."

"Can we start by snooping my way into a good night's sleep?"

Eyolin watched Dale stand, albeit a tad wobbly, and offer her a hand.

"As a trial run to our nefarious plot against Gueah, I have a proposition for that very situation."

Seeing little reason to not trust the human, Eyolin took his hand. She never was one to open up to others. She'd always had reason to hide. But her magik was out in the open now and she was surrounded by wolves. She'd need to have an ally in her corner if she was to survive even a night.

The two of them fell into step behind a few stumbling soldiers leaving the mess hall.

"Your mission," Dale explained, "is to successfully pass as my girlfriend, Freya. Meaning the moment we step into the barracks—you're a human."

Freya, apparently, was sweet, avoided eye contact, and worked as a scribe in Ûnsigra. An easy role to play for someone who had made a living as an invisible barmaid and illegal herbalist's apprentice.

They maneuvered through the human district to the barracks. A line of long wooden structures extended as far as the eye could see. Human soldiers filed through an open door with the elvish symbol, *atorin*, above it. The armory.

Dale's arm slid around Eyolin's shoulder like they did this every evening. His finger twisted around a lock of hair. He must have felt her squirm away from the act because his arm tightened, pulling her close. Every nerve screamed at Eyolin to attack but she swallowed down the urge. She was safe. Dale was safe.

"Remember," he hissed in her ear. "You're supposed to be my girl-friend. Relax. I'm hiding your ears."

Eyolin did her best to relax.

"Good girl," he chided.

Red magik bristled at the edge of Eyolin's vision at the words and she saw every way she could tear the human next to her to shreds. Shock at her own dark urge chilled the bloodlust and she leaned into Dale's embrace like they were old friends.

"That's it," he encouraged. "Almost there."

They passed a good deal of drunk human soldiers. None of them gave them a second glance.

Dale slid a key out of his pocket and unlocked a nondescript door of solid wood. The room beyond was chilly with just a cot and small dresser. The window on the opposite end of the room had metal bars on it. Eyolin could picture the long line of barracks with identical rooms void of possessions and warmth. The human soldiers were so expendable that they didn't even warrant a name plaque outside the door or a spare uniform.

"Home sweet home," Dale grumbled. He quickly removed his arm from her shoulders the moment the door closed behind her and kicked off his boots. "Take the bed, we're up at first light."

Dale didn't allow time for Eyolin to protest. He was curled up on a blanket he tossed on the floor and asleep within seconds.

It struck her how alone both of them were. An elf without a family or bed to call her own and a human who dared ally himself with the one elf seated at the human table, both oddities apart and stranger as a pair.

Eyolin tiptoed around Dale and sat on the edge of the cot, wincing as it squeaked. Exhaustion, alcohol, and food pulled her down into a restless sleep still fully clothed.

That night she dreamt of a world bathed in red. And a man chained to a mountain that spewed fire. Then the Grey, Kipp, running along blackened earth. She would have thought his voice was a part of that same unnerving dream. Would have, except it was very much real.

"Well, this is an interesting development, isn't it?"

Chapter Thirteen

K ipp woke in a disoriented panic. The Twilight had held him for longer than usual. He attributed it to the multiple portal jumps between realms he had made over the past few days and the amount of dwarvish spirits he and the boys had consumed the night before.

He had been swimming through the waters of the Twilight state for what felt like days, looking for a way to the surface and begin his assignment. The gates between the Twilight state and his physical body had been locked until Kipp felt like he truly was drowning. *Jet would find my body*, Kipp had thought. He'd have to drive a seraph blade through Kipp's heart and surrender him to the state between life and death. Then his eyes had opened.

From his room in the barracks, the Portal Tower was a good half-day's run through the city. The sounds that reached him through the walls of the barracks suggested it was mid-day, meaning that the streets would be full of Twilight creatures meandering about. Kipp kicked off the sheets wrapped tightly around his body from the sleep.

The thin folder fell to the floor. Kipp cursed at the sound, sending a glance at Jet's body passed out face down on the bed next to his. He swiped it up and broke the seal. Tingling pain danced up his arm as the Binding magik seared itself to his bones. He flicked through the pages as he pulled on a fresh set of Grey attire, ironically black. The muscle-showing-lady-getter, Jet called it. Jet would be the type to sleep with a target first. His gaze lingered on his sleeping roommate. Kipp would miss him, his idiocy, and unassuming personality. *I'll see you soon, Jet*, Kipp promised silently.

Kipp spun to the door and closed it behind him. He maintained enough composure as he walked through the barrack halls to not sprint. His neck hair bristled with fury and agitation. He didn't want to be a babysitter until the Moon of Sanguis. He spun a counter spell against the Binding that held him to exactly the words of the contracted assignment. The counter spell wouldn't raise any alarms, because no one aside from him knew that such a spell existed. Granted, it was meant for unGifted witches, not a Grey. It worked just as well for him.

Young Grey assassins stood in line for gruel and mush in the cafeteria. They all found a different room to be in when Kipp entered. He hadn't slaughtered most of their home villages and pets to wait in line for breakfast.

He walked and ate, gagging down what he could. Kipp had no issues maneuvering through the crowded streets of witches, frae, demons, and wraiths. All breeds of Twilight monsters gave him a wide berth, no doubt remembering last night's rampage through the streets with Jet, Erik, and Po.

The city gates disappeared behind him. He picked up his pace into a sprint. He didn't know precisely where the girl was—Eyolin Kyenz-ushteira as the file named her. But the tug in his gut had intensified during the Twilight sleep. It could be a good sign, or a very, very bad one. He was inclined to assume a bad one.

He was the only one who could kill the girl, and it would be a shame if she ruined it by dying before he got the chance.

Kipp considered the assignment ahead. According to the client, the more trust she had in him, the more successful the murder would be—whatever that cryptic bullshit meant. Kipp simply needed to guarantee that when the time came, his ascent to the Regency was assured, whether Eyolin died by his hands or not.

It was time for him to set his own plan in motion and be the puppeteer of two games. One a pretty doe of an elf, the other putting him into more power than he had ever tasted. Jet would be his Second, without a doubt, and the two of them, along with Erik, would bring the Grey into a new era.

A few creaking buildings with collapsing roofs littered the road to the Portal Towers. Screams from a young child echoed in the gloom. A syx had its teeth deep into the kid's throat. Kipp hardly turned his head. He was more intent on watching his step on the cracked brick road. The Twilight realm was death where Midriel was hell.

Kipp wished he were in Alagana already. There he could run through the shadows, where his Grey magik carried him through darkness, invisible to those he passed. It was much more efficient than tripping over rocks and bones littered in the streets. The Twilight realm fueled and fed the light and dark magik inside him. When mixed through a delicate combination of blood, it created a deadly combination called Grey magik. Beings in Alagana considered it necromancy or witchcraft but it was nothing of the sort. It was natural to a fault, a mutation thanks to the alternate realm that the Grey called home.

The Portal Tower rose magnificently from the center of a dead, grey garden. The crystals and magik of the structure shimmered with their own light. Crafted by the early scribes and the first Grey, the Portal Tower's three tiers rose, thinner and more delicate the higher it went.

The tiers were built to represent the three classes of Grey. The lowest tier, the scouts, like Po, was made of granite and was embedded with muted emeralds. Dark wood and titanium hugged the granite and formed the base of the Portal Tower.

The next tier was the targisha, like Erik, representing the middle class of Grey assassins. This level of the tower had a solid marble teardrop-shaped section that was smooth without any blemishes.

Topping the Portal Tower was a diamond crystal that reflected the unsetting sun of the realm. It was only to be used by the Regent and his Second. That was Kipp. The diamond shimmered proudly. Its splendor dazzled all who beheld it. It was taught to the Grey that the gemstone was pure magik. A conduit between the realm and those Bound to its power. It was that magik that contributed to the organization's creation of half-human, half-elvish assassins and the channel in which they all sourced their power from.

Kipp felt the magik of the tower prickle his skin. It recognized his power and challenged him. His pace slowed. He released the aura of magik he kept within. Instead of taking his magik as payment of passage, Kipp took the Portal's power for his own.

The journey would have had any targisha or scout breathless. Kipp, on the other hand, breathed in the magik of the tower and let it fuel him, satisfy him like no woman could, permeating through every part of his body.

The solid doors of the tower had no handles. Kipp walked right through the metal. A cool blue light glowed from the walls within the first chamber. The scout portal moved like liquid around the room, sometimes attached to the walls, sometimes to the floor, and other times just hovering in the air. Blue haze swirled around Kipp's ankles as he stepped across the threshold.

The Portal Tower was the only place in the realm that had any sort of color and warmth, so Kipp had always selfishly enjoyed visiting. Once, while admiring the structure, he had fallen into one of the lower two-tiered portals and landed on the wrong side of Alagana, two kingdoms from where he had intended. Once. It hadn't happened a second time.

He thought briefly of the only other portal left in the realms. The one that had challenged him and cursed him in so many unspeakable ways.

Kipp wove around the liquid portal to the golden staircase that spiraled up to the higher tiers. The metal came alive the moment his hand touched the railing. The color of the tower shifted from blue to a deep purple and the staircase carried him into the targisha level. Mirrors depicted varying landscapes that shifted based on the viewer's thoughts. Before Kipp was out of the tier, he caught a glimpse of Eyolin with a human wrapped around her, whispering in her ear. Kipp determined he would be the first kill of the assignment—a way to permanently attach the girl to him so that he could begin gaining her trust. Those brief encounters he had planned between them would have to satisfy the Binding magik of the contract while he worked on other matters, starting with that book he had lost track of all those decades ago.

The staircase rose higher. A golden light beamed above Kipp's head, indicating the Regent and Shadow's portal in the top tier. The light intensified as he got closer, eventually engulfing him. Kipp closed his eyes and quieted his mind.

The diamond-shaped crystal radiated a single golden pulse that spread over the city. Kipp sucked in a breath as the portal enveloped him in magik. The portal responded to the image he had implanted in his mind.

Chapter Fourteen

"What has he done to you, little elf?"

Eyolin blinked awake in the darkness. Grogginess fogged her vision as much as the lack of light, and her head pounded much more physically than any of her previous migraines.

For a moment, she couldn't place where she was or identify the figure that bristled in the entryway of Dale's room. The figure rippled darkness where the shadows breathed in his presence. She tried to convince herself that it was a trick of the light, that she was half-awake and seeing Dale getting ready for the day.

But the voice was unmistakable.

Suddenly, every fiber of her being was alert. She swiped Dale's bow-staff from the side of the bed, nearly tripping over Dale's sleeping body in the process.

"What did you do to him?" Eyolin was seething. The Grey had the audacity to break into the barracks and pick on a human, as if life for Dale wasn't hard enough already. And he was just standing there. Worse was the pull that his presence caused, urging her to take a step forward. She fought that allure with all she had.

"Protective little tiger." The Grey leaned forward, the shadows bending with him. "What would your master think about his prized pony sleeping with the pigs?"

Eyolin hated that Kipp's voice was smooth as butter, almost a purr.

"Get. Out." Magik swelled in response and this time Eyolin didn't care how it snaked over her skin, filling her with fire.

"Easy," Kipp growled. It was a command. His body language was dominant and dangerous—every bit of it the cruel assassin Eyolin had envisioned. She cursed herself for allowing even the thought of his body to enter her mind.

But Kipp's command held. Eyolin's magik bowed to his will. She hadn't felt this magnitude of power pouring off him during their previous encounters. This was lethal.

"Give me one good reason why I shouldn't snap his neck."

Eyolin moved between the Grey and Dale. "You are dishonorable, undesirable, and dishonest. The antithesis of this human here. He the only good left in this world. And I want you to leave."

She threw as much venom into her words as she could.

The Grey just smiled.

Kipp drew in the darkness and stepped forward in full physical form. She hadn't realized he had been *made* of shadows, not just cloaked in them. His hazel grey eyes were dark, lacking that spark of interest they had possessed when he found her in the hallway of the Great Hall mere days before.

A wave of cold emotion hit her. She was dangerously close to losing control. Eyolin swallowed the magik that flared in response to the threat standing in the doorway.

It was imperative that Dale remained unharmed. No one should see two magik wielding elves inside the human barracks. The act alone, if she was caught, would not bode well for the new integration initiative that the High Council approved only yesterday.

"What does he want with you?"

Another step forward meant another step back for Eyolin.

"What do *you* want with *me*?" Eyolin countered. She didn't break eye contact. A challenge. She saw the irritation flash through his features. "Is this supposed to make it three times you've saved my life? Because now I think you're just running up your numbers."

"If I wanted you to keep count, it wouldn't be for this." His face was cold and hard.

"Then do tell me." Eyolin looked him over. "What could I possibly want with someone who's declared themselves an enemy of my kingdom?"

Kipp sneered. "You think me your enemy? Little tiger, if I wanted you dead, you would be."

She was trapped. Getting around the Grey would be futile. Whatever weapon he conjured would cut through the wooden staff like straw, leaving her and Dale defenseless. And why hadn't Dale woken up yet? Eyolin was of a mind to kick him awake when Kipp sidestepped and prowled closer.

"You want someone to blame for all this?" Kipp said, looking through lowered brows. "Someone to fear? Because it will never be me. No, little tiger, you should be wary of your masters."

"I am not a slave."

"I beg to differ. You're being led around on a leash. Taught party tricks by someone who doesn't care to know how deep that magik of yours flows." Kipp's eyes grazed down her and settled on the moontear that had fallen over the top of her tunic. Eyolin's breaths were sharp, her nostrils flaring.

"I know everything there is to know about you," he continued. "The nature of your magik. Where it came from. And where you can get the answers you're so desperate for. Aren't you the least bit curious why you're being tucked away from the High Council? Do they even know what you are?"

His words struck a chord so deep Eyolin thought he had reached into her heart and twisted. She refused to show him that she was rattled.

"Get out of this room," she said. "Go back to whatever cursed realm will take you. You have defiled your body and soul countless times over and I will have no part of your game."

His words had pounded into her like physical blows. They reflected her own thoughts and fears. She didn't know who she was or the kind of magik she was capable of. If she were a different person, one who wasn't so fearful of her own shadow, she would be tempted by his knowledge. But the man before her emanated death. An assassin. A murderer. A killer. She wanted no part of it.

He saw it all on her face. It was as if he were inside her mind, picking through her doubts and insecurities. A part of her whispered how to do it—to breath her mental field around her body like a wave of water. The tug in her gut that she now associated with his presence burned hotter. She pushed the field farther. It was almost to him. One more push and she would wash over his mind and body with her mental field. She didn't know what it would do, but it was the one aspect of magik she could manipulate.

Eyolin took a breath to shove her mental field into him enough to knock him out the door.

In the same breath, Kipp closed the distance between them, grabbed the back of her neck, yanked her head back exposing her throat, and backed her into the dresser against the wall. His breath was heavy. He towered over her; his other arm braced on the wall next to her head.

"You stupid, stupid little elvish girl," he snarled. "You'll learn it's bad taste to leech magik off of a Grey." His eyes were feral.

"That's what I—what are you talking about?" Eyolin sputtered, confused. Leeched magik off him? No, she had just pushed her mental field toward him. The intensity in her stomach was on fire. Her magik seethed and coiled around her veins, cutting off circulation. It needed release.

"You don't know how to use magik." His voice was low and threatening. He shoved her away and her head cracked against the wall. Eyolin winced and bit down a cry. Holding her head, she looked up. The Grey was gone.

"What in the witch-cursed salt ring is wrong with you, Eyolin? I was asleep!" Dale groaned from his fetal position on the floor. Eyolin gaped at how he hadn't stirred for the entire confrontation. The Grey must have enchanted him the same way he had Maximus. How long had Kipp been standing in the room before she woke up to his voice? Her hands shook.

"Sorry, I thought you said first light." Eyolin rubbed her palms up and down her legs repeatedly, trying to rid the feeling of his hand crushing the back of her neck.

"Yeah, to wake up, not induce nightmares of not having toes. "

Dale forgave her quickly, especially once Eyolin distracted him with the prospect of breakfast.

They ate quickly—the dry biscuits and molasses sticking in their throats. Dale offered to welcome Eyolin back that night, so long as she quit it with the jolting morning starts. But Eyolin couldn't trust that the Grey would leave her alone in the human barracks. Kipp was in every shadow they passed by.

At the first sign of scariyai near the city gates, Dale split off with his head down. She wanted to tell him that kind of behavior wasn't necessary, but she'd already meddled with his life enough.

A falcon landed on a post next to her with a parcel wrapped in its talons. Eyolin tried to avoid it, but the bird snapped at her with its beak.

After yelping, Eyolin gave the bird a closer look. It was the same falcon she'd seen Karok whispering to. The recognition in her face made the bird tip its head to the sky and sigh. It was such an unnatural gesture that Eyolin couldn't tell if that was Karok or not.

It wasn't Karok. But the parcel of books was from him, accompanied by a note to find a spot to study and to meet him in four hours.

Any excitement died when she unwrapped the books. This would be a long read.

Eyolin sacrificed a good half hour taking one of her favorite paths to the third tier of Mainwood. Her legs were sore from the horseback ride from the training grounds and the burn now was noticeable. But the view was worth it. She'd been on the ground for far longer than she was used to.

She edged around a tree with a small indent—just large enough for her to curl up in. It was where Arden always used to run off to when she was in a mood. Now it served as Eyolin's private spot whenever she needed some peace and quiet. She needed the respite after the threat from the Grey.

The morning was spent pouring over tomes, the diagrams leaping off the page. It wasn't particularly interesting, but it was something to do. And she didn't mind senseless memorization.

Her back ached after the first hour. A title on caea, wyvern, and dragons lay open in her lap. She scanned the neatly written text around a drawing of a beige sand-caea. The caea's life cycle from egg to adulthood was illustrated in great detail, including bone structure.

Eyolin shivered. If she was going to channel morphing magik, she'd have to change her bones. Not permanently.

As her mind wandered, her right pointer finger ran over the grooves in the wood at her side. She flipped to a new page. *Ugh*, she thought with a jolt. Wyrms. Big ones.

She hastily navigated to a chapter on hatchling dragons hopping around on four legs and flapping feathered wings.

A prick of pain in the pad of her finger brought Eyolin's eyes down. It looked like someone had taken a poker from the fire and dragged it along the wood. The pattern wasn't anything she'd seen in her books, but it was unmistakably a caea. A caea without wings and yet... flying.

Black soot sat caked under her fingernail, bringing with it the scent of fresh tinder lit aflame.

Eyolin swiftly dusted off the residue and scoured every page of every book Karok had given her to figure out precisely what it was she had unknowingly scarred into the tree. Nothing.

She eyed the caea coiling into crude clouds etched over its head. It had wide fanned ears and what looked like teardrop scales. The longer she looked, the more lifelike it became. Like it was changing before her eyes. Enhancing the image until every detail was visible.

Then neatly scrawled letters burned into the wood. One by one. Eyolin held her breath. She didn't see a glimmer or ripple of magik. It was as if the wood itself was writing. It finished writing and Eyolin let the description settle on her tongue: *Aguarot-caea: water dragon, protector of the Falls.*

That was why it looked so familiar. The aguarot-caea was the creature that kept the Falls of Velesah safe. At least that was how the legend told it. A once mighty species, now reduced to one ancient story. It was her mother's favorite tale.

Wanting the memories to stop, Eyolin swiped her thumb over the illustration. The wood yielded to her touch, molding to what she wished. She smoothed over the scarred lines leaving it anew.

After that, four hours passed quickly and Eyolin ended up having to run down to the gate to catch the last horse available.

Eyolin paused at the gates, allowing herself to really look at them. Yesterday, during her return, she had been too tired to keep her head up.

Mainwood's gates stood on individual spires wrapped in vines. Wards shimmered like undisturbed water around the perimeter of the city. Energy rippled from them and if she squinted, she could see the arching wall of magik.

Karok met her at the paddocks of the training grounds an hour later. Immediately something felt off. His brows were furrowed, and his eyes were vacant, lost in some other time. He dipped his head in greeting but otherwise stayed silent—a stark contrast to the bubbly man who morphed into a white rabbit and punched at the air in jest.

Their walk wasn't hostile, simply pensive and quiet. Eyolin half expected another creature to leap out and shatter the silence. Luckily, no tyrono snakes were seen.

They passed by scariyai and scarox working through forms and kata, though their sparring was more reserved than it had been when Master Arendt was present.

Eventually, they came to their isolated glen, Karok sitting down on the same flat stone.

He turned to look at her at last.

"Yesterday you worked with your own mental field. Today, you work with mine."

All the anatomies Eyolin had memorized abandoned her. He couldn't be serious.

"Your mind? What about the—"

"Use the energies of all living things around you. Feel their shape and adapt your own field to morph into it. Once you understand how a mind is built, you can fortify yours to prevent others from breaking in."

Eyolin obliged. The grass was prickly against her mind as her mental field crossed over it. Eyolin reached Karok's mind. It wasn't like the liquid of the city wards or the spikes of grass. His mind was bristling and alive with its own thick skin and black hair and... teeth.

Eyolin recoiled, her chest heaving. Already she sensed the onslaught of a headache.

"That's okay," Karok reassured her. "I'm aware it isn't pretty."

He nodded for her to try again.

She spent hours working on that delicate push and pull of her mind. The energies of the forest were almost too much to ignore, from the pulses in the trees and the squirming of insects in the ground.

Eventually, Karok was satisfied enough to turn to her readings from that morning—testing whether or not she actually remembered anything, or if she had just skimmed.

She was tasked on selecting an image she recalled at random. There was one that slipped immediately onto her tongue.

"Dragonfly."

Karok's mouth quirked. "Tackling wings on your first day."

Eyolin mumbled something about it being her second day, eliciting a grin from Karok.

"Make sure to fall butt first when you forget to flap."

"What if I can't morph back?" It had been nagging at her for hours—since she had incorrectly thought that the falcon was Karok.

"You will always find your way back to your true self, no matter how long it takes."

Vague and unhelpful.

Karok read as much on her face and burst out laughing.

It took time, but Eyolin managed to hold onto the dragonfly form for a heartbeat before her elvish body broke free. He hadn't been kidding about finding her way back. It took far more concentration to hold an alternate body than she'd thought.

That evening, Eyolin stood at the doors of the Great Hall feeling moderately pleased that she had channeled morphling magik, if only for a few seconds. And her mental field was now an ever-present aura that expanded and moved as she willed it.

Karok had sent a bird to Master Arendt requesting rooms be made up for her. Tequerra had agreed given that she had finally shown some promise in shifting forms. Karok had failed to mention how short that morph was. Nonetheless, she had the promise of a place to stay. A room of her own.

Dale had also met up with her as they agreed for dinner. After scarfing down as much as they could handle, they went to the community training grounds within the city limits to go over three of the thirteen katas. Eyolin knew eight, however miserable she was at demonstrating them, but Dale was a fast study. She pleasantly imagined striking a certain Grey over the head. His sandy hair made for an excellent imaginary target.

Eyolin took a deep breath and dipped inside the main foyer of the Great Hall and marveled at the emptiness of it. During the day, it was full of life with parchlim, scholars, and servants bustling about. In the evening, there wasn't a soul. Eyolin craned her head to see if someone would appear, if only to point her in the right direction.

No one.

The wall on the far side of the grand foyer rippled. Eyolin recognized the illusion. These were the same energies that surrounded Mainwood, protecting the city from wandering and unwelcome persons. Eyolin went to the wall and extended an arm toward it. Her hand passed into a hidden chamber.

She recalled Dale disappearing into a passageway in the infirmary and reasoned it could be a way to keep the servants out of sight. Still, she'd have to bring it up with Dale the next night when they met for the next set of katas.

Eyolin had her arm through the illusion when the infirmary doors opened. Traik stepped into view flanked by a beautiful elvish woman with flowing blonde hair and a tightly laced blue bodice. The air around her shimmered like pollen through a ray of sunlight.

Eyolin could just catch what Traik was saying.

"I have told you countless times," the commander said gruffly, "your continued presence here will only cause chaos and up-heaval."

The elf's sea-blue skirts flowed around her ankles like water as she said, "Commander, am I to assume that the disappearance of my kin, my own sister, is of no importance to Aideil? Is the High Council aware of the incompetencies of its leading officers? Do they have no faith in the old magiks?"

Traik's red nose betrayed his offense. But he clasped his arms and beckoned they move on towards a far hallway.

"I have advocated for your presence here to go undisturbed. If you are unhappy with the lack of results, perhaps you should bring it up to your ambassador. Or is his blood unsavory to you?"

The elf's shoulders shuddered and she crossed her arms. "She is my little sister. I will not stop until she is found. Not when our bodies are desired for experimentation."

"Then perhaps you should walk with a skin akin to your own blood. It ought to provide you with more respect."

The air rippled for only a moment, which was all the time it took for Eyolin to see a flash of the blue skinned creature that stood in place of the blonde elf. The ears. The tail. Glimmered back into the body of the elvish woman in a blink.

The woman inspected her nails, long and pointed like claws.

"We have not been seen away from our Isles in nye three centuries. Now many are missing, last seen on your coasts." The woman sighed and dropped her arms, her nails biting into her palms. "I will not be the one to have a circlet stamped into my brow by your people."

The half-giant glanced over his shoulder, making eye contact with Eyolin. His lips pursed and he made quick work of disappearing around a bend.

Eyolin trailed the woman, catching her by the elbow when they were alone in a hall.

"You're the princess everyone's been talking about."

The woman sniffed, her pupils dilating as her eyes went wide. This close up, her alabaster skin was flawless. She did not respond but Eyolin could tell she was waiting with one brow arched.

"Go see the spinner down in the human markets," Eyolin said, her mouth running before she could think twice about it. "Ask him about a girl in chains. He'll know the one."

The woman didn't say a word. Only narrowed her eyes and watched Eyolin retreat back to the grand foyer of the Great Hall.

Alone, Eyolin cursed herself for speaking so recklessly, praying that she had told a friend and not a foe. If she was the same creature as the girl who had been chained in the seer's tent, then the spinner would have to help. Or point her in the right direction. Regardless, Eyolin felt that it was the right thing to do. And, if she was right, this woman, this princess, would provide a useful ally should she ever need one.

A pop and hiccup to Eyolin's side made her start, grabbing for a sword she did not have. The dark blue of the nymph's body was naked except for a bronze circlet atop her bald head. The scars around the metal indicated the pledged servitude to Aideil. Her toes hovered off the ground, floating to compensate for her short stature.

"With me, my lady scariyai." The nymph's voice was so raspy that Eyolin feared the elvish tongue would tear up her throat. Tiny pointed teeth peeked out as she smiled.

With a bob, the nymph skipped through the air, leaving Eyolin scrambling after her. The princess was long gone by the time Eyolin threw one last glance over her shoulder towards the hallway where she had seen her last.

They wove through countless wooden-arched hallways and passed doorways with varying symbols carved on them. The higher they went, the more nymphs scurried around, along with other lower beings the elves had in their service including trolls that mopped sap into holes in the wood, humans carrying linens, followed by rakates and lychtins clutching vials of potions and medicines. Young elvish apprentices hurried by with arms full of books and parchment. Monks and scholars in long dark robes swept by without so much as a glance.

It was the first time Eyolin saw this many lesser creatures in one place. She was used to the dichotomy of elves and humans, always spiting the other, the elves searching for ways to undermine all human existence. She had assumed that the elves in the higher tiers of the city were above forcing servitude by melting metal circlets into the skulls of other intelligent beings. Surely, they were better than that. She had thought wrong. What other assumptions were she not seeing through?

The nymph paused at an arched door carved into the wood, identical to all the rest, except for the design. A sun setting between two jagged mountains was stamped into the wood. The door swung open. The smell of freshly cut pinewood floated over her.

A troll with a box of woodcarving tools flinched at the elf in the doorway. It hastily stored the mallet using its four-fingered hand. As the troll fled the room, Eyolin glimpsed an iron bar on its forehead underneath its greasy locks of black hair.

The room was decorated with a plain desk, dresser, and medium-sized bed. The window looked out on the main square. She dragged a finger along the top of the desk and remarked on the dampness of the wood.

"Freshly carved, lady scariyai. Welcome home. The door will recognize your magik and allow you entrance." The nymph bowed and disappeared down the hall, tiptoeing through the air a foot above the floor.

There was a creak on the other side of the dresser. A creature with pale green skin pulled taut over a delicate frame was finishing filling the drawers with articles of clothing. Eyolin identified it as a syket. Its overlarge violet eyes took up most of its face. It wore a deep green sack dress pulled in at the waist by a golden thread. A woven circlet of silver and gold lay over its braided bun of gold hair. The syket nodded at Eyolin but did not flee as the troll or nymph had. Instead, it bowed and touched a long finger of four joints to the crown of its head where the circlet was melted into now healed flesh. Its violet eyes flicked up through long lashes. When the syket stood straight, it was as tall as Eyolin and somehow managed to make the insulting sack dress elegant and flow like a gown of royalty.

Its dusty green hand rested on the wood of the doorframe. Eyolin flinched as a burst of green magik spread through the room. It was such a casual gesture. Eyolin hadn't even considered the possibility that elemental magik flowed through other beings of Alagana too, in far more powerful ways than the elves let on. Karok was an anomaly, but this was something else entirely. A syket was not considered Gifted, had no gem, and had no High Elvish blood to pull magik from the realm. But maybe High Elvish blood didn't determine that sort of power.

The syket's green magik dissolved into the wood.

"To protect," the syket rasped, the common tongue heavy and accented. "In exchange for salvation, Sarom."

Eyolin's blood chilled. Hearing that title brought a feeling worse than dread. It was full of expectations that she could not comprehend. Suddenly, she wished that the Grey had told her what she was—what she was capable of, if only to ease the knot in her stomach that even so high in the trees, and within the safest place in the city, she felt utterly powerless and afraid.

Part Two

Of Forests and Trees

Chapter Fifteen

A black mist seeped into the room where Eyolin slept. The green shield of the syket whined and strained against it, but it was no match for the power of the fog's wielder. Cracks in the protective magik fissured outward.

The cloud bubbled, engulfing the room until not even the moon could penetrate its wall.

Three figures stepped from folds in space, materializing from the darkness that cloaked them. One was tall and foreboding with red eyes gleaming under a hood. Its head swiveled and assessed the room, a hand hovering over the hilt of a seraph blade. The other was slender with the curves of a woman and hair as red as blood. The last was considerably smaller than the others but was the source of the black haze, the fog emanating from the unnatural cracks in his porcelain skin. The small figure's blackened fingers twitched with strained control.

Red glinting eyes blinked as the tallest figure leaned over the sleeping elvish girl. "Now why would something like this interest someone like you?"

"She'll do what we need," the female said, her voice that of a seductress. She moved farther into the room. "When a god whispers in your ear, you beg for the honor of living."

Those red eyes turned to the figure manipulating the dark mist and narrowed. "You don't look like a god."

"I have spent too long in the pits of hell for such a title. I am everything you can never be—Darkness incarnate."

This seemed to satisfy the man with the red eyes. "And you guarantee I walk away with everything?"

"When we're finished," the man weaving together a sphere of death said. "You will have more power than the five realms."

"No tricks," he said it as a demand, but there was a crack of uncertainty in his eyes.

The female flicked red hair from her face. "The tides of Fate are split into three waves, and we must ensure we ride the winning one. She cannot be allowed to access the magik currently blocked in her mind."

"Unless you fail." The orb cleared into an image of carnage. The man smiled. "I'm sure, by then, death would be a mercy. And we will all suffer for it."

Chapter Sixteen

He was going to kill her.

Magikal energy surged through his body from merely being in close proximity to Eyolin Kyenz-ushteira. It pulsed like it was alive and at war with his own carefully wound Grey magik. The experience felt almost like the ritual that bound the light and dark magik into his half-elvish body in the first place, allowing him to pull as much of the Twilight's essence into himself as he could.

The blink from Mainwood to the outskirts of Aldeyn was not nearly far enough for him to exhaust the building tension his body screamed to release. Once materialized, grey sparks danced over his arms, and he stormed down the empty road in a fury.

His body betrayed him, craving closeness to the source of this unexpected development. She was in every way a magikal battery. A part of him that regretted the role he had opted to play. The aggressor. The antagonist. That was exactly what he was, but she didn't deserve that sort of deceit when he ran a blade through her chest.

He eyed the walled city of Aldeyn ahead. The city lay in the northern region of Aideil where it was all farmland and salty air. The elegant stone and metalwork of Velesian Gold Elves rose above the thick walls in arches, domes and spires. The temperate ocean climate blew salt through the air that stuck inside Kipp's nose.

Kipp circled the city twice, mapping out the points of entry. There were few guards on patrol and the atmosphere outside the walls was ghastly. It would be primarily human farmlands stretching south. He glimpsed elvish country homes to the north that were all but abandoned. The Velesian coastline provided access to an empty maritime harbor.

It was exactly as he planned. Accessible but remote in every sense.

If his calculations were correct, the High Council of Aideil had pulled troops into war camps in Aniöm to bolster the clans' defenses against a ground invasion from Huebeck, thus leaving cities such as Aldeyn ripe for crime.

Even the most careful overseer wouldn't be able to turn him away once they saw how good he was at acquiring and maintaining power. If not, it wouldn't take very long at all to build his own stronghold in the tip of the kingdom.

Yes. Aldeyn would do perfectly.

Kipp veered off towards an inn he had spotted on his first lap around the city. Before he could successfully navigate the politics of taking over Aldeyn from the inside, he needed money and he needed allies—allies that had no choice but to obey. He needed to create more Grey.

Finding new Grey wouldn't be an issue. He had already spotted four street rats that spit at him with such passion that they were practically begging to ascend. One of them, a pickpocket he found fighting a guard for the bread he'd stolen was already under his employ to map out the inner-city streets.

It was in the delicate Binding of the two opposing magiks that he would need help. The Book of Bindings was essential in creating not only a Grey, but more Grey with his level of power. The Regent and he knew the spells, but there was something otherworldly about that book. Something that shifted Fates. And he needed more beings who could pull entire veins of magik from the Twilight realm that answered only to him.

He ducked behind a column of hay as a group of men on horseback clopped by. His assignment regarding Eyolin was under a year from completion. The Blood Moon of Sanguis would grace the skies of Alagana and more than the clouds would bleed red that day. During the eleven months until then, he needed to ensure the upset of the Twilight realm.

The coin purse he kept at his waist was unnaturally light. He almost thought he'd been robbed before he remembered the bet he'd lost to Jet during their exploits in the slums of the Twilight realm.

He conjured a seraph blade, piercing a small hole in the center of his palm. Kipp murmured softly as he started walking again. Words formed in his blood and faded into his skin until no sign remained of his witchcraft.

Dusk had descended by the time Kipp shouldered his way into the inn tucked against the stone walls of the Aldeyn. He was hit at once with a thick wash of grime, sweat, and spilt mead. Men sat curled over tables clutching pints and cards. He'd chosen his den well. These were all men whose business brought them outside the walls at night.

Kipp slid a silver ryke across the bar. The fat dwarvish bartender snatched it up, eyeing the Grey. "Been a long time since one of you have crawled through those doors." The dwarf's hand curled around the coin, no doubt testing it for a fake. "Life getting dull, Grey?"

"Hardly, Tuk," Kipp replied. His grin widened with the recognition that dawned in the barkeep's face. "Miss me?"

Tuk all but snarled at Kipp, his shoulders tense. "Last time I saw you, you were nothing more than a dirt poor pathetic excuse of a human stealing from my customers."

Kipp let some malice gleam in his eyes and took no small amount of pleasure at the way Tuk's throat bobbed in unease.

"I wouldn't have had it any other way," Tuk grumbled.

Realization pushed a dribble of sweat down the dwarf's forehead. Kipp leaned into the bar, lacing his fingers.

"When was the last time you kept your sticky little fingers on your side of the bar?"

Tuk gave Kipp a murderous glare, but only curled a lip over rotten teeth in response. He didn't have the spine to stand up to him. And Kipp needed to start influencing the underbelly of the city—building a reputation and clientele.

The dwarf grunted and slid down the bar. Tuk smacked the silver ryke in front of a customer at the other end of the room. The man lifted his head. A long scar ran down his face into the scruff of a beard.

Kipp grinned. "Who do you want me to kill?"

The man lifted his lips in a ghost of a smile and reached into his pocket, returning with a heavy stack of coins and a lock of hair. "The gods are good to me, if they deliver me a Grey."

"Before long, you won't believe in any other gods than me."

Kipp blinked to the outskirts of Mainwood to check in on his magikal battery a few days later. The sun was just dipping below the canopy of towering trees.

Eyolin's training took place outside the wards of the city, so Kipp made it his duty to patrol the woods for pests who might take interest in her. He didn't make contact for the first few scouting trips—that would've been too much too soon.

But the feisty scariyai had been practicing. She sniffed out his aura within the first week and he had half the mind to bring her a medal. She was horribly undertrained, but at least she wasn't walking around whipping lightning out with every sneeze like she had against the frae.

Kipp couldn't shake the pleasure he felt when her tangled mess of a head whipped in his direction, her eyes squinting into the foreboding woods past the road that connected the city gates to the paddocks of the training grounds.

"What do you want, Grey?" she shouted.

Kipp hesitated, weighing his options. He allowed a shaft of light to hit his shoulder, knowing it would illuminate his frame and make his sandy hair glow.

"Have you decided to give my magik back, Eyolin?"

His grin widened at the startled look from calling her by name. She hadn't given it to him, though he had offered his.

She pulled on the reins of the sleek chestnut mare, halting her trek through the forest. If she'd known how many creatures stalked her out there, drawn to her magik as he was, she likely wouldn't doze off so often. But he saw to it she was safe. At least, when he wasn't distracted in Aldeyn.

"You know this is called stalking," she said. Her nose got so red when she was nervous.

Kipp merely shrugged, content with letting her believe whatever she wanted.

"And I don't have your magik. I have enough problems of my own." That she did.

Kipp felt the gaps in the wards of Mainwood, the same he had slipped through that day with the frae. There were forces within the city that were dismantling the carefully spun protective layers that the old master had planted. If Kipp cared about the welfare of anyone other than his brown haired Sarom, he might have investigated. As it was, Aideil could crumble. Kipp would whisk Eyolin away when that happened, right onto his dagger when the Blood Moon of Sanguis graced the skies.

Chapter Seventeen

For the next week, Dale met Eyolin to go over the other forms she remembered. The result of these evenings was an infuriated Gueah who fully expected to be rid of the human in his care after the first day.

The Great Hall felt emptier with every passing day with only the creatures with their circlets of servitude and parchlim filling the halls. Gone were the scariyai and soldiers that crowded the hall that first day. Eyolin had no idea where they had been deployed. The only signs of life she saw were in the morning when those who lived there left to the training grounds. Even then, it was only perhaps a dozen or so robed scariyai with their heads kept down.

Karok's falcon continued to deliver her books to study to the point where there was an ever-growing stack of tomes under her windowsill. She had half a mind to ask him where he was getting all of them if he never left the training grounds but opted to feign ignorance.

Neither Master Arendt nor Commander Traik showed their faces for that entire week, leaving Eyolin with a pile of questions and more confusion as to her purpose. The princess had not been seen wandering the Great Hall to tell Eyolin whether the spinner had helped her recover her sister. And Eyolin had made minimal progress holding a morphed state before she was snapped back into her elvish form with a splintering headache. A recent development was a few blistering burns marks along her wrists after attempting a feline cat form. She reasoned that it was this continued failure that kept the master from her. She pushed harder, hoping to regain his attention, though he never appeared.

Worse was the lingering assassin who always sat perched in the low branches of the trees along the road to and from the training grounds. He never got too close, the two exchanging words here and there. Logically, she should be wary of him, and in part she was. She even made a show of gripping a dagger in the same hand that held the reins of the mare.

But her moontear warmed in his presence—like the way a fire feels on a cold night or wrapping up tight in a thick blanket against the chill of the morning. The Grey didn't give her reason to be frightened, not the way Traik or Maximus did. Every action the Grey had taken was to help her, and she cursed herself for trusting that his reasons for staying near were not to harm her.

It was like her magik wanted the Grey around. Like he held some precious key, and she was a long forgotten chest with an impenetrable lock on it. That revelation infuriated her even more.

He never revealed what he wanted, and Eyolin in turn bit down every question she wasn't ready for the answer to. Kipp was a Grey. A murderer. They had nothing in common.

But they did. And Eyolin threw up wall after wall to distance herself from that fact.

It was after that first encounter with the Grey that her memories had flared up into full-on damned visions. The mere possibility of seeing Kipp again on her ride to the training grounds sent her into such a state that she tore open the barrier in her mind she had so safely guarded for all those years.

She had held control for days—longer than she had ever gone without the cold sweat of her past creeping from her subconscious.

These scenes were closer—too close to the moment she buried in that dark kernel of shame housed where no one was allowed to see.

A tattered-cloaked figure standing in the doorway of her home with knobby, skeletal hands clutching a polished skull-topped cane.

Eyolin curled over herself in the saddle, willing with all her heart that she would not experience that day again.

This time the memory stabbed some deep part of her beating heart, lodging itself in her core, wound around the same chord where Kipp's presence nestled restlessly.

She should have gone to her mother.

Eyolin's mother stood her ground against the creature that leaked a billowing darkness from within its cloak, leeching the light from the room. Eyolin's entire person shook from her spot in the shadows of the stairs, watching as the morning sun dimmed. The creature took a step forward.

Candles around the kitchen thinned and flickered out.

She should have saved her mother.

The woman, standing stoic in the doorway between her child and the creature, could do nothing as the creature's hand flew up in a sweeping motion, the air rippling like a mirage.

Eyolin's mother whipped into the air, feet hovering off the ground.

Telekinetic power pulsed with Dark energy, sourced from the hell realm of Midriel, clutching Eyolin's mother by the throat until her face turned the wrong shade of red.

What use is all that power if she couldn't use it to save the one person in all the five realms that loved her despite all the pain she caused? Eyolin's mother was the last person left who loved her unconditionally. And she let her die.

Her magik let her own mother die.

The creature raised the skull-topped cane. Black haze flowed out into the room in serpentine ribbons nipping at Eyolin and drinking in her fear like wine.

"The shadows answer to me, and the Mother calls you. The king needs you back." The words hissed through the air.

Eyolin's eyes were glued to her mother, who squirmed and thrashed against the crushing grip of the telekinesis. Her mother opened her mouth to scream—maybe to tell Eyolin to run. But the scream never came.

The creature closed its fist in the air and dropped her mother to the floor in a heap.

It should have been Eyolin who'd died.

Eyolin wrestled her memories into submission and suppressed the last moment of that day, desperate to open her eyes to the reality she had built for herself—a life of quiet disillusionment, tucked safely in an herbalist's illegal establishment, and running stories to and from the ground districts.

She threw herself into training, using all her pent-up resentment to fuel late nights in her room memorizing the placement of bones and muscle until even her dreams lost their horrific undertones in lieu of book pages with moving pictures.

It was a small relief. For years she had been plagued with haunting memories of her family and past, always running from the truth that she refused to acknowledge. At least between Karok, Dale, and the Grey... Eyolin didn't have time nor energy to dwell on her ghosts. Exhaustion brought her close to peace.

Karok masked his frustration with Eyolin's slow progress as irritation that his liponarks weren't growing as quickly as they should. He wouldn't blame Eyolin and refused to snap at her despite the obvious quivering of his right hand each time she failed. They tried other exercises too, working on manipulating the energy fields of the living things around them. Those were slightly more productive, if only because Eyolin was already so adept at identifying plant life.

At the end of that first week, she tied up her chestnut mare at the edge of the training grounds around midday. She noticed immediately how every fiber of Karok's body vibrated. Unrelenting anger rippled off him—so uncharacteristic of the trainer who always looked on the verge of cracking a joke. Even Eyolin's mare let out a whinny.

The crinkled paper in his fist suggested that he had gotten new instructions for Eyolin's training. Eyolin had half a notion to seek out the master herself and demand he give her an end game. Something—anything to work towards other than some elusive Shoutka that was supposed to represent her spirit in animal form. How was morphling magik supposed to turn the tides of the war that had likely already started? How many elves and humans had to die before she was useful?

At their training glen, Karok paced. His breathing was ragged, chest heaving in such a way that Eyolin's own fear spiked involuntarily. She had spent enough time in his presence that she trusted him completely. This change... it was something animalistic. Like one of his forms was pressing against his human skin from the inside.

She remembered how his mind had felt on that second day of training. Bristling and alive. He was a morphling, despite his human blood. She knew that. Surely he had control over the werekey venom that had infected him four years ago.

Eyolin hadn't been assigned any readings on werekey and she was secretly thankful. A part of her deeply feared that her perception of her instructor would be forever altered should she discover exactly what sort of monster lurked on the edge of his mental field, biding its time until Karok slipped up. If the energy it took for Eyolin to hold an alternate form was any indication of the strength needed to keep one's natural form at bay...

"Sit down, love," Karok managed eventually.

Eyolin sat. She trusted him, despite the lingering fear that whatever that note said would change their dynamic significantly.

She squirmed, suddenly uncomfortable with how the rock felt beneath her. Eyolin watched Karok wrestle with his words before he spoke.

"You are not progressing as quickly as the High Council needs," he said at last. "There is... Master Arendt has decided that you need a push."

Eyolin scoffed. The last time he 'pushed' her was when he left her for dead with a three headed serpent crushing the lift out of her.

"I know, love." Of course, Karok knew. He had been her only supporter aside from Dale. "But there is something about your Shoutka that the master needs. I've poured over every ounce of knowledge I've gained to try and figure out why, and it's something about that gemstone of yours that is supposed to tip the scales of this war in our favor. And if accessing your Shoutka is the key to tapping into that power..." He trailed off.

"We've tried, Karok. What if I don't have one?" It was entirely possible. A Shoutka was supposed to be the innate spiritual reflection of a morphling's soul, an extension of herself and a shield against dark magik. But Eyolin had outlined every inch of her mind and there was no secret beast lingering other than her own demons.

"That is why you must meet mine."

Her instructor's tone was dark.

"You've felt it before. Now you must alter your own mind to pass through it."

Eyolin obliged warily. It was what the master deemed appropriate to push her in the right direction. She had to trust that all this work was for her kingdom. To protect against the might of Ïsteldûr.

Karok wouldn't hurt her.

She brushed against the same writhing wall of black hair and gleaming teeth. She hesitated.

Remember, Karok spoke to her mind. *The werekey is a creature that responds to its own. In order to pass through the barrier of my mind you must morph into the same beast. You have not studied them out of my own stupidity and shame, and for that I am sorry. Use the knowledge I have given you. A werekey is not so different from a wolf. Only darker, more fueled by a blood rage. But be careful. For you to enter, I must distract the venom. If you slip for even a moment, the werekey will take over, and I will watch myself tear you apart.*

What?! Eyolin screamed telepathically. She bit her tongue hard enough to draw blood. Already she sensed the wall of teeth snap its attention to her exposed body seated across from Karok.

This is an exercise, just like any other.

Eyolin doubted that was true.

Pass through. Survive the werekey hunting you through my mind. And let your Shoutka rise to your defense. It will be enough to save you.

There was something he wasn't saying. His tone was sorrowful. Full of pain.

You'll be alright? Eyolin asked. She peeked an eye open to see Karok's lopsided smile that was almost convincing.

Of course, Eyolin.

It was the first time he'd said her name.

She launched herself at the werekey before she could talk herself out of it, shaping the edge of her mental field into hair and bones and beady eyes. She had no room for error. One shot. Her moontear warmed in response.

It was everything evil and monstrous. But there was that thread of Karok—his laughter and joy that reminded her he was in there. Somewhere.

Then the werekey's barrier fell away into a memory.

Eyolin stood next to a wood and grass-thatched building on the open plains of Aniöm. She had never seen such endless grass. A caravan of humans piled sacks of clothes and baskets of food onto wagons in the muddy street.

She nearly lost her concentration on maintaining the werekey form when Karok's voice began to narrate the scene, his tone as casual as if they were sitting around a bonfire.

Three Aniöm dragons with their elvish riders alerted our village of a werekey sighting not far from where I lived. It was a poor settlement, barely two generations old.

It wasn't even twenty minutes after the warning when the pack filled the streets with blood.

Two grass dragons were shredded by the alpha, taking their riders with them. The third rider and his dragon made it off the ground with two of our village's youngest children in his arms, another child thrashing in the dragon's claws. They were all orphans by the time they arrived at the castle stronghold to call in reinforcements.

I watched everything happen from a cracked window in our hutch.

My mother barred the door with my dead father's body from the outside, hoping that the corpse would distract the werekeys enough to not seek me out. They were far too thorough. The alpha sniffed me out, hungry for the faint whisper of elvish blood in my mother and I. The High Elvish blood, however diluted, drove the werekey mad like they were designed to slaughter elves.

It tore through my mother first, the bloodlust overwhelming.

I hung from the alpha's jaws when Odelle's reinforcements dropped from the clutches of the grass dragons. Tequerra Arendt was among them, on some diplomatic mission. He bound the alpha to the earth, burying it along with me.

I must've let out a cry. I was so close to death by then. The werekey gave me one last parting bite, its venom dripping into my open wounds to ensure the survival of his pack.

I should have died. I would have if Tequerra hadn't collected me, fearing I would become a mindless monster. I did. And I didn't.

If I was purely human, I would have morphed permanently into a werekey. Instead, that sliver of elvish blood, the one that contained the essence of the High Elves, fought back. It gave me enough autonomy to shift into a Changeling, like a Gifted elvish morphling. There aren't any others like me.

Now, for the rest of my human existence, I fight against the werekey venom that gives me the power to shift forms. It could take over at any moment, at the slightest distraction. Why else would I be kept among the monsters of this forest?

Tequerra took me here to save me, to study me. He wanted to know how a human could shift skins like a true morphling. Four years in isolation is nothing compared to the people I would kill if the werekey was given the chance. At least here, in the training grounds, there are wards against me.

Eyolin choked down a sob as she experienced the brunt force of Karok's memories. The pain of morphing into a werekey as his humanity was stripped away into red fury and rage. More memories flashed by—each more horrific than the last. Screams. Blood. Fear. Karok's internal monologue quieted, and Eyolin retreated her mental field. She connected with a solid, dark wall. Her focus slipped, and she collided again with Karok's mind. Every hair on the werekey's hide on his mind rose.

Elvish blood, it called. *You don't belong in here.* It was like nails were being dragged down her spine. Eyolin pounded frantically against Karok's mind.

Let me out! Karok, let me out!

The darkness peeled away. She was seeing through Karok's eyes. Looking at her. His fingertips went cold as ice and Karok's thoughts became her own.

No. She had to get out. It wanted her. It smelled her elvish blood. Master Arendt was wrong, this wasn't the way. He should have protected her. Kept her safe from the monster. He's going to kill her. He's going to kill her.

Eyolin felt Karok tense up in a last attempt to stall the venom.

The werekey venom seeped into the recesses of his mind, the edges of his vision going red. In moments, he would no longer have anything human left of his mind and body. Canines poked through his lips and punctured his cheeks. Blood flowed down his throat. His fingernails itched and squirmed as they elongated into sharp, jagged, black claws. One more breath and he'd lose this battle.

With a single word, Karok threw Eyolin from his mind.

Run.

There was nowhere to run.

Eyolin opened her eyes, and blood red irises were focused intently on her body where it sat.

But she had been in his mind when he had morphed. She had experienced each bone crack and shift and the bristling mangy black fur grow from his skin. She had felt his claws inch out of his nail beds.

Karok was not in front of her anymore.

It was a werekey.

The monster's mouth filled with saliva as it smelled the sweat that dribbled down her neck. Werekeys were attracted to elvish blood—her blood—sent into a frenzy at the mere proximity. Karok had kept control for a week working with her, suppressing every urge to tear her to pieces.

Now, it lunged.

Eyolin's mind twisted and morphed as the werekey collided with her, every reaction an instinct. She felt her skin ripple and scratch and she sank claws into the werekey's underbelly, kicking up off the ground with long black legs. Her canines snapped around the werekey's—Karok's—neck as she had seen the creature do in the memory. Where Karok's werekey's eyes were blood red, Eyolin's were ice blue and crackled with electricity. It was a beast she pulled from the dark corners of her soul, the antithesis of what a Shoutka should be.

They hit the ground, and she pinned him swiftly.

Green tendrils of Tequerra's magik snaked around the werekey's neck and torso. The wards set up to protect the training grounds finally activated. Distantly, Eyolin wondered at their delay—they had let this battle play out before intervening.

The werekey beneath her whimpered. She snarled down at it.

Release him, she commanded.

She felt the werekey's mind submit, and a savage wave of energy passed into her from the werekey's eyes. The redness dulled. Eyolin's form got stronger. She reveled in the new strength of the body she had morphed into. Venom dripped out of her gums and down her canines. She had morphed into an alpha—she *was* the alpha, precisely as she had seen it in Karok's memory.

Karok made a sharp yelp and Eyolin backed off. She curled her mind in on itself and shifted back to her elvish form. This time, her elvish form was hesitant to return, fearing the bloodlust it had felt in the werekey form as a natural threat.

The werekey relinquished its hold on Karok's mind. His human form curled into a ball as the hair and claws retracted back to the confines of his mind.

The magik holding him down sunk back into the earth. Only once the green tendrils of magik vanished completely did Eyolin approach her trainer.

"Karok..." She had no words of apology or accusations, so she opened herself to pour every emotion possible into that one word.

"Great form, kid." He winced, not getting up. "I thought I'd kill you."

Eyolin swallowed. Her reaction was a primal response to an imminent threat. She'd felt that way only once before, when her mother... It brought her more shame now that that corruption had surfaced. At least this was a beastly form. It was so much better than seeing the monster in her own reflection.

"How did you do that?" Karok said at last. "That wasn't a Shoutka."

Eyolin released the breath she hadn't realized she'd been holding. Hearing confirmation that a werekey wasn't the shape of her soul was a small relief.

"You morphed into an alpha."

"Was that the...?" Eyolin didn't know how to describe the transfer of power that occurred between them. Karok acknowledged the truth with a nod.

"I am forever a Changeling, forced to fight against something I'm not. You have morphling magik. That kind of natural magik can never take power it does not already possess. You pulled an alpha werekey from the energy of your Gift, and for that I am thankful. I cannot kill my alpha."

Chapter Eighteen

Eyolin's morphing lessons were slightly more successful in the following days. She had wanted to press Karok about what exactly Master Arendt expected from her but gained nothing. It was like the master had simply dropped a note and vanished along with everyone else living in the Great Hall.

At least Dale had been getting progressively better at fending off Gueah's stick, for all the good those preparations would be when they met with whatever horrors Ïsteldûr unleashed on them all. It was that looming inevitability that pushed them harder each day. Their meals together lacked their usual banter and lightness, traded for defeated silence and worry.

Always Maximus and Gueah sat preening on their dais, picking at prime cuts of meat while the humans below slopped mush and hard bread onto their plates. If either of them took notice of the female elf tucked among the benches of human soldiers, neither made any indication. A small mercy.

Dale met Eyolin at the end of their second week at the paddock. Eyolin was tucking in the next set of books and objectives for her to read, this time to be taken from the Great Hall's library. She had finally advanced from pigeon post to accessing the historic library.

That, or Karok had exhausted his own books and needed to keep her entertained. Either way, there was a swell of pride that puffed her chest that afternoon.

"Hey, princess," Dale sneered. "Nice ride." He nodded to the mare she was brushing.

"Don't," Eyolin warned, anticipating the sexual joke on the tip of his tongue before he said it.

"Ugh, you're so stiff. Fine. Where do you want to go over the forms today? Gueah has me pounding the fifth, and I want to see if it's right before I have the first match in the arena tomorrow. Figured we could meet here and do some nefarious digging on Gueah after. Just for leverage."

"Sure, I think I remember it well enough. Come on." Eyolin stored the brush in the nearby bucket and scooped up a dented sword from the side of the stall.

On her way out of the paddock, she ran right into a large figure and stumbled sideways into a pile of horse dung.

"Earth-born dirt eater!" Eyolin cursed and frantically wiped her shoe on a pile of hay. She'd lived long enough in lower society to have picked up the vulgar phrases not suitable for a lady living in the Great Hall. Hanging out with Dale certainly didn't help either.

"Didn't realize your elvish tongue was as vile as a human's," the figure said. Eyolin could have moaned in relief. Karok.

"Who's the scrawny one?" Her trainer nodded at Dale hiding behind the mare in the stall. Dale ducked around the horse's tail with a scoff.

"I'm not scrawny you fat—" Dale started, until Karok's eyes flashed and a growl rumbled in his chest. Eyolin felt the werekey venom swirl in his veins and this time it filled Eyolin with amusement.

"Try not to upset him, Dale," Eyolin said. "He might bite your head off. Relax, Karok." She let a bit of the alpha's tone into her voice to soothe the werekey that threatened to consume her trainer. She and Karok had been practicing that too for the next time he needed to be quelled.

Karok's face softened into an amused grin. "You're awfully protective. Who is he?"

"I'm right here, thanks. You can stop talking about me in third person." Dale waved in Karok's face.

"Dale, this is Karok, my trainer. Karok, meet Dale. I'm helping him with some weapons training."

Eyolin paused to see how the two would react. Both were as close to a friend as she'd ever had, but she saw the risk in introducing them.

Dale's mouth dropped. "Why can't I get a human trainer? I'm stuck with the pointy eared devil."

Karok's shoulders started shaking before the laugh bubbled out of him. "You're teaching him combat training?"

Eyolin crossed her arms defensively. The smell of horse shit on her boots wafted over her. "I know enough to be helpful."

"Who's training you, boy?" Karok asked Dale.

"It's Dale—not boy. And Gueah."

Karok's face pinched in feigned pain. "Oof, you won't last a minute in the arena."

Dale's face reddened but he didn't back down; stubbornness and bluster had gotten him this far.

"An elf will never teach a human the techniques needed to kill another elf," Karok elaborated. "Follow me, I'll show you what I can. Hopefully I can give you a bit of an edge tomorrow, eh?"

It wasn't more than two hours later when Eyolin heaved sore legs over a tall boulder. Her arms felt like they were made of lead. This was miserable. She stepped over Dale's legs as he breathed heavily from his spot on the ground. Karok hadn't taken his role lightly, pummeling them in forms and fighting techniques. If they got something wrong, they had to climb boulders and balance on top of them until they got it right.

Though her muscles screamed, she reveled in the deadly dance Karok led them through.

Karok sat perched on top of a boulder in fox form, yipping commands to them telepathically. Dale couldn't talk back and flinched at every word. The best he could muster was to flip the fox his middle finger.

Both Dale and Eyolin's clothes were soaked with sweat from the extra training.

"I'm biting your arm off tomorrow," Eyolin grumbled to the fox.

Dale lifted a fist in agreement, warranting a high-pitched caterwauling laugh from Karok's fox form.

The fox peered down from the top of the border. *You may have to carry him back, Eyolin. I don't think the guy can walk.*

"I heard that, you mind reading asshole," Dale barked.

I know. I intended you to.

"How can you even morph? You're as human as I am."

An unfortunate chain of events I don't recommend.

Eyolin gave Dale a glance to signal not to push any further. Dale conceded and slowly pushed himself onto his feet.

Dale, make sure she does her reading tonight. She must be able to sprout a tail as pretty as mine tomorrow.

Dale took that as his personal invitation into the upper tiers to walk Eyolin back to the Great Hall. He had every intention of snagging something sweet from the kitchens since they had missed dinner.

They made it all of two steps up the main staircase when Dale stopped Eyolin with a hand on her arm.

"Hey," he said. "You heard anything about humans collecting elf ears?"

"What are you saying?" It was the first Eyolin had heard of it.

"There's this rumor going around that elves seen on the ground have come up missing or show up the next day without their ears."

Eyolin's heart beat faster. The shadows leaned in closer, clinging to every word. She could almost see hands reaching out to her. Her mind worked quickly, piecing together what little she had to go on. The frae breached the wards of the city. Magnogogue had ways to get through to her and take down the armies from the inside. Her gut told her that these rumors were somehow connected to her. And her gut was all she had to go on these days. She decided to do some digging.

"Where precisely?"

Dale quirked a smile. "We did agree to get up to some nefarious doings tonight, didn't we?"

"We'll give it two hours," Eyolin agreed. "See if we notice something."

"At last." Dale looked far too excited for the foreboding feeling nagging at Eyolin's stomach. "Let's put these new moves to use."

Going off the minimal evidence they had, Eyolin decided to search the houses nearest the human barracks on the ground, focusing on the thin stretch between the barracks and the border of the city where the wards extended up into the skies. She was close to the market avenue where the dwarvish spinner lived. And where the frae had been.

The streets were empty at that hour—unnervingly so. Lights were out inside the squat stone buildings and the lamps were flickering and dim. It cast the entire ground in an eerie sheen.

Dale kept his hand on the dented bow staff he'd been working with. Eyolin wished she could extend her Gift to him, if only to protect him from whatever it was they found. Although, so far, they hadn't found much of anything.

They passed through the abandoned alleys and streets, keeping to where the light didn't shine. Eyolin admitted that they were an excellent sleuthing team.

Movement ahead froze their steps—coming from where the wards of the city should have hummed with their earthen energy.

A bulky figure took up the entire street. Soft grunts of exertion echoed to where Dale and Eyolin stood peering around a corner.

The figure dragged a horrific sight. A skinned elf slumped in its grip. Bile rose in Eyolin's throat, and she shoved her sleeve into her mouth to stop the wave of vomit.

Beyond the figure was an entire pile of elves, each without skin, but otherwise intact. The atrocity was overwhelmingly evil, dripping of dark magik, there wasn't any other explanation.

Then the hulking figure turned—like he smelled them.

Eyolin's vision blurred red.

It was Commander Traik.

Without another thought, Eyolin ran.

She pumped her arms, vaguely aware that Dale was right on her tail. Faster and faster she ran, trusting some innate sense of direction, hoping she was going in the direction of the stairs. There wasn't enough space she could put between her and the half-giant. The dark presence surrounding him that day in the infirmary, his presence in the human districts that first afternoon with the frae. The anger that rippled off him in the Middle. He was a traitor. A commander of the Aideillian army—someone everyone trusted—skinning elves. Piling them on the border of the city doing some kind of grotesque ritual.

Eyolin's body threatened to shut down from shock. She didn't acknowledge where her feet were taking her until she slowed to a stop. Dry heaving racked her body. There wasn't enough in her to warrant more.

Her secret nook where a few leftover books lay scattered looked cast in a foreboding light. How many times had this spot offered her warmth and protection? Arden had so often left her treats and little notes jammed into cracks in the wood along with her cyphers. Now the entire forest felt different. It was all wrong. She tried reasoning with what she had seen but came up with the same horrific conclusion. Traik was working for the enemy.

A huffing behind her brought Eyolin's head snapping around. Her heart didn't abate, though Dale's face brought a small relief.

He moved toward her slowly either because of the sheer drop to the ground or out of caution due to the wild look on her face.

The two of them sat in stunned silence, waiting for the crunch of a boot behind them or the cool metal of a blade indicating that the half-giant had found them. They'd no doubt been heard by the commander in their mad flight from the wards.

It was well into the witching hour, and no one had come after them, Dale released a breath, breaking their vow of silence.

"He won't touch you, ears." Eyolin turned to see Dale wince at the poorly chosen nickname. "You're untouchable. Master Arendt wouldn't let anything happen to you. Remember that."

That was so far from the truth. Tequerra didn't seem to care what happened to her, especially since she was nowhere near mastering her Gift. Magik wasn't all it cracked up to be—what with all its formal studying and drills that didn't get her any-where.

A phrase Master Arendt had told her, that first time he had spoken in her mind filtered through the shocked dread.

There will always be monsters. It is when they show their face in the light, we realize that we knew them all along.

He might not have been aware of it at the time, but that mon-ster was Traik, his commander. And there was nothing she could do about it. If she had let that frae kill her... she would have ended up in that pile of skinned elves. So why did he spare her?

It was that familiar yet ever elusive voice that chuckled deep within her soul that told her she was missing something.

"What if I'm not safe?" Eyolin hadn't meant to say it out loud. "This is all my fault. Ïsteldûr is after me. They're inside Mainwood because of me."

"No," Dale said. His voice was hard, showing an inner grit that hadn't been there before. "You are not the monster. He is. We can go to an officer. Tell them what we saw."

"You know we can't say anything." Eyolin had dealt with enough death in these trees. As long as Traik didn't kill someone of importance, no retribution would happen. She had gotten pardoned from crimes just as horrific by simply offering Master Arendt her magik.

"Traik is well regarded here," she explained. "We are nobody, the lowest of the low. If we go up against him, there's no telling what kind of dirt they'll dig up on us."

Dale's eyes narrowed.

"What would they find, ears?"

There were some things Eyolin wasn't ready to face. Dale knew her as someone trustworthy. And she had dared accept him as a friend. She'd never had one. And letting him see that part of her was too painful.

"I'm sure they'd come up with something."

Dale clearly didn't believe her, but he didn't press further either. It was a small relief.

They sat shoulder to shoulder until the evening chill bit into them and frost billowed in their breath. Dale helped Eyolin to her feet, their muscles screaming from the events of the day.

"I don't know if it helps," Dale said. "But remember to do that reading Karok gave you."

It was a dry attempt at humor that only reminded Eyolin that she indeed needed to get the work done. She and Dale had agreed that they wouldn't bring up accusations against Traik as they couldn't be sure that he had identified them. Bringing attention to their friendship and snooping wouldn't be wise.

If they were to survive the next days and gather evidence against Traik, they had to keep their heads down.

Chapter Nineteen

E yolin all but sprinted the rest of the way to the Great Hall. As much as she wanted to curl up under piles of blankets, she was covered in crusted sweat and dirt. That, and she had to complete whatever readings Karok required. She had a newfound determination to unlock her Shoutka to get Master Arendt's attention back. If that meant she wouldn't sleep, so be it. Any lingering doubt that the library was closed at this late hour vanished when she beheld the steady trickle of scholars shuffling through the Great Hall.

Her room was littered with books that she took care not to trip over on her way to the bathing chamber. There were dangers everywhere but that room, and frankly the Great Hall, was as close to a sanctuary as she could get.

There was a layer of silt at the bottom of her bathtub by the time she'd dried off. It was a mercy to cleanse the day off her skin. Already the numbing fear of discovering Traik was fading to a memory, replaced by a new anticipation of gaining access to the library.

She scanned her drawers for appropriate attire, thinking on how scholars and ministers dressed. She couldn't wear her beige acolyte training clothes, especially this late at night, without drawing further attention. And she would rather keep a low profile until she was certain Traik wouldn't come after her.

A green dress made of heith fabric caught her eye. Heith fabric was woven near the Seas of Velesah and she could taste the salt water in its very fibers.

She swiftly slid her feet into light brow flats and shifted the dress over her head. It was soft and silky on her skin; finer than any fabric she had been able to afford working for the herbalist. She tied the brown band at the waist and the dress flowed around her knees as Eyolin shook her damp hair free from the towel.

In the mirror, her face was sharper than it had been a month before. Her arms were more toned and her features harder. Speckles of blue and purple were visible on her shins from the day's training. Her knuckles were red and raw from failed sword deflections.

She turned from the mirror and scrunched her hair up to encourage her natural curls to form. She rarely let her hair down from the braid. As she tossed the towel onto the bed, a tiny ding, not unlike a minuscule bell, rang. Eyolin sprang to the bed, ripped the towel up and flung it to the opposite side of the room.

On top of the sheets was her moontear, wrapped in its delicate metal spiral. It must have slipped over her head when she took off the towel. Its coloring was muted and milky. As soon as her skin touched the smooth surface, it lit up like a flame. A rainbow of colors flooded from it and bounced off the walls.

Energy shot from the gem into Eyolin, restoring her drained reserves. She recognized it as the magik she been storing during her meditations with Karok. When the swirling rainbow of light faded, all the injuries from the day were healed. Eyolin sighed and looped the cord back around her neck and tucked it under the collar of the green dress. The moontear acted as if of its own accord at times, like she didn't truly have control, but rather permission. But if that were the case, who, or what, decided when the magik flowed through her fingertips? Theories blossomed in her mind, theories that absolved her of murder and violence. But what good were those kinds of thoughts if they turned out to be false? The hint of hope vanished. Whatever power connected her to her gem was likely more ingrained in elvish blood than acting of its own volition.

The library's massive wooden doors towered over her. She traced a finger along the frame, mesmerized by the smooth red wood that guarded one of Alagana's largest libraries. The doors inched open, and Eyolin's breath caught.

The room was the most spectacular thing she had ever seen. Tall pillars of books curled around the circular room and spiraled upwards, stopping only at the domed ceiling that depicted the constellations as they were seen above the canopy of Mainwood. Stone trees lined the room with branches that allowed for scholars to climb up to the shelves that couldn't be reached by ladders.

She had been right. The scholars of Mainwood didn't sleep. She watched as scholars in white cream robes stood on platforms that rose of their own volition. Tiny alcoves tucked into the pillars were each filled with elves curled up in reading chairs. This was a space that would take weeks to map out, and a lifetime to catalogue.

Scholars swiped books off their racks and piled them high on either side of their persons. Scribes scratched away on parchments, even now in the dead of night.

A handful of stout creatures with tiny blue wings and hook-like feet zoomed back and forth carrying books this way and that. Eyolin flinched as one of those creatures—the librarians—flew past her.

Their skin had a bluish tint that was cracked and slightly scaled. Little pointy ears stuck out from round heads with large, angular eyes. Four-fingered hands with sharp nails clung to the books they carried. The rusted silver circlets that marred their foreheads indicated that though they may have infinite knowledge, the elves did not consider them equals.

"Creepy little bugs, aren't they?" chimed a sickly-sweet voice. Eyolin spun around and nearly bumped heads with the speaker.

"Oh!" Eyolin gasped in surprise and stumbled back a step. She quickly composed herself, tipping her chin up like she had seen her mother do when councilmen came to visit.

Catlee stood at her back with an elvish soldier with gold hair that fell shaggily over sharp blue eyes. Catlee's arm was wrapped around his waist possessively and Eyolin couldn't help noticing her winged eyeliner and penciled eyebrows from how closely she stood. Her blue two-piece exposed a slender midriff that was far more scandalous that anything women wore in this kingdom.

"Or is the little bug just you?" Catlee said, her eyes narrowing. Eyolin ran through every way in which her intel could have been faulty. Catlee had a look of a predator and Eyolin was her prey. When she inhaled, her breath seemed to be tasting Eyolin's skin. Suddenly, Eyolin wished she had brought a knife.

"Quit intimidating her, Catlee," a new voice called from behind a bookshelf. A human boy in tan scholar robes with a white sash around his neck ducked into view, narrowly avoiding colliding with a librarian. "Leave her be like the rest of us." The scholar's brown bangs fell over his round glasses.

"Oh, it's a *her*?" the soldier at Catlee's side remarked. "I thought she was a decoration to adorn the chair."

Catlee's pupils dilated into feline slits as she found the moontear at Eyolin's throat. The distortion was gone so quickly that Eyolin almost thought she had imagined it. The entire evening had been disconcerting to say the least and Eyolin wasn't sure she wasn't seeing things.

Eyolin took a step back and the soldier at Catlee's side laughed. Catlee didn't take her eyes off Eyolin.

"I think you're intimidating our little she-elf, Cat," the soldier murmured in her like a lover. Catlee shrugged off his arm and withdrew her own from his waist, drawing herself up to her full height.

"Leave us, Kristofor," she said. Her voice was as thick and smooth as honey. Her eyes darted to Eyolin's chest a second time. "I'd like a talk with this she-beast in private." She turned to the scholar who nearly dropped his book. "Aaron, escort Kristofor back to our rooms. I'll bring you your books later."

The scholar and the soldier moved with complete obedience, leaving Catlee alone with Eyolin in the middle of the library.

Eyolin was too tired from sprinting around the ground to be confident in escaping if this Catlee was dangerous. Her best bet was finding a more populated area of the library to have witnesses if she attacked.

"Did you find what you were looking for?" Eyolin squeaked.

"I've been looking for you," Catlee mused, moving to cut off Eyolin's retreat.

Eyolin's blood chilled. "What about your sister?"

Catlee ignored the question.

"I had my doubts before. Now I'm certain." She inhaled deeply, her eyes drifting shut for a moment. "How many cycles has it taken for your Gift to be perfected?"

Eyolin's heart raced. Every inch of her screamed that this Catlee creature was dangerous. The librarians and other scholars paid them no heed. Eyolin didn't trust her own magik to come to her aid, she more feared that it would.

"Did you find your sister?" Eyolin tried again. This time Catlee's body twitched involuntarily.

"What's left of it, you mean?"

"She's..." Eyolin couldn't voice it, not when it was the fear she had for her own sister, Arden.

"Dead," Catlee confirmed. "Mutilated. As I once was. Only my little sister was not old enough to regenerate fast enough. Her wounds were too great."

"I'm so sorry." Eyolin's words came out as a whisper.

Catlee looked at her then, exposed for only a moment, but enough for Eyolin to see an ancient lingering pain akin to her own.

"You truly mean that, don't you Sarom?"

Catlee backed Eyolin into a bookshelf, the spines cutting into her side. "What makes you different from the others? Lara was weak in the mind, her Gift fractured." Catlee leveled herself with Eyolin, eye to eye. Any sorrow was gone, leaving the predator before prey. Catlee grinned, her smile not reaching her eyes.

Warmth blossomed in Eyolin's chest, a spearing pain that spread through her. Her magik didn't surface, but it rose to the threat.

"Oh, you are something." Catlee's nose brushed a strand of Eyolin's hair as she inhaled another breath. "I can feel your Fate rippling off your skin like the sweetness of fear. They have no idea what you truly are. What they have let run free in their halls." Catlee spoke into Eyolin's ear, her breath tickling her earlobe and sending shivers down Eyolin's spine. Run, her instincts told her, but her body was held in place by Catlee's presence. "What you are destined to become."

"Who doesn't?" Eyolin asked.

"Oh," Catlee sighed, the breath caressing Eyolin's neck like a kiss. "Your destiny. You haven't felt him?" Catlee pulled back and smiled. It was cold, not the smile of a friend. "Even I can taste his influence over your past."

Bile leapt into her throat at the words. She had to be talking about Magnogogue. Ïsteldûr had to be inside the walls of the city by now, that much was certain if Traik's actions were any indication.

Compared to the frae, this female seemed infinitely more deadly.

Eyolin's control slipped for a heartbeat and her mental field expanded like she was inhaling breath. Catlee's glimmer faltered for a heartbeat, revealing a creature of glittering blue skin and a long, snaking two-pronged tail. In a blink, the creature was gone, replaced by the pale elf before her. If Catlee was aware of this slip, she didn't let on.

"You will know when the time is right. Then seek me out, *Sarom*."

Primal fear speared through Eyolin. She needed to run, to get out of that library. The one sanctuary left for her was her own chambers, and now she doubted even that was safe.

Just as Eyolin prepared to make a break for it, Catlee pulled back and dipped her head in a mockery of a curtsy, spinning on her heel and dipping out of the library without a second glance.

Eyolin shivered against the cold air that filled absence. A monster under the guise of a glimmer walking the halls freely. A creature, no doubt, who knew precisely what Eyolin had in her veins. If there were others with her Gift before her, why had Catlee acted as if they were lesser? A Gift could not recur in Alagana with increased strength. The magik of the realm was fading. Each generation was weaker than the last, the dilution of the High Elvish blood disappearing back into the earth. That blood was what gave the elves the ability to wield the Gifts given by the land. The immortal race of elves that came from the Sky were what gave elvishkind that connection. What Catlee had said didn't align with the history as Eyolin knew it.

The only other glimmer she had seen in the Great Hall hovered near Traik. If they were one and the same, they had been lurking for weeks. Weeks when Eyolin had been mindlessly training, not seeking out the dark presence. Now it was too late.

The sound of beating wings announced the arrival of a librarian and Eyolin filed away her worries as the tiny, blue creature fluttered into view. It flapped upwards in a spiral around a columned book-shelf. Knobbed knuckles tapped on the spines of books as it scanned the titles written in a multitude of different scripts. Light shone through the blue wings as it passed in front of a floating candle, dark blue veins crisscrossing their surface like drawings on fine filmed paper. Eyolin composed herself after the encounter with Catlee and fumbled for the list of books Karok had given her, finding it crumpled into a ball in her dress's pocket.

"Excuse me?" Eyolin's voice came out in more of a squeak than she would have liked.

The librarian's large, round head turned sideways acknowledging Eyolin with a frown. It scratched the top of its head with four-fingered hands, ruffling its white hair. Slowly, as if drifting down a gentle river, the librarian came to her.

"I can't remember the last time one of Master Arendt's students graced the shelves of our library." It sighed tiredly and waved a hand. "Wait here a moment."

A reading chair beckoned at the base of a nearby pillar of books. Eyolin curled up in the red fabric and fingered her moontear restlessly. Robed scholars shuffled past, paying her little attention.

The librarian returned minutes later with a pile of books it its arms. The thin skin on its arms strained as it heaved the books onto a small round table next to Eyolin's chair.

"Now," its voice was raspy, and it emphasized the end of each word and prolonged its *S* sounds. "Here is a variety of folklore, fact, and everything in between, as well as the anatomy of cloud dragons, otherwise known as the yousay-caea, though there are other derivatives. From your mind, I gleaned it useful to include books on other creatures of Alagana that you might educate yourself on." The creature's lip curled in what was an attempt at a smile, revealing yellowed teeth that were filed to points.

Eyolin suppressed a shudder and offered a weak thank you.

"*Life of Alagana* will acclimate you to the beings you interact with on the daily in the city so your mind can be more prepared next time."

A cryptic comment made by a puzzling creature.

The librarian turned its attention to another part of the library and vanished. Eyolin sighed and picked up the top book titled *The Ology of Atremen and Her Children*. The title wasn't one of Karok's assigned readings. Eyolin lifted her head to see if she could inquire about why this was included in the stack but the librarian was long gone.

She lifted the thick, bounded blue cover and dust slid onto her lap. Eyolin coughed and fanned away some of the dust before a scholar materialized from behind the nearest bookshelf, grabbing her wrist. "Stop! The dust from ancient texts cannot be disturbed or the author is said to haunt your dreams."

Eyolin rolled her eyes as the scholar readjusted his own pile of books and disappeared. She stroked the smooth, leaf-shaped paper of the book and flipped through the contents lazily.

She stopped at page twenty-five. Her finger froze on the upper corner of the page. A thin and precise drawing of a creature that bore an uncanny resemblance to Catlee was etched onto the page. The next leaf elaborated on the drawing.

'The daughters of Atremen are a species known to Alagana as the Enchanted. These offspring of the water goddess are protected by the Mist of Velesah. They rarely venture out from the safety of the Isles of Enchantment and lose strength the farther away from their isles they venture.

The Enchanted have the power of Soft Tongue, enabling them to make their victims do their bidding no matter the cost. Without their eyes, an Enchanted cannot use Soft Tongue and loses their ability to enchant others.'

Eyolin felt a rock in her stomach. How could she have been so naive? For weeks she had felt the safe monotony of routine—for the first time in years—only to discover that she was farther away from being protected than a rabbit among foxes. She turned her eyes back to the book, hoping to glean something of use to turn Catlee over. To whom, she couldn't say. Master Arendt was pointedly absent from the Great Hall. Traik was her only other contact of power. The memory of his hands gripping the bodies of skinned elves rose to the surface along with a wave of bile. Eyolin turned back to the book.

There were other phrases that caught her eye in the following pages. An insatiable hunger. Prone to hunting.

Catlee revealing herself was intentional, and Eyolin vowed to discover why. If she couldn't take Traik down, she could focus that energy on Catlee instead.

Chapter Twenty

The knife sliced through the neck of the guard. Kipp caught the weight of the elf and lowered him to the ground silently. Three other elves lay propped against the wall of Aldeyn, each with their throat slit, their blood dripping from Kipp's seraph blade. The dark energy trickled out of their chests and writhed through the air like a snake to a torch. Kipp sliced a lock of hair from each of them and stashed it in his pocket.

He moved toward the woods beyond the city. To kill a wraith all for a few silver coins. If the wraiths he, Jet, and Erik had slaughtered in the Twilight realm had paid a bounty, he would be royalty by now. The people of Aldeyn, however, viewed wraiths to be as dangerous as the most powerful necromancer or rogue witch.

He followed the dark energy into the edges of the forest, his seraph blade glowing at his side.

You're mine, wraith, Kipp promised. His movements were silent, drawing on the power of the Twilight to keep his steps from being heard. He felt the wraith whisk through the air to his right, assuming he could not detect it. A typical mercenary would have been oblivious of the movements of a Twilight creature, assuming the shadows themselves had teeth. Kipp was not ordinary. He was the Shadow, the Regent's right hand, and heir to the limitless power. He felt every flicker of dark magik and knew how to dispose of it. The task was a mere chore.

The wraith swung around base of a tree to the left of the dirt road. Kipp swung his blade in an arc. The head of the wraith clunked onto the ground at his feet. Another execution. He wiped the black ichor of the wraith's blood on his thigh and sheathed his weapon.

Footsteps rustled behind him. He did not draw his blade this time.

"That's how it's done, you see?" Kipp said.

The kid was scrawny, but his heritage was undeniable. Slightly tipped ears and blood split between human and elvish. He was maybe twelve—thirteen. The age didn't matter. All that mattered was that the kid was thirsty for power and had killed three entire families to get it.

His first recruit to his cause. Step one: introduce him to the world of the shadows.

"How long until I get one of those?" he asked. His eyes were locked on Kipp's seraph blade.

"When I'm done with you, you can summon much more than swords."

He beckoned for him to follow, weaving further into the woods.

Kipp had left the confines of the inn with Tuk's slimy fingers a few days ago, opting for an abandoned estate teeming with rouge Twilight creatures that had dripped into Alagana.

Balla had sought him out, following the screams of the dead that infested the structure. The half-elvish kid could see ghosts, as creepy as that was. Kipp had been slightly worried Balla was a bit mad but turned out the kid was just a bloodthirsty little cretin. Balla was bred to be a Grey.

It wasn't without pride that Kipp saw himself in the kid and made it his duty to prepare him for the ritual that would give purpose to his malicious life.

They'd tidied up the estate as best they cared to—which was to say, not very well. Vines still snaked up the interior grand staircase and the chandelier dangled precariously from the ceiling. They'd disposed of the bodies of the creatures that had holed up there, but other than that, it was dreadfully unmaintained.

Balla skittered at Kipp's tail. It was endearing, to have someone mimic his every murderous motion.

Three other boys, each under sixteen, emerged from the shadows at the top of the staircase. The oldest of the three, Jorrith, was still wrestling with the Grey magik Kipp had Bound into him. It was he who stood in front.

"When do we move in on Aldeyn, Kipp?"

Kipp had made it abundantly clear that they were nowhere near ready to tackle the city, but the boys were restless. Only Jorrith had volunteered to undergo the ritual so far, and it would take another few weeks before the others were ready.

The bond he shared with Eyolin told him that nothing was astray in that department, giving him free rein to continue his training of new Grey initiates in the north outside of his evening trips to the outskirts of Mainwood.

Kipp surveyed the two boys at Jorrith's back. Of course, Jorrith had established himself as the ring leader. The one on the right called himself Cole and knew his way around poisons better than most

Grey. Rith practically snarled on the left like a rabid animal but had good connections with the witches inside the walls.

"You think you're ready to topple a city?"

Jorrith stuck his chin out. A challenger. Kipp liked that. But wouldn't stand for it.

A flash of light and darkness exploded across the foyer. The bolt of magik hit Jorrith square in the chest, sending him sprawling.

"I'm giving you invincibility in exchange for your loyalty. You do as I say, and you will—"

"We're with you, Kipp. Don't listen to Jo," Rith said.

Kipp let his magik free of its cage, letting black flames lick his arms and back. The four boys looked at him like he was a god. For all intents and purposes, that's exactly what Kipp was.

"There's a witch I want. She has something of mine. The first of you to find her for me ascends next."

Of course, it was Balla who found the witch. The kid was far too eager to join the Grey's wretched ranks. As a reward, Kipp sent Balla to the post with a few letters to Jet back in the Twilight. He and Jet had a way of communicating while one of them was out on assignment, and Kipp was getting irritated that Jet hadn't been returning any of his reports. He would need to know the state of the Grey if he was to gain control of the Regency once this whole Blood Moon ordeal was over.

The exterior of the building Kipp stood before was unassuming, nearly identical to the rest of the street in the residential district of Aldeyn. Kipp opened the well-oiled door and shouldered through the waterfall of crimson beads that obstructed his view of the interior. *A witch's house, all right,* he thought, noting the dank herbal smell that washed over him and the haze of smoke.

Candles lined the floor of the room, the wooden flooring having been ripped up in a haggard manner. A figure hunched over in the center of a circle of symbols scratched into the hard-packed dirt.

"Knock, knock," Kipp called. "Any rat tongue for me to buy today?"

"Time to move along, Grey." The witch grinned, her splintered teeth jagged and black. "You won't find your supplies here."

Kipp shifted his hand through the air, tasting the magik that clung to the walls.

"Excellent glimmer for an unGifted cretin," Kipp mused as he absorbed and dissolved the enchantment that distorted his view.

The room's features shifted. Lush velvets and tapestries were packed into every crevice. And so much gold. Old books lay open on a dark chestnut desk. In the place of the squatting witch stood a white-haired, milky-eyed older woman.

"All that work for naught, child," the witch spoke in a scratchy voice. Her hands clutched a particularly frayed volume to her chest. Kipp could see the veins in her hands like blood running down paper. Slanted ears poked through the wisps of her snow-colored hair. "Our mother will not take kindly to your prying."

Kipp cocked his head and flicked a seraph blade into his hand from within the folds of space. He scanned the room for any additional source to the witch's power—their kind being verbal, full of incantations and spells—spells that could be found in books like the one he searched for.

"I don't suppose your mother is as charmingly beautiful as yourself?" Kipp had his eye on the battered book the witch clung to. It didn't call to him as the Book of Bindings did, but if he were to trade that tome with the right witch, he may be able to locate the correct one in time. He needed to break the Binding magik that held him to the Regent and unwind the spell the book had woven into his mind.

The witch coughed out a rough laugh. "You know I had hoped the pretty one would come. The one that smells so sweet."

A snarl rose in Kipp's throat. He had competition in Aldeyn. The witch could only be referring to a Grey or a Sister. If it were the former, it meant trouble. The latter could be dealt with.

"Is she worth it, Grey?"

Kipp's blood chilled. There was no doubt about who the witch was referring to.

His jaw tensed. The illusionary magik that Kipp absorbed from the witch writhed against his control beneath his skin. It felt otherworldly—alive. He adapted his own magik to mirror against any negative effects, but it pressed against his power.

The illusion was looking for something, crawling through his veins.

"Will you let her die for your precious book?" The witch croaked. She set the bound pages on the table delicately. Her fingers traced a symbol into the air above an unlit candle. A gentle flame flared up in its wake.

"She is to be a gift to the mother. As she will die, I will be reborn. I have been promised my youth and will not help you keep it from me."

Rage in all its unperfected glory tore through him. The illusion Kipp had absorbed needed to be expelled. And he happened to have just the target for all of it shuffling to a low seated divan.

He would not rest until he unearthed whoever hid the Book of Bindings from him and slaughtered them the way he did the witch, now unmoving and lifeless in her robes.

Chapter Twenty-One

"**W**hat could possibly intrigue you about the Enchanted?"

Eyolin shut the book with a loud bang and winced at the glares from a table of scribes.

Every instinct screamed at her to flee from the shadow towering over her.

Traik's presence froze time itself. She had to hope that the half-giant couldn't smell the terror that trickled down her spine.

"You weren't in your room after dinner." Obviously. Eyolin had been watching the half-giant pile dead elves across the city wards.

He had seen her, or he hadn't. It didn't matter. Traik was there *now*. In the library, in the dead of night. Eyolin couldn't see whether he had the time to wash the blood of the skinned elves from beneath his nails.

Accusations nipped at the tip of her tongue. *He* was the traitor breaking through the wards of Mainwood with what no doubt was some necromantic spell. What other use would the bodies of elves serve in that wretched state? How long had he been spilling the kingdom's secrets to the enemy?

"I'm sorry?" Eyolin said. Her voice was carefully collected, too much so.

Traik narrowed his eyes and Eyolin could see his swift calculations. She attempted to assume an aloof look and had to hope it was enough.

"You and that creature they call a Changeling have been given far too much leeway as to your training."

"We are doing everything we can given Master Arendt's instructions." How dare he ridicule Karok. He had given her a semblance of control over her magik despite her Shoutka.

Think, little Sarom.

There was that voice again. The same that whispered in her mind the day the frae attacked her. The same day she met Traik.

"What is it you do, day after day, in that forest?" Traik took a step closer, his presence amongst the books imposing and dangerous.

The image of him standing with the body of a skinned elf in his hands was too powerful. She felt her resolve waver and her mouth slipped.

"My Shoutka," she blurted. "Master Arendt needs me to unlock my Shoutka."

The half-giant's sneer contorted his face horribly. "And he's failed most spectacularly. I haven't seen one extraordinary thing about you at all."

She was next. Her body would be stripped and tossed lifeless on that pile at the edge of the city. Her face must've exposed her fear from the glint in Traik's eyes. Right then, Eyolin decided she would go out kicking. There was a slight tilt to the column of books at her back. A solid push would bring it toppling down, giving her just enough time to slip away.

But Traik didn't come any closer. Instead, he tossed her a missive scratched on a leaf of parchment.

"I'm taking over your training in the morrow. If I see you've run off... I'm sure there's some punishment worthy of the crimes you so quickly passed off to Tequerra."

Every muscle in Eyolin went numb. The paper fluttered into her lap without a sound. The ink bled red where Master Arendt signed her transferal to Traik's care.

She sat frozen in that velvet chair in the library for what seemed like hours, every part of her numb from shock, until a scholar had to shake her awake.

It was a few hours from dawn.

Traik had taken over her training. That was the one thought that kept repeating over and over in her mind. She was expected in the city training grounds where the armies were underwent their vigorous combat training.

Eyolin sat on the edge of her bed until the morning breeze whisked through her window and footsteps pattered outside. There was no drug potent enough to have gotten her to sleep in the face of the truths she now knew. Traik was a traitor. And she had to pretend that everything was fine or risk being stolen away to be locked up beneath the city as she should have been to begin with.

Whatever fear kept her from unlocking her Shoutka with Karok had doomed her to a public punishment in front of the bulk of the Aideillian army.

Eventually she had to strip off the green heith dress in exchange for her light acolyte training attire. It was time to face her fate.

Nasally voices filtered through her doorway.

"Have you seen the human fight?" someone asked.

"Not once," another responded. "Heard he's been with Gueah this whole time."

A scoff. "Wasting one of our best on a human? If Ïsteldûr kills us all, I blame them."

Eyolin was on her feet and at the door quicker than a blink. In her self-pity she had forgotten that Dale fought in the arena today. She decided then, her hand gripping the smooth wooden door, that she would see to it that Dale walked out of that arena alive and well. Her own fate was scribbled in ink, dooming her to whatever horrors Traik inflicted, but they would not touch Dale.

Her limbs were stiff from lack of sleep, but at least her body was free from visible injuries.

Taking the steps at a run, Eyolin bounded through the hall until she caught up with a pack of scarox who she recognized as the ones who had passed by her room earlier.

No one had given her a proper weapon, so Eyolin kept her single dagger tucked into her belt without a sheath.

She followed the group of men at a distance until a muffled cry caught her attention. To her right, above a rounded door not unlike her own, was a mutilated syket. Eyolin glanced at the scarox disappearing around a bend. They hadn't even noticed.

Nails pierced the syket's wrists, crucifying it to the door. A small band of runes were carved underneath the metal circlet of Aideillian servitude. The lines pulsed with a haunted crimson glow and Eyolin couldn't shake the memory of all those elvish bodies stripped of skin and piled so vulgarly. The elves. Then this syket. Traik must have left it as a symbol of how close he could get to her without getting caught.

Or something far worse was inside the Great Hall.

The door with the syket nailed to it flew open. A girl no older than Eyolin with wine-red hair thrashed against the grip of three fully armored Aideillian soldiers, pulling at the shackles on her wrists and ankles.

She wore the same sleeping robe as Eyolin had folded up in a drawer—the same one she donned most nights. The girl's hair was a mess of red tangles, but Eyolin caught a glimpse of ears clipped of their tips and amber eyes.

One of the soldiers, his face caged in a metal helmet, gripped the girl's neck. Clenched in his knuckles was a tiny ruby on a gold chain. Eyolin pressed her back against the wall, willing herself to fade into the shadows.

Eyolin watched as the ruby glowed fiery red. The girl's smooth skin cracked with dark fissures snaking from her mouth until her shoulders and neck resembled a volcanic mountain.

"Bloody fire-scaled bitch," the soldier at her back hissed. The skin gripping her neck bubbled and blackened upon contact, but he gritted his teeth and held fast.

The air tightened around the group in a sealing bubble, cutting off sound and any hope the girl had of escape.

Still, she thrashed and kicked, embers and smoke unfurling from her mouth.

Eyolin's eyes flicked to the slaughtered syket bleeding freely down the wood, staining a door that could have been a mirror to Eyolin's own. It was unmistakably the syket who had blessed her room.

The soldiers hauled away the first and only Gifted female elf Eyolin had seen in the Great Hall. And Eyolin, breath catching in her throat, just stood there.

It took a great effort to move from her spot on the stairs. Dale needed her in that arena. She needed to get to the combat grounds.

Chapter
Twenty-Two

A spiked fortification rose above her. The combat grounds were in the first tier of the city, closest to the ground, where the branches were nearly as large as the trunks of the Greywood trees. It was a stadium, and a fortress.

The urge to find Dale and get him out of the arena drove her through the gates of the grounds. Nets, ropes, and ladders were strung throughout the branches. Soldiers whacked at spinning wooden dummies with swords, maces, and scythes. Even the elves without magik moved with such precision that their limbs blurred with speed.

Logs rolled down a controlled slope to her left where men leapt and maneuvered in various formations. Ahead stood a quickly expanding crowd—the epicenter of the arena.

Eyolin wove her way closer, taking care to avoid those her Gift identified as scarox. Scarox had a diluted way of predicting the immediate future and Eyolin couldn't risk revealing her intentions.

Bodies pressed in the closer she got to the arena, but she slipped through.

A cold hilt pressed into her hand. A voice whispered to her—Eyolin couldn't tell if it came from her mind or by a mouth at her ear.

"You'll be with the Mother soon."

Eyolin involuntarily gripped the sword, her head whipping around to identify who had spoken. It was a sea of moving bodies—every face represented a possible threat.

She risked a look at the weapon clutched tight in her fist and it was all she could do not to scream. A red ribbon was woven around the hilt and an ornate I was inscribed in swirls on the obsidian blade.

As she stared, the sword evaporated into a twinkling plume of smoke. Elves packed in closer around her, but Eyolin couldn't tear her eyes away from the small envelope that now sat in her hand.

There was a certain kind of darkness that seeped into the marrow of Eyolin's bones as she recognized the serpentine symbol on the front of the folded parchment. The symbol was seared into her memory. She hadn't seen it since the last day Eyolin had ever seen her older sister Arden.

Eyolin hadn't understood it when she'd seen it tattooed on the wrist of an old crone of a woman, but now it was all too clear—the mark of a Sister.

The paper fluttered open in the wind. One word repeated over and over.

Sarom.

The words from that encounter all those years ago surfaced.

"The Sisters will have her collected one way or another."

Sarom, Sarom, Sarom. The pieces started to fit together all too sickeningly. The Sisters took Arden because she would not betray Eyolin. Because Eyolin was the Sarom. They'd known this entire time, biding time until she was alone and forgotten by Master Arendt, disregarded, and thrown to the whims of a murdering half-giant commander. There was a Sister in that crowd—an assassin as deadly as any Grey.

A Sister who knew what happened to Arden that day everything changed.

The ink lifted off the page, wrapping itself around Eyolin's hand and wrist. The enchanted ink soaked into her skin, fading to a lightly raised scarred tattoo. If Eyolin shifted her wrist, the tattoo blurred into the shape of three interlocking circles and lines.

The threat of having a Sister in the combat grounds had Eyolin scanning for any female figure among the crowd. But the space was packed and soon a loud cheer erupted.

Through a small opening between two soldiers, Eyolin saw that the fight had begun. She was too late to prevent the inevitable. It was all she could do not to explode with rage as Maximus sparred with Dale.

Eyolin navigated to the front, her stomach twisting with every step. Maximus moved with the fluidity of water, a graceful dance of lethal precision. Dale, on the other hand, swiped and hacked at the elvish commander without so much as a scratch landing on Maximus' tanned skin.

Maximus moved with savagery as he arched his sword arm over Dale and snapped it down, thwacking the blade against Dale's shoulder.

A loud crack echoed through the arena. Eyolin drew in a breath. She was too late to save him. There was no way for her to interfere, no matter how desperately she clung to her friendship with the human.

Dale's parrying block languished from the pain in his shoulder. Eyolin's breath stilled as Maximus straightened his arm and slammed the flat of his sword against Dale's temple. He crumpled unconscious.

Her eyes fixed on his still body in the dust as the crowd erupted in a chant.

"Maximus! Maximus!"

The commander reached down to grab Dale and a skull pendant swung free of where it sat tucked under his shirt, still crisp and white despite the dust of the arena. Not only had Dale been matched with an elf, but a scarox—the same man who had threatened Eyolin in the Great Hall the day she decided the Kipp wasn't her enemy.

Maximus tossed his sword to the ground and shook off his helmet. He ran a hand through short-cropped brown hair where beads of sweat crowned his forehead. He spread his arms out wide and walked in a slow circle with a cocky grin. Arrogance drove each pompous step, all the way to an expensively adorned elvish courtesan in a deep emerald gown. He caressed her side carelessly, drinking the praise from beating a human to a pulp.

Eyolin rolled her eyes before noticing a tall, slender woman with raven black hair standing at the shoulder of the courtesan. The woman's eyes leered up at Eyolin. Even from where she stood, they were a steely grey that sent shivers down Eyolin's spine. Those were Arden's eyes. But Arden was gone—abandoning her hours before their mother's life was taken. The tattoo on her hand and wrist stung in reminder. A Sister was in the crowd.

The possibility that Arden was that Sister burned through her. Arden would have looked like that all grown up, so like their father where Eyolin was a mirror of her mother.

A familiar blonde woman distracted Eyolin long enough to lose sight of the raven-haired Arden lookalike. Catlee had her arm looped around the tall elvish soldier in her company the night before. Her attire should have drawn more attention than it did—the crowd thirsty for blood, not women—except for Maximus.

Metal swirls constituted the only coverage of Catlee's breasts, and two panels of cerulean fabric were draped over her shoulders, belted with a silver band. She was of the few who did not cheer at Maximus' victory. Rather, her mouth was pinched in a frown as she stared down Maximus like he was a meal. Deep beneath the glimmer that disguised the Enchanted, Eyolin saw slender claws extend around Kristofor's arm. The soldier didn't react, his Velesian armor cut from the skins of whales thicker than most weapons could pierce. No other Velesians were present in the crowd, and the heavy armor must have been stifling in the growing heat of the late spring day.

Eyolin still suspected Catlee's involvement in some underlying plot that had not come to light. While Traik may be using bodies to break wards, someone was still collecting elf ears. Eyolin's bet was on the Enchanted. Catlee looked like she wanted to eat the crowd alive.

Movement in the center of the ring brought her attention back to Maximus. He ate the praise up like a vulture on a carcass. Where she stood in the front row, Eyolin was clearly visible. She sent a prayer to the Grey that Kipp's enchantment held.

Traik's booming voice quieted the crowd.

"Eyolin Kyenz-ushteira will fight next!"

Eyolin searched for the half-giant in the crowd. He stood directly across from her, on the other side of the arena, his face grim and focused intently on her. He nodded to her once. Next to him, Gueah looked obscenely smug.

From the corner of her eye, Eyolin saw Catlee draw herself up straighter, her lip curled in a hiss revealing canines that were just long enough to be noticeable. The Enchanted watched Eyolin take two steps back, wishing she could vanish into the crowd.

This was not training. It was a show. And she was the main attraction.

Her mind flicked to the woman being dragged out of her room kicking, the body of the syket not yet cold where it hung nailed to the door. This fight bore the same tone.

"*Ushteira,*" Maximus snarled. "Of the famed General Kyenz? Do you know what happened to him twelve years ago? Why he never came back?" Eyolin couldn't help but notice the alarm in Traik's eyes at Maximus' words.

Eyolin stood rooted to the spot, anxiety gnawing a hole through her organs. Her father was about to be ridiculed in front of this bloodthirsty crowd—her hero who had worshiped their little family. And there was nothing she could do to stop it.

"Are you going to follow in your dear father's footsteps, little doe?" Maximus used that damned term of endearment as he nudged a toe into Dale's still unconscious form. "Would someone drag this meat out of my ring before it starts to smell?" Maximus searched for

Gueah, pointing at Dale with the point of his sword. "Isn't this yours, Gueah?"

Gueah's face wore a permanent sneer. "Consider this my resignation as his tutor. Unless you think he has potential?"

Maximus dropped his helmet on Dale's back. "Not in the slightest. Traik will send him to the camps in the morrow."

"I don't take orders from you, Max." Traik crossed his arms. "Remember the damage I did to you when we first sparred."

The two commanders stared one another down. Maximus broke first with a shrug, turning back to Eyolin.

"Must I bloody up such a pretty face? I'd quite like to bloody her up in other more savory ways. A scream from a blade is far less satisfying."

Eyolin glanced toward where the mirage of her sister stood. Arden's cold eyes stared back. *Fight*, they seemed to whisper in a challenge.

Maximus swayed back to the center of the arena as two trolls pulled Dale's body away. She took a step forward, glaring at Traik. He knew she wasn't ready for the arena. She hadn't finished her studies with Karok. She hadn't unlocked the spirit form that would graduate her into her next specialty. She'd fight. She'd lose. But not until she showed everyone the monsters that itched under her skin.

Traik sensed her plan. "No magik. No Gifts," he announced. "Remove your gems. Both of you."

For Maximus, the removal of his skull gem would do little to inhibit his skills with a sword, only slow down his movements and take away the intuition of the scarox. Eyolin's moontear was a different matter. The removal of her gem would cut off her access to magik. She had tied herself to the moontear, and now she was without even that last resort.

Maximus dropped his gem into Gueah's outstretched palm. He stalked around the arena as Eyolin handed her own gem to Traik, shrinking from his gaze, pausing only when the slight flicker of pain glimmered beneath his hard exterior. Surely, they wouldn't let her die. Someone would stop the fight if things got too bad.

"It's alright, little doe," Maximus called. He exchanged his metal sword for a wooden blade in a bucket, directing her to do the same. Eyolin reluctantly parted with her dagger. The wooden sword felt clunky, pricking her hand with splinters. The last time she used wood was with Arden when she was seven.

The crowd hushed in anticipation, everyone but Catlee drinking in the spectacle. The girl crossed her arms and scowled centuries of hatred at the commander in the ring. Eyolin's mind raced with the stiff elvish forms she knew—useless in an actual fight. She was intuitive enough to defend herself against a thief—maybe put a drunk on his knees. Maximus was neither of those things. He was a scarox who breathed death and violence in a world tinged in red.

Maximus slid his left foot behind him and shifted his weight forward. It struck Eyolin as narrow and off-balance. She took a tentative step forward.

He cocked his head, looking every bit like the erixsay who attacked her in the Middle, and lunged.

Eyolin froze. She watched Maximus bridge the distance between them, doing nothing to avoid the collision. Some innate survival instinct flared to life and Eyolin managed to twist right as the sword whizzed a breath from her leg. Eyolin brought her right arm up to hit his sword arm, but he had already pivoted away and blocked the blade with little more than a tap.

"An amateur defense. I expected a little more from an elf. But you are a woman." He stepped in and twisted Eyolin's arm behind her. "For example, this position would be so much stronger if we were naked. But you aren't at my level even if you were disrobed." He swiftly brought the butt of his sword down, slamming it onto Eyolin's head. Spasms coursed through her body, black dots speckling her vision. She stayed standing but lost her grip on her weapon.

"This is sparring, not a beating," Traik called. "Teach her."

"Take out her legs before you knock her out," Gueah shouted over the top of Traik's voice. The half-giant snarled down at the elf in front of him. Gueah conceded with a slight bow of his head.

Eyolin squinted through black encroaching her vision to glimpse Maximus shifting his weight to execute a sweeping lunge. She dove over the leg at the last possible moment, rolling away from his sword as it sliced down. She tumbled to the ground, dirt dusting every surface.

She stood up sharply, invading the space between his sword and chest. It wasn't technical but it allowed her to slam her fists into his sternum. Sloppiness aside, Maximus stumbled backward.

He regained his footing in a heartbeat and closed the distance like a shadow. Eyolin's wrists were twisted behind her back with a sharp yank. Maximus kept his sword in one hand, the length of it pressed to her spine. She was pinned to his body. The point of the sword nicked the tip of her ear.

"If you're set on fighting like a human, you aren't worthy of your ears." The cut stung. A trickle of blood ran down her neck. The warmth in the blood sent her mind tunneling inward, grasping at the strings of golden white magik that she had unlocked with Karok. Where was it—where was her magik? Sense and reason abandoned her to make room for the panic that seeped into her joints.

It all happened in a blink. Maximus swept a foot under her, and she landed on her back hard. The weight of him crushed her ribcage where he drove his knee down. He took the blunt edge of the wooden sword and slammed it against Eyolin's temple.

A scream shattered through her lips as her head ricocheted against the ground. Maximus released her and took his time wiping the blood on the blade onto his white blouse.

"She hasn't conceded yet, boy," Traik boomed.

Eyolin's eyes opened into a squint, watching Gueah lick his lips hungrily. She checked for the Enchanted only to find Kristofor's side void of Catlee's presence.

There was no reassuring voice telling her what to do, or Grey to lend a helping hand. They were going to kill her.

Eyolin breathed in at the approaching footsteps. Her body refused to move from where it lay crumpled next to the indent where Dale had fallen. All she wanted to do was melt into the ground, becoming the soil, disappearing at last.

The air shifted as Maximus arched the sword over his head for a blow that would paralyze her if she ever woke up again.

She grabbed fistfuls of the dry dirt, feeling the slight sting where it lodged under her fingernails. Though her mind screamed to get up, her body wouldn't move.

The sound of splintering wood made her flinch. But Maximus' sword never hit her.

Karok crouched over her, his arms outstretched to stay the elvish commander. Chunks of Maximus' wooden sword were clenched in his bare hands, the werekey's strength curling black claws around them.

"Careful how you treat my student," Karok snarled.

The air around Karok bristled as he wrestled the werekey venom under control. The crowd withdrew, sensing the monster lingering under the skin of the human.

He was there—inside the city limits, breaking his deal with Master Arendt. Eyolin tried to tell him to run, but her body was failing her. The last thing she saw was Karok shaking in the center of that arena.

Chapter Twenty-Three

"**W**hat do you mean I'm not allowed out of the Great Hall?" Eyolin yelled at the half-giant that towered over her. "I have to see Karok!"

Fear of the traitor be damned, Traik had the nerve to stand there like he did her a favor, letting her get beaten to a pulp in front of the entire army—an army she was supposed to be a part of.

They stood in a hallway off the Great Hall. Her wounds had stitched themselves back together once Traik had returned her gem and the fury that swirled inside her ricocheted through the moon-tear.

"Your trainer's leash didn't permit him from leaving the training grounds. He broke his deal to save your life."

"You put me in that situation!"

"I had no choice," Traik bellowed. Eyolin's magik pounded in her ears and hissed and pleaded to be released. Traik's head twitched to the side like he heard a sound, and he shoved Eyolin into a hidden hole in the wall before she could protest. Eyolin stumbled into the darkness, her back colliding with wood. She leapt forward, but Traik stood with his massive form blocking the exit.

Someone in the hall had approached Traik. The voice that spoke to the commander kept her from pounding at his back.

"What in the pits of Midriel was that, commander?" It was Master Arendt. "She was hours away from unlocking the Shoutka, completing her spirit form. Karok had been waiting in the training grounds to meet her this morning. When she didn't show up, he assumed the worst and sniffed her out, fearing for her safety considering the recent murders in the Great Hall. Instead, he walked right into the middle of the Aideillian army's training grounds, where he found his devoted pupil getting beaten into the ground by one of our own. The act broke the magik I used to keep Karok secure."

Eyolin clamped a hand over her mouth and stifled a whimper as her newly healed skin stretched painfully. There was no way that Tequerra wouldn't hear or sense her presence. Except Traik seemed to be keeping him occupied.

"We're running out of time, Tequerra. I had a theory that if she was tired enough, it would be easier for her to rely on magik and slip into her Shoutka. Your meditative practices have gotten her nowhere."

"A *theory*, Commander Traik? You risked our entire operation on a theory? To use magik, she needs energy. I tried using a forceful technique and it blew up nearly as spectacularly as yours did. Regardless, all that adrenaline she'd worked up fighting will have burned off when she healed herself. It won't help her slip into a Shoutka like you ill-advisedly assumed."

Eyolin shrank as far back into the crevice as she could. Her mind worked fast, but not fast enough as Tequerra continued.

"Where has the little magikal battery gone, in any case? She didn't show up in the infirmary. She hasn't been spotted entering her room. If she takes her gem and runs, the esthioryn will never be completed. She will fall into our enemy's hands. I will lose the retribution I am owed." Currents of power singed the air where Master Arendt's magik flared, turning the walls around her effervescent green. She expected the master's magik to feel like the earth—damp and unyielding. This felt ancient and cold.

"There's one place she could hide," Traik offered. "The herbalist that lives in the third tier of the city. We have allowed her illicit dealings to go unnoticed but not ignored. Eyolin would go there to find a remedy for any lingering injuries."

"And risk another knowing of her Gift?" The earthen magik shivered, shriveling like the burnt edge of parchment on fire. "We have kept her power a secret thus far. The information cannot be leaked. We've disposed of the lessers that have caught her scent, but there will always be more. Ïsteldûr will steal her from me and I—" Tequerra stopped himself short of whatever he was about to divulge.

Traik shifted uncomfortably. "What would you have me do?"

"You've identified the holes in the wards?"

Traik grunted.

"Then be useful and tell the High Council it was Ïsteldûr. And retrieve my weapon."

Eyolin felt when Master Arendt stepped away. Traik hesitated a moment before moving away from the hidden doorway. The half-giant didn't turn his head in her direction, but that didn't lessen the impact of what he had let her listen to, inadvertently warning her of the danger the herbalist was in because of her. The memory of the syket nailed to the doorway flashed through her mind. Karok had been drilling her on anatomies so thoroughly she almost missed it.

Magikal beings Aideillians considered lessers had an aptitude for recognizing Gifts in others. The syket was murdered as a warning to others, and the herbalist was on the list for harboring her for years. The one person who had given her the illusion of a home and purpose.

Gears turned in her mind. Traik had a head start but needed to send a missive to the High Council to warrant the assault. She couldn't risk being seen. Apparently, Master Arendt wanted her gem to complete the esthioryn. Whatever that was.

Esthioryn...

Eyolin connected the fragmented dots, drawing on knowledge from her years in the shop. Esthyri was an herb she had seen in her mentor's shop. If the esthioryn was a derivation of esthyri, the herbalist would know what kind of weapon Tequerra was building which no doubt would put her higher on his kill list. There was no reason to return to the claws of the High Council who would undoubtedly turn her over to Master Arendt. She had seen what they did to those who no longer served their agenda and had no interest in entertaining their next play. Her moontear warmed at her throat waiting for a command. She morphed into a black cat and tiptoed out of the hidden passageway in the Great Hall.

Eyolin was bounding through the trees of Mainwood, winding down toward the pub near her old home on all fours. The streets were quiet. A few elvish men stood with their backs against shops with metal glasses of mead in their hands. The occasional mother ushered her children across the warm hearths of their tree homes. Eyolin supposed it was around dinnertime.

The sun slipped beneath the horizon by the time she navigated to the shop. The city was cast in green shadows as night pulled across the canopy above. The air chilled, a crisp wind picking up.

Eyolin stayed in the feline form as she approached the pub entrance. There weren't any Aideillian soldiers. No screams. No... anything. The pub was silent, void of customers and the regular bustle of life.

The entire third tier had been quiet as if everyone had been told to stay inside come nightfall. Eyolin expanded her mental field into the pub. The wood of the tree hummed with energy. She pushed further. No living people that she could detect in the chamber.

She stepped through the curtain that lay hidden at the back of the pub. Eyolin's grip on the feline form faltered. She fell to her knees, stunned.

Flowers and stones lay littered on every surface. Pots and jars were smashed and upturned, and the counter was split in two. The herbalist lay groaning against a wall where Eyolin could see her tunic and apron in tatters, like she had been shredded by an erixsay. Her face was intact, but the extent of her bodily wounds brought tears to Eyolin's eyes.

"No," she whimpered. It was too late. Traik had gotten there first. She should have never left the old woman by herself.

Eyolin took a step into the shop. Glass cracked under her feet. She winced at the shards that poked through her shoes. At the sound, the herbalist stirred, emitting a pained cough.

"What have I done?"

The herbalist shifted in place, face tight with pain. "They were after me for longer than you."

Eyolin fumbled through the shards of a ceramic bowl, scooping together what could be salvaged. She needed to keep the herbalist awake and talking. Eyolin rummaged through the littered remains of the herbalist's collection. Her own healing magik was unrefined, only used on two occasions on accident. She didn't trust magik to heal. Not yet. Eyolin found a complete mushroom and ground it into a leaf, mixing a poultice that would bind and clot the wounds well enough. The herbalist was going to bleed out otherwise. Her old mentor's face didn't look particularly worried, or in pain for that matter.

"I have access to illegal substances that I trade directly with the Court of Farindor. And I happen to have ingredients that witches and necromancers require for certain portal spells to and from Midriel." The herbalist paused. "Or I did. Before they came by and destroyed my shop. I managed to stay out of sight of the High Council of Aideil through protective wards made by channeling your magik through wormwood and esthyri. It made me invisible, as it did with you."

"You stole my magik?" Eyolin's head reeled. She wanted to vomit. She had learned that wormwood nullified her magik, but didn't realize it could be redirected somewhere else. Was that what esthyri did?

"Channeled its raw energy, not stole. It was a simple enough spell, and I did you a favor. You did not yet have a gem to control the power you possess, and you wanted to stay out of the High Council's claws. You wanted to remain unGifted and ordinary. I kept you safe."

"You're a witch." It came out more accusatory than Eyolin wanted.

"To be an herbalist with my clientele, I know of witchcraft, but am not a witch. I only cast through your magik to keep us safe."

"You knew I was Gifted. Why didn't you sell me like one of your trinkets?" It was unfair, Eyolin knew, to be demanding answers as the woman lay dying before her.

"You were a loyal worker—until you disappeared and left me scrambling to maintain my inventory. I looked for you, you know. No one could pick up your scent for days. I had all my little creatures keeping an eye out. If you were dead, they would have found your body, so I knew someone was hiding you, just as I had done. That is until a particular syket blinked into my shop to inquire about the size of clothes she should put in your dresser in the Great Hall. You can imagine my surprise when I discovered my apprentice was being locked away by the Master Scariyai of Aideil."

Guilt, in all its glory, was a wicked thing. Eyolin had left the herbalist without a word, judging incorrectly that she would go on with her life as if her apprentice never existed.

"I wasn't locked anywhere," Eyolin replied. "I had a deal to train with the master."

"On what, exactly?" The herbalist looked far too pleased to be that close to death.

Eyolin hesitated. The herbalist had just admitted to crimes against Aideil, using witchcraft, and stealing her magik—a power that Eyolin didn't know how to wield herself. For the past weeks she hadn't questioned learning morphling magik as anything more than a steppingstone to something greater. But she was starting to realize that she didn't know anything at all.

"Ah," the herbalist murmured. "You forgot to doubt. So caught up with being wanted for something that you didn't see their true intentions until it was too late."

"What *do* they want?" Eyolin pressed the bandage down, the poultice oozing over the edges and through the cloth.

"Which one?"

Eyolin froze. "What do you mean, which one? Master Arendt?"

The herbalist chuckled. The laugh brought a dribble of blood leaking from the corner of her mouth. "The poor man tried resisting once. To protect you, I imagine. Now he is nothing. Scrounging at any scrap of power. If the dark one has his way, the old master will never see the light of day again."

"Magnogogue?" Suddenly Eyolin was gripping the shredded bits of apron.

The herbalist winced. "I refer to the demon Magnogogue is trying to catch."

Footsteps pounded through the walls, followed by voices coming from the pub.

"Eyolin, you need to go. Now."

Chapter Twenty-Four

The pitcher of mead was nearly empty. Kipp nursed his mug in the corner of the dark inn he frequented whenever he got a moment alone from training his four little Grey initiates.

His blood boiled, furious from the words scrawled on the crinkled parchment in front of him. Jet's correspondence gave him the notion that the Twilight was tipping toward chaos while Kipp had been removed to Alagana to tend to a babysitting assignment. The upset of power in his absence had sent the Grey spiraling and still the Regent didn't call him back.

Worse was that Kipp was no closer to locating the witch who held the Book of Bindings. If things continued this way, he might have to storm the Pipassê and take the Regency by force. Jet was struggling to keep their ranks together in light of the creatures continuing to drip through the cracks from Midriel. They needed Kipp. His grip on the limitless Twilight magik he drew upon as the Second was waning with every passing day he didn't get that book. Soon, his position would be passed off to another and his primary avenue of channeling from the Twilight would disappear.

He felt it in his bones. His magik was breaking, just as the Regent said. He needed to Bind it back together, or any hope of reclaiming command of the Grey would slip away. Unless he found his client and demanded he be replaced by another.

Mead sloshed at the bottom of the pitcher. Kipp sniffed the flat amber liquid distastefully. It resembled the waves of Eyolin's magik that flowed through his stomach every day feeling like vomit that he couldn't quite get out. He'd been doing his best to shut out the influence her magik had on him—what with attempting to teach Balla and Jorrith how to effectively walk between the folds of space.

Alcohol allowed him to consider how the two of them were connected, alone in that inn with no one to bother him. It wasn't Binding magik, or any witchcraft he was aware of. Necromancy wasn't out of the question but extracting the essence of magik from one Gifted being and chaining it to another was darker a practice than many would dare attempt. His magikal battery was too innocent to be involved with the level of demonic power it would take for that. The witch in Aldeyn alluded to a mother who wanted Eyolin, someone who could raise the dead and instill youth. That was who he should be looking for.

He hadn't tested if it affected Eyolin the same way—if he could somehow pluck the strings that connected them to manipulate her Gift the way his magik flared every time she channeled. If he kept the hounds off her scent for a few more days, he would get the chance to ask her.

No Gift of magik matched the imprint of Eyolin's either. Not in any book or annul. It was elemental—not the skill set of the scarox or beiythron. The aura that surrounded her crackled with a power that should not exist. And she couldn't manipulate any of it.

Kipp reached for the empty pitcher, dry as a bone.

A fresh mug clunked onto the table.

"Miss me?"

Erik slid into the seat across from Kipp, who lifted his head to meet the eyes of his friend. The targisha Grey assassin looked the same as when Kipp had left him in the streets of the city cutting through frae and other demonic creatures stuck in the Twilight realm.

"You got Jet's letter," Erik murmured. He nodded at the ball of paper wadded on the table soaking up sloshed mead.

"Didn't have the balls to mention your assignment yourself?" Kipp grumbled. The mead was hitting him stronger than usual, attributed to his lack of dinner.

"My client has me on a tight leash." Erik shrugged. "I only caught wind of you this morning when some kid with big ears mistook me for you."

"Clearly those boys need to learn to keep their mouths shut." Kipp's tone was harsh, and he didn't miss the flash of hurt on Erik's face. His friend should know better than to encroach on another Grey on assignment. The very suggestion that Erik knew of Kipp's four protégés was dangerous, despite decades of camaraderie between them. They were to be the key to taking over the Grey and controlling the creatures who lived in the Twilight. Now the competition knew of them.

"I would've found them anyway, Kipp. You holed them up in the one house that sits on top of a vein of magik sourced straight from Keystones. Even I felt drawn to it."

"Did you at least secure the Pipassê before you waltzed into my domain?"

"I don't think you have domain anymore, Kipp. The Regent's naming me Second once I finish my assignment."

"Clearly they've lost sight of what power is if you're to steal what is mine."

If Kipp had been sober, he would've killed his friend where he stood. But his mind swirled with grief instead. Erik had timed his arrival well.

"If I didn't take this case, they would've sent someone else." Erik propped his elbows up on the table. A film of flour dusted his dark sleeves. "Someone who isn't as sympathetic to you as I am."

Something about Erik's tone nagged at him. There was something off. Grey didn't practice empathy, especially with the Regency on the line.

"Now why would you be sympathetic if you're after the same thing as me?"

Erik didn't miss a beat. "We're working the same kingdom. The same politics and people. I don't want you to step on my toes and ruin this for me. You're already out. I intend to take up the mantle."

Kipp's skin prickled. His magik pulsed to the rhythm of his heart, torn between hating Erik and knowing he would have done the same.

"Why did you come here, Erik?"

"I needed one last look at you, my mentor and friend, before all this shit catches up to us. What Jet said in his letter was only half the truth." Erik took a long drag of mead, handing it to Kipp after. "You found me and gave me purpose. I never thanked you for that, and I ask for your forgiveness for when our paths cross again."

"If you lay a single finger on my target..." Kipp paused to finish the mead. "I will show you exactly how much I never taught you."

"She's quite pretty, that one." Erik called for another pitcher. "I can't say I wasn't a little excited to finally bump heads with you on assignment."

"Pity to waste all that baking potential."

Erik cracked his neck. He was fidgeting. Nervous. Good.

"You sure there's nothing I can do to get you on my team, Aisolon?"

Kipp sneered into the amber liquid as he said, "I wouldn't bother with the likes of you anyway. I've got all the help I need, and you're the last backstabbing leech I'd ever go to."

"Good to see you still love me, Aisolon." Erik pushed off the table. He was still rubbing his sleeve between two fingers, though his face was a cold mask.

"You sure there's nothing else you want to tell me?" Kipp asked.

Erik leveled a look at Kipp that was charged with everything but sorrow.

"I'll see you soon."

Chapter Twenty-Five

P anic seized Eyolin, her eyes glued to the hidden door of the shop. She needed to move.

The herbalist's breaths came shorter and shorter until Eyolin had to strain to hear the wheeze of air trickling out of her lungs. *Come on,* she told herself. There were seconds, if that, before whoever was after her broke down that door and killed both of them. At least if Eyolin wasn't there, the herbalist might be able to talk her way out of certain death.

"Get out of here, Eyolin. What are you waiting for?" It must have taken the herbalist every ounce of strength to say those words and the pain was visible in the old woman's trembling lip.

Wood groaned under countless boots in the pub.

Get up, little Sarom. The voice Eyolin associated with her magik whispered. *Get up and run.*

Instead, she dipped her arm underneath the herbalist, bracing her back to support the herbalist's bleeding body.

"Come on, let's get you out of here."

Eyolin pulled the woman to her feet. She was dead weight as she shook her head, a sad smile playing at her features.

"You were always meant to get out when the time was right."

"Where am I supposed to go?" Eyolin choked, the sob lodged in her throat. She should have never left the shop. She was no better than Arden abandoning them when they needed her most.

The herbalist planted her feet on the floor, detaching herself from Eyolin's grip. Her wrinkled hand was brown with dried blood where it pressed against the wall.

"Do you have your foraging kit handy?"

Eyolin nodded absently, not pausing to wonder if the small pouch with rations was still where she left it. She couldn't focus. Everything was swirling and pitching. The footsteps were right outside the hidden door behind the tapestry. Could they smell her from the other side of the wall?

"Go get it. And don't look back." The herbalist slid under Eyolin's arm and sank to the floor with a certain finality.

Eyolin was just up the broken staircase when the hidden door shattered inward from a blast. She fumbled around the debris that used to be her room until her hand closed around a familiar leather satchel.

As her feet carried her through the window of the attic, she glanced back.

She shouldn't have.

Eyolin hit the ground at a sprint, running as fast as her heartbeat.

Her cowardice took her to the human districts on the ground, weaving through the streets that once offered safety. Now every shadow screeched and clawed at her.

The clothes on her back were still torn from the fight with Maximus, not having had time to change after making it back to the Great Hall. If the humans she passed wondered at the blood-covered elf sprinting through their district, she didn't look close enough to tell.

Without any forethought, she found herself on the doorstep of the dwarvish spinner.

She was on the verge of hyperventilation when the stout dwarf with a rust-colored beard hanging to his kneecaps peeled back the curtain of a door. He would surely turn her away. She was covered in dirt and blood, looking ghastly.

Shouts of soldiers bounced off the stone buildings and Eyolin threw a pleading look at the spinner.

"In, girl. Quickly." He rolled his eyes and made a point to avoid touching her, backing to the wall as Eyolin stumbled over the threshold.

He coaxed Eyolin to a cushion near the fire. Eyolin heard locks clicking in place followed by the now familiar hum of magik. The spinner was putting up wards. Again, a tiny voice warned her of danger. He may be protecting them from discovery, but also preventing her from escaping.

Words eluded her save for three, "They killed her."

The dwarvish spinner hissed her silent, his ear pressed to the door that she hadn't seen shut. His door was always open. It wasn't now.

He stayed that way until the muffled shouts died and the only sound was a crack of a log in the fireplace. Eyolin watched the spinner approach her and hold out a hand. She eyed it quizzically before noting his gaze set on the satchel at her side. She peeked inside and found it full of rykes—gold rykes. Those certainly weren't hers, making the image of the herbalist's mutilation as she ran that much worse.

She had no use for such money anymore. Any hope of purchasing a home in Mainwood was gone. Her mentor was killed from mere affiliation. Now she owed a greedy dwarf any chance she had of buying her way to a new life. It was almost laughable.

Eyolin transferred the rykes to the spinner's hand. Immediately his countenance changed, eyes lighting up excitedly.

He kept quiet as he dabbed the blood off her face. Of course, he would help her for the amount she'd transferred to his pockets.

The interaction was swift and rough—exactly what she expected. Somehow, she'd known that she would be relatively safe in his care, though she wished he hadn't sniffed out gold she hadn't even had a chance to count.

Distracted, Eyolin lifted her arms to the side for him to measure. The spinner grunted and waddled over to a stuffed dresser. Within minutes Eyolin was dressed in a drab, unassuming tunic and pant set.

"Ready to move?"

Eyolin blinked in confusion. The dwarf looked like he wanted to smack her.

"Do you want out of this city, or should we call the elves with their pointy blades back here to throw you in the cells beneath the Great Hall?"

It dawned on her that he wasn't just a dwarvish spinner, trading songs spun with magik to enchant his listeners with history. Her reports she sold went somewhere. She was about to find out how.

"You're a smuggler."

"And you thought we were friends why? Because you sold me secrets a wise woman would never tell?" He tipped his head to her in a shallow bow that looked more mocking than respectful. "You have powerful enemies looking for you, but stronger allies."

He didn't elaborate further. Eyolin's mind worked in circles. She had no friends of that caliber—not any left alive. But there was that sliver of doubt that made her think of the voice in her head that was so distinctly not her own that flared when she dove into the moontear's power. Of how the Grey always seemed to be there when she needed him. The syket who warded her room in the Great Hall. She had been so caught up in drowning out the pain of her past that she hadn't stepped back and truly seen the saviors tucked in the shadows.

"Ready to run?"

Eyolin shifted in the scratchy material and nodded. The dwarf pulled the fireplace in. The entire metal grating, fire and all, turned on a concealed gear. It opened to a dark tunnel that put every hair on Eyolin's neck on end.

"Keep straight in the tunnels, no matter what you hear. It leads right under a gap in the wards surrounding the city."

Eyolin took a wary step into the tunnel. The walls were damp and the air musty.

"I'd ask what I owe you, but you already took all my money."

The dwarvish spinner winked at her and pushed the fireplace back into place.

It was hours before Eyolin pushed her way out of a hidden entrance beneath a thick bush. The day had turned to night and the clothes borrowed from the spinner felt horribly thin.

She couldn't see the lights of Mainwood, so she trusted her gut and set off in what she thought was the opposite direction. The events of the day haunted her—from the Gifted elvish girl whose skin cracked with molten power to Dale crumpled in the center of the arena. The herbalist's body run through so many times it was morbidly comical. Then the help of a dwarf to a girl who had sold him words perhaps a dozen times.

She hadn't seen Traik among the bodies that had swarmed the shop, but the gold helmets of the Aideillian army were unmistakable. Whatever he and the master were planning would bring the entire realm to its knees, that she was certain of.

Everything she had thought would provide her with safety and a future worthy of her father's title had been upturned within the course of hours. For a race that lived for centuries, the elves sure knew how to flip the trajectory of Fate.

A stag leapt out of the brush sending Eyolin stumbling into the harsh bushes. It looked at her curiously, pawing at the ground with a hoof rather than spiriting away.

The moontear warmed as Eyolin expanded her mental field. Brushing against the familiar werekey wall of teeth, Eyolin could have fallen to her knees in relief.

Karok tipped his antlers and motioned for her to follow.

They sprinted through the forest: a stag and an elf side by side. As the forest deepened, the truth hit her. Eyolin had left the only city she ever knew, abandoned the human who had befriended her, and now ran alongside a man as much an outcast as her. And she wouldn't go back.

The night deepened until the forest was cast in violet and the birds had ceased singing. Eyolin and Karok stopped only when she could no longer see an arm's length in front of her.

A ripple of magik washed over Eyolin and Karok knelt at her side. Neither had spoken during the flight from Mainwood.

"They came for you, too, I take it?" His warm voice was enough to bring tears to Eyolin's eyes and she was glad it was so dark.

"There's nowhere for me to go."

It was an understatement. Saying it out loud reminded her how alone she was in the world.

"I'm headed the same way. Lucky I caught your scent when you passed through the wards, otherwise I might have missed you."

"Don't," Eyolin said, the chill creeping into her bones. "You aren't my instructor anymore, you can go." *Go*, was what she wanted to say. *Please, I can't have you die for me too.*

"Now where would a lowly beta like me go without my alpha?"

Eyolin coughed a rough laugh. "Well, you're released from me. You have my blessing or whatever."

"Nice try, love. You've been through some shit, but you've got to stop playing the pity card. I've seen the strength in the way you show up, day after day. You don't quit. And there's power in that. You have been gifted the opportunity to find out where you fit in this cursed world, outside the safety of this kingdom, a gift not many see through."

Eyolin followed Karok around a creek.

"I'm sorry." For everything. For ruining his position in Aideil, and with Tequerra. For wasting his time with her. For forcing him to save her in the arena. "You shouldn't have thrown away everything on me."

"Way I see it, you saved me from a bargain I made at my weakest. Aideil was never meant to hold me—only provide me answers. It stole four years from me when I could never leave. Until you came along."

It was all Eyolin could do to keep walking. She had never viewed Karok as someone who would stick by her—only as the first instructor of many. She had been wrong about so many things, she wondered what else could surprise her.

"Do we know where we're going?" she asked.

"I like that *we*. And I do. I know of someone who might know a thing or two about your Shoutka predicament."

"I don't have a predicament," Eyolin retorted. "I just don't have one or I'd have figured it out by now."

"You can gloat if I'm wrong." The prickling of energy signaled that Karok had morphed again. He finished speaking inside her mind. *Or go back to Master Arendt. I'm sure he'd be willing to put you under similar restrictions as me. But what do I know? It was only a couple of years before I broke free.*

Chapter Twenty-Six

K arok in stag form pranced into the water of a shallow river a few hours from sunrise. Moonlight glinted off the surface, a rare beam of light illuminating the forest in hues of frosty blue. Eyolin could just make out a road overgrown with weeds stretching into the distance. She hadn't found the energy to morph into a creature after the shock of the herbalist's shop. The use of magik made the loss of her mentor feel infinitely worse.

A branch slapped at her face and scraped her arms where she tried to deflect it. She hadn't attempted to cross the water yet, opting to navigate along the bank until it looked shallow enough to wade through.

You know, you could save us days of walking if you cared to morph into something a bit more mobile.

Eyolin was already getting fed up with Karok's nagging. "Are you ready to tell me where we're going yet?"

We've been walking for less than a night, love. Every minute we spend on the ground is another minute we give whatever Aideillian forces they send out after you a chance to catch your scent, which, may I add, is very distinctive. It's like honey if honey were shat out and put in a ham sandwich to be left out for a month.

Karok's stag reached the other side of the creek and tapped a hoof impatiently.

"I can clear it just as well on two legs as you can on four."

Oh, certainly, Karok said in her mind. *But you could save yourself the wet socks.*

Eyolin, hungry and exhausted, grumbled, "Not everything has to be done with magik."

The stag morphed into a crow. Karok flapped over to Eyolin, landing on her shoulder. She took a step into the river, the water a temperature that put her senses on high alert.

"If you shit on me," Eyolin mumbled. "I will pull out your tail feathers."

The crow—Karok—swiveled its head to look at its sleek black feathers fondly. Eyolin waded deeper until the water was up to her chest.

Instinct told her to look back.

Squinting into the forest was futile, but there were eyes on her, that much she knew. Though they weren't visible, Eyolin and Karok were being watched.

Eyolin leaned against the current, pushing to get to the opposite bank. She was making slow progress.

Karok's crow bristled uncomfortably, its head swiveling around. Eyolin stilled her breathing, focusing on the silver moonlit water. Any sounds of an approaching foe were drowned out by the rushing of the river.

A deep rumbling rose in the crow's chest. Karok commanded, *Run. Now, go.*

Karok's crow rocketed upward as an arrow whistled over Eyolin's shoulder, aimed for where the crow had perched. The shaft embedded itself into a tree across the creek. Eyolin's moontear snapped to attention, inadvertently drawing energy from the forest, siphoning the life from the earth and foliage. The energy converted into the now familiar warmth of unshaped magik. Her mind mirrored Karok's wings and she morphed in a flurry of feathers.

Her falcon form transformed the landscape into a blend of temperatures and hyper clarity. She was moving faster than she could fathom, but her surroundings never blurred. Karok must've been somewhere above the tree line.

Eyolin strained to maintain the aerial form. The wave of adrenaline provided by the arrow was fading fast and she hadn't had a moment's rest in over a day.

There was a break in the canopy, flooding the forest with light from the full moon. Eyolin pumped her wings hard, wincing at the aching in her back. She broke through the trees and out of range of arrows—directly into the jaws of a demon of darkness.

The moon vanished in the face of a night that swallowed the sky and all its glittering stars. It flowed thick as blood and shuddered with hunger. Pearly white teeth snapped from the heart of the mist, and it was all Eyolin could do to bank out of the way and hover in the space beneath it. Nights spent memorizing monsters in her assigned readings let her identify the kaizor, straight from the pages of Midriel.

She didn't have time to question how it got there, or what crack in the realms it seeped through. The smog of the kaizor's body took away thought, its very being an abyss that fed off magik and life.

Eyolin was utterly trapped—from above and below.

To return to the forest would allow her falcon form to lose the kaizor in the trees. While agile, flying beneath the canopy exposed her to an assault from the soldiers on the ground. Choosing to be prey gave her airspace to outrun those navigating the dense underbrush.

Mist swirled around the monster, reminding Eyolin that she had moments before the kaizor attacked.

Blood red eyes blinked open and a rancid waft of dark magik stung her nostrils as the kaizor inhaled. The twisted halo of black bubbled and spit where it touched the air. Eyolin watched in horror as the leaves and branches closest to the kaizor wilted and rotted.

Meanwhile, whoever hunted her from the ground rustled through the brush hurriedly, every step amplified by her falcon form. The falcon assessed the threat, identifying at least a dozen figures. There were mere moments before either attacked.

The falcon form, while lethal in its own right, was not built to withstand the forces pressing in. She needed something bigger. Anatomical sketches and diagrams stitched together as Eyolin spun around in a steeply banked circle. The static of the shift distorted the air and she fed it all the strength she had. Smooth blue scales that reflected their midnight surroundings rippled down a sleek neck and torso. There were no wings to keep her in the air, but still the aguarot-caea slithered through the night sky.

Eyolin's serpentine body twisted and coiled to the side, narrowly avoiding the lunging maw of the kaizor. The dark sources of the kaizor's power hissed to attention, seeking to absorb the dragon's magik for its own and satiate its endless hunger.

The aguarot-caea spun in a circle to assess any flaws in the shift. Eyolin's elongated teeth glinted in satisfaction when a ring of water formed around the smooth body, the wetness gliding over her scales. The moisture in the air was hers to mold as she wished.

The sound of a drawn bowstring—of many bows—brought Eyolin's attention down. Soldiers in golden caged helmets were lined up with their weapons aimed at her. Aideillian soldiers. So many of them, their merciless sights set on her.

She released a snarl and fed the water magik her flaring feelings of betrayal. They murdered the herbalist and now hunted her like an animal, despite the looming threat of the kaizor. The small ring of water swelled into a tempest. The droplets sent the kaizor into a howling frenzy where the water splattered against its dark mist. It dawned on her that a creature of Midriel could be weak against water—the natural opposite of the fiery realm it was raised in. That was the only advantage she had. Her hurricane spit with energy to match the kaizor and deflect the barbed arrows arching into the sky.

The dark demon from Midriel unleashed a wave of power, tendrils licking toward her. The dragon spun and flicked away, taking the tempest with her, and she countered with blasts of water that exploded from the snapping of her jaw.

The Aideillian archers withdrew and Eyolin watched with a sinking realization that there were scariyai in their midst. She knew that where an arrow might fail, their magik would not.

Orbs of magik flickered like miniature suns of varying colors. The archers dipped their arrowheads in the magik and stood behind iridescent shields that rose to block any fallout. Distantly, Eyolin thought of the beiythron in their smithies and labs engineering weapons. From what she deduced from the herbalist, the esthioryn was among the most dangerous of these experiments. Those arrows were no exception and would pierce any magikal barrier she raised, the energy tipping them as good as poison.

The kaizor continued to push her closer to the tree line, each wave of dark energy stronger than the last. It sensed her weakening state. Every moment she stayed in the massive aguarot-caea form drained her. Split between navigating the air and maintaining the fading water shield—Eyolin wouldn't last much longer.

A burgundy-tipped arrow whizzed past her, narrowly missing her scaled hide. Distracted, Eyolin never sensed the telepathic attack of the kaizor until it was already crushing her mind.

Memories flashed against her mind, trapping her mental field inside her own mind. Any control over her morphing magik vanished as the kaizor took her will. Every ounce of sorrow extracted in an agonizing jerk, the last of her strength leaving with it. She tried to throw the kaizor from her mind, but her control had already diminished to a dull pulse.

The aguarot-caea plummeted from the sky and through the jagged, dead canopy. She couldn't see through the eyes of the dragon anymore but felt the impact into a forked branch that scattered her blue scales across the forest floor.

Out of direct sight, the kaizor lost control over her mind. Eyolin expected to snap into her elvish form, but her body had taken too much damage. Silver-hued blood dribbled from where the bark punctured the hide, her dragon form bent at incorrect angles.

Eyolin squirmed against the wood. Where was her magik? She reached for the kernel of light that sat in the center of her soul—nothing. She recoiled from the monstrous roar that rattled the night sky.

Above, the kaizor circled. Below, she waited for the scariyai's magik to splinter through her heart.

She was injured, trapped, and yet no one was attacking.

Hooves snapped through leaves and the soldiers on the ground parted. The scariyai with their shields and orbs retreated. A sole horseman raised a crossbow, aimed at Eyolin's neck.

If she had been in elvish form, she wouldn't have picked up on the distinct scent of the horseman. As it was, every nerve went on high alert. Not from the crossbow. From the man. Her dragon form snapped its jaws, the fanned ears flattening against her head.

Maximus.

She threw everything she had into dislodging from the tree. Anything to escape the scarox's range. A ball of water pooled at her nose. Eyolin urged it to swell with energy and grow. In tandem, the kaizor raised its own mass of dark magik.

Both creatures released their respective magiks at the same time Maximus fired. Eyolin tensed, waiting for the impact that would cut through her neck. It never came. He hadn't even been aiming at her.

Her ring of water shredded through the trees, deflecting by the wave of darkness, the energy washed by her without harming a scale. The same could not be said for the two rows of Aideillian soldiers.

Scariyai braced behind their transparent energy shields. Their gemstones glowed with the channeling of their Gifts. But the kaizor's attack was stronger.

Upon impact, the scariyai were flattened to the earth, their life forces whisked upward in plumes of smoke. A few archers stumbled back, blindly shooting magikally enhanced arrows at the kaizor. Eyolin had been forgotten in the face of the demon. She still had a chance to get away. If she could ever break free from that damned tree.

The kaizor loosed a screech as arrow after arrow sank into its shrouded form. Even demons felt pain.

As Eyolin struggled, her eyes were drawn to movement by none other than Maximus. The commander drew twin blades, his eyes fixed on the sky above Eyolin, where the kaizor bled ash and night. The flecks coated the ground, slick where it mingled with the lingering water.

Maximus crouched in the sludge, twin blades poised to decapitate. To kill. Despite the splintering pain that laced her existence, Eyolin was struck by how gracefully the curved blades suited him. He did not exude the arrogance or hatred she had grown accustomed to. No, the red glint around the rim of his irises was the scarox magik he channeled. She did not know the depth of his Gift, only the certainty that he was an apex predator, staring down a demon with nothing but lethal intent.

The elves under his command lay scattered behind him. Those without a Gift sunk inward, their skin ashen in death. The scariyai fared only slightly better in the aftermath of the kaizor's mass slaughter. Maximus secured a foothold in the mud and glared at the kaizor through the thin slits of his helmet.

He stared the kaizor down with such intent that Eyolin truly believed that, when the demon withdrew into the night sky, it was from the pure violence in the commander's eyes.

Without the kaizor to take the brunt force of the scarox's attention, Maximus turned to Eyolin, viewing the aguarot-caea beast as one might a stray dog who bit a child. The rest of the company was in no shape to kill a dragon. But Maximus was.

Maximus slid into his stance just as the branch snapped under Eyolin's weight, using the intuitive instinct he activated through his skull pendant.

Flowing with the momentum of the fall, Eyolin angled herself into a spiraling dive. Her aguarot-caea form twisted, avoiding Maximus' sweeping blades, and wrapped her tail around his right arm to bring down his guard. With that same motion, Eyolin rammed her thick neck into his back. She was bigger this time and had every motivation to inflict as much damage on the man who had beaten her so publicly and haunted her in private.

Maximus sprawled into the slick ashen ground. His swords clattered into a bush.

A crossbow clicked into gear at her back.

Eyolin had been so lustful for revenge that she failed to register the scariyai at her back, hand raised, levitating an armed crossbow. More soldiers emerged from the brush. More, she realized, than had initially led the assault. An entire squad encircled her in moments, each step in sync.

Dread crippled her anger. They had watched a dragon attack their commander. And had her trapped.

Bows raised, each with arrows tipped with the greens, reds, and blues of the scariyai's magik. The same enchantment that had frightened off the kaizor, if not killed it. The scariyai who had survived raised a solid shield with their other fist pulled to their chests. Each unique Gift manifested around their knuckles in preparation for an execution. It didn't matter if she was Eyolin or an aguarot-caea dragon. She was a threat.

"Hold your fire," Maximus commanded. Eyolin, unable to magik her way into the skies, snaked into a tight ball as far away from the commander as she could while avoiding the sizzling shield.

"Fall back." Maximus' mouth twisted into a smirk. "I'll dispatch of the beast myself."

He feinted to the side, swooping up the discarded twin blades and in the same motion flung one at Eyolin. The steel pierced the scales and muscle of the aguarot-caea's tail, buried to the hilt. Eyolin couldn't even roar before Maximus drove the second sword up in a clean arc. Agony crackled out of her throat in a jagged cry as the tip cut up her spine, a bleeding gash blooming in its wake.

The sword in her tail pinned her. The blade in his hand dripped with her metallic blood.

"No wings to fly," Maximus observed. He dragged the flat of the blade up her belly.

Eyolin made one last attempt at reclaiming her elvish body to no avail. She wouldn't die as a Silver Elf—but a monster of her own creation. All she could manage were animalistic spasms of anger like that of a cornered cat.

The woods cleared of the legion. They were more than confident that their scarox commander had a pinned dragon under control.

"Did you eat the little elvish girl?"

Silver blood gurgled in her throat. She wouldn't be conscious for much longer. Eyolin lashed out, her jaws snapping at air. Maximus only chuckled.

"I could kill you," he mused. "But there is a legend with your kind. One where, by sparing your life in the face of death, you owe me a debt." He cocked his head. "Is that true? Are you truly intelligent enough to know when you are beaten?"

Eyolin hissed and snarled as he approached. She tugged against the sword in her tail, the pain blinding. She tried reaching it with her teeth.

"You are intelligent enough to spar like an opponent would, I'll give you that."

The scarox drew a short dagger and dragged it along her scales. The tip reached the long gash across her back. Eyolin threw every ounce of energy into freeing herself from that damned dragon form to no avail.

"Will you honor the bond of magik that links you to me? Will you answer when I call?"

A ridiculous request. He was mad.

Like hell I do, Eyolin spat. From the look on his face, she realized she'd spoken directly into his mind. Maximus had never heard her speak before—he didn't know her voice.

"A female," he said. He removed his helmet with a touch to the side releasing the mechanism. "I never knew you could speak." He pointed the dagger at her forehead. "Bow to me, caea."

Her aguarot-caea's lips curled over slender, pointed teeth. A guttural growl rumbled in her throat, and she felt her Gift stir, stemming from the last emotion left within her. Hatred. It sharpened her power into a point. Every fiber of her body locked onto the commander's body. She would destroy him, reduce him to less than air. As Fox's friend, he had cost her an apprenticeship. As a man, he had violated her. As a commander, he had beaten her from the respect of an army. Even now he sought to enslave her in a new form.

Her body glowed white, the scales illuminating with magik that flowered from the hatred in her heart. This time, she did not swallow it down. Quelling her power had betrayed her thus far. There was one certainty left. To wield magik was to reap destruction. And she wanted to obliterate the man with a knife to her head.

Magik flowed through her, hot as lightning.

Maximus backed up a step. She saw the haughtiness of the scarox commander slip. In its place... concern.

"What made you like this, caea?"

He lowered the dagger to the blood-soaked earth, standing again with his hands raised. She might have thought about the spectacle of a water dragon wielding anything other than tides and oceans. Might have cared that blood and smoke seared the inside of the form she was trapped in. Might have worried about mixing the elemental magiks if it didn't feel so good.

"Easy," he said, reaching a hand toward her.

A black ball of fur and teeth crashed into the commander, the brush of his fingertips lingering on her neck. The mass of an animal dragged the scarox into the brush and out of sight. Shock snapped her out of the rage she clung to. The veins of the aguarot-caea form dried where electricity and fire had seared through them. Hatred could only take her so far. The blade in her tail. The gash on her back...

The pressure ebbed.

Eyolin's head snapped to her left. The pain and dizziness vanished with the removal of the steel from her body.

"Just follow the howls of death and screams of battle to find you curled up in a bloody heap on the forest floor. I don't know why I'm surprised, princess." Dale tossed Maximus' sword to the side and caught Eyolin's large, blue head as she collapsed.

"Come on, up you go," his voice coaxed. Dale pushed the scaly dragon head up, cradling her.

"She can't handle the shift," Karok's honey-glazed voice said. He knelt next to the long wound in Eyolin's back. "We need this mended, and quickly."

"I delivered your message. Am I supposed to be the escort as well?" Dale's voice was short and snappy.

"If you did as you were supposed to, where is she?"

Eyolin coiled the aguarot-caea dragon's serpentine body in on itself. The numbing effects of fatigue settled in. She wasn't alone. She was safe. Dale was there. Karok had come back. She could rest now.

Chapter Twenty-Seven

K ipp woke to a knife at his throat.

The moldy bed creaked under the weight of a second body. "Is this where you meet all your girls?"

The voice chimed like bells. A jingle he recognized well.

"Countess de la Luna." He'd fallen asleep at the inn, too drunk to make it back to the estate. "Is now the moment you profess your undying love to the lonely soldier?"

"You're no more a soldier than I am a bat," she scoffed.

Kipp risked opening his eyes. Luna was clad in her signature leather jumpsuit, black hair slicked into a skin-pulling bun. Her curled lip marred an otherwise pretty human face.

"You're out of your lane, Grey."

She withdrew the blade from his neck, and he got a better look at her. Last time he saw Luna, she'd been little more than a stab-happy moody young woman following her sister Mariah around, or Countess de la Lynn as she was known now. The years had filled out her leathers at least and Kipp would have liked her to keep the blade to his chin a moment longer if it meant she continued straddling him.

"I'm a lucky man to be so popular this early in the morning," Kipp said with a stretch. He gestured to the room. "As you can see, I'm on holiday."

"Any recollection in that small male brain of yours of a witch in Aldeyn? Ugly and old type."

Kipp shrugged. He was naked beneath the thin bedsheet and made a show of shifting the sheet down as he sat up. The motion pushed Luna to the edge of the mattress, her hand drifting to what was no doubt a hidden sheath. "I didn't think you were so insecure. You know I only like my girls branded." He nodded to Luna's tattooed wrist. The Sister quickly covered her order's symbol.

"She was one of Lady Weiy's contacts. When she didn't deliver, a group of us were sent to investigate why."

The mead from the evening pounded through his head. Kipp shot a sliver of magik through his body to nullify any lingering effects. The knife under his pillow could be reached if the Sister made a move.

"And what did you discover?"

"Two Grey lurking in Aldeyn. A dead witch. And rumors of a new Sarom in Mainwood."

Kipp slid a relaxed had behind his head to be within range of his knife. "There's hardly anything connecting the three, so I ask again: are you here to satisfy more than an itch? Or is this an official notice?"

"Your Grey companion marked the door for us. Seems like your cadre have finally turned you over to our hands."

"How very capable those hands are."

A blade shot out of Luna's sleeve, jumping into her hand. "He didn't want you anywhere near Mainwood in the coming days. But from the look of you..." Luna sniffed, no doubt smelling the mead on him. "I don't think you're a threat to anyone anymore."

"But you don't believe that." Kipp mulled over the intel she had given him, inadvertently exposing Erik's interest in Mainwood. For Erik to have alerted the Sister put the two organizations under the direction of a single client.

"I know what you are," Luna said, her voice low.

"Smart girl." Kipp felt for the handle of the dagger. His fingers wrapped around it as he sat forward. The bedsheet fell away, and he brought his face within a breath of the countess, his own dagger dancing at her throat. She didn't so much as flinch as the cool metal touched her trachea.

"I need to know what your involvement is in Aideil. And how much you need to get out of it."

"That's a poor excuse to sneak into my bed, Luna," he purred.

She recoiled from the name with a hiss. "You reek of demons and mead."

"Never stopped you before." Kipp uncorked the invisible power that manipulated the folds of space, seeping his magik into every crevice. He dragged a phantom finger down the Sister's back. There was no small amount of pleasure watching Luna fight from leaning into him.

"You will lose, Kipp Aisolon, if you continue to be a player in this game."

Kipp looked her over slowly, mulling over his words, and reveling in how quickly he could kill her or slide her into his lap.

"Who says we're playing the same game?"

"You want her," she said. Luna pressed into the dagger until her lips ghosted over his. "How badly do you want to keep the Sarom girl alive?"

Kipp planted a hand next to Luna's thigh. "And what makes you think I want you less?"

"You insult me, Aisolon."

"I've done much more than that." Kipp conjured a seraph blade into his other hand.

Luna's mouth twitched. "You're dead."

The Sister withdrew from the bed and the edges of his blades. Within two strides, the door closed behind her.

Kipp fell back onto the mattress. His body was fully awake. Itching. Alive. Images of his target and her intoxicating power mixed with the physical closeness of the Countess de la Luna. He slipped his hands back beneath the sheets and closed his eyes, reveling in what his mind created. He'd have to work on getting closer to Eyolin before long.

He didn't get too far before realizing he couldn't feel the tug of the girl's magik. He sat up, heartbeat racing. Even when she hadn't explicitly used her Gift, he had felt her, like a nagging itch. Everything was quiet. Too still. Empty.

Where was the girl?

* * *

"Drink."

Eyolin's nose wrinkled at the mug held in her face. Her consciousness swam through the dark recesses of her mind as the dream of the Grey assassin faded.

Icy hands brushed her stomach. A cool sensation spread through her body, tingling as it passed through her heart. Shivers sent goosebumps down her arms. Her eyelids still refused to open.

The hands on her hardened. Nails dug into the soft flesh of her abdomen. Eyolin arched off the surface she lay on. Her mind screamed where her mouth could not. White, red, agony. The pain ebbed and her spine flattened.

A similar sensation dragged her to and from consciousness repeatedly, stitching together each fiber of her body. She didn't stay above a dream state for longer than a few minutes. If the treatments lasted longer, she had no way to gauge it.

Minutes or days could have passed by the time Eyolin's mind snapped taut and catapulted her body into a gasping fit. Her muscles were sore but lacked the overwhelming pain she had grown accustomed to. At first, the scene was blurry, her surroundings a slurry of browns. Then her vision cleared.

She sat on a bed in the corner of a small wooden cottage with a few closed doors leading out. The pungent aroma of medicine reminded her of the herbalist's shop—and the murder she'd witnessed there. A small fox slept in a ball on the windowsill, its fur bright from the sun.

Eyolin scanned the tiny bottles on the old, stained table at her bedside. She recognized a few tinctures. Many possessed an energy of their own that pulsed and swirled.

A silver basin and bucket of water sat on a teetering wooden bench. Above was a cupboard with rusted hinges and a few scrolls of parchment stuffed between books that threatened to fall. Each item confirmed that the resident of the cottage was involved in healing arts—except the door.

The doorway was lavishly ornate with polished iron locks, carved arches, and gold paint. It so starkly contrasted the humble surroundings that Eyolin could have imagined it. The air hummed around it and it didn't take long for Eyolin to catch the ripple of an enchantment drifting around the edges.

The cloth of her shirt itched horribly as Eyolin shifted. They weren't what the dwarvish spinner had outfitted her in. These articles were bags of cotton. She whipped a hand to her throat to find the moontear resting at her clavicle.

Eyolin swung her legs off the bed and grimaced at the ache that shuddered up her spine. A ghastly reflection blinked back from the silver water basin. Her eyes were stained by dark circles and her once full cheeks were pronounced and gaunt. Blood leaked out of a crack in her lip, but other than the obvious hunger and aches, she seemed safe. However, Eyolin couldn't rule out some new danger lurking behind the enchanted door.

Items that could be used as weapons were everywhere, so whoever left her there must not be worried about an attack.

She drifted to the window, testing out her legs. The trees outside indicated a forest. She squinted at the unfamiliarity of the way the trees branched out with spindly needles and long narrow trunks. They were closer in resemblance to the trees she encountered in the Middle than anything she'd seen around Mainwood.

The enchanted door crackled with golden magik as a barrier fell away. Eyolin slipped back to the bed, prepared to feign sleep but stopped when a cloaked female figure stepped through the door as if it were made of liquid. Curiosity kept Eyolin's attention.

The woman kept her back to Eyolin, hanging her cloak on a peg and kicking off grass-stained boots in exchange for slippers. Eyolin kept her mouth shut as she noted the woman's bright auburn hair pulled into a tight bun without a single strand left unattended, her elvish ears on display. She spun on her heels, peering at Eyolin through grass green eyes, her fair skin speckled with freckles. Each feature on her face was tight with wariness.

She spoke in a dialect that Eyolin could only shake her head to. The woman's mouth pinched with irritation. She tried again, speaking slower. Eyolin met her gaze blankly, lips parting with confusion. The woman spoke again, this time in the Aniöm dialect. Eyolin didn't know the words but at least recognized the accent, since that was Karok's native tongue.

"Not a subject of the queen or a lost pup from Aniöm," the woman said at last in the Common Tongue. "Aideillian to the core. Knowing nothing but their own decreed monstrosity of a watered-down language."

She took two strides to a cabinet nailed to the wall. Her hands tinkered through glass vials, grabbing a few and stacking them precariously in her palm. Eyolin identified a blend of duskshadow petals and emberot, both known to counteract magikal ailments and boost immune systems. The herbalist had sold the mixture as tea to Gifted elvish mothers who were pregnant.

"You're a healer?"

"Should I also tell you when I leave for the toilet?"

Oh, Eyolin didn't like her at all. This elf was the cold stereotype of all she hated about elvish society. Bitter and cruel from generations of breeding out emotion.

"Who are you?"

The woman pinned her with a glare dripping with ire. "A healer, like you deduced." She moved to a table and measured out small portions from the assortment of ingredients at her disposal. Starthistle crushed from its prickly spikes with a few drops of water to make a paste. "You're up earlier than expected."

Eyolin studied the healer at work. Something nagged at her mind like a dream she couldn't quite remember. Her mouth was running before she could stitch it shut.

"Are you ever in Mainwood?"

The corner of the healer's mouth pinched inward. "Why would I go to that pit of snobbery?"

"You look... familiar," Eyolin said lamely for lack of a better explanation.

"Is this where the Silver Elf remarks that all those who live in Farindor look the same?"

'That's not—I wasn't saying..." Eyolin started but gave up.

The healer let out an exasperated breath and shoved the glass jars back in the cabinet. "Save your questions for my sister."

Eyolin observed the woman pour the tincture through a funnel into a syringe. The healer moved to the basin next to Eyolin's bed and pulled down a spout from the bucket. A stream of water poured over her cupped hands and the healer went about scrubbing stains from under her fingernails. When finished, she grabbed a wooden bowl and steaming cup, and made a show dragging a chair over to Eyolin's bedside.

She shoved the mug into Eyolin's hands.

"Drink it," she said sharply. Bitter wafts of boiled roots made her eyes water. "Why in the Sky's name would you smell it? I said drink."

"There's uva barna in this? The contraceptive?"

"The little Silver considers herself a practitioner. How quaint." The healer clasped her hands. "You are incorrect. And you will drink it. I sweetened it with honey, and you won't waste it."

Not up for an argument, Eyolin tipped the mug back and drained the liquid, smacking her lips from the film of honey at the bottom.

"How's your back?" The healer raised an eyebrow.

"My..." Eyolin trailed off. It ached but other than that it hadn't occurred to her that something might still be very injured. Had she been unconscious for a day? Longer?

The woman tutted and brusquely rolled Eyolin onto her side, lifting her shirt up to access her back. Eyolin heard a string of curses that were recognizable in any language.

"Your beiythron have been dipping into powers they should never tamper with. Not even my sister was able to get rid of that scar."

Eyolin opened her mouth to ask further questions but found words slurring together on her tongue. Sleep infringed on her mind, dragging her under.

The next time she came to, she sensed a familiar presence lingering outside the cottage—Karok.

The enchanted door shuttered and Eyolin grabbed the mug at her side to use as weapon for whoever broke through that door. She didn't trust the elves of this kingdom to keep her safe. Not when

Aideil had already deployed its forces. Farindor might very well be at war as well. She tiptoed until her back was to a wall. A figure stumbled through the doorway and Eyolin cocked the mug back to strike.

The woman had long hair that resembled flames concealing her face and her breathing was labored. In her arms was a limp body wearing blood-soaked armor. The style was identical to the green of the Farindor guard who had interrupted the High Council meeting.

"Away from the bed," the woman commanded, and Eyolin shuffled to the side, still holding the mug like a club.

The female soldier's chest rose weakly, each breath labored and wet with blood. She must've had a collapsed lung.

"Are we under attack?" Eyolin asked. They didn't appear to have pursuers, but this was a wild kingdom. Those who resided outside the cities of Farindor lived in constant fear of the ancient beasts as old as the realm itself. If the rest of Alagana's magik had faded, Farindor and their queen held onto a reserve that preserved the old ways.

The thin-lipped healer from earlier stepped through the liquid doorway. Her head was tipped forward slightly, hands clasped behind her back. She didn't approach the injured elf as a healer was expected to, content to let the other woman undress and treat the patient.

Gold shoulder plates clattered to the ground bearing the royal insignia of Queen Daetheiri. Where Aideil favored more bulky armor that covered soldiers from head to boot in metal, Farindor used green and brown leather with minimal adornment other than two leaves of precious metal across the shoulders and a corset of metal around the waist. Even in its bloodied state, Eyolin admired the artistry of the armor, which perfectly blended into the topography of the forest. Lethal and flattering.

"Nina, get the boy inside," the woman with the flaming hair said. Her hands moved over the injured soldier without touching her. "Have Karok check the wards and guard the perimeter. I don't want whatever got her to get any closer."

"Karok's alright?"

"You're full of questions, aren't you little Silver?" Nina said with a frown. She disappeared through the door with long strides.

A heartbeat later, Nina returned pulling Dale by his ear. Eyolin gaped but closed her mouth when the red-haired woman spoke, her hands held over the worst of the soldier's injuries.

"Come. Hold her down for me."

Eyolin, feeling useful at least, moved to the other side of the bed, putting the lingering questions on hold to assist the woman. She used her weight to pin down the soldier's shoulders. Behind her, Dale shook off Nina's grip and tucked himself into the corner of the room, clutching a broom.

The woman's hands glowed a brilliant golden yellow. Runes floated around her knuckles as she murmured in low tones, eyelids half closed. The magik intensified. Eyolin expected the prickling sensation that the energy caused. In its stead was a smooth warmth that felt like a soft blanket.

Eyolin tried to identify some of the larger runes that encircled the injured body. The soldier thrashed against the healing magik that wove skin and blood together. The injury on the soldier's chest looked like barbed whips had shredded flesh from bone and there was a distinct black ichor mixed with blood that stuck to what little skin was left.

The Gifted healer's entire person glowed brighter. Even her hair lifted slightly with static. Eyolin marveled at the strength of her magik, the pure energy of it astounding. It was what her younger self had always imagined magik to be. An extraction of black sludge pooled where the healer held her palm. Once the droplets gathered, she shot it into an empty glass vial that shut upon contact. A silver lock at the lid kept the dark magik from ricocheting out.

Her hands moved swiftly from there on out. Wherever she touched and twisted her fingers, the skin knitted itself together. She was a sculptor with clay.

Movement at the window claimed Eyolin's attention. Karok jogged past with Nina at his side. Beyond was a neatly maintained garden landscape within a glen. The trees loomed as a castle wall would. Karok and Nina strode across a delicate bridge arching over a trickle of a stream and out of sight.

"It's done," the Gifted healer announced.

"Cool, can I go outside now?" Dale piped.

The woman lifted her head and pushed a sweaty hand through her hair. Wary recognition darkened her eyes as she glanced at Eyolin, but she turned to the human, assuming an amused mask.

"You could have gone with the last patrol. But you would've been eaten."

Dale gawked and Eyolin couldn't have been happier to see him. At that moment, she didn't care that they were both in a strange—possibly hostile—kingdom. He had gotten out of the city. He was still alive after the fight with Maximus. They both were.

"My best friend was dying—as some blue alligator snake. We'll come back to that. Then the gods-damned teleportation from the mean elvish twin had my head in a bush for hours. No one had bothered explaining why I can't go take a piss in the woods for some peace and quiet other than vague death threats. I've seen more immortal women in the past week than any human should. Also—any repercussions for summoning you with the twigs? I don't know how debts work here, but trust me, I have nothing you want. And a girlfriend. Who I need to get back to. Speaking of girls. Eyolin. What the bark-fucking drunk elf is going on?"

Dale would have likely continued to ramble on if Eyolin hadn't crossed the room and wrapped him in a hug. She hadn't thought about how he got there, but it was clear he had come for her. He hadn't abandoned her. Neither had Karok.

By the time Eyolin managed to compose herself, the Gifted healer had removed her cloak and was dabbing a damp cloth over the soldier's forehead and neck. The resemblance to Nina was uncanny, though her hair was more sun-bleached and far wilder. But those green eyes were the same. As was the narrow chin and face spattered with freckles.

"You didn't summon us, human. Nina was already on her way and managed to blink you three here before your friend bled out." She turned to Eyolin. "You destroyed an apple tree before Karok managed to get you back into elvish form."

Dale wasn't convinced. "You sure? I did the triangle stick-in-the-dirt thing Karok said to do. That wasn't portal jumping?"

"No."

"Which brings me to my next point," Dale said, his arms waving around. He glared at Eyolin. "Why were you two leaving without me? Deserting without your mascot is the greatest form of disrespect."

The woman turned to Eyolin. "Are humans always so irritating?"

Eyolin and Dale spoke at the same time.

"Yes—"

"No—"

"For the sake of an explanation, human," she started.

"Dale," he offered.

"Dale," she continued with an amused eye roll. "You and your companion, Karok, have displayed admirable behavior in standing by your friend and the queen has decided to turn a blind eye to your presence."

"You shouldn't have come," Eyolin whispered. Dale looked at her incredulously. "I am the reason Karok broke his bargain with Master Arendt. I'm the reason you were sent into that arena. Traik was trying to get to me through you and..."

The Gifted healer spoke while she wiped down a counter with a rag. "In the tapestry of existence, a single act, seemingly inconsequential, may be interpreted as an act that rewrites the very fabric of Fate. A seemingly impulsive gesture, devoid of explicit intent, can carve destinies in ways unforeseen. We cannot know until we are the ones looking back if that moment was the turning point of it all."

The woman hummed to herself, unaware of how those words struck a chord in Eyolin. How every moment from her past constantly haunted her. What could she have done better to prevent the sorrow that followed in her wake? Fate was a cruel thing, twisted and changing with infinite possibilities. Kingdoms rose and fell on whims. Children were orphaned in the absence of love. Still such cruelty laced every future. And her own life proved that some Fates repeated themselves until exhausted—that all those who loved her would die.

Shouts from outside broke through her reverie.

"Are we under attack?" Dale asked, gripping the broomstick handle as he would a bow staff.

"Nina and Karok. The worst war of all. He was supposed to come here weeks ago."

Weeks of training flashed in Eyolin's mind. The constant work, the distracted moments, the grueling drills.

"He stayed because of me."

"Oh, Nina is aware." The Gifted healer refilled a few jars with ground leaves. "She took pleasure stitching your back together where I could not."

She unlocked the enchantment on the door and moved to exit. Eyolin stopped her with a hand to her wrist.

"I didn't catch your name."

The woman weighed her words for a few beats. "You may call me Cara. It's a pleasure to meet you, Eyolin." Something about her tone told Eyolin that there was much left unsaid. Cara back-tracked to her hanging cloak, pulling a leaf-wrapped parcel from a pocket and the image struck her.

"You bought the esthyri," Eyolin exclaimed. "In Mainwood. I traded a capper mushroom for you."

Cara looked uncomfortable as she responded with, "Mm. Right, that must be it."

"Do you still have the esthyri?" Tequerra had been building something utilizing the herb and if Eyolin could study it—maybe extract some understanding from the plant itself—she would know how to disarm it. With time she didn't have, she might be able to put together a way to shut it all down. She wouldn't be the one who buried an entire kingdom.

Cara lifted a brow and assessed Eyolin, letting the pleasant mask slip for a moment. "The esthyri is all around us, the very foundation of this safe house."

"How...?"

"Your master never told you?" Cara swallowed hard. "You have been exposed to the esthyri's influence ever since you came under the care of the herbalist I purchased it from. Her wards were laden with it."

Slowly, the pieces of the puzzle fit together. Not quite enough to reveal the entire picture, but enough for Eyolin to glean that the herbalist had been hiding from someone. An entity worse than the High Council or Magnogogue. Someone with reach into all their lives. Someone that fit the description of a master of magik, who coincidentally, had been abnormally absent from the Great Hall in a kingdom on the precipice of war. Eyolin truly had forgotten to doubt. To see the master as anything other than a benevolent leader, a general cultivating his kingdom's assets.

"But you use esthyri for wards, not weapons."

"There are theories that the properties could be weaponized. There was a Gifted fire scariyai a few centuries ago. She worked with a beiythron to manipulate magikal energies into a contraption that would offer amplification in the face of weakening Gifts. Esthyri was a component, but the device was never completed." Cara paused and moved over to the sleeping solider, rubbing a minty salve on her newly formed skin. "The scariyai claimed that esthyri functioned much like a needle. It can stitch up a wound, or slice open a deeper one. Similarly, esthyri can protect, as well as create little tears in a realm's barrier."

"You mean it can cut into realms?" There was every chance that the increased number of demons slipping into Alagana was a direct result of someone attempting to complete the esthioryn. If Master Arendt was attempting such a feat, he would be able to revolutionize warfare, reopening an elvish-made portal system.

"In the practice of my people, the children of the forest, it is believed that the esthyri is a soul herb that connects our realms, drawing strength from those that we extend a hand to. For instance, our wards pull protection directly from our ancestors in the Sky realm, however faint the connection is. As the Sky is the farthest away, the protection pulls minute filaments from the Twilight and the Middle on its way to our wards." Cara shrugged. "That is, at least, how it reacts to our magik. Depending on the Gift, other realms and spirits are called on."

Eager for as much information as possible, Eyolin asked, "How about channeling morphling magik, such as a Shoutka form?"

Cara's body shuddered once—her aloof mask donned immediately after. "When an elf touches their Shoutka, it splits their body into two separate beings with one made of pure magikal energy. I would assume that if a Shoutka can be contained and the essence of the elf's power extracted from it... that kind of power could permanently split the realms, cleaving our reality into pieces."

"I'm guessing no one has ever faced this before?" Dale spoke up at last.

"If anyone knew anything," Cara replied cryptically, "it would be Queen Daetheiri. She doesn't speak of how her two mothers died, but it had to do with closing all access to Midriel."

Dale's grip on the broomstick hadn't loosened. Eyolin couldn't blame him.

"You mean to tell me demons could just waltz into Alagana?" His face was comically pale.

"Creatures of dark magik could act through a vessel. They knew that convincing elves and other magikal beings to ingest esthyri would allow them to control the body of that whom they entered. The more powerful the host, the larger the tear between the realms. All access was said to be cut off with Midriel after the first Blood Moon of Sanguis but with the exposed energy of a Shoutka from a scariyai such as you... the result would be catastrophic."

Nina barged through the doorway followed by a sheepish-looking Karok. Eyolin reeled with the possibility that Tequerra and Traik were building a device that could shatter the barriers between the five realms, releasing whatever horrors existed within them. Alagana was woefully unprepared to face legions of demons such as the kaizor or frae. Eyolin also knew that worse things would follow. Creatures like the one that had broken into her home as a child.

Eyolin cleared her mind enough to hear the end of Nina and Karok's report. Twelve Farindor guards were found slaughtered just beyond the wards. Only the one in the cottage managed to get out in time. The realms were already cracking, the space holding one realm from falling into the next collapsing. Between the necromancers in

Ïsteldûr pulling up legions of demons and raising the dead and Aideil building a weapon that would unleash hell itself, every living thing would be wiped from existence.

"I have an idea of how to stop it," Eyolin announced.

"What are you talking about?" Nina snapped. Karok shot Eyolin an apologetic look for the tone of the woman at his side.

"The esthioryn. But I need help working out one crucial detail."

Chapter Twenty-Eight

Kipp's body screamed from the sprint. The walls of Alden were a flat smudge on the horizon behind him. He had to hope that Jorrith received the letter he spirited to the estate explaining his absence and the importance of staying out of sight until he could get to them.

The Terrot Mountains rose in the distance in all their jagged glory. Firelight glinted off the sheer cliffs of Keystones from the castle city of Ûnsigra. One thought dominated his mind. *Where was she?*

The moment Luna left his room in the inn, the absence of Eyolin's magik was chilling. Whatever tether held them together was gone. Not broken. But effectively nestled beyond his reach. One kernel of energy remained. For a single night he had been selfish and, in that time, Eyolin went missing, Erik showed up making threats, and the Sisters were on his ass. He'd gotten complacent. Soft. It was time to go on the offensive.

His lungs and legs couldn't maintain this speed. It was an instinct that told him not to blink. There was something he was missing. The muffling of her magik felt intentional. If he were to blink, his actions could trigger her body to be moved. This was groundwork.

The night without food gnawed at his stomach and even his Grey magik was dwindling drastically. He needed to find the Book of Bindings fast if he were to permanently tie the Twilight's energy to his body. After getting Eyolin out of whatever hellhole she waltzed her pretty curls into.

Roads webbed out from the spiraling castle spires of Ûnsigra. Each building was carved of stone chipped from the sides of the mountain. Kipp slowed his pace to a casual walk as elves on horseback galloped his way. There were no trees or shrubberies to hide in this far from the woods of the valley. Keystones itself stood proud amid the dry brown grasses and pokey weeds, reminiscent of the true might of the High Elves—of Alaina whose spirit created the falls at the mountain's heart.

Kipp took the rest to dive inward, examining each crevice of his mind for any sign of Eyolin. The connection was so faint, he'd almost missed the draw of Ûnsigra. The thought of Erik holding her sparked a hatred he hadn't anticipated. Kipp would have difficulty not skinning whoever touched her. Even leaving Maximus unscathed tormented his dreams.

He pushed deeper, pulling into the darker parts of his magik. Dammit, where did she go? He swore at the emptiness where her kernel of light had lived for weeks.

The gates of Ûnsigra were open upon his arrival. The guards lazily reclined at their posts. Kipp glimpsed cards in their hands. One guard was about to lose the small pile of silver rykes piled on a stump between them. Kipp flashed the illusion of papers in their faces and kept moving.

His body was strained to the point where red edged his vision. Rest. Then food. He wouldn't be of any use to Eyolin if he keeled over. He fingered the rykes in his pockets, weighing enough for a nice city room that had security who wouldn't let scum like the Sisters into his private chambers. As much as he enjoyed waking up to a woman in his lap and a knife to his neck, he'd prefer her with less of a knack for disemboweling him before breakfast.

The city streets were full of afternoon life. Merchants had carts set up with their wares, mothers dragged their children along by the scruffs of their tunics with heavy bags slung over their shoulders. Kipp slipped between them, adjusting the assortment of knives on his belt, conjuring one and vanishing another until it was perfect. He spotted an appealing vendor with a cart full of meat pies when the full force of the vision hit him.

Kipp hadn't been susceptible to the visions as often as he had when he fought his way into the portal at the heart of Keystones. Now, that mountain was reminding him how deep its hold on him really went—and why he needed that book to break it. One immortal god's vengeance was relentless. Worse was that now he identified the central figure in all of them.

A midnight abyss swirled in front of him where the street of Ûnsigra should have been. His feet moved across plates of obsidian that sputtered with cracks of steam and magma. Veins of fire and molten earth pulsed like a beating heart and that same purring voice scraped talons down his spine.

"All of this death, all of this destruction can end before it has even begun."

He expected the vision to end there as it had so many times before. It did not. One more step and he was falling into endless darkness.

The voice spoke from the impenetrable black, "Bring her to me, Kipp Aisolon."

His eardrums thrummed with the sound of hundreds of flapping wings. A red moon glinted in between charred trees. Everything was on fire—people, earth, the very air itself. And there was a girl kneeling in the center of it all with her head bowed. Thick chains looped around her neck, wrists, and torso. Every drop of her blood that touched the obsidian fizzled into steam. Then flames licked above her head in the shape of a tree. Then into that of a crown.

The vision tunneled through the perspective of an eye, the darkness and flames contained within a single unblinking iris. That eye squinted at Kipp, and he felt the full presence of a god weighing down on him. An endless power trapped as Eyolin was.

This god was furious.

Kipp flinched against the grips of two Ûnsigra guards, the vision melting away with a blink. The Aideillian elves with thick furs pinned to their shoulders hauled Kipp into an alley, away from the mothers shepherding children away from a convulsing half-elf.

His head throbbed from the onslaught of the vision. He put his full weight on the Silver Elves who held him. This could be some nasty hangover from straining the leash that kept him close to Eyolin, but Kipp wasn't particularly grateful for the reminder.

He glanced at the breastplate of the guard who supported him. The guard was saying something, but Kipp didn't care to tune in. Their armor was spotless though, not a speck of grime on any surface. Kipp tilted his head. The alley and shadows hid the three of them from onlookers.

The Grey conjured two short seraph blades and drove them through the soft necks of the guards, right between their helmets and furred shoulder plates. He lowered both to the ground silently and the seraph blades retracted into the shadows of his magik.

Flickers of red and cracked earth danced across his vision. The voice. It grated through his mind in hisses and clacks. The visions from the Book never had her in them.

That had been the voice of a god. And it knew his name. There was one god who would be depicted clothed in the fires of Midriel. One High Elf above all others who might need the Blood Moon of Sanguis to unlock a gateway back.

Kipp had assumed that Magnogogue was the mastermind behind Ïsteldûr's designs on Aideil—on Eyolin. The western king was the last true fire scariyai with the greatest necromancer of their age at his side. But no, Magnogogue did not hire him of his own volition.

He was acting on the whims of the fire god. The King of Midriel.

Suddenly, those rivers of lava and scorched earth that bled red were clear. That voice—the eye—it was the one who led the Betrayal that spawned the five realms. And he wanted to be rid of his hell-scaped prison.

Kipp slunk away from the lifeless bodies and into the main avenue of Ûnsigra, the city of scholars. A flick of his wrist and the bodies in the alley dissolved into mist. It was time for Kipp to narrow in on his pretty magikal battery and unlock precisely what the King of Midriel wanted with the power in her blood.

He followed the faint whisper of her magik, the thread leading him deeper into the city and away from the warm rooms and food he so desperately needed. The slums of Ûnsigra pitched unevenly as the Grey faded into the shadows.

Chapter Twenty-Nine

"If you're the last hope of stopping the esthioryn, we may as well surrender to Magnogogue now." Nina crossed her arms, leaning against the cottage walls. The loud crunch of the apple in her hand seemingly echoed through the entire Hågenveihr forest. Eyolin's strength had recovered significantly, but Nina's sour moods made her feel weak.

Eyolin sighed with irritation, and opened her eyes. Karok sat across from her, his legs crossed in meditation.

"I'm trying," she grumbled.

"Shouldn't you be trying to master lesser magiks before attempting to access a Shoutka?"

Eyolin glared at the woman. "Are you certain you *want* me to unlock my spirit form—what with the possibility I'll accidentally activate a device that shatters the realms?"

Cara and Nina had been busy trying to figure out the cause of Eyolin's seeming lack of magikal ability. It was a risk exposing her Gift and moontear to another kingdom, but one that Eyolin was willing to take. Based on Traik's behavior, the esthioryn was nearly finished. Without her Shoutka and moontear to complete the esthioryn design, it would drain the fading magik of the city. It was only a matter of Eyolin dismantling the weapon before it destroyed the realms.

Right now, Cara was deep in a text so old its pages were crumbling, leaving her prickly twin sister Nina to sour Eyolin's mood. Nina rolled her eyes while picking apart an apple.

"You'll be a tasty snack for the demons Magnogogue has lurking around Foxwood. I can't even leave this glen without spotting their grisly hides."

Nina stalked around the side of the cottage and out of sight. Moments later, the soldier who had been recovering for the past two days sped off on a horned mount, no doubt with some message reporting on the threat of Aideil's esthioryn and the presence of three Aideillian fugitives holed up in the depths of Foxwood.

Two days of work with Karok to figure out her Shoutka had proven to be more testing than Eyolin anticipated. They'd dug around her psyche and even tried hallucinogenic herbs to try bringing her spirit form to the surface. Absolutely useless.

Karok suggested that her body was too battered to focus, but Eyolin felt the resistance of her magik whenever she brushed against the moontear. Every avenue was frozen and detached, a film of ice that refused to warm to her wishes. That deep in the forest, isolated from the outside world, brought every worst case scenario to the forefront of her mind. Elvish bodies piling up along the border of the city disrupting the wards. Some creature collecting the pointed tips of ears in some sick game. The deterioration of elvish-human relations and the abuse of the human legions. And she was sitting in a peaceful little spot in a forest, utterly useless.

"This is pointless," Eyolin snapped. "I might not even have one and this has all been a waste of time."

"Master Arendt doesn't seem to share that sentiment, and he is a Master of Magik." Karok fell onto his back dramatically. "He can likely smell your Gift, and the power your Shoutka holds."

"Or he's too old to smell anything at all."

Her plan was taking too long. And she was no closer to figuring out why her moontear was refusing to allow her to channel.

"What is his Gift, exactly?" Tequerra could blink between the Middle and Alagana, but that only signaled that he could channel enough power to make the jump. Any powerful scariyai could blink if they practiced enough. He had a connection to earthen magik, but then there had always been something different about him.

"You never learned to see the auras of those around you to determine their Gift?" Cara asked from the doorway of the cottage. Eyolin shook her head. Lesser magiks were something many elves could access to varying degrees, but she had adamantly avoided anything of the sort.

"Earth," Cara explained. "It has a brown sort of haze. Tequerra Arendt has the Gift of earthen magik, strong enough to pull any form of the element he chooses."

"Many earthen Gifts manifest though vines and chlorophyll charged energies, making them such a vibrant green," Karok said next. "But there are also earthen Gifts that take the form of rock manipulation or sand. Even grass and floral patterns have their place among the earth element, though we usually only acknowledge magik that can tip the scales in a battle."

"An elemental magik," Eyolin mused. Training with Karok was solely morphling magik—often considered a lesser magik. Anatomies and metal fields and shifting forms. Nothing even remotely connected to the elemental magiks of Alagana.

"Of course, there used to be more than just one Master of Magik," Cara continued. "Fire died off with the loss of the fire agate gemstone. The only god capable of granting a fire agate refused to allow anyone to harness more than what obsidian can channel. But there are records that pure, undiluted fire Gifts could burn through cities and wipe out entire battlefields. Now not even the fire sprites born of the land can hold a flame for long."

Eyolin thought of the elvish woman in the Great Hall with the tiny ruby of a gemstone, how her skin had cracked and blazed against the guards' hold.

"What about the others?" Eyolin asked. "The other elements."

Her mother once told her a story about the six elements that were divided between the children of King Jenthius, but she couldn't remember what they were.

"You know already of earth and fire," Cara started. "The four others were water, air, space, and consciousness. "

"How is consciousness an elemental? I thought there were mind and skill."

Cara smiled and moved over to kneel where Karok and Eyolin sat. She drew a few symbols to depict the six elementals. "Each kingdom teaches it differently. Mind and skill are one and the same in our tradition. Two sides of the same coin. Consciousness manifests itself in many variations. The master of such an element is a master of the mind, as well as the minds of others. A master of the body and all its deadly and sensual uses—a master of the living. Branches of consciousness you may be familiar with are the scarox, the beiythron, morphlings, and me. A healer."

"And no one is the master of that?"

Nina stalked back around the side of the cottage, chiming in, "Consciousness and space are the two elements that can rewrite realities, and as such, only a High Elf has ever been able to harness the full scope of them. And they're all dead." The way Nina said the last word dripped in loathing.

Cara managed a pained smile as she explained for her twin. "Fire, too, has never been Gifted to someone without pure High Elvish blood, but that is solely due to the greed of the god who holds it. The three races of elves left are mere reflections of a once immortal faction of gods. Where humans and dwarves crossed the seas to the magikal realm of Alagana, the High Elves came from the Sky. Away from their ancestral plane, they were forced into the skins Alagana gave them, stripping away true immortality. It is said that if the High Elves still existed, they could drink the magik from Alagana to maintain everlasting life."

Eyolin nodded and formed the map of Alagana in her mind. The Farindor tale was similar enough to the one of Aideil her mother had spoken in whispers. The talk of the masters of the elemental magiks captured her interest. It was possible that there were scariyai out there who had stayed hidden with Gifts rivaling the masters of old. The Master of Water would likely stay near the coast, in the sea kingdom of Velesah. Air would make the most sense in mountainous regions such as Aideil and Mendia. Or perhaps the plains of Aniöm with their grass dragons. She didn't know where Master Arendt came from, but the trees of Mainwood thrummed with earthen power.

Dale—who everyone had taken to be napping—let out an exasperated breath from his spot in the grass in the shade of a tree.

"Magik is so boring." The three elves around him raised their eyebrows. "You sit around in little circles and talk about all this power when all you do with it is bicker and try to dethrone one another."

"And what is your Gift, human?" Nina asked pointedly. "Sarcasm?"

"A true master," he responded and closed his eyes.

Later in the afternoon, Nina busied herself sorting through inventory in the cottage while Karok and Dale hunted in the surrounding woods, taking care to avoid the shifting shapes of demons. Eyolin hadn't moved from the indent she'd made in the grass. Her brow was slick with sweat from focus. Cara had found some books on Shoutkas, but nothing in the pages had gotten Eyolin closer to accessing hers. Cara, with her Gift as a healer, had at least confirmed that if Eyolin's magik was the key to activating the esthioryn, it was also possible that Eyolin could absorb the energies from the device and redirect them. If she could split herself into the Shoutka, her elvish form could extract the energies of the esthioryn while the Shoutka kept it open and exposed. That would require her to be able to hold the two forms simultaneously and pull energies into her moontear. She could do neither. But that little voice in her said told her she could. That if Master Arendt claimed she was the key, then she would prove him right and stop him.

This had to be some divine punishment. Her moontear refused to warm to her touch. Eyolin tugged off the gloves she had on to keep warm in the late dusk. There on her wrist and hand were those inked symbols from when she'd touched the letter from the Sisters that marked her as the Sarom. The lines and circles shimmered slightly, invisible at some angles, and distinctly black at others. She hadn't told the others about it, though Cara certainly knew of it from the days and nights she had tended her while unconscious.

Maybe she deserved to be a Sister—trained to assassinate men in high ranking positions, navigating courts and fineries. People around her had a tendency of dropping dead. It was no wonder that her moontear had gone silent. It recognized her curse and responded by cutting her off from her one channel of hope. At each crossroads of her life, she let people down, or was directly involved in their death. She was constantly a failure to her masters over the years. To her family. The resistance blocking her from her gemstone was a culmination of every event where she had taken the wrong path. Chosen wrong.

The Sarom title was nothing more than a fluke. Magik had so deteriorated in this realm that Grandmother Tree made a mistake. A powerful scariyai such as the Sarom didn't—couldn't—exist anymore. And the moontear knew that. She didn't even have a Shoutka. Simply morphing into as many forms as she'd managed was a miracle in and of itself.

The grass rustled next to her. Cara spread out a blanket on the damp grass and sat.

"May I?" Cara asked in a whisper. Eyolin pulled herself out of her swirling self-doubt and covered the ink on her wrist. Cara's proximity to Eyolin brought Nina to the window of the cottage like a beacon. "I wanted to apologize, Eyolin. You have been lied to, and I am ashamed that I contributed to the confusion you're feeling."

Eyolin peered at the healer, brows furrowed.

"You are the spitting image of your mother. I thought it was a coincidence. It had to be, but Karok confirmed your last name, and something I read today connected it all."

Eyolin blinked away tears as Cara enveloped her in a hug. Eyolin couldn't breathe. Couldn't move or return the embrace. The memory of the day her mother was torn from realm of Alagana threatened to break through, the one failure worse than all the others.

"Your past is fractured and blocked, not by grief but by magik." Cara held Eyolin at arm's length, her touch reverent. Eyolin's breath caught. "Your fear of your past, of your power, created a prison within your mind that prohibits certain avenues of magik. Morphling magik did not have pain attached to it until the aguarot-caea shift, and now you cannot morph."

"What does a block on my mind have to do with that?"

Cara's breath was shaky, but the healer squared her shoulders. "There is a prism in your mind, trapping any magik that has ties to pain. It is an ancient practice no one has attempted to replicate in centuries but..." Cara paused.

"You think I can lift the block?" Eyolin finished for her.

The healer shrugged and Eyolin all but threw herself into the arms of Cara for the hope she presented. "Something happened in your past, an event so filled with horror that you may have unintentionally called upon that ancient power to prohibit you repeating any magik with ties to physical and emotional pain." Cara took out a small glass vial. The liquid in it swirled with ribbons of energy. "I was the healer that accompanied your mother into the faërfalls before your older sister's birth. As such, she burdened me with the vision the waters gave her. It may be the trigger you're looking for."

Eyolin was shaking her head before she could stop herself. If there was a block, it was there for a reason. She couldn't withstand the agony of reliving her mother's death. Not even with the answer cupped in Cara's hands.

Cara did not wait for Eyolin's consent. She cupped Eyolin's hands in hers, wrapping the amber ring in Eyolin's palm. The vial opened of its own accord and linked powers with the healer's magik. Glittering golden magik sparkled and coated her skin and Eyolin's mind was no longer her own. It felt similar—familiar, like smelling the pages of an old book or the aroma of a stew in a cauldron.

The vision consumed her whole.

Vialett's eyes opened under the surface of the water. Pearly strands of magik entered her consciousness.

A small elvish girl knelt before her. She had a stick frame, the build of Vialett's partner, the father of the child. The child's hair floated around her head like black seaweed. Almond eyes turned up. The sight of her mother furrowed her brows. Abandonment. Fear. Betrayal. Each glinted in tears that leaked out her eyes.

The mirage of the child washed away with a flick of the faërfall's magik. A new child appeared when the water settled. This elvish girl had her mother's buoyant orange and gold curls. A smile lit up her face. Her palms were cupped around a dewdrop of light. Magik. Her second born was to be a Gifted child. Electricity zinged up the child's arms. She looked up with eyes that crackled with lightning that faded as she beheld her mother.

Vialett's firstborn stepped from behind a curtain of water, years older now, with a woman's body. She gazed at her sister with a pointed sneer and stalked around her with weapons belted and strapped across her waist and back. The younger daughter met her sister's gaze. Her eyes glowed with embers, but she did not move.

It was Arden all grown up in the same garb as she had appeared in the crowd of the arena in Mainwood. Eyolin clung to the image of her older sister fiercely. It was all she had left.

The water blurred the scene. It cleared as Arden charged, hands gripping an iron sword. Hazy figures rushed alongside her. The younger child—Eyolin—dropped to her knees and screamed, hands clutching her head and ripping out fistfuls of curls. A light pulsed from her. A single blast of power.

The pool surrounding Vialett flashed into a burning wasteland. Trees crumbled.

A family covered in ash and blood limped away. Dark tendrils wrapped themselves around an older Eyolin's wrists, dragging her down. Her skin crackled with black veins as her knees reached the charred earth. Fissures in the dirt opened around her. Creatures with pointed talons and leathery, scarred skin rose from the gaps. They perched around her.

Madame Kyenz-eihra had spent years training to heal nature as a water lily. She had learned to feel the auras of the living in her presence. And she could feel the white aura that radiated from this child. A child of light, who reaped such dark destruction.

She looked deeper. A kernel of deep purple sat in the center of her daughter's bright aura. 'What are you?' Vialett mused. 'What is your Gift? Your purpose?'

Her mother's thoughts trickled into Eyolin's own. Despite being sucked into the vision, Eyolin knew that tears streaked down her face at hearing that voice one last time.

In answer to her mother's question, the purple spread. It wiped out the light, surrounding the water lily in a midnight black space, her daughter nowhere to be found.

Vialett made to rise from the waters, but a new tendril of magik holding her down. The vision wasn't over. Her elder daughter rushed from behind the water lily wielding two swords. And ran directly into the midnight abyss of magik. Beasts snarled and snapped. Only their black jaws were visible through the fog of magik.

Water entered Vialett's throat as she screamed out a warning. The magik, either the faërfalls or her second daughter's, not even conceived, held her head beneath the surface. Invisible hands reached up from the depths of the pool and pulled her farther down. The faërfalls would not let this child be born.

The water lily thrashed her arms up, fingers barely breaking the surface of the pool. She choked and squirmed against the strength of the hands.

A delicate voice whispered in her ear, "All of this death, all of this destruction can end before it has even begun. This power needn't walk the earth."

All she needed to do was give up.

Her spark refused. The spark inside her that let her create life with her hands in the sweeping gardens of Siochanta and breathed magik into wilted leaves until they were flowing with energy. Fundamental to her work as a water lily was the belief that nothing was permanently Fated or rooted in Darkness.

Her daughters were to be no different than the flowers of Alagana. They may wilt at times. May need extra care. But nurtured, they would flourish. The innocence of life could not be tainted by this cursed vision. The faërfalls showed one outcome, but not all of them. Fates were subject to change, each tendril of Fate tied to decisions made by those they affected. The darkness and destruction need not ever occur. The darkness was seeded in her daughter's magik, that much was clear. A magik that consumed souls and devoured worlds. But also pulsed bright and clean. Her children would fight for each other, not against each other. They would break the darkness that was coming.

By the time Vialett had made up her mind to fight for her daughters, she had run out of time. Water flowed down her throat. She thrashed for air. Tightness wrapped around her throat.

Eyolin's eyes cleared of the vision. The forest felt different. Brighter and sharper than before, and infinitely louder. She still sat with Cara's hands in hers, that golden healing magik pulsing in the space between them.

Her mother had known that her magik would reap death but had loved her in spite of that. Her mother had believed that her magik could be an instrument of good in the face of the impending darkness.

The warmth and love shown by her mother was a sacrifice, till the very end. Cracks in the block she never knew existed blossomed outward, encouraged by the golden light of Cara's magik. She needed to remember. She needed to face the moment that created the wall.

Eyolin stood frozen, her eyes fixed on her mother unmoving on the floor—unconscious and fading fast.

The creature stood looming in the doorway. Dark tendrils of magik snaked over her mother's body and slithered toward Eyolin. She tried to scramble away. One ribbon wrapped around Eyolin's ankle, jerking her leg from under her. Upon contact, the creature's hood flew back.

Eyolin's blood chilled. Never would she forget the silhouette of this monster. Its face was a sheet of solid bone, the shape and texture of an egg. No eyes. No nose or mouth. But it saw and spoke. Its movements mimicked that of a reptile bobbing back and forth, assessing its prey.

No matter how hard Eyolin kicked, she could not rid herself of the magik that dragged her to the creature. Dark magik snagged her skin, biting at her soul, leeching out the lies and fear from her short life. Each memory was devoured, the mass of shadows swelling.

Reliving the moment, Eyolin recognized the creature as something other—not a demon or a frae or a creature of Midriel—but a hybrid of two realms. Something made, not born. She watched her younger self curl up on the ground, pinned by shadows. Her body was so small. Only seven years old. Tears leaked from the eyes of her seven-year-old self as the child rocked back and forth. She had thought Arden would come bursting through the doors—that her mother would wake up and save her. They didn't.

The dark tendrils reached Eyolin's chest and pressed deeper into her subconscious, claiming her mind and soul.

She couldn't take the pressure. The pain. Guilt that wasn't hers plagued her. Memories that she never experiences flashed through her fragile mind.

She did the only thing she could.

She screamed.

The scream cut through the dark magik like a sharpened knife, the ribbons falling away into smoke. A brilliant, white light emanated outward from her small body.

It pulsated in bright spasms, drowning out the memories. It was a metronome of magik that flowed out of her. It washed over her mind in calming waves. She could feel the life in the wood beneath her. In the small insects that buzzed in the branches outside the window.

The creature before her hissed and screeched. The bird skull flaked away into nothingness. Eyolin squeezed her eyes open and looked to where her mother lay.

Eyolin held back for a moment, afraid of the guilt that seeped through her exposed mind.

"Eihra!" *Eyolin screamed.* "Eihra, where are you?"

Eyolin scrambled to find the warmth of her mother, the safety her mother provided. She would be there, just two more steps. The white light flared brighter with the panic that fed it.

Her tears splashed to the floor in droplets of golden light. She closed her small fingers around her mother's apron, desperate for the embrace that would erase her every fear.

Instead, her fingertips found bone.

The light ebbed. Her mother's dress was splayed around a neatly arranged skeleton. The bone Eyolin clutched in her palm crumbled into dust and an eerie chill filled the room. The pulsating light ceased.

Eyolin scrambled back. Her entire body shook. She couldn't think. Couldn't grasp what had just transpired. Her mind was blank. Numbed. Empty and hollow. She felt the absence of the creature that had gripped her in darkness. But she felt the absence of her mother's warmth more.

Eyolin had flinched away from the chirping of songbirds, clutching at the fabric that contained what was left of her mother's body. It was then that the block occurred.

An elderly man stepped across the threshold, whispering hushed words in a language charged with magik. The power muted any Gift that may have existed in her blood, save for a small kernel. The man scooped her away from the handful of bones that remained of her mother. Only he witnessed the murder of Vialett Kyenz-eihra, and only he knew of the block on the young girl's mind.

Though he wore simple grey wraps with lightly tattered edges, Eyolin recognized him in an instant.

And the betrayal was all the more potent.

Murmurs to her left caught her attention, pulling her from the vision.

Returning from his hunt, Karok gaped at her in disbelief. Eyolin opened her mouth to ask, *What?* The feline snarl that ripped loose from her startled everyone, including Eyolin.

Then she felt the shift of her soul from her elvish body into another. The arc of claws, the silken fur rustling in the breeze.

"I think you've unlocked your Shoutka," was all Karok said.

Eyolin's elvish form shook with fury as she said with certainty, "I'm going to kill a Master of Magik."

Chapter Thirty

No guards ventured that deep into Ûnsigra's underbelly, and there certainly weren't any elves outside the wooden warehouse that Kipp had tracked Eyolin's magik to. It was a foggy connection, not at all taut and humming with energy as it should have been. Poison was at the forefront of his mind. That, or a cloaking spell to muffle her magik. Hell, it could be the fiery omniscient god from Midriel rearranging Fates.

The roof of the warehouse caved inward in places. Every bit of it smelled of rot, salt, and blood. Kipp cocked his head and grinned. Fatigue melted away with the excitement of the hunt. Just another witch hunt. His fingertips twinkled with magik, and seraph blades warmed his palms as they materialized.

Kipp slid into a narrow gap between buildings and ran a hand along the outside of the warehouse. He expanded his field into the shadows of the inner chambers. It was full of ungifted elves and humans—all of them female.

His lip curled and Kipp blasted a hole through the wall with enough force to send the splintered wood and fractured stone foundation through the next two buildings.

"I hate it when the Sisters take my things," he snarled.

The Order of the Sisters turned their heads in unison.

Kipp spun and whipped his arm around him in a horizontal arc. Glittering crystal daggers shot through the air where he willed them.

Metal fans with needle-points flicked out. Arrows shot daggers out of the air. Swords flicked the blades to the side. Titanium sleeves crossed in an x before the daggers could pierce skin. Four assassins hissed from dodging too slowly. Two fell without eyes. One slumped to the ground, her head rolling away.

The air rippled as Kipp drew the shadows from the corners of the room. They had taken her—that much seemed clear enough—and they were armed to the teeth to keep her. All the more target practice for him. Daggers slithered and circled through the warehouse like puppets on strings.

No one moved. Heartbeats were the currency of time. Kipp blinked through the warehouse, leaving a phantom shadow in place of his body, maintaining the illusion of stillness. The string of the girl's magik was there. But not on that ground floor.

He spotted the stairs. Before he could make it there, a strong, veined hand raised from the railing of the second level. The wall of power that slammed down crushed Kipp and the rest of the assassins flat on the ground.

Erik clomped down the stairs. Kipp waved a hand, breaking the hold Erik's magik had on his physical body and stood. Kipp's blood pumped with fury.

"Weren't you warned to stay out of my way, friend?" Erik came flush with Kipp's chest as he said it.

Kipp's eyes were dead cold. "Were we ever meant to be friends?"

"As friendly as a master to a pup," Erik spat. "You were always stronger, faster, better. I never questioned why that might be."

"Erik, Jet told me—"

"Jet?" Erik sneered. "He was the first throat I slit. The Regent sent you that letter, testing to see what you'd do. He told me all about your little Silver Elf and the magik to be harvested from her. Who knows, I might even take her to bed after I dispose of you. You know how I get after a fight. Then her kingdom will crumble, and all others will follow."

Kipp's heart stopped. The Regent had sent Erik to Alagana not for a single girl or a single mission, but to create war. The Grey never dipped their fingers in widespread warfare for the same reason a snake does not dive into a vat of acid. The Grey were solitary killers, never soldiers. "You can't destroy an entire realm for spite, Erik."

"Who said it was spite? When Jet's blood soaked into the soles of my boots at the Regent's orders, I gave him an assassin's death. It is what we all face as one of the Grey. Better me than someone lesser." Erik motioned at the Sisters struggling against his hold. A few were attempting to scratch witch symbols in the dirt, their knuckles snapping backward from the pressure.

"Was baking a ruse as well?" Kipp slipped his magik beneath Erik's hold on the Sisters. He molded his shield into Erik's and slid a film of air under for the female assassins to breathe. The Order of the Sisters would attack them both, but... their attention was now fixed on the broad shouldered Grey assassin whose raised hand sought to extract their souls from their bodies.

Erik took two steps away. There was nothing of the man Kipp knew in Erik's eyes.

"You've stood unchallenged as the Regent's Second for too long. You taught me how to be a Grey, but you also taught me how to destroy masters. Destroy kingdoms—though you never wielded the power, coward that you are. As you flaunted your titles and magik, I grew stronger in the shadows that you so passionately claimed as your own."

"A true child of the Twilight," Kipp mused. He made a shallow bow. "The Regent will be so proud."

"Patronizing until the end."

"Perhaps," Kipp said with a smile. His hold on Erik's magik exploded. The Sisters spread their weapons like wings as they leapt up from the release.

As he predicted, the Sisters launched themselves in a flurry, swarming the staircase. A barrage of weapons flew. Erik sliced with untethered grey magik. Shadows and darkness curved with each swipe of his hand. He backed up through two Grey stances before he was overwhelmed.

Kipp tugged on the minds of the female assassins who closed in on his former friend.

Injure. Incapacitate but do not kill. That was his command. Those who resisted were manipulated by an image Kipp pierced into their minds. Despite Erik's hostility, Kipp wanted him to live to see the full failure of his mission. To suffer through every rip and tearing muscle when he lost. It would be by his hand. Just not that day.

Two scrawny but lethal arms wrapped around Kipp, pulling him into a dark corner. Wood and stone groaned against the impact of his back against the wall. Almond shaped eyes were ablaze above the Sister's curled lip.

"Who is this girl you're looking for?"

"Shouldn't you be helping your Sisters, assassin?"

The raven-haired elf had him pinned. Her knee held him still at his groin and a blade curved up his spine. Her lanky arm pressed against the pressure point in Kipp's right shoulder, rendering his physical body fairly useless. He'd never seen *this* Sister.

Kipp considered incinerating her. Then locking her in between realms to suffer for an eternity as her body tore itself apart. At that moment, the magikal tug he had been following pulled taut.

That was Eyolin's magik he felt in her. Not power like a Gift, but the same magik in her blood.

She leaned in. Her head swiveled on her neck with serpentine movements. A killer, trained just as he was to savor the kill. She smelled of bergamot and smoke from a woodfire, each breath washing over Kipp like an unrelenting tide. It smothered his magik as he riled it to flare against her. Somewhere in her blood was the same ghost of the girl he was tracking. He had kept watch in such a haphazard manner that she was likely on death's door at this point. If he dared to defy the Binding of the assignment, he would know for sure, but guessing wrong would flay his skin from his bones. Not ideal.

But this woman—this assassin, his organization's sworn enemy—she pulled him from the clatter of the brawl with Erik, into a quiet hole in the wall, like she had been waiting.

"The girl," she spoke in low tones. "The Aideillian Silver Elf. What do you want with her?"

Kipp's head swam. A magik that tethered itself to another, muffled by distance and wards. A blood relation. She was likely marked as dead if the Sisters had her and, therefore, was as invisible as he was.

He scoured his memories of his target's file until he had to contain the smirk.

"Have you been in contact with your sister recently?"

"Look around you," she spat with a nod over her shoulder. "Take your pick."

A clever brat, Kipp thought. "No sister by blood, I take it? Feisty little thing, killed her mother, older sister dead, left to the perils of the tree-city alone... Ring any bells?"

His gamble hit home. A slim dagger slid out of her sleeve from a mechanical trigger and nicked Kipp's trachea.

"Better one learns to survive alone than be sold into slavery for one's talents. Isn't that right, Grey? You had one taste of the magik that the Twilight realm offered and gave your soul for more. Now you're leashed like a mutt."

Kipp couldn't hold back as he pressed into the knife at his throat. "You left your child of a sister to die."

"I left her to live." The assassin pulled the blade off his skin and pushed him further into the narrow hallways, farther into the dark. "Do you know what the Sisters would have done to her? Lady Weiy would have cut her open and stored her blood in jars to be sold to the witches. Her skin would have been sold to the darkwalkers to wear. What was left would have been burned to awaken spirits from Midriel. You're a smart dog, Grey, and yet, you have failed to see behind the masks of those in power."

Kipp's face felt numb. A witch of Lady Weiy's caliber could be who he was looking for. Except Lady Weiy wasn't a witch. She was an unGifted Sister who scoffed at the reliance of magik like the rest of her disciples.

He had read reports on Lady Weiy, the Mother of the Order of the Sisters, a leader like the Regent was to the Grey. She was ancient, even for elvish standards. An old Gold Elvish crone found living in squalor in Volbourge. No family, no registered Gift, and extremely well-connected in the high courts and houses of Ïsteldûr, Farindor, Huebeck, and the rest of them. If the leader of the Sisters happened to be a witch, a primary objective would be to eliminate the competition. She would know precisely how to drain him of his magik. Given that she had eluded the Regent and the Grey for so long, she would have a solid base of power amassed. And she wouldn't have left a warehouse full of her assassins—her daughters—defenseless.

"Sky shit on me and rail me from behind," Kipp muttered.

The assassin paused with her fist balled in his tunic. She shook her head at him in irritated disgust. "What?"

"We aren't leaving this building alive."

The salty tang he smelled in the air around the warehouse. The mud mixed with rot and blood. Salt and blood were the foundational ingredients in spell casting. Too easy to get in. Impossible to get out. There hadn't been any obvious bundles or symbols or markings on the building, so the witch who hexed the warehouse would have buried the spells or built it into the very stones of the building.

Lady Weiy had known that someone would come for the Sisters tonight. They had been waiting, for what Kipp could guess at later. Since Erik was the one who had the most to gain in the Regent's favor by slaughtering the rival Order, it was a trap ripe for him. Erik wasn't sloppy. He wasn't traceable—a trait Kipp had whipped into his bones when he trained him. That left one player holding all the cards. The Regent. The Grey. Jet was dead, a fact Kipp did not have time to dwell on. Kipp had been sent on his last assignment. That left Erik as the last of the fully trained Grey. The newest two cohorts were untested in their first decade of training. They wouldn't be ready to leave the Twilight for another fifteen years if they were strong. He and Erik had been sent to Alagana on suicide missions, neither meant to return. If Erik succeeded in whipping the realms to war, he would perish in the conflict. If Kipp succeeded in killing the girl under the Moon of Sanguis, what that death unleashed would likely take him along with it.

He and the assassin sister of his target reached the end of the narrow hallway. The sounds of Erik and the Sisters' clashing echoed distantly.

"I have no intention of perishing this day," she said frankly and stomped down hard onto the floor. Dust shivered and fell into the symbols that commanded witchcraft. Two circles with intersecting lines creating obscure points settled in the dust and grime. Salts, Kipp realized with a frown. The Sisters already knew witchcraft. The Regent had done nothing to eliminate the threat.

The raven-haired assassin knelt and used her sword to push the lines of salt to form two triangles with their points touching. She looked up from her squat and gestured to the wall next to the symbol.

"After you, Grey."

"How do I know this spell doesn't enslave my mind and make me your Lady's pet?"

"You don't."

She was behind him so quickly that he thought she must have been Gifted with magik and blinked through space. She shoved him into the ring. He felt layers of earthen blood magik peel off his body—or coat it. His grey magik swirled and roiled around him.

"What—what did you do?" He gasped. Air in his lungs popped and compressed, the unnatural witchcraft causing a negative reaction with his magik.

"Get my sister out of there, you complete imbecile," the assassin grumbled. "They're coming for her." She turned and vanished into the darkness, heading back to where Erik still fought whatever Sister still stood against him.

Kipp coughed blood. The symbols siphoned off his power, growing stronger. He hadn't encountered a spell that could extract magik from beings who were naturally Gifted. He had now. His vision danced with stars. His hands tingled as though he had stood on a frozen mountaintop for the past six hours.

He flicked his hands out to summon his seraph blades. The triangles licked up his magik like it was dry sand blowing in the desert. Kipp lifted a hand to the wall that—wasn't there. His weight threw him forward and he slammed head-first into a massive tree trunk.

The witch-bitch had learned how to create portals.

Chapter Thirty-One

"**R**epeat exactly where the entrance is to the servant's laundry room again," Eyolin said to Dale from the center of the floor. Crude maps, drawn by Dale, lay strewn around the cottage, framing Eyolin in a flurry of parchment. The Great Hall and its tree were just another puzzle. Another map hidden along the borders of parchment she encrypted for the spinner. From what the five of them had figured out, there was a singular, albeit slim, way of getting into and out of Mainwood without a hitch. Everything just had to go according to plan.

Nina sipped tea in a chair looking irritated. Karok had his nose in a book, avoiding eye contact with Nina. Cara rolled a piece of sharpened charcoal between her fingers as she thought. Dale tiptoed through the papers to squat at Eyolin's shoulder.

"There." He pointed at the heart of an illustration of the Great Hall. "You can get fresh clothes in that far chamber. From there you'll be invisible to whoever you see in the halls."

"You'll need to gain access to wherever they are building the esthioryn," Karok said. "It'll be secure. Somewhere only the Master of Magik could access."

"The cells!" Eyolin exclaimed. "They're deep below the city and maintained by earthen magik."

"How are they accessed?" Cara asked.

Eyolin shrugged. "That was what worried me about getting arrested. If I wasn't executed as an undocumented Gifted, there isn't a known way out of the cells. They're warded. Without doors."

"You're telling me the famed Aideillian prisons are holes in the earth with no way in or out?" Nina did not look convinced.

"That's not true," Dale piled in. "Prisoners need to be fed. That's where the tunnels and servant passages come in handy."

"Do continue, human," Nina cooed. "I'm fascinated by the mundane."

He nodded at the spheres drawn underneath the roots. "The earth scariyai have the subterranean holding cells set to move counterclockwise throughout the day, never staying in one spot longer than a few minutes. There was always one cell we were never supposed to enter."

"It's that one," Eyolin interjected. "It has to be." She'd wished she had more experience with lesser magiks and glimmers to offer an additional disguise, but Dale reminded her that Mainwood was a city built and sustained by magik. If she were to use even the smallest amount of power, triggers would go off alerting the kingdom of her location.

"Or the cell holds someone very, very bad," Karok commented.

"You'll be able to feel the pull of magik when you're close," Cara reminded Eyolin, her charcoal tapping her lip, leaving a black smudge. "The device will be unstable, trying to absorb the magik that surrounds it. That is why they need your gemstone to stabilize it. To direct it."

"When does the cell arrive to be serviced?" Eyolin asked.

Dale pinched the bridge of his nose in concentration. "Hour before midnight."

Nina rolled her eyes. "How convenient. The only useful human in the world was a food boy."

"Sorry, your Gift is...?" Dale said with feigned innocence.

"Dale's intel makes sense," Karok said with a grimace, turning the book to face the others. "Dipping into Midriel is easiest at midnight. All Tequerra would have to do is activate the esthioryn when in aligns with the hollow center of the tree."

Eyolin shuddered. "And the tree would become a portal to Midriel."

Eyolin smoothed the map out and drew her finger around in a circle at the top of the stairwell that led to the cells. "Then I enter here."

Dale rubbed his neck and nodded. "That's the best we've got. The tree changes the glimmered servant entrances constantly, except for one opening at the top of the inner stairs. I marked it with an X. Right behind the High Council chairs they use for public events."

Karok closed the book with a clap. "You intend to infiltrate the Great Hall of Mainwood, sneak down an inner stairwell in the middle of the night, and break into an unknown cell?"

"I'll redirect the energy of the esthioryn and bury it in the ground. I'll be out before it strikes midnight."

"And you get out and meet us in Aniöm," Dale said with a pat to Eyolin's shoulder.

"Easy peasy," Eyolin breathed. She didn't tell them how she planned on luring Tequerra into the cells the moment she triggered the blast. That she had figured out on her own. He would pay for blocking her magik. Of the intrusion on her mind.

A messenger slipped to them in the night. The queen of Farindor's gold and green insignia of spirals and ancient runes was stamped into the wax seal. Cara shook Dale awake from his fetal position in the corner of the cottage; he had refused to sleep in one of the cots, claiming that the witches would carve him open and store his organs in jars. Karok and Nina emerged from a separate room, tousled, with bags under their eyes. Eyolin jolted up from the same bed where she had been operated upon days prior. The scar on her back splintered with pain.

Cara's face was pale and her hands glowed with golden magik until Nina got some candles lit.

"They're almost here."

Dale spoke first. "Who?"

"The Sisters," Cara murmured. "Along with a host of creatures we do not have record of. It seems all those demons lurking in Foxwood have been summoned by their master."

Karok began arming himself. "Where?"

"A dozen Sisters appeared within the northern border of Foxwood at the second hour of moonrise. Someone must have blinked them in past the enchantments. Each were accompanied by their own guard of... dark entities... The warning doesn't specify what exactly is protecting the Order, but you have been ordered to leave immediately. Daetheiri will not risk Hågenveihr forest if Foxwood falls."

"The queen knew?" Dale asked, distrust in his eyes. "It's not even the third hour, how would word reach her so quickly?"

"She knows everything that happens within her woods," Nina said.

"We need to leave." Karok stepped into the candlelight. "Eyolin, their orders had to have come from the West. Magnogogue is making a move."

Eyolin's stomach dropped. "Ïsteldûr..."

"Or Mainwood. Maybe one of us sold you out for coin," Nina offered. The rest of them glared at her. Nina shrugged. "You're worth quite a lot. I checked."

"It's been nearly a week since you disappeared," Karok started. "Your blood was littered all the way to the border of Farindor. I'll ask you this once, Eyolin: do you have what it takes to disassemble the esthioryn without us?"

"I think what he means to ask," Nina interjected, "is if your Shoutka can be relied upon to not shatter the five realms and bring us all to our deaths?"

Cara cut her off. "We are all divided. We have done all we can to aid you, Sarom. And you, in turn, must do all you can to prevent that weapon from activating. Nina and I will stay here and ensure the Daetheiri is prepared for either outcome. Whatever Master Arendt did to keep your Gift hidden was not all craven nonsense. Not with the strength of Midriel backing Magnogogue and the instability that exists between each of the kingdoms. Many have not forgotten the last war and will not hesitate to retaliate against Aideil for pushing their forces to claim Annjeih Castle as its own."

"Aideil can't declare war because a single scariyai went missing," Eyolin argued. "Do you think it has anything to do with the block on my mind lifting?"

"I wish I knew more, Eyolin," Cara said. "The truth of it is, I wasn't even sure showing you your mother's vision would work. It was the only avenue we hadn't tried. A gamble."

"Aren't there laws that protect against all-out war?" Dale asked.

"All laws between kingdoms are mere formalities," Nina replied, her bitter tone never ceasing. "Farindor has remained at peace because our queen has no designs on expansion. The same cannot be said for the others. It is no secret that Magnogogue has long sought the Old Throne. Aideil is Ïsteldûr's counterpart, dating back to the Beginning. Matthieus founded the kingdom of fire. Alaina built Aideil. Neither will stop until the other is destroyed. "

They were silent for a moment. The candles flickered warm light on their solemn faces.

Dale spoke first. "So, there's a host of assassins headed our way and a war about to break loose if we engage because one girl decided the hell with it all and ran away?"

Nina nodded. "The human sees at last the great game. It was never how to maintain peace, but who would make the first move."

"How can I be sure to get out of the forest alive?" Eyolin asked. "I was unconscious when I was brought here. Unless you mean to tell me Farindor's forests aren't as deadly as the tales say"

Nina smiled. "You run."

"And you will be alright? Even though the Sisters will track my blood here?"

"Our wards can easily overpower anything the Order of the Sisters throw our way," Cara assured.

"You said there were how many?" Eyolin watched Karok's mind work through a soldier's analysis of the coming threat.

"Does it matter?" Nina replied.

"It matters knowing who holds the blade to our throats, Nina," Karok snapped. "You have immunity with the queen if you run to Jothya or Threinsfold, but what of us? We are not sworn to your crown. We three have our names in ledgers that quantify our worth to our kingdom as pieces who will be used when it best benefits our superiors."

Eyolin looked to her trainer and felt the werekey within him flare with rage. Dale blanched at the words as well.

Karok pressed further. "Your benevolent queen and the wild kingdom of Farindor has never stood with the other six kingdoms but rather profited off them. What will happen when the world lays beneath smoldering ashes? Will the selfish elves of the woods look to their kin then? Will anyone? Will anything be left?"

"Leave the forest," Cara said. Her voice was no more than a breath that flickered the candle on the table before her. "Run. Flee and save yourselves. Mendia is a wasteland of mountains and ice, where there are caves deep enough to withstand the darkness ahead."

"You said yourself that the esthioryn wouldn't spare any realm from ruin." Eyolin's lip trembled as she finished speaking. It was her. It was always her. She had assumed that it was Aideil who would wreck the world with their tinkering experiments, but Alagana stretched far beyond the borders of her kingdom. Perhaps the mountains of Mendia would withstand the tides of war, but who would she be if she alone stepped from the rubble to a world of smoke and ash? The dice were still rolling across the table; not yet settled or decided. She only needed to keep the odds ever-changing—do something unexpected that would disrupt the cycle of destruction.

Aideil was not at fault, nor was it faultless. And Mainwood was the one place she knew like the back of her hand. The city was close enough to Master Arendt that she would have a chance at locating and disarming the esthioryn without raising alarms. Mainwood was her home, at least until it burned to the ground. Then the city would be her grave.

Chapter Thirty-Two

"**Y**ou realize that an entire hostile forest, a mountain range, and the same soldiers that carved up your back lie between here and Mainwood, don't you?" Dale said. The pack in his arms made his knees buckle from the weight. "And remind me again why Karok and I aren't allowed to come with you?"

Nina answered on Eyolin's behalf, wincing as she heaved a saddle onto a horned stag. "Karok is formally exiled from Aideil. And you, are a useless human who will slow her down when that spot between your legs gets sore from riding. She travels fast and alone."

"You're more than welcome to stay here with us," Cara called. Nina's eyes narrowed with disapproval.

Karok intervened. "I'll take him to Grösgir, I've kept in touch with a few households that can take you in."

"No," Dale sputtered. "I'm not leaving Eyolin, and I'm not leaving the humans of Mainwood to fend for themselves. The cells beneath the Great Hall are in the ground. Do you know who lives on the ground? Humans."

"You go back, you're as good as dead," Nina said in a low tone.

Eyolin spoke over Nina pointedly, "Stick to the plan and go to Freya in Ûnsigra. I can meet you both in Slétum, right across the border." Eyolin turned to the twins. "How do I get out of the forest?"

Dale shrugged. "Same way you came in?"

"You had us that time," Nina said. "The forest does not harm those who were born here."

"I fly then," Eyolin suggested. "The falcon form navigated the trees outside Mainwood—"

Cara held up a hand to cut her off. "The flare of magikal energy it will take to morph will trigger a defense system. Our forests are already on high alert."

"Sticking to the ground then," Eyolin said with a huff. "Good old fashioned run. Through a wicked forest."

"It isn't wicked," the twins said in sync.

Karok pulled Eyolin to the side, his hand rough and firm. "You've only shifted into your Shoutka once. It was trauma that caused the snap, not control. How can you be sure that you stand even a hint of a chance?"

"I have to try, Karok." Eyolin's blood thrummed. The moontear on her neck warmed her skin. "If I don't go back, if I run, I risk Aideil burning this forest to the ground, using whatever soul-power that the esthioryn generates. İsteldûr will unleash whatever horrors they've been breeding in response. And this world, all Alagana, will be gone. I saw my mother's vision, the one from the faërfalls. It's not quite a map, but it gives me something to work from. This plan has minimal casualties. No one will even notice I'm there until it's too late. By then, I'll already be halfway to Aniöm."

"Stand strong, love," Karok said, his arms wrapping around her tightly. "Even a mouse can scare a lion shitless. And you are one fearsome rodent."

Eyolin shoved him back as he grinned.

Nina frowned. "Queen Daetheri will ask a favor in exchange for warning you rather than collecting you. Be prepared to pay it when she calls."

The Fate Cara had shared with Eyolin was ripe in her mind. There would be a time when the Queen of Farindor joined the fray. By then, it would likely be too late for all of them.

The warning from the twins to *stay on the forest floor* had lasted perhaps an hour before Eyolin had been forced to abandon her supply pack and mount at the edge of a river rather than be eaten by a snapping scaled lizard.

She'd morphed into a bird and fled from the haunted woods before sense could stop her.

Now her back ached from the flight, skimming over the tips of Foxwood as a flinorock glacier bird. At times, Eyolin felt like the branches reached up to grab at her ankles. Sleek icy white feathers coated the length of her body. Two head-tails extended down her back, and her curved talons were curled tight to their body. Her magik sung through her blood, mixing with the ice that the flinorock could summon with a powerful thrust of its wings.

The longer she flew, the more she sensed the hostile probes of magik that reached for her like the venomous fangs of a snake.

With the passing leagues and never-ending forest, Eyolin let her mind wander. Cara had found a link that had eluded her. A determination to prove her mother's vision wrong, a purpose that she could mold into a new Fate. She wanted answers as to why the Master of Magik had placed a block of magik on her mind and then pretended to be ignorant.

A wind current from the changing geographies pushed her up. The land stretched out before her like a blanket, the clouds distant over the plains of Aniöm.

To her left spread the remainder of the forests of Farindor, divided by the light yellow-green of Aniöm. On the far horizon was the hint of the mountains of Mendia. The Galan Valley stretched before her, with the towering Terrot Mountains flanked by the delicate Pipete Mountains. In between grew the ancient trees that led to Mainwood.

Eyolin felt the shudder of exhaustion wash over her. The day's flight had covered the distance of two to three days on the ground. Stone buildings broke the horizon beneath the first of the Terrot Mountains as she glided over Theony, the outermost southern city in Aideil.

She banked down in a spiral, relishing in the rush of wind and weightlessness of the fall. The flinorock landed at a farm, behind a hay bale, a league away from the stone city. A flash of magik and Eyolin fell to her knees. Weariness tied her to the prickly hay she knelt on.

Sleep blanketed her as the sun dipped closer to the horizon. The pull of hunger didn't even register, and Eyolin shut her eyes, curled against the hay.

Eyolin rubbed the grogginess from her eyes hours later as her stomach clawed her awake. She picked hay clean from her green tunic, and made her way into Theony. She brushed a hand over the neckline to ensure that her jagged scar was concealed. She adjusted the glove over the ever-shifting ink on her wrist and fingers.

Theony was the first settlement Eyolin had stepped foot in other than Mainwood. Stone had been manipulated using earthen magik, shaped into smooth domes and spires. The roads were worn and muddy with cart and horse tracks chopping up the ground. Rock had been twisted into garlands adorning doorways and arches. Fire-light replenished regularly by fire sprite slaves that twinkled through windows. Mainwood kept servants of the lesser magikal creatures to maintain the façade of equality and decency to visiting officials. Here the lessers like the sprites were treated like stray dogs. The air was dense and dirty, different from the leafy breezes that floated through Mainwood.

Aideillian Silver Elves clad head to toe in armor strode through the mud with swift steps, each with their spears tucked tightly to their side. There weren't many regular people on the streets, and the ones who were actively avoided the soldiers. Eyolin feared that she was too late, that someone else had filled her void and given Tequerra Arendt a weapon to tear open rifts between realms.

Eyolin eyed a tavern at the far end of the road. Muffled sounds of glasses clinking and laughter encouraged her toward it. She tugged a few strands of hair loose to cover her ears. Better to keep her anonymity and dance the line between elvish and human in foreign towns. Her face was grimy enough from sleeping in the haystack that her features were unrecognizable. She didn't know if these Theony soldiers actively sought her, if Master Arendt was searching for her. There were other powers who could be on her scent. Ïsteldûr likely had spies in every alley. If they deemed her a worthy bargaining chip, there was no doubt that they wouldn't hesitate to snatch her. Eyolin didn't trust her moontear to come to her aid outside of morphing and running. Broken block or no, she still had little control over her magik. The aguarot-caea dragon had fared well against the kaizor and attack force from Mainwood but was a bit conspicuous. And if these soldiers carried weapons that prevented healing magik, a scratch of poison could kill her.

Wooden walls shuddered against a crash and a roar to her right. Eyolin flinched away from the stable, slipping slightly in the mud. Consoling whispers drifted out of the open door.

A deep male voice rumbled behind her. "Toracyl smells the wind on you. Thought you were another caea."

Eyolin turned, finding a dark-skinned Amber Elf whose black hair was twisted back. His large eyes held reserves of skepticism but looked down at Eyolin with curiosity. Hard flying leathers fell in flaps around his legs. A skirt of chainmail clinked around his waist. His forearms were covered in braces with hooks near the wrists.

"You're from Aniöm," Eyolin said without thinking.

"And you are not a dragon," he mused with a smirk. "Though rolling around in the hay is definitely a beastly attribute."

Eyolin's cheeks heated, yet she stood her ground. Elves, neither Gold, nor Silver, nor Amber, ever addressed her so frankly in Mainwood. She had been invisible in the tree-city until her run-in with Traik that sent her life spiraling. He noted her silence and dipped his head in a slight bow, eyes not leaving hers. A gentle symbol of supplication between elves that made Eyolin step back. She'd had enough of kind faces manipulating her, and she didn't have Karok or Dale to speak for her. In this place, she needed to survive. Food, shelter, and information. The elf stood, and Eyolin gave a slight nod of recognition.

This rider was less threatening of an option than entering the tavern alone. Aniöm was full of clans who all allied with Aideil individually. Eyolin flinched from a deep crack of thunder in the skies. The building at his back shuddered under the weight of the creature inside for a second time, and the rider took off on long strides.

"You'll have lightning in a minute," the Amber Elf called over his shoulder, making his way into the stable. "You're welcome in to wait it out in here. Or return to whatever dung pile you came from."

"It's not going to rain," Eyolin retorted, unable to stop the nagging words. Immediately the skies opened and poured down on her. She was soaked through in an instant.

Worse was that the gorgeous Amber Elf had stepped under an awning, untouched by the pelting rain. He took a long inhale, as if relishing in the freshness the rain brought. When he opened his eyes, he ducked into the building, leaving the door open behind him.

Eyolin weighed her options. She had no money and no food. She told herself that she followed the rider inside because there wasn't anything to rob her of.

Hot air puffed in her face. Water sprang into her eyes from the blast. Blinking the tears away, she came nose to muzzle with a grass-caea dragon. Long green feathers rustled along its narrow body, every muscle bred for speed. Its diamond snout was cold as it nudged Eyolin's chest. Books about these grass dragons didn't do the species justice.

The Amber Elf ducked under a soft wing, his hand running against the lay of the feathers. He nodded toward the door, which Eyolin shut.

"Why did you invite me inside?" Eyolin demanded, her tone harsher than she intended.

"Toracyl wanted to meet you," he said, pouring from a jug of water.

"You ride for a clan of Aniöm?"

"You may call me Agatio," he said with a smile and went to tidy up the large room, kicking hay and blankets toward Toracyl's clawed feet. He nodded at the dragon. "Toracyl and I are more like siblings. We grew up together, my father allowing me to raise Toracyl as long as I one day joined Aniöm's riders."

"Why trust me to enter your space?" Every alarm in her body was going off, but the presence of the elf was unnaturally soothing, like he was always meant to help her. And that terrified her.

He looked at her quizzically. "Toracyl frightened the stable hand so thoroughly that she abandoned her biscuits and meat stew. I can't begin to eat all of it, and I leave at first light. Would be a shame for it to go to waste."

"She's beautiful," Eyolin murmured. The grass dragon's face softened into a content smile. Its head slid into Eyolin's arms. The weight of it took Eyolin by surprise. When she recovered her footing, the Amber Elf was staring at her with a slight gape.

"You can tell a caea's gender?"

"I like to read."

"Have you read any of Thower's works?"

She shook her head. "I've only recently gained access to a library. There wasn't time to read for pleasure."

"Pity. You must find me again when you do. I've been itching to pick someone's brains about him." Agatio handed her a bowl. The contents of meat and chunks of bread were steaming. "You look as if you haven't eaten in days."

Eyolin tucked her feet underneath her on a cushion across from Agatio, who tipped his own bowl to his lips and drank the stew as if it were water. Toracyl crawled behind Eyolin's cushion, tail curling around her back and flopping into her lap. Agatio observed out of the corner of his eye. She took a tentative sip of the stew, then another until the bowl was drained.

Rain pattered against the roof and walls. Agatio and Eyolin sat in silence, the only sound rumbling out of Toracyl's chest in rhythmic snores.

"My name is Eyolin," she offered, breaking the silence.

"Food makes the tongue loose, doesn't it?"

She shot him a look through narrowed eyes.

"You traveled here alone. From Farindor if your clothing is anything to gauge by. But your accent is Aideillian. You are well read and hold yourself well, possibly of noble blood, but not acknowledged since you didn't have the self-righteousness of a Silver Elf when you addressed me, an Amber Elf, from the barbaric grass clans. Some affinity to beasts with jaws that could snap a neck, suggesting you are Gifted with some natural magik that draws animals to you, or you have no sense of self preservation. Possibly both. And you have no idea how to execute whatever plan you have lurking in your eyes. How did I do?"

"Do you enjoy hearing yourself speak, Agatio, or are you that desperate for friends?"

Agatio grinned. "Oh, I have no use for friends. But Toracyl and I want to prepare ourselves for the gala and how we will navigate the seas of maidens sending us off to battle."

Eyolin quirked a brow. "Your caea decides on your women?"

"She chose you, didn't she? Are you doubting her judgment?"

Eyolin snorted at his arrogance. "What did you mean before? What gala?"

"You're young enough to not have been of age at the start of the last war. What I refer to is the war gala of Mainwood—the swan song of warriors from any allying town and village, gathering in the seat of the High Council of Aideil to revel and fuck and drink and become true blood bound allies. Where towns, cities, and clans from across Alagana gather to show allegiance."

Eyolin's mouth dropped open. She had never heard of such a gala, not in any stories of soldiers in pubs or in the mess hall after training. "And Aniöm stands with Aideil?"

"My clan does, yes. Our lead rider sent me as the emissary."

Sides were being taken; she was too late. But there was another avenue for preventing war, at least for a little while. "What about the seas of maidens? You sure you haven't been bathing in dwarvish spirits?"

"A taste for them all," Agatio murmured, leaning back on his elbows. "Any proven elvish soldier, from Gold to Amber, is invited. The gala is a night where any and all indulgences may occur. The High Council of Aideil spares no expense at the spectacle. One final night of peace before war. A setting that takes the edge off of months and years and decades away from the warm beds of home."

"Why do you speak like you're writing an epic?"

"Why speak plainly when one can speak like the god of poets?"

"A god of poetry on the battlefield. How... poetic."

"Judging by your shock, you grew up in Mainwood." He was good. "The gala is kept silent. Very hush hush. Families believe that their soldier husbands are attending an important briefing, obtaining their stations and squadrons. Not a whisper outside the halls."

"And the maidens?"

Agatio leaned forward, elbows on his knees. Eyolin didn't miss the gleam in his eyes. "Looking to participate, Eyolin? You're welcome to be my escort."

"I wouldn't be attending as a maiden."

"Even better. We can share." Eyolin wasn't completely turned away at the vibrating purr of that last sentence in his mouth.

"I just need to get back to Mainwood." She swallowed, ensuring that she didn't expose more than she should. "My ride ran off, and it wouldn't be proper to arrive alone." Not to mention dangerous.

"How fortunate you found yourself the second rider of the Welle River clan. You may be more capable than you let on."

Eyolin made a show of patting her pockets. "I don't have any payment."

"I didn't ask for any. Though," he said with a smile, "if I catch you at the dance, you'll owe me."

"I'll be sure to bring fresh steak for Toracyl as thanks."

Agatio tipped his head back in a roar and it was music to Eyolin's ears. "Don't go bribing my dragon off me, you cruel queen."

A smile tugged at Eyolin's mouth. She hadn't felt so careless and easy with her words in—she couldn't recall when. Lately, it felt like there was always some hidden agenda in every interaction. There wasn't a breath of conspiracy in this rider and his dragon. Parrying coy words against the backdrop of the rain. He truly did have a poet's touch. Eyolin's smile drooped slightly. Rider and dragon would likely perish if the war was truly upon them.

A war gala hosted by the High Council of Aideil, Eyolin mused. It disrupted her plan to infiltrate an empty Great Hall, but that just moved her into better position for the second leg of her scheme. If there was someone else who could activate the esthioryn, they would be herded into the Great Hall like sheep to slaughter. The perfect spot for both key and weapon to go missing from enemy hands. Or be activated by friendly forces.

Again, she reminded herself that there was no reason for her to go back. She could hide. Karok and Dale would be waiting for her just across the border. But that would bring the assassins on her tail to Dale. He had already been put in harm's way because of her before. She had decided on Mainwood as where she would make her stand, even if it made her a traitor to her home. She had been isolated in the Great Hall, kept away from the others. No one was likely to notice her return, if she kept away from scariyai who could sniff out magik and the commanders, and—actually quite a good number of elves, humans, and servants would recognize her. If she came back as the soldier they had grown accustomed to.

Her eyes refocused to find Agatio gazing at her.

"What do these maidens wear?"

He grinned again.

Chapter Thirty-Three

Kipp despised every Sky damned piece of bark in the tree-city. The bitch-assassin-sister-of-his-target-part-witch-apparently had blinked him onto a lower tree road in Mainwood, right underneath the spout depositing sewage from the entire shitting city of elves.

He was going to level this forest. Damn the repercussions. Then hunt that bony almond-eyed elf to the ends of every realm. His blood sizzled, magik pushing against his skin to be released. A horrible idea, but one that Alagana would thank him for in a few centuries.

Every inch of him dripped with sour liquid and noxious chunks. He peeled off a layer of slime with a swipe of magik and took a few steps out of the sewage drain. If he used his power to clean himself further, he feared the built-up tension would tear through his skin and eat through the wood beneath him. He wasn't particularly keen on falling a few stories down to the ground. Neither was the mudslub that inched through the piles of filth, hissing at him. Hideous blobs of dirty bones and teeth. Kipp hissed back.

Three young men stumbled around the corner of the tree Kipp clomped toward. They were young. They spat at his appearance. Kipp tunneled into their minds and melted them. The release took the edge off his rage. He crouched over the bodies, trying to decide which had the cleanest clothing. Kipp shrugged out of his sewage-drenched attire and tugged one of the young elves' sweat-stained cotton top over his head. The arms were tight. The neckline threatened to choke him. And his chest strained against the narrow torso. But it would have to do.

He looked up through the canopy of the city. The sunlight suggested it was late afternoon. Soldiers would be training, then dining, giving him adequate time to get settled.

The tiny, cramped room in the human barracks was exactly how he remembered it. Just with two less occupants this time around. His target hadn't been there in weeks, judging by the faintness of her magikal footprint. A few drawers were left open next to the unmade cot, their contents a mess. The bow staff was gone. Boots with them.

A procession of humans trudged past the sole window, shouting blasphemy and treacherous things, damning the elves and damning Aideil. A revolution of humans in the heart of the tree-city would be a glorious sight to behold.

Kipp rifled through the clothing that remained, tossing a few options onto the crumpled sheets. He and the human were around the same size, thankfully, though, the kid's legs were a bit thin. He scooped up the pile of clean clothes and scrubbed his skin raw in the bathhouse.

The soldiers in the bathhouse discussed the riots and division between the ground and the branches of Mainwood. There were a handful of elvish murders that had piled up with fingers pointing to the human faction. Something to do with a black market for pointed ears. Listening in, Kipp formulated a plan.

* * *

"*Cito*," Agatio commanded the grass dragon. The grass dragon lowered into a pouncing position and Agatio brought his head down to Eyolin's ear. "Hold on tight."

The wave of energy tunneled through the air. The world blurred and tilted. Then the wall of air ripped against Eyolin's skin, and they were airborne. Mountains flickered by like the pages of a sketchbook. Rivers looked like bands of ribbons in a breeze. The great trees surrounding Mainwood whipped by underneath.

The world slowed a minute later, the earth closer than it was before. She recognized the training grounds surrounding Mainwood where the stables were kept. Toracyl tucked her wings to navigate the forest descent. The mossy green ground rose too quickly. The grass dragon lurched to a halt, and Eyolin tumbled over Toracyl's neck and harness. The narrow neck bent under her weight.

The Aniöm dialect reached her ears with the same silky tilt of Karok's voice. "*Mo wa binu pę, a ni won waye soke. Toracyl, proinde eam.*"

The dragon's neck slid out from under her and the ground rushed toward her. Strong arms stopped her fall, halting her shriek of terror.

Eyolin opened her eyes to find an Amber Elf with straight, shiny black hair pulled into a ponytail. Delicate bronze coils were melded together into an intricate elven circlet atop his head. His dark face looked like it had been shaved hours ago. Bright hazel eyes glinted down at her. "*Pischa nirotin*, Agatio? *Sei bey ēy?*"

Agatio swung his leg over Toracyl's saddle and pushed off, falling the remaining few feet to the ground, landing as silently as a feather. Toracyl clacked away from the trio, following her nose towards the nearest feeding bin.

"Agatio, *sey lout oh, choush uo nay. Keh ske aei, gersue thrym nopiel.*" The words meant nothing to Eyolin. In Mainwood, people spoke the Common Tongue. Eyolin had wrongfully assumed that the kingdom sharing the longest border with Aideil would have a similar dialect.

Agatio and the other Amber Elf continued their conversation, with Agatio beckoning Eyolin to follow as they moved deeper into the stables. Eyolin hesitated. There were a few horses left in the stables for scariyai and scarox to return to the city after any last-minute training prior to the war gala.

Eyolin slipped to the side of a stallion, running her hand along his coat to alert the horse of her presence. She had the saddle strapped on a few minutes later. Agatio hadn't come back for her, either caught up in his discussion or intentionally leaving her be, not intent on chasing her.

She galloped out of the stables toward Mainwood before someone in the building spotted and identified her.

She was quick and efficient in navigating to the Great Hall in the upper tier of the city, frequenting the paths she'd used to keep hidden all those years. This time, as she moved through the branches, the life forces of every living thing sung to her soul in greeting. Her magik had been dampened for over a decade, so long that she had forgotten how beautiful the songs of nature were.

Eyolin slid through a side entrance into the Great Hall, praying that the planned festivities would keep that entrance unguarded. She was rattled momentarily by the servants, both human and creature, hurrying through the corridors. It was a miracle none of them collided. Fabrics and tiles and candles on platters fluttered past, all to prepare for that night's war gala.

Following Dale's instructions, Eyolin navigated to the laundry. Piles of neatly folded linens were stacked to the ceiling and a vat of steaming liquid bubbled over a fire. She checked the room, confirming the one exit she'd came through.

A voice chimed in her ear before Eyolin could snatch a set of servant's clothing. "You've caused quite the ruckus in the Great Hall since you ran off."

Eyolin suppressed a flinch, not bothering to turn towards the immortal Enchanted behind her. Right on time.

"I'm surprised you're not the cause of this war, Princess of the Enchanted. Or do they really believe you're Velesian royalty?"

"Ah, you did your reading. Good girl."

Eyolin scanned the hall behind them. No guards. No sign of Catlee's two companions.

"Where are your pets?" Eyolin asked.

"Busy." Catlee waved a hand and brushed past Eyolin and into the laundry room, closing the door with a wave of her hand.

The air hummed around the Enchanted, evidence of the glimmer she had coating her skin, altering her appearance. Eyolin had half a thought to tear into it, to reveal the creature lurking underneath with its large yellow and green eyes and glazed blue skin. The moontear at her throat warmed with the idea, but Eyolin shoved it down. No violence. No magik. Dale said there'd be wards to alert the High Council of any use of magik within the Great Hall. They'd likely be tailored to recognize *her* Gift. The last thing she needed was for Tequerra to get wind of her before she it was in position.

Catlee beckoned her to follow, unaware or unconcerned with the magik roiling against her under Eyolin's skin. "I'll tell the boys you asked after them."

The Enchanted placed her palms flat against a span of wall and pushed. A slab of wood slid to the side to expose a doorway.

"How'd you know I was here?"

Catlee looked up under long lashes and smirked. A folded letter danced between her knuckles. Eyolin's curiosity got the best of her and she swiped at it. Catlee merely raised her hand out of reach and vanished into the secret tunnel.

"Wait!" Eyolin hissed after her, scrambling to hurdle over a heap of clothing.

The door slid shut, locking Eyolin in with Catlee. The Enchanted's yellow eyes blinked in the darkness. A moment later, the air shimmered a light blue. Catlee's body—her true form—illuminated the narrow space.

"Now that we have privacy," Catlee said, offering up the letter.

Eyolin nearly tore into it. Air rushed from her lungs as her eyes raked the familiar scrawled writing, written in the cypher Arden had created.

"Where did you get this?" Eyolin gritted out at last.

Catlee's eyes blinked. "Where'd you think? You helped me find my sister. It's only fitting I be sent by yours."

"This was all a test." *Arden was alive.* Her sister had orchestrated the blue Enchanted in chains for Eyolin to find, somehow knowing her every move. It was her greatest puzzle yet.

"Naturally. Now come." Catlee moved, taking the eerie blue light with her, leaving Eyolin little choice but to follow.

"Arden found me skinned alive on a table, left for dead because my body wasn't regenerating fast enough from infection." Catlee paused to look over her shoulder at Eyolin and it took every effort for Eyolin to keep her mouth from gaping. "She knew of an Enchanted girl who was set to be auctioned off here in Mainwood. My little sister."

"Arden freed you."

Catlee nodded. "In exchange for a favor. Clever thing, your Arden. She knew the price a debt held with my people. In exchange for my freedom and my kin's location, I had to confirm that you were alive."

"Did she say anything else? Any clue?"

"No." Catlee lay a hand to the wall. "We're here."

"Where's here?"

"Somewhere we can get you looking presentable if you're Midriel bent on going to the ball."

"How did you—?" Eyolin started.

"My duty to Arden is complete. Your debt however is still lingering. I cannot leave this forsaken city until I pay forward the kindness you showed me in locating my sister. *That* and my obligation to assist the Sarom."

With that, Catlee vanished through the wall, taking the light with her. When Eyolin followed, the elvish glimmer was back in place, the girl's blonde hair flowing in loose curls down her back.

Eyolin's eyes went wide. "Why are we in my rooms?"

This was the last place she wanted to be. The last place she should be. It was exactly how she'd left it: bed unmade and the top drawer of her dresser open.

"Haven't you been paying attention?" Catlee ridiculed. "An Enchanted cannot break a promise, the same way an elf cannot go without water." She leaned in and gave a slight gag. "You hair is heinous and you have a working bath. It was this or throw you in with the dirty laundry. Here at least you have nice soap."

Catlee picked up a plain dress from the dresser, gave Eyolin's body a once-over, and flicked the clothing once. Magik popped in Eyolin's ears and she was looking at a black lace gown. The Enchanted snapped, the lesser magik making the bed, then she flattened the layers of the dress on top.

"There," Catlee said, "this should work marvelously. But we're missing one detail..." She hummed to herself, eyes searching every corner of the room. She held a pair of trousers between her fingernails like they were about to snap at her. Next, she plucked a book from a stack and tore it in half.

Eyolin's gasp was audible.

"Relax." Catlee balanced the mutilated book in her palm and spun it. In its place sat a black mask of swirls and smoke.

"I didn't know lesser magik could alter shape like that," Eyolin said in awe.

"We didn't teach the elves all our tricks, or they would have no more use for us."

Catlee tossed the mask on the bed, the black whorls catching the light.

"Why the mask?" Agatio hadn't mentioned anything about a masquerade.

"The idea of anonymity. This way, lineage and station are gone for a few precious hours, before the majority of them die in battle. And a good number attending the gala are betrothed or married or mated. The mask allows them to forget that."

"How obscene."

Catlee picked at her cuticles. "A few centuries ago they were a work of art. Now they're tacky and cheap. You should have seen the spectacle when Aideil was ruled by a proper Queen."

"Aideil had a monarch?" That detail was conveniently left out of the modern histories.

Catlee hummed and returned to rifling through Eyolin's things. Eyolin accepted defeat and left the Enchanted to her search. There was hardly anything damning amongst her clothes.

The bathwater had turned cold by the time Eyolin detangled her hair from the nest that the flight with Agatio had created.

"Done yet, little monster?"

Eyolin sank lower in the tub at the Enchanted's voice. Catlee's head popped in. She whipped a towel at the side of the tub, jolting Eyolin into a yelp.

"Out. Or this elvish orgy will get out of hand without you."

"I'm not getting dressed for an orgy," Eyolin grumbled, but accepted the towel discarded next to her.

"Obviously, if you thought you were going in that shit-splattered chic outfit from earlier."

Eyolin scrubbed the dampness from her skin and shuffled into the main living area where Catlee sat on the windowsill with one of Eyolin's books. A few shrugs and tugs and Eyolin slid the black gown on.

Catlee peered at Eyolin through thick lashes. "Are you going to indulge me as to your plan? It couldn't possibly be to dance your dreams away."

Eyolin eyed the letter from Arden sitting next to the vanity. Arden had offered up the Enchanted's aid. Eyolin should make the most of the opportunity.

"I expect the gala is happening in the same room as the entrance to the servants staircase. I'll need the slip through unnoticed." Eyolin left out the finer points about the esthioryn and murdering a Master of Magik.

"Oh, you'll be noticed," Catlee commented with a look at Eyolin's chest over the lip of the book. "But they won't be looking beneath the mask." Eyolin would never have dreamed of donning a gown like this, let alone attending a gala of every powerful scariyai, beiythron, scarox, and commander of Aideil in it.

The Enchanted's smile drooped when Eyolin turned to fit the mask on her face. The jagged scar shredded down Eyolin's back, on clear display through the fine lace of the dress.

Rummaging around, the Enchanted transformed a plain cloak into a cape of black silken lace, pinning it to Eyolin's shoulders. Her finger brushed down the length of the scar, goosebumps shivering down Eyolin's arms and neck.

"Why come back at all?" Catlee asked. "You have the world at your fingertips. You could have sought out masters to delve into your power, but instead you came back here. To the place that has scarred you so thoroughly, both your body and your mind."

"If I leave Mainwood—leave Aideil—I will forget my mother's face." Eyolin wasn't sure where the confession came from, or if she should be exposing herself in such a way to the Enchanted. But she couldn't stop herself. "She clings to the branches and leaves in the mornings. Ever since... I now feel where she once walked. The wood she healed with water magik. I don't have anyone left if I leave that trace of her behind."

"She's dead, Eyolin." Eyolin flinched from the words. "Come." Catlee stood in the doorway. "The men of this war await."

Chapter Thirty-Four

Eyolin had never once ventured into the upper tier of the Great Hall where the war gala was being hosted. She had been so fixated on proving herself that she had failed to observe the finer points of her surroundings. Just as she had failed to doubt. To see. She had pushed her body to the breaking point trying to please a man she now sought to kill.

Eyolin had to force her face into neutrality as she rounded the sloping staircase. The burning rage melted into awe as she looked at the grand ballroom in front of her.

Harps and violins and cellos and drums all echoed off the walls, contained by spell to only be audible by those in the ballroom. Not once had Eyolin heard such symphonies and, just for a moment, she allowed herself to float upon each note. The weapons and wars could hold off for a little longer. Right then, Eyolin was blissfully happy.

Music sang and wove through threads in the air, the notes shimmering in their wake. Across polished wood spun a crowd so elegant it was fierce. Delicate sun sprites bobbed above the orchestra and dance floor, casting dancing figurines of sunlight through the air. And towering platters of rich meats and sweets lay along tables against the walls.

On the far side of the ballroom, the High Council of Aideil sat upon a raised dais in deep velvet chairs. They were all there. Every parchlim, scariyai, minister, and general. The High Council noblemen at least pretended to enjoy themselves. They mingled with the others, wearing immaculately spotless dress suits with long tailcoats, dripping with the wealth of the kingdom.

Eyolin turned back to the dancers who moved so gracefully, she would have thought it was all an illusion, delicately created just for her. Dark skinned Amber Elves from the clans of Aniöm spun women in two-pieced gowns that glittered with precious gemstones and beiythron captured magiks.

Aideillian Silver Elves caressed the backs of their dance partners, accenting every dip with a sensual brush of lips to necks—As if death would not claim all of them the moment the esthyorin was activated and Eyolin redirected the device's power to take down Tequerra Arendt.

Eyolin pressed her back to the nearest wall, pulling herself back to the task at hand. She made a point to avoid the gaze of anyone who took notice of her. There were so many people crowding the room, there was no way she was going to be able to get to the secret tunnel entrance on the other side. Dale had said that there were servant passageways all the way down to the cells beneath the tree from behind the High Council's dais.

But she was hopelessly unprepared to squeeze her way through the twirling crowd without being noticed. Even Catlee as a dance partner would be preferable to taking on the floor alone.

Eyolin swiped a glass of sparkling wine from a passing servant and drained it in a single gulp. She'd drunken it too fast and gas made her want to explode.

"Might I suggest something a bit stronger?"

She knew the deep ebony face that accompanied the question without needing Agatio to take off his mask.

"Well, if it isn't Agatio, my savior." Eyolin grinned despite herself.

Agatio returned the smile in turn. "You do owe me a dance."

Eyolin plucked the glass from his hand and took a burning sip. Tiny fire sparks flowed down her throat and chest from the dwarvish spirits.

"Do you always lurk around the edges of galas?" Eyolin breathed through dwarvish spirits working their own magik on her.

"I had to make sure you made it."

"And your companion from the paddocks?" Eyolin asked, trying to keep him talking until she figured out a way to the other side of the room.

"They can join us later." Agatio held out his hand. "Shall we?"

Her mind was practically screaming, *No!*—but she still accepted his invitation.

Movement across the room caught her eye and she placed a hand on Agatio's shoulder. There Tequerra was, shifting his weight onto his right hip. He had forgone wearing a mask lest anyone forget who the Master of Magik was. Green detailing wrapped around tradi-tional scariyai fighting gear—the armor usually hidden under the scariyai's vibrant cloaks.

Tequerra swirled a crystal glass in between his fingers, eyes prowl-ing the room. The parchlim seated to his left tapped his knuckles on the arm of his chair, receiving a murderous stare from Tequerra until he stopped. Also notable were the three commanders that stood at his back, none of them wearing masks and all armed to the teeth.

The dais she had hoped to slip behind was full to the brim with the entire High Council. The threads of her plan unraveled.

Agatio pulled her into the first circle of the dance, whipping Eyolin out of her daze. Before she knew it, Agatio's lips were at her ear.

"Don't fight me, Eyolin. Where do you need me to get you?"

The dwarvish spirits twisted in her stomach along with the bubbles of the wine. There was no way for her to actually survive this dance. But Agatio, while whisking her through the sensual dips, did not once touch her beyond what was appropriate. She leaned her full clumsy weight on him. Agiato did not once let her fall.

"Where, Eyolin?"

She pulled back enough to see his face. There, beneath the plaster of ecstasy and haze were sharp eyes that scrutinized every dancing pair.

"You didn't come here for pleasure," Eyolin breathed in realization. There was bound to be a spy in a room full of supposed allies. It was what she would have done in Ïsteldûr's shoes.

Agatio's hands gripped her tight enough that she couldn't escape. The gravity of what she was about to do settled uncomfortably next to the spirits. All these people. So many lives. Now, every person in that room was at risk of the esthioryn's influence. Of the portal the tree would become if she did not deactivate it in time. Of the havoc that would ensue. The pit in Eyolin's stomach grew. "Let me go."

"This finery pleases me. Who are you looking for?"

Bodies closed in around Eyolin and Agatio and sticky sweet air settled on their shoulders. It was a familiar haze that rocked her forward. Agatio refused to let her fall.

"Quickly, now."

Her head spun, from the dance or the mixed alcohol or lack of food or the dress she was altogether uncomfortable wearing. She was going to be sick. The plan would fall apart in this breath or the next and she was losing her nerve. Agatio tipped his head to the side and his eyes flared with sudden understanding. Lip curling up ever so slightly, the Amber Elf cupped Eyolin's chin, the only force holding her stomach down and her body up.

"Don't scream," was the only warning he murmured before his mouth smashed into hers. His tongue pried her lips open. A crunch of bitterness ground into her teeth and dripped to the back of her throat. Eyolin gagged. *He's drugging me*, she thought in a panic. *He's drugging me, he's drugging me, he's drugging me.*

Agatio pulled away. His knuckles stayed lodged under her jaw to keep her from screaming or moving away. Eyolin couldn't see his mask beyond the blurriness of her tears. Agatio maintained the rhythm of the dance, holding and moving her entire weight. He swiped her tears away when they escaped beyond her metal mask.

"Swallow it," he demanded.

Eyolin waited for her magik to boil up to save her—to kill someone for her. Not a single spark in the cold moontear. Her mind immediately went to the esthioryn and how it needed to harvest magik. Did Tequerra already have her magik? Maybe walking into the ballroom initiated the extraction. Or the spirits or... Eyolin felt her body shaking.

She involuntarily swallowed when the saliva became too much.

"No." It escaped her lips as little more than a whimper.

The music shifted. The circles of partners spun faster, then the men twisted their women into new arms. The rotation reached them and Agatio spun her into new hands.

This new partner towered over her, an Aideillian soldier, with callused hands. Her eyes were stuck at collarbone level. The soldier's chest shone from buttons carelessly popped open. His skull and bones pendant swung at his neck marking him as a scarox, but without any visible weapons on display.

Eyolin lost sight of Agatio within a measure of the new dance. She felt the coolness of the drug work its way down her throat and through her stomach. Her eyes fixed on the soldier's chest in front of her, trusting that he knew the steps and submitting her body so that her mind could work out the adjustments to her plan. She needed to follow a servant into one of the ever-changing entryways. The closer she was to the center of the tree the better.

Tequerra Arendt hadn't moved from his seat on the dais. She hadn't spotted Catlee, nor Traik, nor any soldier she recognized from her meals in the mess hall.

Her head pounded but was otherwise clear. Eyolin waited for the drug to hit, for her mind to be washed away into oblivion. She needed to work quickly before she lost control.

She felt a lag in the tempo and stumbled intentionally on the soldier's ankle. His hand dug into her back to keep her upright, a grunt the only sign of irritation.

"I—I am so sorry. I really need to—" Her words died in her mouth when she looked up at the masked face. So much for the anonymity of masks.

A leather mask was pasted over Maximus' cheekbones and eyes. His hair was slightly longer now, eyes glassy and hungry from alcohol. The scar on her back twinged with phantom pain, recalling how in his bloodlust he had driven his blade into the dragon's tail and back. Her back.

The genuine worry in his eyes indicated that he did not recognize her, probably thanks to however much he'd had to drink that night. From the look of his pupils, it had been a lot. As he spun her, Eyolin remembered all the terror he inflicted. Possible ways of fitting him into the events of the night worked through her mind. But none of it mattered if she didn't find where her magik was being hidden.

Maximus' voice tickled her ear, the same tone as when he'd pinned her in the hallway all those weeks ago. This time, though, it had less of the sadistic bullying in it and more of the purr of a lover. It sent thrills through Eyolin's scar that prickled with his presence. "You are simply the most beautiful creature I've lain my eyes on."

Eyolin scrambled to put words in her mouth before she snapped his leg out of vengeance. "All. Yours. My lord."

"Not a lord, my lady. Your eternal servant."

Maximus was less graceful in his dancing than Agatio. More rough handling her, pushing her about rather than moving with any rhythm.

"You're drunk like everyone here." Eyolin felt like vomiting for real, no drugging required.

Maximus swiped a glass of sparkling wine from a nearby table and tipped it to her lips. "Everyone includes you."

Eyolin sputtered and coughed. Some got down her throat. The wine tasted normal enough, without the bite of any toxin. Maximus didn't resist when she slipped beyond his grasp and pushed backward into the nauseating spin of the dance circles. The commander chuckled and brushed off the wine that had gotten on his shirt.

She was still too far from the High Council to access the tunnels directly, but there had to be alternate routes. Eyolin had made it all of three steps out of the ballroom into a side hall when Agatio stepped in her path. His arms were crossed, and he looked far sourer than he'd been earlier.

"You think you can drug me the moment you get me in a gown?" She fed every ounce of spite into her voice, but that anger was already fading. Agatio noticed the shift and stepped to the side, letting her pass.

"It isn't every day that Aideil opens its gates to foreigners. Tell me, Eyolin, when should I have come to hunt the demon who killed my mother?" Eyolin halted, her momentum nearly toppling her. "They call him the Prince of Midriel."

"What would a demon be doing here?"

The dead elves, skinned and stacked across the city's ward. Rumors of something eating ears. A demon hiding in plain sight.

Eyolin crossed her arms over her chest. "I suppose you know where this Prince of Midriel is, Agatio?"

The rider grimaced. "Almost. It's been a bit difficult not to kill the body it inhabits. I quite liked the original owner."

"You assumed I was possessed so you drugged me to find out?"

Agatio looked furious, though none of it was angled at her. "Dammit, Eyolin, they were smoking the entire gala with an incense to take away the Gifts of everyone in attendance. Do you think that is how I wanted to kiss you for the first time?"

She ignored his words and focused on the familiarity of the haze that had settled over the dance floor. So similar to a daily tea she grew up on.

"But all of Aideil and our allies are here," Eyolin said. "All preparing to obliterate the creatures that Ïsteldûr has been breeding. It's the last place a demon would hide." Or the best. A demon in Mainwood didn't explain the accusation that the High Council was absorbing magik. Unless they knew already and wanted to flush out a starving demon. All the missing servants, the slaughtered sykets—they were all magikal beings of Alagana. The High Council covered up the presence of a demon by baiting a demon to target specific rooms. Repeatedly. It was why Tequerra was so adamant on activating the esthioryn. To send the demon back to Midriel if they couldn't destroy it. Was she damning a distant mentor, or killing a demon? Before it was obvious. Now, not so much.

Agatio smiled grimly as he leaned against the wall. "And how convenient for the High Council to showcase their strength when only those with the antidote have access to magik."

"What showcase—what are you talking about?" The pieces weren't connecting. A demon powerful enough that a Master Scariyai and the entire force of Aideil's Gifted couldn't get rid of it. Unless only the High Council knew. A demon that could hide in plain sight in a body everyone knew well. A demon that the High Council knew would attend the gala.

Except one hadn't shown up. Where was Traik?

"All that accumulated magik has to be funneled somewhere," Agatio continued. "Any idea where that might be?"

Eyolin didn't reply. Gears clicked in her mind. The herbalist had extracted Eyolin's magik through wormwood and esthyri tea and had built wards around her that kept even a Master Scariyai from finding her. That was just her magik. The amount of power from all Aideil's Gifted military was astronomical. If Master Arendt thought he had lost access to her Gift as a way to activate the esthioryn...

"Holy Sky."

Chapter Thirty-Five

Eyolin sprinted down the corridor driven by the one frantic thought that she had just killed them all. Her black silken dress billowed behind her, and she desperately wished for her acolyte clothing. Agatio kept pace with ease and caught her arm before long.

"Talk to me, Eyolin," he yelled. The sound bounced off the walls making Eyolin cringe at the exposing loudness of it. If Eyolin's blood wasn't already boiling, she would have snapped his neck from the threat of violence that twinkled in his eyes.

Out of breath, Eyolin backed down and whispered, "They're going to kill us all to send it back... Or I'm going to open it and kill the man who took my magik."

Agatio's grip on her arm faltered. "How?"

Eyolin shook her head. They didn't have time for this. If she didn't get down to the cells before the esthioryn opened to redirect its blast, the five realms would crumble, and she would not have her vengeance.

How much time had she lost in the gala? How long would it take for her to get to the cells?

A familiar chime twinkled down the empty wooden corridor. "About time you became useful, little elf."

Eyolin glared as Catlee sauntered down the hall, swirling a glass of sparkling wine.

"Agatio," Eyolin murmured. She hid the thrill at figuring out how to get rid of them both. "What sort of demon have you been hunting?" Eyolin raised her voice so that Catlee could hear, "An awful lot of skinstealing has been going around. Is that really you under than glimmer of yours, Catlee?"

Catlee shook off the mirage of a glimmer. Her blue body was lithe and long. Two feline ears complimented her wide violet eyes and the long canines in her mouth. And on that immortal mouth was a snarl.

"You think I would allow someone to walk in my skin?" Catlee took a single step forward.

Agatio pulled Eyolin into his chest, angling her body away from the predator in the hallway. The Enchanted tasted the air with a deep inhale.

"Let me tell you a secret, Amber Elf. My kind deal in gifts and promises and debts. We are the eternals that outlasted the High Elves. And *I* am not your enemy. *They* are." Catlee's voice dripped with Soft Tongue that caressed Eyolin's nervous system and left her waiting for a command. Without the elvish glimmer to dampen its influence, Eyolin's body bowed to the Enchanted.

"Do you swear you are not a being of hell, Enchanted?" Agatio spoke with such force that Catlee stood up straighter, her eyes wide. "Swear it on your isles."

Catlee rolled her eyes and dismissed him with a wave. "Honestly, Eyolin, you should have known that I was about this deep in a delectable nobleman. I'm sure he would be thrilled to demonstrate."

"Later, perhaps." Agatio regarded Catlee for a moment as he might his dragon. "My mother told me a story of the time the Enchanted aided magik in the crusade against evil. To honor her memory, I believe you are not the demon."

"How kind," Catlee said. "Look in there." She nodded to a broom closet that Eyolin knew hadn't been there before. "Enna can take you to the esthioryn you're so bent on finding." Eyolin's jaw dropped. "Your mind was screaming it. Good thing no one had their magik but me. Well, me and one other person."

Eyolin huffed in irritation as she yanked the closet door open. Inside, a grey syket curled under a sack in the corner. It took one look at the two elves and the Enchanted and hissed, teeth sliding out of gums and eyes blackening.

"It's okay," Eyolin tried saying gently. The syket sniffed once. Immediately, it relaxed into wary silence.

"*Eihra* found me," it rasped.

Agatio was looking Eyolin up and down like he'd never seen her before. She'd deal with him once this whole mess was over.

"Enna," Eyolin said to the syket. "My name's Eyolin, I—"

"*Eihra*," Enna interrupted.

Eyolin tried again. "Can you show us where the magik is being stored, Enna? Beneath the Great Hall?"

The syket held a hand to its forehead where the circlet of servitude sat. Catlee moved into the closet, sending Enna into a frenzy of hissing. The Enchanted ignored each flailing limb and gripped the circlet firmly. She pulled up, and a horrible burning smell filled the small space. With a pop, the circlet of servitude tore from Enna's skin. The effect was immediate.

Enna walked out of the closet and toward a solid wall. A dead end and yet—Enna walked right through, vanishing from sight. Agatio put an arm in front of Eyolin to stop her from following. She wasn't sure if she should tell him that following her would likely end in his death. There was only a slight chance that she would make it out of the cells alive, let alone with company. Then again, he had drugged her.

The air buzzed and Eyolin turned to see Catlee in her glimmered body once again. She had to admit that she preferred the ears and teeth. It suited the Enchanted much more than the delicate body she hid behind.

"This is where I leave you, Sarom." The Enchanted blinked through space with a wink, away from the entryway to the tunnels.

There were a multitude of ways things could go wrong. And yet, she did not fear any outcome. If there was even a chance to use her cursed Gift to stop the esthioryn from tearing the realms apart, she had to try. A recompense for her mother. Her father and sister. For everyone who had died loving her.

Eyolin stepped through the hidden entrance, Agatio right behind her. The tunnels were as dark as she remembered. They had no way of navigating the passageways other than following a general downward direction. Agatio swore something in the Aniöm dialect.

"The syket's gone," he commented. The shadows pressed closer. "There's no way that we don't get lost in here."

Eyolin smiled. And her moontear answered. She tunneled into her magik, snaking tendrils of her mind to feel out the map of the many passageways that stretched around them. The left was light and loud from the gala, but the right forked into a spiraling stairway straight into the heart of the tree. The auras of the servants that scuttled through the maze felt like Eyolin had dipped her hand into an ant mound.

She wrapped a hand around Agatio's wrist. "Time to let me lead."

They made it all of two minutes before the wood shook violently. She lost her grip on her map of magik and the narrow handrail. The tremor only increased in magnitude. Desperately, she tried to find a foothold.

Eyolin could do nothing as she slid down the steep, slick stairway, down the center of the Great Hall tree.

Agatio crashed into her and lost his footing in the dark. Eyolin heard him bite down a cry as he fell into the darkness. Gone without a sound.

Eyolin's hand clawed at the wall hoping—praying—there was a single crack that would keep her from following Agatio. She did not hear a crash, so he was very likely still falling. She lost a few feet of ground, bringing her treacherously close to the drop that she hadn't realized was on either side of the spiraling stairs.

The tremor lessened, but now the slant of the stairs was steep enough to pull her weight down on its own. Her fingers kept slipping over the lips of each step, unable to slow her down.

A segment of the wall on her right side gave way, and she flung her body toward it. She tumbled into an empty hall somewhere in the Great Tree. She had lost her cape. And Agatio. Another person who trusted her enough to follow her into a wall and fall to their death.

Eyolin stood on shaky legs, bracing herself on the solid part of the wall. She fixed her askew mask and checked herself for any injuries or tears in the gown, focusing on anything other than the growing dread.

She was in an empty chamber somewhere far below the gala.

And she knew with absolute certainty that there was someone behind her.

"There you are, my beautiful creature," a voice cooed, ancient and cruel.

The wood browned and decayed in fractals from the spot where the voice spoke. The energy in the tree recoiled and shrank back, crumbling away.

"You..." Eyolin breathed. The woman wore the same straight green dress as the day Eyolin spied her speaking with Arden. Her grey hair was longer, braided into a single thread down her back. It was the dark purple hue of the woman's lips and fingertips that struck a chord of fear, like the woman drank darkness.

"Lady Weiy," the crone said. The bow was low and mocking. "At your service, my Sarom."

Eyolin's wrist and hand felt seared with pain from where the partially glimmered tattoo marred her skin. The tattoo was very much visible now, the three circular symbols flaring to the surface.

"It was you." The certainty ran deeper than any magikal ability. It was as if the very fires of Midriel roared in her veins. This woman was the puppeteer behind the device that sat charged beneath the Great Hall.

"He was nearly as old as I when he sniffed me out of hiding."

About to dive into the tunnels and risk the drop, Eyolin paused. Did she mean the demon, or Tequerra?

Lady Weiy looked down at Eyolin with revulsion. The slippery film of the crone's mind against hers was nauseating as the woman extracted a scene from Eyolin's memory without consent. One where a kind scariyai named Mageiyro complimented a seven-year-old Eyolin on her fighting stance outside a post shop. He had always been nearby during those years, a prominent earth Gifted scariyai. Until he disappeared. The rumor mill had it that he ran off to Velesah after a scandal.

But that wasn't the point of the memory. Eyolin remembered the decaying trees of Mainwood regaining full health the day after Mageiyro had claimed that the city was crumbling. He and a team of scariyai, all Gifted with varying earth elements, had worked day in and day out in their attempt to slow down the disease.

Until Lady Weiy showed up, poisoning Arden's mind, causing the older sister to abandon them. Until Eyolin killed her mother. Until Master Arendt, disguised as a beggar, put a block on Eyolin's magik.

She visited the post shop regularly back when she believed her father would write them, and the tree that housed the shop had deteriorated faster than the others.

It was her. The magik in her blood was the venom that had threatened her home. It always had been.

The trees ceased withering and homes stopped tumbling down through the trees. It had never occurred to her that it was all her fault.

Lady Weiy withdrew her clammy memory. "Mageiyro always kept an eye on you, Sarom, protecting you from the attention of others. He even managed to interfere with my collecting what was rightfully mine. You."

"You don't own me," Eyolin spat. Despite every nagging thread of horror that twisted inside her, the magik she channeled through the moontear was hers and she couldn't give a damn what kind of sick claim this monster held over her. Her power was a disease, and if needed, she would infect the Mother of the Sisters and bring them all with her.

The crone took a step forward. "Your eyes are a window to power, aren't they? So much like your mother."

Eyolin felt an odd thrum through the tree, a breathing mass of energy that extended a tantalizing hand toward her moontear.

She resisted the strange pull that seemed to want to drag her through space and time. The esthioryn was reaching for magik, just as Cara said it would. Eyolin should have been nearing the prison cells by now. She was out of time.

"Your father ran into Hågenveihr forest in a panic to escape an arranged marriage. For weeks, no one heard from the Gifted prodigy. Then Lord Kyenz emerged with your mother, a creature of this world and others. Pure magik knitting together every fiber of her body." Lady Weiy's eyes had gone distant. "You should have seen how her flesh glowed, with those eyes..."

The drugs Agatio had given her—to nullify the wormwood and esthyri haze or to overwhelm her, she couldn't say—made her stomach gurgle in protest. And Lady Weiy continued, content to revel in Eyolin's discomfort. Metal gears roared in Eyolin's ears from some psychic connection deep in the roots of the tree. Souls screamed in her ears to be freed, and some howled for blood. It took all her concentration to not be sucked through the ground. To focus on Lady Weiy talk of a woman Eyolin killed.

"She came to me in order to bind her life to an elvish body." Lady Weiy scoffed and took another step toward Eyolin, who was barely holding onto her grasp on reality. All the pent up magik beneath her cried for her to join them. "A water sprite who gave up an immortal body. Kin to the High Elves of old, tied to the rivers and morning dew of Farindor's forests, now wishing to curse her existence for a few years with Lord Kyenz of Mainwood."

Eyolin hung on to the memories she had of her mother, flowing freely now that nothing prohibited her channeling of magik. Her mother's frizzy curls. The lullabies and warm meals around a table in their modest home. Her mother, Vialett Kyenz-eihra, the woman who raised her with such love and devotion that she gave her life without hesitation for Eyolin to have just the slightest chance.

I love you, eihra, Eyolin told the spirit of her mother.

She knows. The voice was so like her father's, warm as embers and unmoving as a mountain. It was that voice she clung to.

"I never feared the task," Lady Weiy said. She was within reach of Eyolin, but she merely strode around her, content that she wasn't going anywhere. "The Book of Bindings. So tricky it was to find the right spell to extract the essence of an immortal and supplant it in a body of my own making."

"You," Eyolin hissed, her chest tight. "Will not. Talk about my mother."

"Foolish child. How do you not see?" Lady Weiy's breath sizzled on Eyolin's cheek as if her very spit was toxic. "She *was magik.* The very essence of life itself. A water sprite. Only the elves need gemstones to channel magik. Do you know that, girl? Only two drops of water magik, Bound by the Book to tie her permanently within that skin remained of her life force, of her magik. All within a stitched shell."

"What do you mean *stitched*?" Eyolin snapped. She had to hold on a little longer, the wave would pass. She could control it.

"Vialett was my best work." Lady Weiy continued to circle her. "The bones were collected only from the most powerful of tombs, the skin from only the most beautiful Enchanted. The blood part was tricky."

The woman snatched Eyolin's wrist as Eyolin struggled under the influence of the esthioryn.

"Your father used his own blood at first." Lady Weiy dragged a sharp black fingernail down Eyolin's wrist that bore the tattoo, drawing blood. Eyolin gagged as the woman licked her fingertip, Eyolin's blood on Lady Weiy's violet lips. "But someone had to supplement the rest. The blood of your mother is mine."

Icy numbness spread from the wound, snaking up her arm and shoulder. She couldn't move. Could barely breathe as every conception of reality she held was stripped away.

"And you blew my creation to the pits of Midriel." Lady Weiy's tone dripped with loathing. "She flew so far from the realm of the living, I'd be surprised if she made it to the realm of the dead at all. I'd thought that your sister would bring you with her as I'd asked. But she left you instead."

"What have you done to Arden?"

"I thought her a waste of resources for a time but... she proved useful in finding you after all these years. How clever it was for her to send the frae after you."

Her sister had sent that thing to kill her—to collect her, she didn't know. Arden.

Lady Weiy was enjoying the torment that crossed Eyolin's face. "The Sisters wait for you, daughter."

Eyolin met her with blazing eyes. "You may have pumped blood into my mother, but you will never have any claim to mine."

"Yes," Lady Weiy flashed a cruel smile. "You will serve me in completing what the Book requires."

"You can break me, force me, but I will never help you."

Eyolin pushed against the vortex of power amassing in the esthioryn somewhere far below.

"I've had longer than twelve years to plan this moment, Eyolin."

The shadows grew clawed hands of ebony night that slashed at the fringe of Eyolin's black lace dress. The blackened wood circle around Lady Weiy stank of rotten flesh. Eyolin glimpsed a trickle of obsidian salt trickle from the woman's fingers and Eyolin realized with sudden certainty that this was the being stealing the skins and ears of elves. Not Traik or Tequerra. And that realization sent her spiraling the same way that the blink had the day she teleported to the Middle.

Chapter Thirty-Six

The blackening walls of the Great Hall melted away as Eyolin fell through Lady Weiy's unnatural portal. It ripped and tore at the essence of her soul. There would be shreds missing if she ever walked from the pit she was dragged into.

The moontear at Eyolin's throat choked her of air as if it too was trying to escape the drowning darkness.

Then, suddenly, she could breathe.

One look around the underground chamber made her wish she had never stopped falling through space. At least three dozen young elvish girls knelt around her, wrists bound to their ankles and clothed in tattered sacks. None could have been older than Eyolin.

Deep red hair caught Eyolin's attention. She identified the elf who'd been arrested the morning Eyolin sparred Maximus. Her skin, once crackling with fiery power, was now gaunt and grey. And her eyes... they were milky white.

Eyolin tripped over another girl in a similar state on her way to frantically escape the rows of women. At the apex of the chamber's domed ceiling was a massive shard of reflective crystal encased in iron gears that spread in a fractal spiral. At regular intervals, tiny specs of the rainbow gleamed. Gemstones. One for each of the Gifted young elvish girls that now knelt bound around her.

Without needing confirmation, Eyolin knew this was the esthioryn that Master Arendt had built. Crafted from the Gifts of all would-be female scariyai from his kingdom. This was why there were no women in the Great Hall, no women among the ranks of the Aideillian army. She had always been meant to kneel among them.

All the magik of these elves was stolen, siphoned as a substitute for her moontear because she had failed in mastering her power in time. Because she had hidden and ran and feared her magik for too long. These girls were damned because of her.

"Familiar, isn't it?" Lady Weiy cooed to Eyolin's right. The skin stealer inspected a girl with coal-black skin and eyes coated in a glaze. "The kiss of death that comes to those around you. It needn't be that way." She gestured broadly to all those in the room. "You can transform these young girls, liberate them and lead the most powerful host this realm has known. They will write songs about you."

Eyolin tucked her knees against her chest, pushing backward with a trail of smeared blood in her wake. She needed to get out of this room full of living corpses. All she could see was her mother's vision that Cara had shown her. Her mother's bones had disintegrated in her hands. Pain erupted from the scar etched across her back.

Lady Weiy moved to another girl, inspecting the specimen as one would a calf to slaughter. "My champions need viable hosts. Do you not agree that these talented young women deserve a chance to serve a greater purpose? Imagine. So much power stripped away from them. Their Sky given right, stifled."

The lump in Eyolin's throat grew thicker. She had found the esthioryn, the weapon that had the potential to rip tears in the fabric between the realms. She had uncovered what became of Gifted women in her kingdom, the Fate her mother shielded from her. This skin stealer had confessed to trapping a water sprite in the skin that walked the land as her mother, Vialett Kyenz-eihra. She had toyed with the darkest of magiks and witchcrafts Alagana had ever seen. So blackened was her Fate and soul that there was nothing elvish left of the shell that now strode through the rows of young girls without a glint of compassion.

"You seem to be having difficulty making your choice, Sarom," Lady Weiy snarled, suddenly holding Eyolin upright by the chin, moving with preternatural speed that had no place in that realm. "Allow me to give you a little nudge. My children are growing anxious."

Eyolin twitched against the woman's grip as the space in the center of the chamber rippled. An all-too-familiar face was drawn from the folds between shadows. Dale was held suspended in the air by invisible hands.

Lady Weiy rotated her wrist in a jerking movement, releasing Eyolin and drawing Dale closer to the two. His mouth was squashed by the same force holding him in the air, prohibiting him from speech or movement.

"Your choice will decide the Fate of your dearest, and only, friend, who happened to be apprehended by my girls as he fled Hägenveihr forest."

Dale. The one person Eyolin had let in during all these twelve years.

"It'll never work," she croaked. "You'll lose."

Her heart was shattering. This was Dale. He had no reason to trust her. To befriend her. But he showed up day after day. He was her friend. The unmoving living corpses of Gifted girls were a blurred backdrop to the decision Eyolin couldn't bring herself to make. She had come there to destroy both the weapon and the man who made it. Now she couldn't be sure she would make the right choice.

"Puppet," Lady Weiy said, dragging a bloodstained nail along Eyolin's jaw. "It's okay. You couldn't have known that we had already won. My greatest general has been walking with the face of Master Arendt for decades, spying and readying our hosts for you. But the old man somehow managed to break through twelve years ago when your power was last seen." The witch gestured to the elves around them. "My children need magikal mortal blood to stay in this realm. It is a source of food. The stronger the Gift, the stronger my children become, and thus can remake Alagana to suit you, Sarom."

"Why is he here?" Eyolin hadn't taken her eyes off Dale. The dread in his eyes kept her frozen. One wrong move and the skin stealer would suck the life from him.

"Motivation," Lady Weiy cried gleefully, clasping her hands, and taking a joyous leap back. "You either open the gates for my children to take these elves as hosts, or I summon a demon already of this realm to crawl inside this very mortal human and shred him so completely there won't be anything left."

"You want me to shatter the realms." For Eyolin to release not just her magik, but the Gifts of every elf at the gala above...

"I lied, you know," Lady Weiy purred. Eyolin tore her gaze from Dale at last. The smirk on the skin stealer's face was darkness itself. "You were taking too long."

"What have you done to him?" Eyolin's voice was a ghost. There wasn't time for her to tell him how much she cherished his presence. There weren't words to describe the way Dale reminded her that she was worthy of love, despite everything. He was human. She an elf. He was no one. Neither was she. But together they were something. A force to combat the injustices that tore them down daily.

But because he loved her, he would die for it.

Lady Weiy put an ear to his chest. "He doesn't have long now, in any case. His human blood would never have survived. But..." The witch knew that at that moment, Eyolin would do anything. "A stronger scariyai could extract the dark matter," Lady Weiy offered with a nod to the chained women. "And choose a host from all these lovely faces."

The sobs in Eyolin's chest jostled the moontear at her throat. Sensing her distress, it warmed. But what could her magik do but destroy?

"What do I need to do?"

"You cannot do anything, my dear." The skin stealer's violet-black lips parted in a smile that sent hopelessness spiraling down Eyolin's spine. "You need to be broken."

Chapter Thirty-Seven

All Eyolin saw was blood. A fine mist spread from where Dale's body combusted from the force holding him and the demon within. She felt the warmth coat her face, her lashes heavy with sticky wetness. The beautiful black lace forever stained with the blood of her one person.

Her mind was a hum of ancient cold whispers. Dale was dead. Not a glimmer of who he was remained in Alagana. And Eyolin was numb with fury.

Lady Weiy, the skin stealer, who had implanted one of her demons inside her human friend, stepped backward into a fold in space and vanished from the chamber, a smile glinting in her ancient eyes.

Eyolin lunged at the dissolving mirage of the witch, her hands closing around nothing. She looked for an exit where there was none. Tunnels did not venture to such a depth. These were the prison cells of Mainwood. The short window for getting in and out had passed.

Fire and hatred bled her vision red while rage burned cold as ice. Dale's death stripped her of reason, the blindness of wrath a comforting blanket. She could not bring back the dead. But she could prevent the demons from entering her realm that housed people like those who had dared love her—humans and innocents that were threatened by a monster who they could not best.

Her eyes turned to the spiral fractals of gears and that infernal crystal that reflected the scene beneath it. She was on her knees, black lace gown soaked with the mist of red, snarling. The host of unmoving girls bent their heads.

Lady Weiy wanted her broken. Broken, she would take them all with her. At the edge of her power, she felt the fragility of the esthioryn. So delicate a weapon. The preparation that required a decade of lies and death. All it would take is a thought and she would make it cease to exist.

Lightning charged from her core. The moontear melted from its chain around her neck, molding with Eyolin's breastbone. There was no pain that she registered from the sizzling of flesh. Her blood was lightning, skin a mere conduit of power. The scar across her back burned.

Eyolin raised a hand above her head, pointed at the center of the crystal. One blast to shatter it. Then she would bring down the walls of the chamber, giving these living corpses a burial rather than a sentence of slavery to demons.

She leaned into the voices that guided her power, more intoxicating than any spirit. The moontear responded by unleashing a blast of magik directly into the heart of the esthioryn where the might of the Aideillian scariyai lay prisoner.

Red sparks crackled to life from the center of the reflective crystal, the surface molding into a liquid plane. Shapes gathered beyond it, red and black.

And one humanoid figure appeared at the center of the crystal's mirror. She did not fear it. Because she did not hesitate to obliterate any chance at it breaching the barrier between the realms.

A blind attack of undiluted power erupted from within her, directing the full force of the stolen magik into an explosion. She felt her fire blaze through the bodies of the milky-eyed Gifted women around her reducing them to nothing. The esthioryn dislodged from the ceiling in a great groan. The sides of the chamber cracked.

There wasn't a reason to fight the death that pressed in around her. Dale's blood soaked into the lace of the dress and pooled in her collarbone. Her friend's blood. If Karok wasn't with them in that room, he must have died fighting. They never even made it out of the forest.

The cracks in the wall widened. Dirt and roots exploded through the wood in a wave. Bitterly, Eyolin smiled through the carnage. As the last Sarom was taken by a hurricane, she was to be lost to the earth, buried for none to recover.

Soil covered her ankles, then her knees. The air was already oppressively toxic. Eyolin leaned into the pain in her chest as her vision darkened.

* * *

Kipp groaned with the weight of the entire tree imploding into the earth and genuinely wondered how he managed to get himself into such a compromising situation. Again.

His evening had gone according to plan for the first seventeen minutes. Infiltrating the Great Hall and the opium den of a gala was easier than cleaning blood off a blade.

Inside, he watched the masked soldiers lounge on cushions, engaged in various debaucheries, the dance floor mainly abandoned. Then, his luck and fortune wore out. He caught his charming elvish battery fleeing the room through a side hallway with a distinctly dark Aniöm man right on her tail. The pursuit of a desperate drunkard.

A metal buckle clicked against a button to Kipp's left. Too acutely. The sound was so deliberately targeted to his own triggers that only one other would dare exploit it. Kipp felt the moment his friend stepped from the folds of space and shadow.

Erik emerged near the dais holding a High Council member with heavy opium-laden lids. The seraph blades in his hands danced and twinkled as Erik swirled them lightly in his palms, fingers nimble. Kipp felt the energy of Erik's Twilight magik before his eyes saw it. Two slim darts, so slim that only a single flicker from a nearby candle betrayed their existence, slashed through the necks of a parchlim member of the High Council and a scarox general. Their heads rolled forward, bodies slumping in their velvet chairs. They could have been asleep. No one noticed.

The old Master of Aideil, seated one chair to the left of the two dead Council members, breathed deeply but kept his eyes straight ahead, trained into an observing boredom. If his elvish ears or nose picked up on the clean, cauterized wounds that seared the windpipes of his associates, he did not reveal it. A thin trickle of blood ran down from the corner of the dead parchlim's mouth. His two personal guards glimpsed the maroon ribbon far later than bodyguards should.

A single note rang out through the hall. All Aideillian soldiers and commanders rotated toward the High Council's dais in unison, trained so well that a single note had the power to pull them out of a drug-induced trance. Their Aniöm allies crouched instinctively and slunk to the sides of the room, sealing in the women they had in attendance in the center of a protective circle.

A high-pitched scream crackled through the air, ending in a muf-fled gurgle. Erik released his grip on a woman in a silver gown. She fell to the ground, eyes frozen wide in fear behind the stunningly crafted metal mask.

Aideillian soldiers marched into a diamond formation, pushing all allies to the edges of the room. The scariyai slunk through the lines like snakes in grass, each perfectly spaced to ensure that any attack would be met with a solid shield. But no sparks of magik flared. None of the scariyai or soldiers apprehended the black clad assassin who blinked out of sight. In fact, their gemstones sat dull and mute as ordinary stones with no flickers of magik. They moved from muscle memory alone, with no weapons and no power. This was a gathering of the most famed league of magik wielders in Alagana, bred and fed to wipe out armies. Yet, they did nothing but act like trapped rats in a sewer. Sweeping the room with a flick of magik, Kipp realized how powerless each one was. Their magik was dormant, as silent as his little target had been when he panicked days ago in Aldeyn. Even if their magik was readily accessible, they were too intoxicated to locate the right side of a sword to hold. The kingdom of Aideil was falling before his eyes.

As if on cue, the room chilled with an atmosphere that whispered of death. Kipp wanted to curse the kingdom for his damned luck.

There was no more music. The musicians were ushered into a corner by sharp-toothed slaves. The only weapons in the Great Hall belonged to the few guards not permitted to partake in the festivities. Those and what Kipp had strapped to his belt and chest. One such guard was a beast in stature who had to have been more than half giant; his eyes sliced through the crowd sharper than the broadsword at his side. There was no need for a Gift of magik if one could cleave a horse in half with a swing of an axe, a feat this giant-bred beast would make look easy.

A presence not of that realm tickled the edges of Kipp's power. Right as he locked on to its location—at the heart of the mass of soldiers and Councilmen—the entire tree shuddered.

The tree as ancient and all-enduring as the realm of Alagana, cracked.

A single slice ran through the center of the floor and up the High Council's dais. In tandem, a blast of his magikal battery's power erupted in Kipp's chest so powerfully that it singed his throat and blackened his fingertips with a wave of rot and anguish. His Twilight magik flared in response, grey starlight and shadows twisting around the decayed nails and counteracting the wrath that threatened to shred his innards, remaking them anew.

He held to the torrent of power like he would to river rapids and tumbled towards its source, falling into the tunnel of space. She was in every way summoning him into the depths of the earth, closer to the realm of Midriel than he would have preferred. Binding magik or not, he would find her. He was compelled to.

The lack of oxygen hit him first. Kipp blew a sphere of power around himself, clearing away the debris of what had once been a cavernous room. He waded through what was left of the bodies of young women until he got to the girl that glowed as hot and bright as a sun. She could have been the mother of flames the way the light burned a protective sphere around her. Her eyes were closed, arms clutching her shoulders in a desperate hug.

Her light glinted off broken shards of murky crystal, poking up from crimson-colored earth. Kipp had little control over his actions as he reached for the beacon of power. Upon contact with her shoulder, the fiery light flooded over his skin. Kipp expected to be burned. He did not, however, anticipate the cool pinpricks that raced over his arms and face.

This magik did not hurt him. It should have disintegrated him like the rest of the room he expected this girl had imploded. There was no reason for her to be alive beneath the weight of the entire Great Hall of Mainwood. But not even the earth and darkness had dared to touch her.

Without the consent of his rational mind, Kipp scooped Eyolin into his arms, a glowing orb in the darkness. His Twilight magik surged and swelled the longer he stood with her, so much so that he feared hurting her himself if he did not find somewhere to set her down and break this intoxicating contact.

He pushed off the ground hard, blinking through space to the last spot he saw Erik before getting sucked into the vortex of the girl's power. He would suffer for taking Jet from him and as long as his magikal battery was near, he needn't worry about his magik breaking.

Chapter Thirty-Eight

The Great Hall's gala was in a further state of chaos than when he'd left it. Kipp stepped through the blink carrying a burning Eyolin. She literally glowed.

The crack in the wood had spread to the width of a carriage. The darkness of the crevice sucked light from the hanging chandelier and the sprites that hadn't managed to flee. A High Councilman lay skewered on his broken chair.

Kipp's mind whirled. What had she seen in that chamber deep beneath the Great Hall that had caused such an explosion? Further, how was her magik not hurting him? It was almost as if it recognized his power and welcomed its dark origins.

He had mere moments before eyes found the two of them.

Quickly, he covered her glowing skin with a discarded cloak, tucking her inside while she shook. Meanwhile, piles of weapons were being dumped in heaps near groups of sweaty Aniöm riders. The women of the gala were filing out of the room in groups of eight to ensure that the stairs out of the Great Hall would not get overly congested. No one knew how the crack in the ancient tree would affect the health of the tree as a whole. It could have cut off the life force that held up the entire capital city of Aideil. Kipp watched a servant shuffle along behind a group of women, studying the iron circlet seared into their skin. Kipp hissed to himself at the sight, vowing to one day rip out the throats of those who considered themselves masters enough to mutilate their servants in such a manner.

One of the Aideillian men staggered to a nearby pile of metal. His shirt hung together by a single button as he bent over to retrieve two slim swords. Maximus, Kipp identified. Still kicking. Even from a distance he smelled of sex, liquor, and idiocy. But no violence twisted his features, all emotion numbed from his face.

Other commanders and soldiers shuffled from the neat lines that they had initially formed, some cognition reminding them that they needed weapons. Swords and axes and daggers were gripped in slick palms. Hazy eyes and sluggish movements.

Kipp assessed them all within moments. These soldiers were not the threat, not with them moving like chess pieces being set up in tidy little squares. Erik was still in Mainwood. He could feel the likeness of his Grey magik swirling in the shadows. Ïsteldûr had made a move to take the kingdom's stronghold... or another power he had not sensed had finally stepped into the game. The darker parts of his magik whispered that was the case. That he was close. So close if he only looked harder.

His eyes found the half-giant snarling at soldiers to move as he clomped toward the Master of Aideil who had positioned himself atop the dais next to the crack in the wood. Arendt's gaze was clear, sizzling with his green earthen magik. The master's power swirled around him like a living beast, but the earthen magik did not look to close the crevice in the wood.

The master's sword was not drawn, and no one stood near him; almost as if none dared approach the head of the kingdom as he whispered commands into the minds of his officers. Indeed, Kipp realized, no words were being spoken aloud. The only sounds were jagged breaths and the scrape of metal. That and the half-giant's spitting comments as soldiers shifted into his path, arms heavy and mouths slack.

The gold and white-skinned elves of Aideil mixed seamlessly with the brown and black elves of Aniöm. Too seamlessly. Too few words. The only magik Kipp felt in the room was emanating from two spots. In his arms and on that dais where the Master of Aideil breathed steadily, eyes twinkling green.

None had noticed the Grey assassin appear with a conspicuous body in his arms. It was a small relief that her skin had stopped glowing bright as the sun beneath the cloak.

Kipp located that otherworldly power that his own magik had flared against before he fell into the torrent of Eyolin's explosion. It was fluttering beneath a thin blanket of magik. Hidden beneath the illusion of earthen magik was something much more sinister. There it was: a masterfully concealed glimmer.

A puppeteer, enslaving the minds of the entire Great Hall with a single nudge. The Master of Aideil had them all on strings. All without the magik to resist.

Kipp fortified his mind further, confident though he was that none could break down his mental walls.

He remained in the shadows, watching. The half-giant had almost reached the dais, pushing and disarming soldiers as he went. Kipp could just make out the words he was saying. Commands to stand down. Orders to lay down weapons. Furious curses when none paid him any heed.

Two figures appeared in the far-right doorway: a female in red and a black-skinned rider. The latter had blood running down from his temple and a badly split lip. The female's arm supported his weight at his waist. Neither appeared under the influence of Arendt's mind control. Kipp felt a film of power around the woman in red and was reaching to push beneath it when commotion at the left side of the room demanded his attention.

Another rider, identical to the other man save for the sleek hair, was dragged through the hall held by two emotionless scariyai. He wore classic dragon leathers with green and gold plates, hair braided up into a top bun. The rider's face was badly beaten but his eyes shone clear. He was thrown to the ground before Arendt. The master's green eyes simmered and narrowed as blood smeared the floor.

The whispering voice of the master scariyai commanded kneeling. Not just from the rider at his feet, but from everyone in attendance. They were all in such neat military lines that provided beautiful symmetry when they dropped to their knees. Kipp and Traik were only two slightly delayed in doing so.

A sputtering cry brought Arendt's attention to the other rider, struggling to stand on his own. He looked like he'd fallen off a cliff. Even so, the elf surged forward like he could defeat the world if it meant protecting the captured rider, who was no doubt his brother.

The female in red, unburdened of the rider, scuttled into the shadows.

Two soldiers in the nearest line fell out of position, grabbing the rider by the arms.

A familiar swelling of magikal energy surged from where his little battery sizzled with power.

"No. No, no, no," Kipp murmured. He watched in dismay as power surged through Eyolin Kyenz-ushteira and exploded through the room in rays of sunlight. All of it directed toward the two soldiers that dragged the Aniöm rider toward the dais and Arendt.

The absence of her power left his mouth dry, and skin cracked. Hollowness entered where her magik had filled him so completely. It might have been the Binding that connected them so, or something much stronger. Whatever it was, his core needed to be near her.

Each step she took didn't quite reach the wood floor, her body floating.

Master Arendt's green gaze slid to her. The puppet soldiers didn't so much as turn their heads.

"My child," Arendt's voice crooned across the room. "You've awoken at last."

* * *

She didn't acknowledge him. Didn't hear him. Her focus was on Agatio. A friend who was alive. Alive and hurt. Bleeding out in the grip of two soldiers who had no mind of their own. She had failed Dale. Failed her mother, her sister, Karok. Everyone who entered her life, who gave her a chance, died.

Her moontear hummed with life and death and power where it sat seared into her breastbone. Seared like the iron circlets on the heads of the slaves Aideil called servants. Servants who were slaughtered alongside Gifted women. Women she had stolen the life from.

Everything she was led to death. If death was to be her curse, she would slaughter them all if it meant that Agatio would live.

Roaring sounded in her ears, her magik swelling. Tequerra wanted her broken, to use her like a weapon.

He stood at the head of Aideil's army like a king. He had hunted her like a beast. She had stood her ground against a kaizor and a legion of scariyai and scarox. All without allowing her Gift to take control.

Master Arendt chose to treat her with such malcontent and manipulation. He had allowed all those Gifted women to be rounded up like animals, Gifts ripped away. In those moments before she exploded beneath the Great Hall, she had felt every fear and pain that those women had felt. The cruelty and torture they endured as their Gifts were picked apart and tested for purity.

All of that pain flared in her chest, her moontear crackling with energy that snaked down her arms. She knew that Tequerra saw the pure lightning that glowed from her irises. Let him see a glimpse at the terrible power that she had suppressed for years.

And he smiled. A horrible, gleeful, and ancient smile.

It undid her.

She had control of her elvish form as her Shoutka engulfed the space around her. Forearms and legs lengthened into white furred legs striped in black, the size of a liponark's. Long canines grew from her gums, and her head rose ten feet above the host of motionless elves, each as glassy eyed as the Gifted women had been when Eyolin disintegrated them.

The massive white tiger moved where she wished, a second body for her to control and direct to her bidding. Her mind and body were split in two. The Shoutka shielded her elvish form, glowing with rage, pacing with deadly intent. The tiger locked black and gold eyes on the Master of Aideil.

Eyolin and her Shoutka pounced.

Chapter Thirty-Nine

Never in all Kipp's years had he seen a tiger of that size. He knew that a select few Gifted could unlock an ability to manifest a Shoutka, but it hadn't been seen for centuries, and he was certain none were as violently beautiful as the one that prowled the air at Eyolin's back.

He glanced between the elf and her Shoutka, two sides to one soul, separated momentarily and projected into existence. Kipp's stomach dropped. Kill one, and you kill the other.

One leap took the white tiger across the dark expanse that cracked the wood. Kipp saw Eyolin's elvish form fused to her Shoutka's center like she was encased in armor. She moved in a blur through ancient forms that Alagana had forgotten about. Her feet and arms shifted and struck. Lightning and fire crackled along her limbs.

Beautiful. Absolutely beautiful. Kipp could have gotten on his knees.

Where Eyolin's power surged, it manifested on the white fur of the tiger. All four of her eyes fixated on the Master of Aideil, met by Arendt's hungry gaze. The old man wanted this. He wanted her unleashed and vicious.

Kipp felt the air shift as the Aniöm rider got dragged to join his kin at Arendt's feet. If the old man goaded her enough, Kipp suspected Eyolin would tear a hole through the very fabric of the realm. Kipp didn't move yet. No... he was utterly enthralled with that amount of limitless power that circled her like she was the sun.

Finally, Kipp's body moved toward the fray. The Aniöm elf squared off against glassy-eyed soldiers under otherworldly control. Kipp ran one of them clean through with his blade.

He gave himself over to the fight. His body was more than capable of executing any who raised an arm against him. Killing them would be too easy. But keeping that Aniöm rider alive seemed to be in his best interests. He needed to be close to Eyolin's power. It was an intoxicating drug. And he wanted to overdose.

Kipp shifted into the shadows along the edge of the room as he defended the back of the Aniöm rider. He was an excellent fighter and the two complimented one another's preferred styles. Kipp's slaughter with the rider's evasion. The more they cut down, the more dazed soldiers stumbled in to fill the space.

None of the puppets fought to kill. More than a few twitched inwardly, like there was something trying to crawl out. Any morality left Kipp at the thrill of the hunt. He was bred for the slaughter of gods and monsters. These were mere men.

* * *

Eyolin latched her power onto a strand of Tequerra's mind that had frayed from the rest of his magik. She sucked it into her chest. The master's mind fragment reflected off her moontear that still sizzled with warmth and strength. It was an overwhelming sort of power and nothing about it was connected to an elvish mind. Eyolin tore through the mind of the demon inhabiting Tequerra, hungry for any pain she could inflict. Any hope she had built burned into hatred that focused on one goal: the death of the man and the demon inside.

The veil over Master Arendt's treachery shredded before her. Eyolin saw everything in that cavernous demon mind that battled constantly against the trapped Master of Magik. The true soul of the master fought, but chains of runes from the Book of Bindings prohibited anything more than a whisper of defiance to leak through. Those drifting thoughts from Tequerra's true self spoke to her. Of a skin stealer who carved his flesh from bone. The screams of pain and agony. His imprisonment in a different realm. His straining muscle against red hot restraints.

He showed her a burning wasteland with rows and rows of cells. More and more horror revealed through stolen, painful thoughts from the battered master.

He fought. But the Prince of Midriel, a king amongst all things dark, pulled the strings too well.

And for that Eyolin decided that he would die. Both Tequerra Arendt and the Prince of Midriel. She would not despair for killing a deceiver who betrayed her as the master had. In the moments he'd been in control twelve years ago, he'd taken that time to block her magik and memories. Both the man and the monster were instrumental in Dale's death, and all those women whose magik was harvested. They did not deserve clemency.

A swell of dark magik reverberated off the wooden walls of the ballroom. Eyolin was forced out of his mind in order to meet the army of nightmares.

Darkness erupted from the crack. Winged creatures with bat-like skin and ink black eyes that took up most of their skulls launched into the air. Eyolin raised a hand and a white shield blanketed her elvish and Shoutka forms. She watched as their claws danced off her shield, though more and more swooped toward her.

Crackles of lightning and white sparks of energy kept the demons from completing their dives, her shield as impenetrable as a master scariyai's. More and more power Eyolin channeled through the moontear to the point where her tears twinkled of starlight from the magik that created them.

She hardly registered the hordes as they dove at the lines of soldiers. One by one, the demons picked their hosts. These were the children Lady Weiy had wished to bring into this realm from where they bred in Midriel. The esthioryn must have opened wide enough for them to crawl through. Eyolin's tears of starlight made a glittering path down her cheeks through the splattered mask of Dale's dried blood.

Cold fury had Eyolin curling her fingers, latching onto a strand of Tequerra's green power. She devoured the magik, shriveling that ribbon of the master's making. She wasn't displeased with the spark of shock in Arendt's eyes.

Pushing, Eyolin blew through each haunted memory. She watched the demon take possession of his body. She wanted him broken the same way he had broken the wills and minds of all the victims he controlled. Both beings would die. The moontear hummed with agreement.

Tequerra's face contorted, and his green magik flickered to black, shoving Eyolin from the mind of the master and the demon. She couldn't tell the difference between the darkness of the demon and the light of the scariyai.

"This realm used to be mine," the demon snarled through Tequerra's mouth. "Mine until Jenthius severed the connection to dark magik and cast me into Midriel." Tequerra's green magik surrounded them in a bubble of power. Her own sphere of energy barely kept it at bay. The Shoutka pulled against Eyolin's restraint. She could still finish this. One last explosion. One last kill. She just had to hold onto it.

Eyolin grasped to see the mayhem beyond the master's barrier. She managed to glimpse demons clawing their way into the souls of the Aideillian Silver elves who were slaves to the will of the Prince of Midriel.

She rallied a blast of concentrated energies to break through the Binding magik that held the soldiers captive.

Eyolin dove into her moontear's powers, dredging up the hope that she could beat this demon out of sheer overwhelming will. The enveloping warmth of an ancient presence met her halfway. It guided her through forgotten katas that brought cresting magik to her fingertips.

Wrath fueled her channeling, every blast meeting Tequerra's equally. She could pull more. Could more have saved Dale?

The scar on her back throbbed from the licking whips of thorny vines that stung where they landed.

Master Arendt's voice dropped to a scratchy tone cut with clicks and a guttural hum. "My people ate the humans like lambs, snatching them from cracks in the realms when they wandered too close. The dwarves were like caea hatchlings, soft and supple and full of life. But then we tasted elf..."

Eyolin watched the demon Bound inside skin and bone stretch against Tequerra's weathered body. It gestured at the demons slipping into the skins of the waiting Aideillian soldiers, and the Aniöm riders trying to protect them.

"For the treachery of the High Elves..." The demon licked its lips like it was tasting the Master of Magik. "I will enslave every Gold, Silver, and Amber Elf to serve my people until the end of Fate."

Eyolin broke the mind control of a select few as he spoke.

She released a slew of bolts of magik at Tequerra, each more charged than the last. If her power had given Tequerra the leeway to fight back all those years ago, she had to access the same magnitude of strength that had murdered her mother.

She pressed closer, blowing through wall after wall of runic protection, each darker than the last. This was the Prince of Midriel, a creature that required a host as strong as a Master of Magik to be contained. The rings of dark matter entrapping him grew stronger with every step. She wouldn't make it close enough to obliterate him.

Her elvish form finally severed from her Shoutka. She had done it only briefly outside the healer's cottage and the dizzying sensation sent her stumbling. Instinct had her covering her body in an iridescent shield while her Shoutka sprung into the air. The tiger danced off air as it climbed the wall Tequerra had her trapped in.

The tiger snapped and lunged.

The wall did not contain it.

Winged demons of Midriel were snapped in half where the tiger's jaws closed. Where a flock swarmed, fiery lightning charred them from the inside.

It was disorienting to have half a soul, part grounded and part free. Eyolin felt the draw of falling into the tiger and bounding freely through the air. But if she lost her elvish form, she would not have the moontear to focus the killing blow.

Still, the Shoutka's perspective fluttered across her vision.

The white tiger leapt over Maximus and Traik as they cut their way through the hosts of demons like chaff. The half-giant roared and Eyolin's Shoutka cleared a path for them.

Maximus blocked a strike from a soldier that would have sunk into the tiger's haunches. His twin blades sliced through the soldier's neck and into a flying demon, severing wings at the base. The two commanders left death in their wake. Demon limbs and soldier heads piled at their feet.

Eyolin's elvish form focused on the Prince of Midriel who stalked toward her in a lazy challenge. He drew upon all the earthen magik that the master could control. An arc of green magik swirled around him. Eyolin watched his eyes flash between black and grey. Master Arendt was fighting.

"When it became apparent that the elves only sought our extinction, I took my bloodline and built a residence in your hell ream." The demon talked through the spasms. "In Midriel, we starved. Our skin charred from the rivers of flame."

Distantly, she watched her Shoutka avoid the desperate elves who could not survive the demons that inhabited them. Her tiger form barreled through a cluster of demons gathering near the chandelier. Creatures of hell clung to her flaming white fur. Two were crushed in her jaws. She shook off the rest and barreled toward the elves that had gathered in the center of the space.

With every step, she broke more and more of the barriers that dampened magik and condemned minds. Before long, a luminescent sphere expanded around the group of soldiers putting up a final defense. Spears and swords of the scarox were backed by scariyai with glistening orbs, chunks of earth, and spirals of water. Ice and wind and light swirled around the scariyai as they picked off demons that dove too close. Sweat and blood slicked their brows. Satisfied she had given them enough time, Eyolin pulled back to her elvish form being battered by the Master of Magik puppeteered by an immortal being of evil.

The Prince of Midriel looked genuinely excited as he continued his lecture. "When the High Elves died off, their descendants grew fickle. The vain ones dabbled in necromancy and magiks that begged me for power. Naturally, we answered their calls. I gave those select few a taste of the strength we creatures once possessed."

Eyolin had to assume he meant the practitioners in Ïsteldûr who had created a similar rift near Volbourge. The black splotch covering the Ash Plains that day in the war room on that enchanted map. Ïsteldûr had opened the gates, and now Aideil would pay the price.

Eyolin burned through another layer of symbols with a brush of her hand. The wards sizzled against her skin, but she couldn't find it in her to feel the pain. She had experienced too much of it to have its effects slow her down. Eyolin channeled a blast that would mirror the destruction that had activated the esthioryn and opened the rift.

She was more than willing to level the entire city if it brought Dale's memory some peace.

A cresting wave of power hit her before she could release it.

"Did you know," the Prince of Midriel spat at her, "that Alagana was too hostile an environment to inhabit flesh built for Midriel?" The manipulated whips of Tequerra's magik held her wrists to the floor, forcing her into the same position of supplication as the women under the esthioryn. "When the shards between realms are thinnest, we send scouts. One found Lady Weiy waiting with open arms."

Eyolin heard the shouts and sounds of battle somewhere behind her. She couldn't bring herself to look. To see Agatio strewn among the dead. Her Shoutka forced her to see the carnage and bloodshed that marred the once glorious room.

Her white tiger form was too far away from Maximus to help him dispose of the flock of wings and arms. Luckily, Traik heard the call. The half-giant split from the circle of soldiers he had rallied. Eyolin's Shoutka ran alongside him, two Aideillian scarox, and a scariyai. They were a unit that leveled a clear path through the sea of black, Eyolin's white fur a star streaking through night.

Demons swooped down at them from their cloud formation near the ceiling. The scariyai dispatched eight by tracing a pattern and launching a ball of sand shards through their breastbones. By the time they reached Maximus, two scarox had fallen.

Eyolin's tiger form dragged the remaining elves up the steep wall of bodies that Maximus had been amassing. She trusted that, at that moment, anyone fighting Midriel was an ally, and these commanders were strong ones.

They stood on the lip of the crack that reached all the way to Midriel and watched the endless cloud of death swarm them.

Chapter Forty

Kipp flinched as the side of the ballroom burst inward in a splintering boom. An evening chill washed through the Great Hall. The treacherous drop bisecting the ballroom grew wider with every passing minute.

Then the floor shook, rattling the weapons of the dead that lined the foyer.

A sound not unlike the snap of a bowstring cracked through the air. Flashes of forest green zoomed in through the opening in the Great Hall. Kipp could have hollered in victory as the full host of Aniöm dragons arrived to aid their riders.

Silken feathered caea swooped and dove for their riders. Others spiraled into the heart of the blob of demons, each straight and sure as arrows. They exited the mass with demons in their teeth. Then there was his magikal battery's Shoutka tearing through creatures with rabid efficiency. The white fur was slick with black ichor and crimson blood, a haunting sight as demons dangled from her jaws.

Kipp spun closer to the rider, his makeshift companion through his chaotic battle. They had killed more than their fair share. Kipp slid through shadows while dissolving demons with a touch of his magik.

He had needed the release ever since he felt Eyolin's power pull him into the depths of the Great Tree.

Behind him, the doors of the ballroom fell off their hinges. Kipp glanced in the direction of this latest commotion. A daisy yellow liponark bounded through with a blue streak of a woman on its back. Kipp hadn't seen an Enchanted in years. Frankly, he thought they'd all died. But there one was, leading a charge of all manner of wild beasts from the forest.

Kipp extended his mind in offering. The Enchanted's eyes found him immediately, homing in on the Grey's presence.

We fight together for once, Grey. She motioned at the animals and creatures tearing into the far flank of the demons, some of them still walking in the skins of the more powerful elves. *The elves and humans not in attendance have been alerted. They're on their way if we can hold on a little longer here.*

Kipp nodded in confirmation. A green dragon dove right at him—or at the rider at his side. The dragon pivoted into a spiral and flipped upside down. The rider, without so much as looking, gripped a notch in the dragon's shoulder and twisted himself onto her upturned back. He left a hand outstretched for Kipp to join him, dropping his short sword to help the Grey into the saddle.

Instead, Kipp conjured a glimmering seraph blade and pressed it into the rider's hand. The rider had no choice but to abandon the Grey to the battle being waged on the floor. At least he'd left the rider with a blade that would cut through bone like butter.

He took off at a run, his movements blurring as he danced through space, only materializing to make a kill. He ran alongside the giant liponark with the Enchanted on its back. There wasn't time for Kipp to help the elves whose shimmering shields broke at the attacks of the demons.

And still more flooded over the lip of the crevice, their progress barely dented by Maximus and Eyolin's Shoutka.

He and the Enchanted took a stand near an unguarded doorway where demons were slipping through. Letting any number of them roam free in the city would be catastrophic.

* * *

Eyolin was trapped in her Shoutka's form while the Prince of Midriel slashed down on her elvish form without any mercy or reason. It was a relief to not feel the wounds that sheared into her body.

So, she leaned into the Shoutka's form with what little magik she had left and away from the pain of it all.

Eight thick demons heaved a monstrous lump of blackened flesh from the depths of Midriel. Black ichor sputtered from the crack in the lump's flesh that had to be its mouth. Its labored breathing was so distinct that she realized the air was toxic for many of the demons without a host. The larger the creature, the less time they had to Bind themselves into a body.

Her tiger form roared in warning, sending a blast of understanding into each of their minds. Scariyai who were closest to the mass of flesh shot a wall of razor-sharp spindles at it. The barbs covered the front of the creature, wobbling like a fat porcupine. The elves retracted their magik with a pulled fist.

The outer layer of flesh tore away like seaweed.

A long-limbed figure crawled out as if it were hatching from an egg. The inner membrane stuck to the figure like a cloak. Spindly hands of bone clawed at the film roughly. A featureless face of bone leered at the sack of flesh it had emerged from. It lifted a hand, inspecting each knobbed knuckle, and flicked. The dead flesh that birthed it was thrown to the opposite side of the crevice, the mass crushing a column of winged demons.

Eyolin knew this creature. It plagued her nightmares.

The sheer force of its telekinetic power was crippling. The same power that had blown through her home twelve years ago. The creature who she'd obliterated as a child had been reborn.

Eyolin watched through her Shoutka's eyes as elves broke off from the protective sphere in the center of the ballroom, moving in diamond formation to meet the newcomer. Translucent shields lengthened and fluid magik hardened into naginatas and whips with spikes on the ends, each weapon specific to the magik and scariyai who wielded it.

The remaining elves within the sphere moved as a group, one step at a time, advancing on the crack to Midriel. Though clearly exhausted, the Aideillian forces fought with lithe precision. Above, the Aniöm riders circled the flock of black wings and teeth like sharks. The riders jabbed borrowed weapons into the fray, hurling whatever carcass they stabbed to the claws of their dragons.

She felt rather than saw the Grey along the far wall of the ballroom and wished to call out to him. Eyolin's Shoutka form glimpsed him through breaks in the battle. His blades twinkled through the black cloud that surrounded him. His eyes had gone cold, devoid of emotion. A large liponark fought at his side with a familiar Enchanted slashing winged demons to bits from the dog's back.

Screams of the dying brought her attention back to the crevice where half the remaining troops hung suspended by the creature's telekinetic grip.

Eyolin's tiger form shoved the growing tower of bodies. It tipped slowly, crashing over the head of the creature from her nightmares and creating a bridge across the expanse. Traik threw a few more onto the morbid expanse. They needed a scariyai that could manipulate the earth to seal the gap.

Within a breath, Eyolin's Shoutka could control anything.

She shouted her plan of closing the rift into the minds of Maximus and Traik and they moved into position behind the tiger's form. Channeling magik through the Shoutka was different—more savage in nature. With every injury her elvish body took from the Prince of Midriel, she inched closer to losing her hold on her true self. She wondered if Karok experienced something similar every time the werekey surfaced.

Minutes ticked by while Eyolin focused on stitching together the rift between her realm and the one beneath. The Aideillian forces on the ballroom floor took control of two-thirds of the room.

The elves who survived under the possession of the demon hordes were the strongest of the Gifted. These puppets gathered to the bone-faced creature, who telekinetically cleared space from them with a brush of his hand. The otherworldly magik was lazy, a predator stretching its legs.

Eyolin's elvish form thrashed against the prince's hold on her. Her fits of magik were frantic and wild. Fire spewed from her mouth and electricity crackled and singed her nostrils. She flung light and darkness and any other element she could muster, all to break his restraints.

But she was no match for both a master and a demon.

Her magik beat uselessly against the green of the master's, the Prince of Midriel controlling the earthen magik with lazy movements. He had grown almost bored in his methodical assault. He wasn't the least bit worried about the mass slaughter occurring in the ballroom. The esthioryn had been activated. The realms were shattering.

Tequerra's body convulsed. His wrist snapped back with a crack and his knees bent out. Eyolin watched, blood pouring down her face, as Master Tequerra Arendt fought from a cell in a different dimension, battling for his own mind and body.

He bought her enough time to turn back to her Shoutka and weave the wood together like Cara might have done to a wound that needed to be healed.

* * *

Kipp made one last push to get to Eyolin, watching as the creature with a face of bone approached her Shoutka form from a break in the tide of fighting. He would kill both commanders for leaving his battery's soul vulnerable like that.

It happened in slow motion—the demon flipped into an impossible leap, closing the distance. It gripped the tiger's neck in both hands. A wave of telekinetic power rippled through the entire ballroom.

Eyolin's Shoutka roared. Hurting her physical elvish form was one thing. Striking at the very soul of her being was devastating. Kipp felt the agony wash over him. He let it fuel his pursuit.

The blast that followed the assault on the tiger shook the roots of the Great Hall. Eyolin's elvish form absorbed the Shoutka with a cry that would forever be stamped into his mind. It was that sound that made him decide that he could never kill her.

Every blood-soaked muscle of the tiger rushed back into her body. Her agony flooded the bond they shared. He caught a glimpse of her body curled over, her skin brighter than the sun. The rest of the fighting was drowned out by an explosion he felt in the marrow of his bones. All green magik crumbled to dust. The crevice into hell sealed shut.

Where Eyolin's magik touched, dark matter was stripped away to nothing. The flocks of winged demons dissolved into mist. To Kipp's dismay, the telekinetic creature blinked from the room before the cleansing light touched it. There was no sign of the old Master of Magik, either. Kipp's attention instead settled on a young elvish girl experiencing all the pain that her fractured soul had withstood.

Somehow, her blast did not affect the soldiers who had fought at her side. They stood now, wary of the unnatural silence that hung over the bloody landscape.

Then the cries of terror began.

Soldiers rushed to the gaping hole in the side of the Great Tree, staring out at the tree-city of Mainwood. Three Aniöm riders swooped away on their dragons, vanishing into the skies the moment they saw that they would not be pursued by winged creatures. The Aniöm riders that remained landed behind the ranks of Aideillian soldiers.

Kipp watched the Enchanted slip away down a hall and couldn't blame her as smoke billowed into the ballroom. It was that smoke that clogged their lungs first. Then the immense heat. Flames licked at the ancient Greywood in the absence of the magik of the master.

Kipp glanced out of the gap. Down below, the remainder of the Aideillian army were locked in battle with an advancing army clad in red and black.

Metal contraptions were littered throughout the enemy ranks. Each device required two or more beasts with blackened skin and red eyes to pull them. Kipp recognized them as werekeys likely enslaved from the Ash Plains. Where normal werekeys had dense hides, these had their fur scorched off their backs and replaced by armor seared into their flesh.

Black cloaked scariyai with metal masks moved into position at the backs of the circular cannons. Their hands glowed red hot and Kipp wanted to believe it wasn't true. With a single touch, the cannon erupted with a torrent of fire. The western kingdom had manipulated the weak fire Gifts and had amplified a spark into a weapon that incinerated the soldiers hurrying forward on the tree branch.

The elves standing at the edge of the room all started talking at once.

"The wards of the city are down!"

"We're under attack!"

Kipp couldn't imagine the amount of cunning it took for Ïsteldûr to execute this invasion completely under the radar of the High Council—though, they did have a Prince of Midriel as their leading general. That must have put a damper on their judgment skills.

"Commanders, get to your regiments!" It was the half-giant who screamed. Kipp started towards where Eyolin was curled up on the dais. She needed to move. To get up. She couldn't be dead.

Chapter Forty-One

Eyolin—in her elvish form—was vaguely aware that Maximus was at her side. He gripped her by the bicep, hoisting her limp body upright. He handled her roughly, smacking her face to bring her around. She was so bloody, and she couldn't tell whose it was. The black dress she'd worn to the gala was torn clean away from her back leaving most of her body exposed. Maximus transferred his shirt to her, waving an officer over to give him a proper fighting tunic.

"You done, solider?" He posed it as a question rather than a haughty remark or insult. He kept his eyes trained on her, urging her to show some fight. Eyolin knew that there was nothing but drained defeat on her face. She was completely slumped in his grip.

"You get a hold of yourself," Maximus said. "These men can't do what you just did. Show them that there is a chance. We still have an enemy out there, and we could use all the help we can get." He shook her by the shoulders. "Come on, little doe. I know there's more fight in you."

Maximus shifted his hand to support her back and button up his white shirt over her tattered gown. He felt the scar he had carved into her back. His eyes widened and Eyolin wished he would just leave her to pass on into oblivion.

Instead, he pinched her. Hard.

Every muscle in Eyolin's body snapped to attention to the point where the very air sizzled and cracked. The moontear at her chest hummed and glowed as Maximus put his mouth to her ear and whispered, "We're already on fire. Make them burn for it."

He gave her a shove and leapt back as Eyolin exploded forward and through the opening of the Great Tree. She was not quite whole, more of a wraith of magik. A conduit to the wrath Maximus' touch had triggered.

Eyolin flew through the air toward the tier below. Through the smoke and flames, line after line of Ïsteldûrians marched. They were everywhere, on every branch. Mainwood had been surprised by both assaults, blinded by the Prince of Midriel, leaving the city unprotected for the western kingdom to invade. Eyolin could only assume that they had slipped through the holes in the wards where Lady Weiy had piled her skinned bodies.

It was a beautifully crafted assault stemming from decades of preparation. Ïsteldûr had never planned to leave Aideil with their victory in the last war. They wanted the eastern kingdom flattened. This night would be one that the dwarvish spinner would sing of for as long as he lived. Eyolin wondered if she would have a mention as the one who caused it all.

Now the Prince of Midriel was free, roaming with Lady Weiy and the Sisters. The gap between this realm and the one below had been closed, but she couldn't gauge how effective her sealing had been. That night had reaped more bloodshed and death than any Fate could have foreseen.

Worse was that the war over Alagana had only just begun.

Eyolin was a streak of power, flying to liberate Mainwood of the invading forces of Ïsteldûr. She'd focused on taking down one of the masked scariyai dripping with dark magik. It was a sloppy attack, but that was all she knew. An arc of blood and lightning erupted over her head as she fell towards the heart of the Ïsteldûrian army and a general who saw her coming.

The masked man raised a hand. Eternal night as sure as death gathered at his fingertips.

That was all she knew.

She drifted unconscious through the ether. She couldn't tell if her body was still falling through the trees of Mainwood. If perhaps her Fate was to never stop falling.

But then she felt the rope loop around her chest and arms with its poison inhibiting any access to magik.

Eyolin couldn't hold on for long. There were small indicators that she was alive. The dampness of a forest. The smell of moss. A croaking toad in the dead of night.

At one point, she held herself on the edge of consciousness long enough to feel fresh poison being poured onto her restraints. She fell back into oblivion gratefully.

It could have been days or weeks she passed in darkness never waking fully enough to feel the full extent of her injuries. She wasn't sure she wanted to wake up at all. What had become of her home in the trees?

A violent shivering woke her at long last. Her head lolled on the bank of a small creek. Her body had cramped in the bound fetal position until the blood flow had been cut off entirely. There was not a single part of her body that was not covered with blood and dirt.

Eyolin squirmed toward the steady flow of water beside her. She managed to dig her right elbow into the ground to use as leverage in her grinding path to the water.

She collapsed with only her fingertips dipping into the creek. There was no point. She distantly felt the eroding hunger that tore through her. The way her veins had shrunk from dehydration. In the morning, her body would give out. The beasts of the forest would smell her as meat. There was no one coming for her. As her eyelids drifted shut, accepting the sweet caress of death, she felt its arms lift her. Weightless, Eyolin fell into the void.

Chapter Forty-Two

olden light set her head screaming in pain.

Eyolin curled in on herself, shrinking away from the glare. The movement made her flinch. Her legs were no longer bound. The shreds of black lace from her gown didn't rub into her torso and Maximus' shirt was no longer sticking to her bloody body. Rather, a silken tunic of emerald green had been slipped over her shoulders that were scrubbed clean. There were no signs of the bleeding cuts from Master Arendt's whips, or any scars—she should have had scars.

Two delicate metal bands were linked at her wrists. A pulsing, white energy chained them together. Eyolin followed the chain to a bolt in the wall. She gave them a tentative tug. The metal warmed to the point of burning her skin. Eyolin bit down a yelp and stopped struggling. Almost instantly, the metal cooled and the wounds healed, although pain still pulsed through her arms.

The bars of the cell were tightly braided metal that looked luxuriously out of place. Even the cot she had woken up on was soft as down. The walls were deep chestnut, carved with columns of symbols in a language Eyolin didn't recognize.

Looking up, Eyolin saw the source of the golden light. An orb as bright as the sun hovered near the ceiling that tapered up into a pyramid. It bore the same energy as the chain, though this orb's purpose seemed only to emulate sunlight as a timekeeping device. She couldn't help but wonder at the scariyai who created such an apparatus, as well as the kingdom who would bother with something as thoughtful as time and sunlight for a dungeon full of prisoners.

"She's awake," a whisper echoed.

"Grand, let's announce it for everyone without eyes to see," muttered an irritated voice.

Both voices felt vaguely familiar to Eyolin. Like something out of a dream. One from which she would like to wake up. She had felt herself die in the forest. Alone and beaten. Bleeding out and so very tired. But if the pain from the handcuffs was any indication, she was very much alive. In that case, she wondered, where in Alagana was she? Was she even in that realm? Had she, in death, drifted into the Sky where her spirit was condemned? That would explain the lack of scars on her arms and the unfamiliar characters etched into the deep red wood.

Those same voices reached her cell again.

"We're still alive because of her."

"And, little rider, we were captured in our attempt to rescue said damsel."

"It was a foolproof plan. How was I to know—?"

"Quiet, you fool! Do you know nothing of this court?" A pause. "We'll be executed the moment she opens her mouth and admits that she's useless."

Eyolin tried her voice. "Hello?" It came out cracked.

"Eyolin! You're okay?" Agatio. That was the first voice. But who was the second?

"Would you please, respectfully, shut up?"

A blurry memory pressed against her mind. Just as the features clarified, the glowing orb hovering in her cell blinded her. Her vision was spotting when she heard metal groan. The magik tether lifted her hands above her head, forcing her to stand.

Soft footsteps led her stumbling forward. Eyolin blinked furiously to clear away the swirling clouds in her eyes.

She heard a faint click that jostled her magikal tether and those footsteps receded.

A massive throne sat in the center of a colossal hexagonal room large enough for the guards stationed on the opposite side to appear no larger than Eyolin's thumb. The throne itself was raised on a single column of the same maroon wood as the cell. No stairs led up its length, and it was far too high to climb. From Eyolin's distance, two small crowns of gold were fixed on the rear two legs. Fractal patterns exploded upward in the metalwork creating a fan of abstract coniferous branches.

Eyolin craned her head up. The room opened into the afternoon sun at the apex of the geometric ceiling. Gold and silver inlays ran upward in the shape of leaves.

The floor was a marmoreal mosaic with lines running from the hexagon's corners. Five slender pillars stood tall. Red wood had been manipulated with marble to create a spiral effect.

Her head still buzzed, a dizziness pressing into the backs of her eyes. She shouldn't be there. All grandeur and spectacle. She should be burning with her city, feeling blazing fire licking at her skin.

Eyolin closed her eyes, scrunching her eyebrows as the pain intensified. Any memory she had of the outcome of the battle against both Master Arendt and Ïsteldûr did not exist in her mind. It was a vast void in her subconscious. Karok had taught her the intricacies of navigating her mental plane, sifting through memories like a library. She approached the near past, lingering on Dale's face as he looked at her before the demon inside him wiped him from the world of the living.

The memories went blank the moment she leapt from the Great Hall towards the neat lines of enemy soldiers. Eyolin grasped at any fragment that may remain as a clue. But there was nothing.

Dainty clicks of heels on marble brought her gaze back to the throne room. Queen Daetheiri was unmistakable. Long green panels of fabric fell around her figure like water, displaying everything and nothing at the same time. Gold bands rested on her upper arms. Two thin braids wrapped around the base of her five-pointed crown. The rest of her amber hair fell in silken locks, brushing against her lower back. Little bronze points were fitted to the curve of her ears.

But her skin made Eyolin's heart pound in earnest. The moontear seared into her chest warmed ever so slightly. Daetheiri's skin was pale as moonlight. Delicate designs were inked across nearly every inch of her. Her arms, torso, and neck. The patterns tapered off to frame the queen's face. Something seemed alive about the ink. If Eyolin spent too long looking at one spot, the patterns almost shifted.

This was the Court of Farindor. Stronghold of the oldest monarch of Aideil. A kingdom that prized their female military strength, where the Amber Elves and their Gifted healers were most concentrated, with a forest more wild and unforgiving than any other.

Queen Daetheiri stalked behind where Eyolin stood, feet fused to the marble beneath her. One breath in. One breath out. She was okay, she told herself.

Eyolin, so enamored by the Queen and the throne room, hadn't registered the two other prisoners at her back.

Agatio and Kipp stood shoulder to shoulder. The former, upon making eye contact with Eyolin, gave her a small wave. The Grey bristled with agitation that seemed to affect the air around him. The two men had not had their injuries tended to as Eyolin's had been. A blackish bruise reached up from Kipp's right shoulder to his neck. Any additional wounds were hidden beneath his black leather tunic. Agatio had not fared as well. A cut in his riding leathers revealed where an arrow had skimmed through muscle.

Daetheiri examined the two men as one might livestock at a market. She hooked a ringed middle finger underneath the Grey's chin. Kipp didn't meet her gaze.

The Queen straightened and moved in front of the trio. Her throne rose behind her. Her eyes narrowed at Kipp.

"Your presence here is due to a simple Binding. You couldn't leave her if you tried." Queen Daetheiri waved a hand in dismissal. "But you..." Daetheiri turned to Agatio with a serpentine intent. "You have no clear motive for your actions, making you the most unpredictable of all. Why are you here?"

"Off on holiday, Your Majesty." Agatio bowed deeply, eyes never leaving the Queen. "You know how arid the days get in Aniöm this time of year."

"Unlikely." The Queen cocked her head with a calculated smile. "But you are pretty with your courtier's words."

Eyolin felt the full breadth of Queen Daetheiri's attention like her body had been thrown off the side of a mountain. She fell freely into the eyes of this Farindor royal. The queen had lived centuries beyond any other Bronze, Silver, or Gold Elf who walked the lands of Alagana. Her presence was as endless as the night sky.

And when Daetheiri grinned it was no pretty thing. It was as if Eyolin stared into a chasm without light and without end.

Her knees buckled under the pressure of the Queen's gaze. Sinking to the floor, Eyolin's bottom lip trembled in a whimper.

The Queen of Farindor knelt in front of her, cupping her face in her palms. Endless power swirled through the tattooed patterns of the Queen's arms. The three symbols on Eyolin's left forearm stung, and a single teardrop ran down her cheek.

"My child, you will pay for the war crimes your powers have unleashed on this realm."

Acknowledgements

Thank you to each one of you who took the chance on this reimagining of my debut novel. For those who have been here since the beginning, when *The Moon Tear* was titled *Aideil: The Shattered World,* thank you. Your support has been the backbone to this project that has sat near and dear to my heart since its conception. This is the story that my middle and high school self always dreamed of reading. To feel the complexities of the characters and see their passions shine on the page is mind blowing.

To the Beta readers who trudged through old drafts that have since evolved into a story worthy of the characters, thank you. My editors, Jeff and Connolly, deserve as much credit as me for wringing out the true essence of *The Moon Tear,* even when, at times, I would rather scrap the whole thing and try again another time. Then there is Josh, the artist behind the beautiful cover, who took the soul of the manuscript and made it into a visual masterpiece. The map of Alagana couldn't have evolved into the stunning landscape it is today without Daniel Hasenbos either.

And to you, Reader, for entering the fantastical world of Alagana, with its new creatures and heavy world building, you make the work worth it. There are many stories to tell in the five realms of Alagana, and I welcome you to the adventure.